THE WONDER OF YOU

ALSO BY DANI ATKINS

Fractured (US title: *Then and Always*)

The Story of Us

Our Song

This Love

While I Was Sleeping

A Million Dreams

A Sky Full of Stars (US title: *Gone Too Soon*)

The Wedding Dress

Six Days

The Memory of Us

Always You and Me

Perfect Strangers (a novella)

When I Awake (a novella)

THE WONDER OF YOU

DANI ATKINS

LAKE UNION
PUBLISHING

Published by Lake Union Publishing, Seattle

www.apub.com

EU product safety contact:
Amazon Media EU S. à r.l.
38, avenue John F. Kennedy, L-1855 Luxembourg
amazonpublishing-gpsr@amazon.com

ISBN-13: 9781662539985
eISBN: 9781662527500

Cover design by Emma Rogers
Cover image: © Flavio Coelho © gitusik © Yana Iskayeva / Getty

Printed in the United States of America

Contents

Chapter One

There were two of us beneath the tree that day. We both survived . . . and I still don't know how. Some people called it a miracle. Maybe it was.

The last thing on my mind as I hurried across the park that morning was the possibility of my life changing in any way, because I liked it just as it was. In fact, the only thought in my head as I left the path to take a shortcut back to the office was the mansion house flat I'd just viewed. I'd played it cool with the clients, but it had been hard to hide my excitement about the prospect of adding it to my company's listings. I was so busy thinking about how to stage the elegant apartment for the video I'd post on social media that I scarcely noticed how the wind had suddenly whipped up, scooting grey clouds across the previously blue sky.

I wasn't dressed for cutting across the slightly damp grass, and with each step I could feel the turf sucking hungrily on my stilettoes. They were an integral part of my work wardrobe, as much as the elegant designer dresses that I bought pre-loved on Vinted and eBay. Everything about Ellie Harker Properties was carefully curated to project a certain image – and that included me, Ellie Harker.

Owning my own estate agency had been my dream for as long as I could remember, and every time I saw my name emblazoned across the website's home page, I felt a glow of pride for having spotted a gap in how high-end homes were being sold in my local area and finding a modern way to fill it.

The wind ruffled my hair, disturbing the sleek red strands of my shoulder-length bob as a single fat drop of rain fell on my upturned face. Damn. I had another client consultation in less than an hour, and drowned rat was never a great look when you wanted to make a good first impression. It's said buyers often choose a new home in less than eight minutes, and an estate agent even quicker.

It had taken a long time and a great many outtakes before I'd finally been relaxed enough in front of my phone's camera to feel happy posting my videos on Instagram and TikTok. It was hard to believe how uncertain and nervous I'd been in those early days, when now, switching my phone to video and chatting to my followers – who'd grown to over ten thousand – felt as natural as breathing.

That's not to say there hadn't been some initial hiccups. 'How come neither of you ever mentioned there's something seriously weird about my voice?' I remember asking Mel and Jackson, my two oldest university friends, who'd insisted on taking me out to celebrate when I officially launched the business three years ago.

'Everyone thinks that,' Jackson had reassured me, snapping shut his laptop. His help with the technical side of setting up my agency and the website had been invaluable.

'Everyone thinks my voice is peculiar? Terrific.'

Jackson had giggled at that. It was one of his most endearing qualities. He was in his thirties now but still laughed with the abandon of a giddy six-year-old.

'No, dummy,' he'd corrected, flicking his hair like a young Hugh Grant, 'everyone thinks their voice is terrible. The jury's still out as to whether yours is actually worse than most.'

'Don't listen to him,' Mel had said, already half tipsy from two glasses of Prosecco. 'You sound great, and you're going to be rich and successful and will probably end up being far too busy and important to mix with the likes of us.'

I shivered at the memory, which had proved a little too prophetic for comfort. Not the rich part, but the bit about not mixing with my old friends. Weeks had developed a nasty habit of sliding seamlessly into months, and before I knew it, over half a year had passed and I was only calling Jackson when something went wrong with my software, and I honestly couldn't remember the last time I'd spoken to Mel. The thought made me far more uncomfortable than the fast-falling rain.

Drops were landing like ink-spots on my navy shift dress, and I suddenly regretted not paying more attention to the breakfast TV presenter that morning, who'd stood beside a map decorated with lightning bolts and grey clouds. I'd left home without a jacket or even an umbrella, as though playing a dangerous game of dare with the elements.

'It's not going to rain,' I told the chirpy weather girl, glancing through the window at a cloudless blue sky before taking one last swig of coffee and switching off the TV. I hurried from the kitchen, which was in its usual immaculate state – so pristine it could probably double up as an operating theatre if the local hospital ran out of space. I kept my home as though buyers were waiting on the doorstep to view it and liked everything to be just so . . . which I'm sure some counsellor could happily spend months unpicking if I had time to spend on discovering why, which I didn't, because the agency was like a greedy sponge, sucking up every free moment of my life.

Around me people were pulling plastic macs from bags, erecting pop-up umbrellas, and running in every direction like disturbed bugs from beneath a log. I considered joining the throng heading towards the outdoor café, with its large canvas awning, but however fast I ran, I would be one of the last to arrive. Mums with prams were ducking and diving like kamikaze pilots to get their offspring out of the rain, while dog owners were scooping up tiny pooches and tucking them inside their jackets to keep them dry, which I found infinitely cuter. And that's something else an analyst would probably have a field day working on.

The rain was falling in earnest now and a loud crack of thunder stopped my dithering. Impulsively I stepped out of my heels, hooked the straps over one finger, inched my dress higher, and took off at a sprint towards a group of tall oaks beside the park's boating lake.

It had been years since I'd run like that. Somewhere, in some long-forgotten drawer in my mother's house, there had been a collection of medals I'd once won for competing at county level. But that was then and, contrary to the old saying about it being like riding a bike, every single muscle in my body had forgotten how hard running could be. My sides were heaving like a racehorse by the time I finally reached shelter.

It was only a moment or two before I was joined by a second rain refugee. He approached the oak at a run that didn't appear to have winded him, dressed in jeans, jacket, and white trainers that I doubted would look the same after today. I couldn't make out his features – the sky had now turned a shade of charcoal and the overhanging boughs effectively stole what little daylight remained. He was tall though, I could see that, and broad-shouldered, because the jacket – whose collar he'd lifted to keep out the rain – was stretched taut across his back. He was standing on the periphery of the oak's shelter, scoping the park for the next cluster of trees. He kept checking his watch, and everything about him said he was in a hurry.

The rain was cascading off the leaves and the man shook his head, spraying droplets like a dog after a wet walk. There was plenty of free space farther beneath the canopy, but he kept his distance from me. I wondered if he'd even noticed there was anyone else beneath his tree. He certainly seemed preoccupied.

Even so, we both spun to our left as a bolt of lightning, more vivid than any I'd ever seen before, lit up the entire park like a photographer's flashbulb. I saw panic on the faces of the people who were still out in the open as they faltered in their stride, not knowing which way to run.

Poor them. They should have sheltered under here, I thought, before the idea was shunted aside as the man with the white trainers glanced back and our eyes met. His were green, I remember that, almost as vivid as the foliage we were standing beneath. And there was a warmth in them as he flashed me a smile that I interpreted to mean Well, this is shit, isn't it?

Thunder exploded like a bomb overhead and for a moment I swear I felt the earth beneath my feet shuddering from the soundwave. It had come so quickly after the lightning, far less than thirty seconds, and some half-remembered fact from aeons ago told me that was significant, maybe even dangerous, but I couldn't remember why.

The man turned slightly, and from the way he was bouncing on the soles of his feet, I could tell he was intending to move on, which bothered me on a level I never did have a chance to explore. He lifted a lightly tanned forearm, exposed by the rolled-up cuffs of his jacket, and checked his watch once more, and that's when I saw the takeout coffee cup in his hand. Scrawled in thick black sharpie letters across one side was the name Rhys, which I remember thinking really suited him, when suddenly everything changed . . . irrevocably and forever.

There was light everywhere. It felt as though I'd been picked up and dropped into the centre of the sun. The tree branches were gone, so too was the park and the man who was beneath the oak with me. Everything was swallowed up by the light and then an intense jolt lasered out from above, below, and beside me, and I felt a tremendous power lift me off my feet. I don't remember hitting the ground.

◆ ◆ ◆

'Are you okay?'

That was definitely the most ridiculous question I'd been asked in a very long time.

'Can you hear me?'

I moved my head slightly in what might have been an attempt at a nod.

It seemed to please the stranger who was bent over me. I'd thought at first it was a bear, which in my confused state seemed perfectly normal for a city park in the UK on a weekday morning. But my eyes were still dazzled from the light. There were swirling shapes and dots dancing across my field of vision, behind which a person – or possibly a talking bear – floated in and out of focus.

'Okay, she's back with us,' the voice said, moving a little to one side, which allowed me to confirm it wasn't a bear at all, but a man with thick curly hair and an extremely bushy beard.

'How's the guy doing?' the non-bear man called out to someone unseen.

'I still can't get a pulse,' called a female voice, full of fear and concern.

'Be right with you,' the bearded man said, glancing over his shoulder at a woman who was working on someone on the ground. I couldn't see who the casualty was, but they were wearing white trainers. My vision was clearly still impaired, because it looked very much like the one on the left foot was smoking.

My bearded rescuer got to his feet to join his companion, who now appeared to be grunting out something that sounded curiously like the Bee Gees' 'Stayin' Alive' as she bent over the figure on the grass.

I had no idea what had happened to me or the other casualty on the ground, but I knew it was bad long before I heard the wail of approaching sirens.

I lifted my head from the sodden turf, confused to see a circle of onlookers gathered around the cluster of trees. Someone broke through their ranks, carrying an object roughly the size of carry-on luggage.

'The café had one,' the teenage boy said in triumph, thrusting the case towards the bearded man.

The low-level mutterings of the onlookers died away as a robotic female voice spoke from the device, giving out instructions that the bearded man and the woman dutifully followed. I still couldn't see properly and struggled to sit up, which was a bad idea, although admittedly not as terrible as the decision to shelter beneath a tall oak tree in a thunderstorm.

A thick black velvet fog was beginning to descend. Before it engulfed me, I heard the bearded man call out 'Clear' and I responded with the first word I'd been able to summon up since hitting the ground.

'Rhys!'

Chapter Two

I remember almost nothing about the ambulance ride to the hospital. Afterwards they told me I kept drifting in and out of consciousness throughout the ten-minute drive to the nearest A and E, where a small army of medics were waiting on the pavement for us to arrive. When I was awake, there was only one word in my new, limited vocabulary, which I recited like a mantra to the accompanying wail of the siren. For some reason the name of a total stranger had been seared into my brain by the lightning, and I couldn't seem to stop myself from repeating it, with absolutely no idea why I was doing so.

The haziness continued for some time. I remember dazzling overhead lights and ceiling tiles flashing in and out of view as I was wheeled speedily down a hospital corridor. Gradually things became clear enough for me to marvel at just how many doctors were crammed into the treatment room. There was a feeling of being an exhibit in a zoo, because most of the white-coated individuals were just standing around observing me, as though I was some sort of oddity. None of it made any sense until I overheard one of the doctors explaining my condition to a new arrival.

' . . . struck by lightning.'

'What?' It was the first thing I'd said that wasn't the name of a man I'd never met.

'It's okay,' said a female doctor with a soft American accent. 'You're going to be fine, Ellie.'

I frowned, wondering how she knew my name, before remembering the wallet full of business cards in my bag.

She looped a stethoscope around her neck in a slick manoeuvre that suggested she'd done it a thousand times before. As most of her colleagues looked young enough to still be in school, I took comfort in her expertise.

I was wearing a hospital gown that I had no recollection of being changed into. The doctor carefully moved it aside to reveal my left shoulder, which felt sore and oddly warm. A feeling like pins and needles on overdrive was radiating down my arm.

'You've been incredibly lucky today,' the doctor said. Several people in the semicircle nodded their agreement. 'The tree took the main strike, and you received a side flash. Thankfully that made you a secondary target; a short circuit for the lightning, if you like.'

'Lightning?' I said, my voice a horrified whisper. 'I got hit by lightning?' Each word climbed half an octave higher. The doctor slowly nodded before summoning up a comforting smile.

'But shouldn't I be dead now? Isn't that what usually happens?'

For one moment I wondered if I was, and that's why everything felt so weird and disjointed. There were an awful lot of people in the room wearing nothing but white.

Unbelievably, the doctor chuckled, but I found none of this even remotely funny. Suddenly I wasn't so sure if I liked her, after all.

'Actually, about ninety per cent of victims survive a lightning strike. You're probably surprised to hear that.' To be honest, it wasn't a topic I'd ever given a passing thought to before. 'I saw many people who'd been struck just like you were today, when I worked in a Houston emergency room.'

The medics in the room all craned forward, clearly hanging on her every word, but I was still struggling to get my fuzzy head around what the hell had happened to me.

'We're going to run a few more tests, and I'd like you to have a CT scan before we discharge you. But the good news is that your heartbeat has returned to its normal rhythm, and we believe everything else will stabilise just as effectively. You should be able to go home before the end of the day.'

'Home?' I said, my voice wavering as though for a moment I couldn't remember where that might be. I corralled my scattered thoughts and managed to summon up an image of the top-floor flat in the Victorian house where I lived.

'Everything just feels so confused and not quite real.' I hated how helpless I sounded but was powerless to keep the tremor out of my voice.

'That's perfectly understandable. You've had a big shock. No pun intended.'

That produced smiles all round, and several of the young doctors even chuckled a little, but it was way too soon for me to appreciate that kind of black humour.

'Is there someone we can call for you? Someone you'd like to have here with you?'

Like a wheel in a game show, my thoughts cycled through possible candidates, but each of them clicked past and the wheel never came to a stop.

'No. I live alone.'

Did I? For a moment I couldn't actually remember, but it felt true. Not knowing was frankly terrifying.

'You don't want us to call . . .' The doctor hesitated and glanced down to check on a clipboard that was lying on the bed. 'Rhys?' she suggested with an encouraging smile.

'Who's Rhys?'

That wiped the smile away.

'We assumed he might be your partner, or perhaps a friend?'

I shook my head, feeling increasingly as though I'd walked into a really confusing TV show, somewhere mid-season.

'It's just that you've been saying that name on and off ever since they brought you in.'

'I have?' I certainly didn't remember doing so. I blinked several times as though it might help the cloud of crazy to drift away. It didn't.

Perhaps the doctor meant Ash? He was my boyfriend. Almost as soon as the thought landed, I knew it was wrong. Ash and I had dated when I was in my twenties. We'd met just after I graduated and then we'd . . . The thoughts and memories were like wisps of smoke that slipped out of my grasp before I could secure them.

I wasn't with Ash anymore, was I? We'd broken up. Or had we got back together again, and I'd somehow forgotten? I didn't like the sudden panic that clutched me amidst the swirling confusion. Shouldn't I know if I was someone's girlfriend? Or fiancée? I snatched up my left hand. It was bare of any rings.

'What's wrong with me? Why can't I remember things?'

The doctor nodded wisely. 'Memory loss is a common symptom in cases like yours. Happily, it rarely lasts long. And, as I said before, you were one very lucky young woman today.' Her eyes darkened for a moment, which made me think the same might not be true for everyone who'd been standing beneath that tree. The name Rhys echoed through my head like a slowly tolling bell. I bit my tongue to stop it escaping once more.

The CT was scary, and everyone involved in the scan was clearly a dab hand at poker, because I couldn't read anything from their faces when it was over. If the lightning had damaged anything on its passage through my body, no one was saying.

They carried out other tests, but my mind kept wandering, as though its tether to the here and now had been severed. For someone who had turned multitasking into an art form, who could juggle two phone calls and simultaneously rattle off an email without thinking, it was all a little terrifying. Everyone was very kind, speaking to me slowly and carefully, with big round enunciated vowels, which just made me feel worse. This wasn't me. This wasn't who I was.

I especially hated the wheelchair they insisted I use to transport me to and from Radiology. I hated how my day had gone from one in which I was in total control to one where I was reduced to a statistic – albeit a rare and interesting one.

The nurse who accompanied me back to the treatment room politely pretended not to notice the tears that began to fall in the lift. I rarely cried, and the quiet, hitching sobs had a field day at the sudden release, wracking their way through me. She laid a hand gently on my shoulder as the lift doors slid open.

'It's just so . . . so . . . disorientating,' I finished helplessly. It wasn't exactly the right word, but it was the closest one I could find. 'I don't know how to explain it, but everything feels so strange and off-kilter.'

'I'm sure it must do,' she said, finding a folded square of tissue from somewhere and passing it to me. It took a further two before they came away without black streaks of mascara all over them. I felt wrecked, both inside and out.

'Maybe there is something that might make you feel a little better.'

I looked up from the wheelchair, red-eyed, scarlet-nosed, but curious.

'Okaaay,' I said, sounding so unlike my usual confident self even my own mother wouldn't have recognised me. The thought immediately made me feel even worse than before, which was saying something.

Like a getaway driver on a heist, the nurse pivoted the wheelchair with a one-hundred-and-eighty-degree spin. 'We probably shouldn't, but . . .'

I had no idea what she was proposing, or where she was taking me, but for a few minutes at least it distracted me from worrying about the gaps in my memory. She wheeled me down a new corridor, glancing frequently over her shoulder as though we were being pursued. I was definitely intrigued now. Then came to a stop beside a row of curtained cubicles.

'I should probably check if he's okay with this first,' she said, looking like she might be regretting her impulsive decision.

'Who?' I asked, but I think part of me already knew the answer.

My heart, which had been beating perfectly satisfactorily – according to the monitors – suddenly picked up its pace. The tingling in my arms intensified, and I saw the fine downy hair covering them was standing on end, as though electricity was once again travelling through my body. The air certainly felt charged as the nurse reached for the curtains. Through a gap in the fabric I saw a bare arm, attached to a drip. But it wasn't the medical paraphernalia that caught my attention. It was the intricate and detailed tattoo that was etched onto the skin of the man's arm.

A stab of disappointment pierced me like a dart. I'd guessed wrong. My memory might be sketchy, but I was certain that when the green-eyed man had checked his watch, there'd been no full-sleeve tattoo on his arm.

The nurse was still holding the curtains, like a magician's assistant about to perform a big reveal. She spoke in a whisper that was no way quiet enough.

'Actually,' she said with what appeared to be a last-minute change of heart. 'Perhaps it might be better to do this another time. I think he's asleep, anyway.'

'No, he isn't,' said a voice from the bed.

His eyes were just as green as I remembered. At least I hadn't forgotten that.

'Rhys.' His name burst its way past my lips in the manner it had apparently been doing all day.

The man in the bed was bare-chested. Well, that wasn't entirely true. There was no hospital gown covering his torso, but it was anything but bare. I tore my eyes away from the mesmerising network of fern-like etchings and twisting vines that decorated almost every inch of visible skin.

'It's you,' Rhys said, somewhat artlessly. 'The girl with the shoes in her hand.'

It was no longer an accurate descriptor, for my shoes were somewhere unknown, presumably with the rest of my clothes, and my feet were currently clad in lurid blue hospital socks.

'Hi,' I said, feeling shy in a way I truly don't think I'd done since I was about sixteen years old. All at once I regretted turning down the offer of a blanket to cover my legs, which suddenly felt horribly exposed in the wheelchair.

'So, it got you too?' Rhys asked, his eyes mercifully fixed only on my face.

'The lightning? Yes, it did.'

The man in the bed nodded, looking as shell-shocked as I felt. 'It's pretty surreal, isn't it?'

'I can't get my head around it. The doctor said the odds of being struck are less than one in a million.'

We shared a look that only survivors would recognise.

'This was a good idea,' said the nurse, more to herself than either of us. Her glance went from Rhys to me and she gave us a look of encouragement before pushing my chair even closer to his bed.

'Why don't I leave the two of you to chat for a minute?' She swept the cubicle curtains around my wheelchair, cocooning us in an illusion of privacy as though everything we said couldn't easily be overheard. Before either of us had a chance to protest, she slipped through the opening, leaving me alone with a semi-naked man, currently looking just as confused as I was.

'Does she think that we know each other, or that we're . . . ?' I trailed off, leaving my hand, which was flapping in the space between us, to finish that sentence.

'I think she might,' Rhys said, immediately on my wavelength in a way that rarely happens between strangers. And yet this man didn't feel like a stranger. The exact opposite, in fact. 'Although I've no idea why she'd assume that.'

There was no way of stopping the blush. It scorched my cheeks like a flame.

'Erm . . . that might be my fault. Apparently, I came round murmuring your name. I saw it on your coffee cup before the accident and it's kind of got stuck in my head. They tell me I've been saying it a lot.'

I swear if my face got any hotter, they were going to need a fire extinguisher on it. I waited for him to reach for the Call button; to have someone evict this clearly deranged person from his cubicle. Instead, he just smiled, and it was so engaging it took me right back to that moment beneath the oak tree.

'Why do you think that is?' he asked.

'I've absolutely no idea.'

His eyes left my face as he looked me over, in a way that made me feel shy again.

'Were you injured in the strike?' he asked.

'Not really. I was unconscious for a minute or two and I've got a small burn on my shoulder.' I only just caught myself before I pushed the fabric aside to show him. The fact that I didn't know this man kept slipping out of my head even faster than everything else I appeared to have forgotten. 'That's about it.' For some reason I didn't mention the memory loss. 'I think you got it worse than me.'

'So they tell me.'

'In fact, I think your heart might have stopped.' I gasped at my indiscreet, runaway tongue as I realised too late it wasn't my place to reveal such devastating news. What the hell was wrong with me? Had the lightning burnt all good sense away?

I must have looked every bit as mortified as I felt, for Rhys lifted one hand and laid it lightly on my forearm, which – even though it had no business being there – had somehow found a place to rest on his mattress. He patted my arm reassuringly, and it was strangely comforting to know that we were both guilty of crossing personal boundaries. We were behaving like old friends, rather than two people whose sum total acquaintance amounted to less than ten minutes in each other's company.

'It's okay. I already knew.'

I gazed down at his hand, which was still resting on me. The strange tattoo markings even extended to his fingers, and I had to squash a totally inappropriate urge to trace the curious vine-like trail across his knuckles.

Someone drew in a sharp breath, and I truly don't know if it was him or me.

'But you're okay now, though?' My question sounded more anxious than I'd expected.

'I'm fine.' Rhys gave a small rueful laugh that took me by surprise. 'It's been a good day . . . apart from the unexpected cardiac arrest and the full-body tattoo markings that certainly weren't there when I woke up this morning.'

'The lightning did that?'

Rhys nodded.

'My mates all got tattoos when we were eighteen, but I was too chicken to go through with it. I've got this thing about needles. Getting struck by lightning I can cope with, but I almost passed out when they put this drip in. And having these marks now . . . this is a lot.'

My gaze followed the pattern that began at the base of his throat, covered the skin of both shoulders, his entire chest, and travelled the length of one arm, right down to his fingertips. The other arm was tanned and, bizarrely, totally unmarked.

It was a visual and sobering wake-up call of what we'd experienced.

'We could have died,' I said, my voice scarcely more than a whisper.

'But we didn't,' Rhys said, and I suspected that even before the lightning struck, he was a glass-half-full kind of person. 'Someone up there must have been looking out for us.' He flicked a quick glance towards the ceiling, but I doubted he was referring to the medics on the next floor up.

His words made me shiver. I'd always been fiercely pragmatic and level-headed, never believing in anything remotely woo-woo or spiritual. In fact, with years of friendship between us, it had been the only red-flag topic between Mel and me. Our views on the subject were polar opposites. She'd filled our shared university house with healing crystals and incense to cleanse our auras, while I'd maintained the only thing that legitimately needed cleansing was the drains. In the end we'd agreed to differ, but even now, any conversation that steered towards things other-worldly made me distinctly uncomfortable.

'Are you okay?' Rhys asked, leaning in close enough for me to smell a warm, woodsy aftershave above the pervading hospital antiseptic. 'You kind of drifted away there for a moment.'

'I'm good,' I said, not entirely sure if that was true.

There was a sound of a chair scraping across the floor from beyond the cubicle, and I shot an anxious look over my shoulder. 'I think I'm about to be taken back.' The regret in my voice was embarrassing.

'We should have said we were a couple. Maybe then they'd have let you stay.' It was a totally inappropriate suggestion that felt completely right.

'What? Lie, you mean?'

He nodded.

'I'm an estate agent. I never lie,' I said with a grin, pleased to see a matching one break out across his face.

'Are you a good one?'

'Excellent,' I said, but the usual pride in my voice sounded strangely forced.

'I'm sorry,' said a disembodied head as it popped through the gap in the curtains, 'but I really do need to take you back now.'

'Okay.' I tried to ignore the immediate feeling of disappointment sweeping through me.

'I'm glad you're going to be alright,' I said to Rhys, feeling oddly shy in front of the nurse, which was daft because she'd probably heard every word of our conversation from her sentry position outside the cubicle. She was looking decidedly twitchy now, and I wondered how many hospital rules she'd broken in bringing me to my fellow victim's bedside. But her instincts had been good. I didn't understand why, but seeing Rhys and knowing we'd both survived this incredible one-in-a-million experience really had helped.

'Ditto. It was nice meeting you, Shoe Girl, even if it was in the weirdest possible circumstances.'

I was being wheeled slowly backwards, away from his bed, away from him, and that was just as it should be. So why did it seem so wrong? I'd felt so much better when this total stranger had been next to me, and there really was no explanation for that. Nor was there for the way I impulsively asked the nurse to stop.

She halted the wheelchair in a squeak of rubber wheels on lino. Rhys was still staring at me from his hospital bed.

'My name is Ellie. Ellie Harker. You can find me on Insta.'

Chapter Three

You can find me on Insta.

The words circled in my head for about the fiftieth time in the two hours since I'd said them. It was no good, they still sounded as laughably pathetic as they'd done when I'd uttered them in the hospital corridor. What an idiot, I thought as I flopped back on hospital pillows so hard they could probably double up as sandbags.

'Do you need help getting dressed?' the kindly nurse had asked. I think she felt sorry for me. After all, how many people successfully cheat death by lightning strike and don't have a single friend or family member at their bedside to accompany them home?

'My sister will be coming to stay with me for a few days,' I'd lied to the doctor when she'd expressed concern about me going home alone. 'It'll take her a couple of hours to get there, but she's already on her way.'

The doctor had looked relieved, and I was glad that whatever else I'd forgotten, I didn't appear to have lost the ability to creatively embellish the truth. My days as a successful real estate agent could well have been numbered if I had.

Of course, this was more than just a little bending of the facts, because there was no sister. I was an only child, something I'd always felt was my fault. 'It was a difficult birth,' I could remember overhearing my mother tell someone, when I was still too young to know the facts of life, much less what a birth – easy or otherwise – had been. 'She was such a fretful baby that I never felt the need to go through that again.' It had taken me until my mid-teens before I stopped feeling guilty about all the little Harker siblings that never were, because of me.

Of course I thought about phoning my mum from the hospital. I even got so far as scrolling through my mobile for her phone number, but something stopped me from making the call. Would she insist on coming to stay to look after me? Or worse, that I move in with her until I'd fully recovered? I shivered at that thought despite the near tropical temperature of the hospital ward. We didn't do well under the same roof, my mother and I. Things got uncomfortable whenever the space between us was reduced to partition walls.

And as I lay on the hospital bed, with my mobile in my hand, I was shocked to realise I couldn't actually remember the last time we'd spoken. The memory of it was something else that had been seared away by the lightning. Were we currently at odds with each other? Had there been another disagreement about something that probably, in hindsight, had never been worth arguing over?

I couldn't remember, and so I didn't call Mum, because there was no casual way of saying, 'Hey, guess what? I got hit by lightning today. Just thought you might like to know.' Because the biggest fear, the one that really crippled me, was what if she didn't?

'Have you got everything?' asked the nurse, looping the strap of my bag over my good shoulder, mindful of the neat white dressing applied to the minor burn on my other one.

'I think so,' I said, bending down to slip my feet back into my shoes. As I did, my thoughts took a brief detour back to Rhys calling me 'the girl with the shoes in her hand'. A smile settled on my lips. Perhaps that Insta comment hadn't been so awful after all.

'Are you sure you don't want us to call you a taxi? It's no trouble.'

I glanced towards the window. The afternoon had slipped into early evening by the time they'd finally said I could leave. This morning's rain had long since dried up and the sun was now hanging low in the sky, painting everything in warm, golden hues. I had an uncharacteristic urge to find an empty bench somewhere and just sit quietly, doing absolutely nothing except enjoying the warmth of the sun on my skin.

'I'll call an Uber when I'm ready. Thank you so much for everything you've done for me today,' I said, feeling strangely unsure of the correct protocol here. A handshake felt too cold, a hug too intimate. I usually knew exactly how to navigate my way through any social situation, and this uncertainty was almost as unsettling as the memory loss.

'You take care now,' the nurse said with a smile. 'And stay away from tall trees in thunderstorms.'

'I will.'

'I tell you something else you might want to stay away from,' said a passing colleague. 'And that's the front entrance. There's a bunch of journalists and photographers waiting to speak to the lightning-strike victims.'

'There's paparazzi?' exclaimed my nurse. 'Oh, that's a bit exciting, isn't it? Kind of like being a celebrity.'

A senior member of the ward, who everyone appeared to be a little scared of, looked up from the chart she was reading and gave a scornful laugh. 'I don't think anyone who works for the Gazette or the Chronicle can justifiably call themselves a pap. But you might want to avoid going out right now; unless you want to be interviewed, that is.'

Did I? For someone who spent an awful lot of time curating a social media presence, I was weirdly reluctant to share what had happened and see it splashed across the local paper.

'It's not just the local rags,' added my nurse, who'd gone to a window that afforded a better view. 'There's a van from the regional TV news station.'

Her colleague nodded. 'They're quizzing anyone in a uniform if they know the names of the two people hit by lightning this morning.'

With legs that no longer felt steady, I sank back down on the bed and pulled out my phone. I went straight to the most popular social media sites and keyed in the words 'lightning victims'.

It didn't take long before phone footage, taken by various members of the crowd who'd gathered in the park, was playing on my screen. As luck would have it, the torrential rain had made it difficult for clear images to be obtained, but the videos were sharp enough to see two figures lying on the ground, both being worked on by two off-duty paramedics, one of whom bore a striking resemblance to a grizzly bear.

I set aside the phone with a feeling of distaste. Those filming the scene and posting the images hadn't known there'd be a positive outcome. How could they? And yet they'd happily continued recording, as though the internet had a right to see the moment when we could easily have died.

But we didn't die, a voice in my head reminded me, a voice belonging to a man with brilliant green eyes.

'Why don't I make you a nice cup of tea?' suggested my favourite nurse, giving my uninjured shoulder a gentle squeeze. 'Then maybe by the time you're done, they'll all have packed up and gone home for the day.'

I didn't think journalists – even local ones – gave up on a story quite that easily, but she was being so kind I took her up on the offer. There were a couple of mouthfuls still left in my cup when a tall male nurse strode purposefully onto the ward and approached the clerk at the desk. I was too far away to hear their conversation, but I knew he was asking about me even before the clerk pointed in my direction.

By the time he reached my bay, I was already on my feet.

'Ellie Harker?'

'Yes.' There were threads of reticence in my voice, as though everything today might be open for debate. I couldn't remember a single time in my life when I'd felt less certain about absolutely everything.

He smiled, instantly diluting the adrenaline flooding my veins.

'This is for you.' He held out a folded square of paper that looked as though it had been hastily torn from a lined pad. I looked up, my eyes full of questions and my fingers trembling as I reached for the note.

Two words, written in bold strokes on one side of the missive, answered one question, but raised a whole lot more.

Shoe Girl

I'd told Rhys my name, but the jokey title hit the exact tone that I imagined he'd intended. My fingers were still a little unsteady, but now for a totally different reason.

I unfolded the note.

> Hello Ellie. I don't know if you've heard, but it seems we're kind of minor celebrities after what happened today, and there's a bunch of people waiting outside to interview us. If that's your thing, then great. But it's definitely not mine, and my good mate Olly – who's standing in front

> of you – has offered to sneak me out of a service entrance at the back of the hospital, and I wondered if you wanted to come with us? If you do and fancy sharing a taxi, just let him know. If not, make sure they spell your name right in the papers! R.

I read it twice before looking up at the man Rhys had sent to find me. It wasn't a big deal, just a small act of kindness, but try telling that to my eyes, which were suddenly full of tears. Was I stuck in Rhys's head in the same inexplicable way he was lodged in mine? Was this a result of the lightning, because I really didn't think I'd be acting so weirdly if I'd met him under normal circumstances. But nothing about today had been normal. And opting to escape from the hospital with him certainly wasn't, but just seconds later that's exactly what I agreed to do.

It was only a ten-minute walk to where Rhys was waiting, but it was long enough for me to know that I really liked his friend. Olly filled every second with irreverent, humorous chatter, which was entertaining but also a little frustrating as it gave me no chance to shoehorn in a quick question or two about Rhys.

When the lift doors slid open, Olly stuck his head out first, comedically checking the corridor as though we were about to be ambushed.

'It's like breaking Bonnie and Clyde out of prison,' he said with a grin that I had a feeling scarcely ever left his lips.

'Apart from the bank robbing and shooting people bit,' I said, still trying to tell myself that my pulse was racing because of what we were doing and not who I was about to see.

We'd gone a different, circuitous route to the place where I'd last seen Rhys, so it threw me for a moment when we rounded a corner and found him leaning up against the wall, waiting for us.

It was hot in the hospital and Rhys looked distinctly uncomfortable, with the sleeves of his jacket rolled down and the collar once again raised. But despite all his efforts, the curious markings were still visible at his wrist and throat. Rightly or wrongly, I found the lightning marks mesmerising and was strangely disappointed they were hidden. I tuned out the voice in my head that annoyingly wanted to ask just how much of his skin they covered, because there was no way to slip that one innocently into a conversation.

'This is really kind of you,' I said instead, directing a grateful smile at both men.

'Aww, no worries,' said Olly, and it's a measure of how distracted I must have been that it was the first time I noticed a distinct Aussie twang. 'Smuggling patients out of the hospital is my favourite part of the job.'

I enjoyed the amused expression on Rhys's face.

'And I kind of like being known as the guy who helped the Park People avoid the press.'

'Park People? Is that what they're calling us?' I asked, turning to Rhys and just about managing not to be dazzled by the intense emerald of his gaze. How did anyone ever concentrate when they were talking to him? Or was it just me?

'Apparently. Until someone digs deeper and uncovers our names.'

We followed Olly through doors he had to swipe with a pass to open and along twisting labyrinth-like corridors. I made the mistake of glancing down one of them and saw a pair of swing double doors with the word Morgue on them. How easily our journey today could have ended up there. A shiver travelled the entire length of my body, just like the lightning had done. Olly was too busy leading the way to notice, but Rhys saw, and his eyes darkened to the colour of a midnight forest in concern.

'Are you okay?' Three words and that was all it took for me to feel seen – really seen – in a way I didn't think I'd ever been before. From the boys I'd dated who'd never understood me, to the men who'd slid in and out of my life and my bed, had anyone so effortlessly managed to scythe through my protective carapace before?

Old me, the person I'd been before thousands of volts of electricity had flowed through me, said I was talking nonsense. Except 'nonsense' felt like my life before this morning.

'The exit is just up ahead.' Olly's voice cut into my thoughts as we entered a corridor with sack barrows lined up against both walls.

'Wait.' Both men stopped so abruptly they almost collided into each other like dominoes.

I closed the gap between Rhys and me, not knowing why, and my panic immediately subsided. But my heart was still skittering in my chest as all at once the enormity of the day caught up with me.

'We were so lucky today.'

'I know,' Rhys said, and I felt like another link was silently forged in the chain binding us. The very real possibility that after we'd shared a taxi ride together I might never see him again was inexplicably terrifying.

This wasn't me. I was a long slow burn in relationships. I'd heard it too many times to ignore it or believe it was wrong. I didn't do spontaneous; everything was controlled and measured, and I had no idea who this impulsive, reckless person was who'd jumped into the driver's seat of my life. Or how the hell to get her out. Or even if I wanted to, I was honest enough to admit.

We all blinked like moles as we emerged into the dwindling daylight through a service exit at the back of the hospital outbuilding. We appeared to be in some sort of delivery drop-off area, but right now the only vehicle there was an idling blue taxi.

'Ah good, your ride is here,' said Olly with a satisfied nod, who'd clearly masterminded our covert exit.

'I owe you one for this, mate,' Rhys said, pulling Olly in for a short, hard hug.

I watched, fascinated. It had always seemed a shame to me that British guys didn't embrace each other more, and yet Rhys looked totally comfortable as he held on to his friend with what appeared to be genuine affection.

'Remember what I said.' Olly's voice was low and suddenly serious. The men exchanged a meaningful look. 'You have to call, Rhys.'

'I know.'

They were being frustratingly cryptic, and I only just managed to bite my tongue before it ran away from me and asked what they were talking about.

Olly turned to me and held out a huge bear-paw of a hand. The man truly looked more like an Aussie rugby player than a medic.

'It's been a pleasure meeting you, Ellie Harker. Take care of yourself and don't overdo things for a while. This kind of trauma takes time to get over.'

I nodded, as though I knew all about how to recover from a day which so easily could have been my last.

'I'll be in touch,' Rhys said, one eye on the empty delivery bay and the other on the taxi, whose driver was starting to look a little impatient. 'We'd better go.' He reached for my elbow and, gently cupping it, guided me towards the cab. It was old-fashioned courtesy, the kind he'd probably afford to an elderly grandma or a maiden aunt, but it did something to my stomach that made me wonder if my internal organs were entirely safe in his vicinity. As I slid into the back seat beside him and his thigh inadvertently brushed against mine, I decided that I really didn't care.

Chapter Four

It was probably childish of me, but I rather enjoyed the moment when our taxi drove straight past the cluster of newspeople still congregated at the front of the hospital.

'I wonder when they'll realise we've gone,' I said, swivelling in my seat and watching as the group got smaller and smaller in the back windscreen.

'I hope the hospital security is tight and no one reveals our names. Or at least not until we've decided who we want to tell.'

Rhys was looking at me with an enquiring expression, as though he wasn't sure if his next question was appropriate but was going to ask it anyway.

'Do you have family or a partner in the area? I was kind of surprised there was no one with you at the hospital today.'

'I could say exactly the same thing about you,' I batted back.

His laugh was equal parts irony and humour, seasoned with a pinch of admiration.

'My parents live in Jersey, far enough away that they won't have heard about what happened today. I think it might be best to wait and tell them in person.'

He raised his eyebrows and gave me an encouraging it's your turn now look.

'My mother and I are . . . we're not exactly . . .' I blew out a long breath that probably explained things far better than my faltering, incomplete sentences. 'I'm going to go with your "tell them in person" thing. Probably. Eventually.'

Those brilliant green eyes could easily be my kryptonite. I could feel them lasering straight through my emotional defences and seeing the uncomfortable truth far more clearly than I wanted him to.

'I told the hospital staff that I'm going to be nursed back to strength by a non-existent sister I don't have.' I made a big show of checking my watch. 'She'll be at mine any minute now.'

Rhys grinned even while he was shaking his head and tutting at my lie.

'Speaking of which,' he said, 'we need to give the driver your address. The only one he has so far is mine.'

The urge to say 'We could go back to yours' was so strong I had to bite my tongue to stop the suggestion tumbling out. That, and the fact that Rhys hadn't given even the smallest hint that he wanted to extend our time together.

Could being struck by lightning regress a person so far into adolescence that they actually forgot all the good sense they'd accumulated as an adult? I resolved to look that up online as soon as I got the chance.

My cheeks were warm with embarrassment as I leant forward and gave the driver my address.

'So, do you get on well with your fictitious sibling?' Rhys asked as the cab changed direction and began threading its way through the early rush-hour traffic towards my part of town.

'Incredibly well. Probably better than I do with most real-life people.'

I hadn't intended my answer to be so revealing, nor for it to be delivered with a plaintive quality in my voice that I swear I'd never heard before. I rushed to self-correct.

'But that's probably because for the last three years I've put everything on hold to concentrate on getting my business off the ground. It's been both a passion and an obsession.'

My answer brought tiny frown lines between Rhys's eyes, and it set me on the defensive.

'Not that I'd change anything. It's been worth the effort. I just meant that's the reason why there isn't a crowd of people queued up to collect me from the hospital. I've kind of dropped off the friendship radar recently.'

I'd been examined and scrutinised by doctors and specialists for most of the day, but I don't think any of them had looked at me as intently as Rhys was now. Forget kryptonite, Rhys's gaze was more like Superman's X-ray vision, and it was starting to make me feel uncomfortably exposed.

I had every intention of turning the tables on him and asking why there'd been no one at his bedside, except for Olly, who didn't really count as he worked at the hospital, but I never got the chance. Without noticing it, we'd already travelled the length of my road, and the taxi was manoeuvring into an empty parking space right in front of the converted Victorian townhouse where I lived.

'Oh. That was quick,' I said, fairly certain even the cab driver could hear the disappointment in my voice.

Rhys leant a little closer to the window to view the building, which was catching the last of the sunlight at all the right angles.

'Nice house.'

'It's only the top floor that's mine. But the rooms are big and airy, and it has a great view of the church on the heath,' I said, reaching into my purse and extracting a ten-pound note that I attempted to press into his hand to cover my half of the fare. Rhys gave me a slightly disappointed look and gently shook his head.

'That's okay. I've got this.'

I gave a small laugh that didn't come as naturally as I'd have liked.

'Well, I'll pay for the next cab we share, then.' And that came out all wrong too. It really was time to get out of the taxi before I managed to squeeze my other foot into my mouth.

My hand was on the door handle, but curiously so too was Rhys's on the other side of the back seat.

'Could you just wait here for a minute, while I walk her to the door?' he asked our driver.

Rhys was out of the cab before I could protest that I walked unaccompanied to my front door every single evening, often quite late into the night if I'd been working. As charming as it was, I wasn't used to this kind of chivalry. Except, when his hand came to rest lightly at the small of my back, every single protest appeared to have got stuck somewhere between my brain and my mouth.

Never before had I been so glad that we had the longest front garden in the street. It extended my final moments with a man I should probably never have met, and who I already knew was going to be hard to forget. The meter was running on the cab almost as fast as our minutes together were ticking away.

My key was in the lock of the main front door, but I didn't turn it.

'Well, thank you once again for the prison break . . . and the getaway car . . . and the . . .' I was running out of felony comparisons and my words dried up. I bit my lower lip and looked up into a face I was going to miss in a way that made no sense whatsoever.

'This is wrong. This is all wrong,' Rhys said, looking from me to the building, taking in the basement flat, the ground and first-floor ones, and not stopping until he reached the level that I called home.

I followed the route his gaze had taken.

'No. This is it. This is definitely where I live.'

He gave a crooked grin that only occupied one half of his mouth. I knew that because I'd been spending far too much time looking at his face.

'I mean it feels wrong to just leave you here on the doorstep when there's no one to keep an eye on you. What if you have a concussion?'

I didn't. The hospital had already confirmed that. But even so I nodded solemnly, as though he'd just uncovered a colossal hitch.

'You could slip into a coma, and someone needs to be there to call an ambulance . . . and we can't rely on your imaginary sister to do it.'

'She is, admittedly, rubbish at stuff like that,' I confirmed, already feeling a fizz of excitement bubbling in my veins.

'And your heart could stop again,' I chipped in with. 'Clearly you shouldn't be left alone either. What if you need CPR?'

'Do you know how to do it?'

I shook my head. 'But I could google it on my phone. I can type extremely fast.'

He was all-out smiling now.

'Seems to me that, having cheated death, it would be nothing less than irresponsible if we parted ways right now. We should at least spend a few hours monitoring each other.'

'Well, when you put it like that, we really don't have a choice, do we?'

He took a step back on the short flight of marble stairs that led to my door. His eyes were locked on mine. 'This is crazy, you know that?'

'I don't do crazy. Ask anyone. I was born middle-aged and sensible.'

Rhys descended a further two steps and for a horrible moment I thought he had changed his mind. But instead, he spun around and ran lightly down the remaining four treads.

'Don't move,' he said over his shoulder as he jogged towards the cab, already pulling his wallet from the back pocket of his jeans.

◆ ◆ ◆

'Wow. This is a really incredible flat.'

The estate agent in me warmed to him even more at that. The rest of me was already a lost cause.

There had been a fleeting moment of sanity when Old Ellie had elbowed her way back into my consciousness. Halfway up the three flights of stairs leading to my flat, she questioned the advisability of inviting a total stranger into my home.

You don't know this man, she insisted on the second-storey landing. He could be a con artist, a burglar, or something a great deal worse, she pointed out darkly as we crested the final flight of stairs. You're too street-smart to be this unbelievably gullible, was her final thrust as I slid my key into the Yale lock. That one almost hit home. In my job I was careful never to be alone in a building with a man I didn't know, and yet here I was, happily breaking my own rules.

Because you know this man. Even though you'd never met him until today . . . you know him.

It made no more sense than surviving being hit by lightning had done. But I trusted my instincts every bit as much as I trusted him.

I felt a glow of pride when Rhys complimented the period details of my home, the ones that had made me fall in love with it. The intricate ceiling roses, the painstakingly restored shutters, and the polished wooden floorboards all won his admiration.

'In comparison, my place is a functional, dull, soulless box,' he admitted.

'Why did you pick it then?'

It didn't seem like a tough question, but it certainly made him look uncomfortable.

'Circumstances.'

He wasn't looking at me but was studying the walls I'd splurge-painted in Farrow and Ball's finest.

His gaze travelled to the corner of the room where a chrome and canvas designer chair was artfully positioned. It was all strange angles and sharp edges and the moment I'd seen it featured in a high-end magazine, I'd known I had to have it. The price tag had made my eyes water back then – it still did – but I'd maxed out my credit card to buy it.

'Cool chair,' Rhys said, making his way towards it. I shook my head.

'I wouldn't,' I said with a rueful expression. 'I think it might have been modelled on a rack the Spanish Inquisitors used for torture.'

The rich tones of Rhys's laughter filled my lounge, and I truly couldn't remember the last times these walls had heard that sound.

'If it's so uncomfortable, why did you buy it?'

'Because it looks great and all the top designers who I follow were raving about it.'

I felt naked under the scrutiny of his eyes, knowing my reply had revealed far more about how I lived than I'd ever intended. Thankfully he seemed to sense my vulnerability and changed the topic.

'So how does a person find a flat like this?'

I gave a half-embarrassed shrug. 'Well, it helps if you happen to be an estate agent. When the good listings pop up, you nab them for yourself.'

'Perhaps the next time one does, I should ask you to hold it for me.'

'Are you thinking of moving?'

Please don't be about to leave the area.

Please don't be engaged to a supermodel.

Please don't be a mind-reader.

The last was perhaps the most important, because one glimpse of the ridiculous thoughts cycling through my head would have had any sane man running for the hills.

'I've been considering buying for a while,' Rhys eventually replied, as though the answer had taken time to pin down. 'I'm renting right now, but I've always owned. It's starting to feel like the right time to do so again.'

There was a look in his eyes that took him away from me and my flat to somewhere else altogether. Intuition suggested his answer had something to do with the cryptic comments I'd overheard between him and Olly.

'How about some tea?' I asked. 'Unless you fancy a beer or something stronger?'

'Probably best to steer clear of alcohol, after everything that's happened.'

It was a sensible answer, but I couldn't ignore the feeling that he was gently retreating from that delicious romcom moment we'd shared on the doorstep. He was steering us back into the friend zone, and even though friends might be conspicuously thin on the ground in my life right now, it still wasn't somewhere I wanted us to go.

'Milk and sugar?' I asked, pasting a cheery smile over my disappointment.

'Please.'

I took one last glance at him as I left the lounge and really wished I hadn't. He'd already pulled his mobile from his pocket and was keying in a number.

The soundproofing in my flat wasn't great. I knew exactly when the couple in the flat downstairs were running their washing machine, flushing the loo, or having sex, so hearing what was being said in my lounge was hard to avoid. As I waited for the kettle to boil, I turned on both taps full blast and instructed Alexa to increase the volume of the music currently playing. I had no desire to inadvertently eavesdrop on Rhys's private conversation, even though I was practically combusting with curiosity to know who he was calling.

Despite the distracting background soundtrack, I could still hear the low rumble of his voice. The words weren't clear, but I could pick up on the emotion behind them. He sounded agitated.

The tea was made and beginning to cool, and yet it didn't feel right to barge into the lounge and interrupt his privacy. *Scared of what you might hear?* Old Ellie was becoming a proper nuisance, and it was getting increasingly hard to shut her up.

'Would you like a biscuit with your tea?' I called out in a carrying, sing-song voice when I decided I'd hidden out in the kitchen for long enough. I'd given him advance warning of my reappearance, and yet Rhys still looked startled when I rejoined him. I smiled as though I wasn't perfectly aware I'd walked in during the middle of an awkward conversation and placed the mugs on a low table beside my highly impractical white sofa that I never sat on without a throw.

'Just message and let me know when I can call,' he said into his mobile. His voice sounded a thousand times wearier than it had earlier.

He looked up, splitting his attention between the phone call and me. 'No thanks,' he mouthed in reply to my offer of a biscuit, which was just as well as I didn't have any in the flat. He gestured towards his phone and mimed another word, 'Sorry.'

I gave a *don't worry about it* shrug and pointed to the door, to indicate I'd leave him to finish his conversation in private. He shook his head and reached for my forearm to stall me. I jolted. The touch of his hand set off fireworks inside my nervous system. While I couldn't remember exactly how it had felt when the lightning had struck, it surely couldn't have been more electrifying than this?

And it wasn't just me who felt . . . whatever it was. Rhys's eyes widened when his skin connected with mine. What the hell was happening?

'Just turn on the news or check the internet,' he mumbled into his phone. 'There'll be something about it on there. I've got to go,' he said in a rush before disconnecting the call.

'I'm really sorry about that,' he apologised, apparently unaware that his hand was still encircling my wrist.

'No. It's fine. I didn't want to intrude.'

Green eyes that had turned worryingly chilly were now growing warmer.

'It's your home. I think I'm the one who's intruding.'

I took a single beat to see if I wanted to think twice before answering that and then decided that if you were going to lose your mind, there were worse ways to go.

'Except it doesn't feel like you are.'

Two seconds, three, and then four passed before those arresting eyes met mine.

'No, it doesn't, does it?'

I can't remember which one of us suggested ordering a takeaway, but it seemed dicing with death and missing lunch gives a person an incredible appetite.

'Does everything that's happened today make you feel kind of . . . discombobulated?' I asked Rhys while we were prising cardboard lids off takeaway containers.

He paused in the task of opening the crispy beef and gave me a smile that had no right to affect my pulse in the way that it did.

'You might be the first person I've ever heard casually drop that word into an actual conversation.'

I gave a slightly embarrassed smile. 'I was looking for a more appropriate one, but if there's a better way to describe this feeling, then I must have forgotten it.'

I teetered like a lemming on a cliff edge, wondering what would happen if I proceeded, and then decided to risk it.

'Actually, that's not the only thing I seem to have forgotten.'

'Really? What else can't you remember?'

I gave him a Homer Simpson-worthy 'D'oh?' and we both laughed, not loudly, or even for long, but it was a welcome pressure release from a conversation that had suddenly taken a slightly darker turn.

'Okay. Let me rephrase that,' Rhys said, setting aside our takeaway dinner and giving me his full attention. 'What makes you think the lightning has affected your memory?'

'Well, aside from the numerous accounts on the internet where people reported their memory was definitely affected after being struck—'

Rhys held up a hand as though he was stopping traffic. 'Aside from the Google "experts".'

I bit my lip, fairly sure he'd have scoured the exact same websites I had done while waiting to be discharged from the hospital.

'Alright. It's not like I have amnesia, well, not like you see in the movies, where you get a bump on the head and can't remember who you are. I know my name, I know what I do for a living, and what I ate for breakfast yesterday morning.'

'So far, so good,' Rhys said, leaning back against my kitchen worktop and giving me an encouraging nod.

'It's more the personal things that are . . . fuzzy. Like I can't remember when or how my last serious relationship ended. For a while, I wasn't even sure if it had.'

Rhys frowned. 'Should I be worried that some angry ex – who isn't an ex at all – is about to come barging in here and demand to know why I'm having dinner with his girlfriend?'

I saw what he was trying to do. He was trying to lighten the mood and talk me down from the ledge I'd unknowingly stepped on to. I realised in that moment that Rhys was probably very good in a crisis.

'It's more about things I should know – things about people who are important to me – that seem to have evaporated.' My voice sounded weighty with gloom. 'Or been electrocuted away. I can't even remember when I last spoke to any of my friends, or took a holiday, or visited my mum.'

Rhys frowned, which surprisingly did little to diminish how extremely attractive he was looking right now. The gentle concern on his features, if anything, made him even more good-looking.

'And you told the doctors about this?'

I nodded. 'As well as I could explain it. But they just said to give it time. Partial memory loss isn't unusual. Allegedly,' I added, like a sceptical barrister in a courtroom.

'It sounds like you've been given sensible advice. This is all very recent and raw, for both of us.' He glanced over at the clock on my kitchen wall. 'Ten hours ago, none of it had even happened. We weren't in the park, or caught in the storm, or beneath that tree. I think you're going to have to listen to the medics on this one and give your body a chance to reset.'

'But what if it doesn't, Rhys?' Damn it, why did his name still sound so right on my tongue, like I was always meant to be saying it? 'What if it doesn't go back to normal? What if the lightning has done something permanent to my brain, something really bad?'

I wasn't expecting his arms to come up and fold me against his chest. He moved so smoothly, so fast, that being pulled into his embrace instantly felt like somewhere I was supposed to be. His body was a rock, and I wanted to cling to it like a human limpet. But as comforting as the hug was, my concerns were real, terrifying, and weren't going away.

With more reluctance than resolve, I gently eased myself out of his hold before I did anything that would very likely embarrass both of us.

'It's just . . . I don't understand why I've got these gaps in my memory, and you don't.'

Rhys shrugged. 'Perhaps for the same reason I now look like a finalist in a tattoo competition and you're unscathed. It affected us in different ways.'

'Tattoo competition? Is that even a thing?' He was doing it again, trying to claw back some levity into the moment, and this time I let him.

Rhys smiled, clearly pleased that I was no longer spiralling even further into panic.

'Maybe there are things I've forgotten too,' he conceded, 'and I just don't know what they are yet.'

He was trying so hard to make me feel better, although if I was being totally honest, the hug had achieved more to that end than anything he could have said.

That was the moment when I fully realised that Rhys was not only a nice person, but quite possibly the nicest person I'd ever met.

We'd ordered enough Chinese food for four people, and yet there were scarcely more than a couple of mouthfuls of sweet and sour pork and one lonely dumpling left in the foil trays that were strewn across my breakfast bar. We'd eaten straight from the containers, and it hadn't even occurred to me to transfer the food to plates or give a second thought to the drips and spills that could easily stain the marble countertop.

We chatted like the old friends that we weren't, and none of it felt at all odd. The experience we'd lived through seemed to have sped us straight from new acquaintances to the kind of friends who were allowed to ask each other personal questions.

'Those marks the lightning has left on you—'

'Lichtenberg figures,' Rhys supplied, using the official name for the pink-red fractal patterns that were clearly visible under my kitchen halogen lighting.

'They're sort of intriguing,' I said, reaching out a finger – that should have known better – and gently touching the markings on the back of his hand.

His breath hitched.

'I'm sorry. Did that hurt? Are they painful?'

His eyes locked on mine, and looking away right now would have been nothing short of impossible. 'No.'

There was a long pause as though we'd both ventured onto quicksand and neither of us knew our way back onto solid ground.

'The hospital said in most cases they simply fade away after forty-eight hours or so. It's rare for them to last longer.'

'And they don't know why some people get them and others don't?' I asked, already knowing more about the weird phenomenon than I was letting on, thanks to a thorough internet search earlier in the day.

'No. They're kind of a mystery. But the sooner they go, the better,' Rhys said, and there was a note of unexpected concern in his voice. I didn't think it was vanity, because he didn't seem like the type to be bothered about stuff like that, but the marks were obviously worrying him.

'They're not unattractive,' I said, trying to reassure him, and stepping over so many boundaries I should have had trespasser tattooed on my own forehead.

'I think some people might find them scary.'

'Narrow-minded people,' I said, hoping to make him feel better.

He took a beat or two before replying, and maybe that should have prepared me.

'I think, to a child, they'd look kind of terrifying.'

Everything went quiet. Alexa was still playing music, the large American fridge-freezer was still humming in one corner of the room, and the distant thrum of passing traffic from the road outside was still there, but none of that could be heard over the sound of the shoe that I had a feeling was about to drop.

'I expect that would depend very much on the child,' I said, still holding on to the hope that he was talking about random encounters in the street.

Did the lightning fry all your brain cells? Old Ellie suddenly piped up with. He's been subtly checking his phone for messages throughout the meal. He's waiting to hear from someone. How did you miss that?

I hadn't exactly missed it, but I had been guilty of ostrich-like behaviour. I'd asked loads of questions in the time we'd been at the flat, but not the ones I should have asked.

I think Rhys was on the point of explaining everything when a ringtone that wasn't mine went off like a siren. He snatched up his phone as though it might have been planning to escape. A picture lit up on his screen. She was blonde and extremely beautiful. I'd feared there'd be a girl in his life, that his heart already belonged to someone else. And it was obvious that it did, as his features rearranged into a smile that was so beautiful it made me want to cry.

She was the love of his life; I knew that without question.

There was a moment of apology on his face, and I really don't know if it was because he was getting to his feet to take the call in private, or because he'd not been entirely truthful with me.

'I'm just going to step outside to take this,' he said, nodding towards my front door.

'Sure,' I said, my focus on the photograph I could still see on his phone screen. He was two steps away from the hallway when he accepted the call.

'Hello, sweetheart,' he said in a gentle tone that confirmed everything I'd already guessed.

'Daddy!' cried a voice, so loud and excited that I could hear it even as he was walking away from me.

And just like that, the fairy-tale romcom I thought I was starring in took a totally unexpected detour.

Chapter Five

When Rhys returned from talking to his daughter on the phone, I was sitting at the breakfast bar, sipping on the glass of wine I'd poured, regardless of whether the doctors would have approved or not.

He looked sheepish, and he had no need to be. Not really. I hadn't asked the right questions, and he hadn't volunteered the missing information. I'd assumed that because there was no significant other at his hospital bedside, there was no significant other. I was usually cannier than that, and I couldn't blame it on the lightning this time. I hadn't asked, because I hadn't wanted to know. Of course a man like Rhys was spoken for. It was obvious.

'I'm sorry. I had to take that call.'

It wasn't his fault that I'd gone so far down the wrong path. That was all on me. Faster than the lightning that had struck us, I reined in my expectations.

'What's your daughter's name?'

Rhys had the look of someone who'd been floundering in the water and just been thrown a life ring.

'Tasha.'

I had no siblings, so there were no nieces or nephews in my life, but I still knew the right questions to ask.

'Do you have any photos of her?'

It was an icebreaker – one I regularly asked clients before getting down to business, and it always worked.

His eyes were twinkling. 'I might have one or two on my phone,' he confessed before revealing a collection so vast it would have taken me until dawn to view it all.

'You're going to regret asking,' he said, thumbing through endless photos to find some recent ones.

'Not at all.' I was fascinated by how his face lit up as he shared his phone's gallery with me. Tasha was a beautiful little girl, with huge china-blue eyes and long curly blonde hair. Like most people who don't have children, I was rubbish at ageing anyone under sixteen, but I took a stab at seven and surprisingly hit the bull's-eye.

'I'm trying to see if she looks like you,' I said, taking his phone and tilting it to better scrutinise one of the images and then looking beyond it to study Rhys.

'Not really. She's more like her mum.'

Every question I was dying to ask must have been written on my face.

'We're not together right now.'

His answer felt like a slamming door, and I wondered if he realised how telling his choice of words had been. I'd certainly have preferred 'anymore' to 'right now'. 'Right now' felt messy and complicated and the kind of situation I should avoid at all costs. 'Right now' was the kind of thing that got a person's heart broken and it would take more than a pair of arresting green eyes and a dazzling smile to make me disregard my one unbreakable rule: never become part of a triangle.

I took one last look at the photo, and my annoyingly vivid imagination conjured up a woman in her early thirties with the kind of face that probably gave men whiplash every time she walked down a street.

'Did you tell your daughter what happened to you?'

Rhys shook his head. 'It's half term and she's away with her grandparents for a few days. It'll be less scary for her if I explain it properly when she gets home. And hopefully these will have gone by then,' he said, looking down at his forearm as though it belonged to someone else.

I nodded, hoping the media attention would allow us to remain anonymous for that long. Which, for someone who spent as much effort as I did on publicising their life on social media, was an unusual thought.

It didn't surprise me when a short while later Rhys announced that he should probably call a cab and let us both get some much-needed rest. The phone call with his daughter had altered the dynamics of the evening, and the events of the day were finally catching up on me.

'Let me give you a hand clearing this lot up first,' Rhys said, surveying the takeaway detritus that was spread across practically every kitchen countertop.

'No, that's fine. It won't take long. You should go.'

The Uber he summoned arrived in record-breaking time and suddenly there was no opportunity to say any of the things I'd thought of saying. And maybe that was just as well. I followed him to my front door.

Despite knowing there was a car idling at the kerb outside my building, I don't think either of us knew how to end this most unusual of meet-cutes.

'I hope everything works out okay for you – especially with Tasha,' I said. I think I scored extra brownie points by remembering her name.

'For you too. And don't worry about the memory thing, Ellie. I'm sure everything will come back.'

We were struggling. How did you tie up the ends of something that never really was?

'It's been . . .' Rhys began and then faltered.

'Electrifying?' I suggested, going for the easy pun, because leaving each other smiling seemed like the best thing to do at this point.

'Exactly,' he said with a grin. A blast of a car horn from the street made us realise there was no time left for anything else.

'Look after yourself, Shoe Girl,' Rhys said, laying a hand on my good shoulder and giving it a gentle squeeze. He turned towards the stairs and ran lightly down the first half-dozen treads before suddenly stopping and climbing back up again just as quickly. I had my phone in my hand, and he reached for it before I realised what he was doing.

His fingers flew hurriedly over the screen before passing it back to me.

'That's my number. Just in case you feel the need to talk about what happened with someone who gets it. We're a club with very few members, I think.'

'Thank you.' There was more I probably could have said, but my throat was feeling curiously tight, and I had a horrible feeling that I might be about to cry.

He left then. I waited until I heard the clunk of the car door closing and the engine firing up before I sent a message to the newest number in my phonebook.

And now you have mine . . .

I thought long and hard about whether to add a single x to the message, but good sense decreed that was somewhere I really shouldn't be going.

My tread felt weary as I returned to the kitchen after Rhys had gone. It was messier than I'd ever seen it. There were black bin bags beneath the sink that I could be filling, and a bottle of the antibacterial spray that I used so frequently I should have bought shares in the company. But I reached for neither.

In a day of shocking experiences, the one that stunned me the most was when I simply turned off the kitchen light and headed for my bedroom without clearing away a single thing.

I had no idea who this new, laid-back, it can wait until tomorrow person might be. But she certainly wasn't the same Ellie Harker she'd been this morning.

◆ ◆ ◆

Despite falling exhaustedly into bed, I chased sleep for hours before I finally managed to catch some. But it wasn't enough to save me from the panda-like rings beneath my eyes in the bathroom mirror next morning.

Feeling like a very old person and aching almost everywhere, I stood beneath the hot jets of the shower and tried to wash the previous day off my body. But it wasn't going anywhere. I felt different, and even though my only wound was the relatively insignificant burn on my shoulder, I felt marked by an event I still didn't understand. Admittedly, not marked in the same way Rhys had been, but the lightning had got to me in other ways.

The previous day kept playing on repeat in my head as I briskly towelled myself dry, and as hard as I tried to extract Rhys from those thoughts, he was entwined in every memory.

There's someone he shares a child with. And his words implied they might not be over yet. No good can come of this. The voice of my conscience was particularly salty as I tugged a comb through the long damp strands of my hair. It was way harder to dismiss than the tangles.

Leaving the takeaway remains to congeal overnight had been a bad decision and I was so busy scrubbing sticky smears from the worktop that I almost missed the segment on the local TV news that was playing quietly in the background.

'Just yesterday, this peaceful-looking park was a scene of panic and mayhem when two members of the public were unexpectedly struck by lightning during a freak summer storm,' said a young TV reporter.

I lowered the antibacterial spray as though surrendering a weapon and stared with a mixture of horror and fascination at the screen as the park and the youthful presenter disappeared and a grainy piece of footage began to play. It didn't matter how many times I'd already viewed it online, it still felt like watching a horror film, the kind you know will give you nightmares.

'We understand that both of the casualties were discharged from hospital yesterday.'

The camera swung back to the presenter who was closing the piece, which she kept referring to as a 'modern-day miracle'. Her words made me uncomfortable, a sensation that only got worse when the camera zoomed in for a close-up, making it feel as though she was staring right at me through the plasma screen. 'The names of the victims might be a mystery, but there's one thing we do know about them: they are, quite possibly, two of the luckiest people alive.'

Her closing words lingered in my head as I finished tidying the kitchen, and were still there when I nibbled on a slice of toast that was as appetising as buttered cardboard. Even my much-loved morning coffee tasted wrong. Being half of a miracle had left a decidedly bitter taste in my mouth.

Chapter Six

Normally I enjoyed walking to work, but today my nerves were jangling like wind chimes in a gale. My eyes kept going to the clear cerulean sky. There wasn't a single cloud to mar the expanse of blue, but that meant nothing. Yesterday's sky had looked just as innocent. I tried to imagine a future where I was permanently scared of storms, and it didn't look good.

I shaved almost eight minutes off my usual journey time but the vague feeling of unease still lingered as I reached the door of the agency.

My fingers stilled for a moment at the keypad to silence the alarm system, suddenly afraid the lightning might have stolen the code from me. I closed my eyes and muscle memory took over, keying in the correct sequence. I sighed in relief. Perhaps all my missing memories were still there, just waiting for the right prompts to nudge them back into place.

Once inside I surveyed the tiny high street office that I'd rented for the past three years. The familiar feeling of pride and achievement, which hadn't really dimmed since the very first morning when I'd opened for business with a thousand dreams and a grin that refused to leave my face, was a little harder to locate today.

Starting my own agency had been a huge gamble, but I'd been bolstered by confidence, a decent bank loan, and the support of my two best friends. It might be my name above the door, but Mel and Jackson had been right there beside me. They'd given up weekends and evenings to help me decorate the office, not because they loved DIY, but because they believed in me. The furniture I'd sourced from flea markets and obscure auctions, with a long-suffering Jackson at my side, still looked great, as did the hand-stitched scatter cushions on the client sofa which Mel had presented me with just before we opened.

The sudden sting of missing them took me by surprise. When had I stopped replying to their messages? Or started making excuses when they suggested we get together? Why had I prioritised the success of my business over the very people who'd helped me get started? Why was I so terrified of failure that I'd allowed the agency to steal so many evenings and weekends that I should have been spending with people I actually cared about? I wound my arms around my waist, needing a hug in a way I hadn't done in a very long time. I might have a thousand 'friends' on social media, but none of them meant as much as the two real-life ones I'd carelessly kicked to the kerb.

Stop this. Stop this right now. You have work to do. There was no doubt at all which Ellie that was. But she was right. I wasn't the moping kind. Yesterday I'd survived a one-in-a-million, life-threatening event. And if I was strong enough to do that . . . well, I was strong enough to deal with a few moments of self-pity without falling apart. Or worse, reaching out to the only person who might understand what I'd been through.

I went through the motions: opening emails, listening to messages, and reading contracts, but subconsciously I was waiting for Old Ellie to put in an appearance, because the new one was acting like a clueless work-experience student on the first day of her placement.

For inspiration, I scrolled back through old Instagram posts for the agency, wondering who that put-together, composed redhead was in the reels. She was smart, personable, and incredibly business-savvy. She understood how Instagram and TikTok were used by so many of her clients and had tailored the content perfectly. She was the reason why the agency was gaining traction in an already overcrowded market. She was clearly great at her job and knew exactly what she was doing. She might look an awful lot like me, but I wasn't sure that pretending to be her would fool anyone. Because today I felt different, on a deep, molecular level that made absolutely no sense.

After a fruitless few hours flitting from task to task and basically achieving nothing, I was ready for a break. The coffee shop felt familiar and welcoming, in a way that my own office hadn't. Maybe I should quit property and retrain as a barista, I thought, with possibly the first smile I'd managed to crack all day.

Happily, my patchy memory still remembered my favourite coffee order, and it was only when the man behind the counter picked up a sharpie to write my name on the paper cup that everything went off-kilter again.

'Name?' He sounded tetchy, as though he'd had to ask me more than once.

It wasn't a hard question but forcing myself to say 'Ellie' rather than 'Rhys' – which would have raised numerous eyebrows, including mine – was surprisingly hard. I thought after this many hours his name would be out of my head, but apparently not.

I left the shop in a strange, almost trance-like state, nearly tripping over a homeless man and his dog, who I must have passed so many times he'd become almost invisible to me. But I saw him now, and for the first time I felt something that I probably should have felt a very long time ago.

I returned to the coffee shop, emerging again a few minutes later with a second coffee and a bag containing two of the biggest paninis they sold.

'I got one for your dog. I hope he likes cheese,' I said, feeling clumsy and awkward as I placed the goods on the pavement beside him.

'You're an angel,' said the life-beaten man, with eyes full of gratitude.

'I think I nearly was,' I said, smiling at his confusion and feeling better than I had all morning.

It felt like a reward for the small good deed when my phone rang before I'd drained even half of my caramel latte.

Rhys Davies was displayed on my phone screen, and my heart immediately forgot how many beats it was meant to do in a minute and squeezed in a dozen or so more.

Leaving my desk, I crossed the room to take the call on the client sofa. It was positioned beneath a small stained-glass window, bathing whoever sat there in jewelled hues. Surrounded by a kaleidoscope of colours, I answered.

'Hi, Ellie. It's Rhys. Is this a convenient time to talk?'

'It is,' I said, smiling at the sound of his voice. 'Just don't tell the boss, because I've done practically no work today.'

I heard his soft chuckle and suddenly felt like I was fifteen years old all over again and the boy who everyone fancied had just shot a smile my way.

'Is she a tyrant?' He was joking and had no way of knowing that he wasn't that far off the mark. I was the hardest taskmaster I'd ever worked for.

'She can be,' I said. 'What can I do for you?'

He drew in a breath and suddenly I knew this wasn't just a social call.

'Annoying news, I'm afraid. I just had lunch with Olly, and he told me one of the journalists from yesterday was poking around at the hospital this morning. He even faked an injury to get into A and E and somehow managed to get some information out of the staff about us.'

My stomach gave a tiny lurch. 'What did he find out?'

'Not our names, thankfully, no one was that indiscreet. But I think he now knows what we look like. One of us, apparently, is a heavily tattooed guy in his thirties, and the other a beautiful redhead who owns a local business.'

My head wanted to worry that my identity wouldn't be difficult to uncover from that, but my heart had got itself stuck on the 'beautiful' bit. I really wanted that to be Rhys's spin rather than anyone else's.

He gave a dry, humourless laugh. 'I'm probably okay, because according to the internet, these marks should be gone in a few days, but you might be easier for them to identify.'

'I suppose I could always dye my hair.'

'That would be a sacrilege.'

Another smile that had no business being there landed on my face.

'Did you get the colour from one of your parents?'

The smile froze. 'My mum's a redhead – she's practically the same shade as me,' I said, feeling suddenly uncomfortable. 'But I've no idea about my father. I never knew him.'

'I'm sorry. That must be hard. I—'

I cut him off, a technique I'd learnt from a grand master.

'It's all ancient water under the bridge.' My tone made it clear I was shutting the door on the topic.

There was a long moment of silence, and I suspected there was more he wanted to ask. Well, Rhys had his secrets, and I had mine.

'How are you feeling today? Any peculiar after-effects?'

He'd taken the wheel and steered our conversation in a totally different direction, and I was grateful.

'No. No new ones anyway, but I've felt kind of out of it and inadequate at work today. As though I wasn't supposed to be there.'

'Maybe you weren't. Perhaps you should have taken a few days off.'

'I'm a one-man band. I don't do time off.'

'Not ever?'

'Not recently.' I gave a small laugh. 'Or maybe I've just come back from a fortnight in the Maldives and I've forgotten all about it.'

'Well, that would be a shocking waste of money.'

I laughed again and realised I did more of that in his company than with anyone else I'd spent time with recently. Or as far as I could remember.

It felt like our conversation was reaching a natural conclusion and I wanted to go before we reached the awkward umming and ahing bit.

'Anyway, thanks for the warning about the journalist.'

It was the point where Rhys was supposed to say goodbye, but he didn't seem in a rush to do so.

'I was thinking,' he said, 'that it might be sensible if we keep in touch over the next week or so. Just to check in and compare any weird symptoms we might have.' He gave a despairing laugh. 'You should know that sounded much cooler when I practised it earlier.'

'You rehearsed it?'

'I had to,' he said with disarming honesty. 'It's been a while since I've done this kind of thing.'

'What kind of thing is that?'

'Ask someone if they want to have a drink with me.'

'Oh, is that what we're doing?' I teased. 'I thought we were conducting some kind of scientific observation?'

'Well, that too, obviously,' he said, and I just knew he was smiling.

It was just as well we weren't on a video call, because my grin already looked like I'd swallowed a coat hanger.

'I suppose a drink after work would be okay,' I said, aiming for breezy and failing miserably.

'Great. Why don't I give you a call in a couple of days? There are some nice pubs not far from here.'

'That sounds good.' And it did. Very, very, good.

The smile took a long time to fade after we hung up. And when I passed the mirror hanging on my office wall, I noticed my cheeks were wearing an attractive flush. It clashed with my hair. The hair which he liked. As a child I'd hated the colour, hated the playground teasing, but today I was grateful to the woman whose genes had given it to me. Hers was threaded with grey these days . . . at least I think it was. With a frown, I reached for my phone, not sure why I was suddenly overcome with a need to hear her voice. I summoned up her number from my phone book before giving myself time to question my motives.

The phone rang six times before I heard her familiar voice in my ear.

'Hello.'

'Hi, Mum.'

'Well, this is a bit of a nuisance for you, but I'm afraid I'm not here right now. Although I imagine you've already worked that out for yourself.'

I blinked at the phone as though it was guilty of pulling a particularly cruel practical joke. Voicemail. Was this a new outgoing message? I had no idea.

‘I’ll call you back,’ my mother’s voice continued. ‘Just leave a message at the beep.’

It was hard to reconcile the warring feelings of disappointment and relief that she wasn’t around to take my call. Maybe it was just as well. Trying to hide the lightning strike from her would have been pointless. She had a knack of unearthing secrets almost as effectively as she managed to keep them.

Chapter Seven

The café had a few outdoor tables, and I was there early enough to snag one ahead of the Saturday morning brunch crowd. I fiddled nervously with the menu in its stand and rearranged the bowl of sugar sachets and the condiments so many times I fully expected the waitress to swoop down and take them from me.

He'd been shocked to hear from me when I'd phoned this morning and hadn't bothered disguising it with his opening words.

'Well, hello there, stranger. It's been so long, I was beginning to think you'd died.'

I deserved that one, so I didn't tell Jackson that two days ago I very nearly had. That would have just been mean.

'What's it been? Nine months since we've heard from you? Were you going for some sort of record?'

I bit my lip guiltily because that was a hell of a long time to ignore your friends, and also because I had no recollection of when exactly we'd last been in contact.

'Something like that,' I mumbled.

It might have been even longer if it hadn't been for Rhys. When he'd called the previous night to arrange our 'definitely not a date', one of the pubs he suggested was a place I used to visit all the time with Jackson. The memory had caught me off guard, and I was sleepy, which perhaps was why I accidentally let slip that I'd not seen either of my two closest friends for longer than I cared to remember.

'Why?' Such a reasonable question, but I had no acceptable answer to give him.

'Like I said, I've been kind of absorbed with work for a while now. The business was taking off, and keeping the social media side of it going takes up practically all my free time.' I gave a wry laugh. 'I guess I pushed some things onto the back burner.'

'Things like your friends?' Strangely there'd been no judgement in his tone, as though he understood the trap I'd fallen into. But that didn't change how bad I felt about neglecting the two people who'd always been there for me.

'Why don't you reach out to them now?' It was a good question, and one I'd already asked myself about a thousand times.

'Because they're going to be mad that I've ghosted them for so long.'

'And will that get better the longer you keep up the silence?'

He had me there. 'No. It'll just get harder as even more months slip by.'

'I can't tell you what to do, Ellie,' Rhys said, in a way that made me realise – as if I hadn't already worked it out – that he must be a really good dad. 'But I think that's your answer right there. It will be even worse if you let those months slide into years.'

That had shocked me and been the prod I'd needed to finally set aside my fears and contact my friends to do some serious grovelling.

I tried Mel first, because those bonds were stronger, and the roots of our friendship went deeper. Perhaps that's the way it always is with the first friendly face you find on Day One at university. There'll always be an unbreakable connection with the person who'd unfailingly held back your hair when you'd drunk too much cheap cider, and who'd venture out in the middle of the night to buy paracetamols for your crippling stomach cramps. They would always be your forever person . . . even if you hadn't spoken to them in what felt like forever.

Mel hadn't picked up, and the horrible suspicion that she'd seen my name on her caller ID and chosen not to answer crept into my head and refused to leave. I left a message – knowing it was still antisocially early to be phoning anyone.

Four hours later, when I'd still heard nothing from her, I'd called Jackson.

'It would be great to meet up for a coffee sometime,' I said hesitantly, never for a moment anticipating his reply.

'I could do today.'

I swallowed down a gulp of surprise.

'Perfect. I'm free too,' I replied hurriedly, giving him no chance to change his mind.

He strode across the car park towards me now, and I sprang to my feet. His hair was a little longer and scruffier than I remembered, and the new style really suited him, as did the neatly trimmed beard he was sporting. Was that new, or had he had it the last time I'd seen him? My patchy memory is so much worse than 'normal' amnesia, I thought, giving the word the kind of air quotes I had always hated. I knew how many sugars Jackson took in his coffee, that he was allergic to shellfish, and snored like a rhinoceros after only a couple of beers. But I had no idea when our last conversation had been. Or whether he was still mad at me.

He came to a stop beside my table, not reaching for me. The hug I'd been so ready to give him suddenly felt awkward as my arms dropped disappointedly back to my sides.

'You look good,' I said, nervously shifting my weight from one foot to the other.

He surveyed my face, as though compiling an inventory of my features.

'You look tired.'

I took comfort in the fact that he was pulling the friends don't lie card rather than just opting to be polite.

'I didn't sleep well.'

He nodded solemnly and for one awful moment I wondered if our entire meeting was going to be like this.

'I've . . . I've ordered us coffees,' I said, my eyes darting to the restaurant entrance. 'And pie,' I added, because Jackson's sweet tooth was something else my Swiss cheese brain had decided to retain.

'Pie,' he repeated.

I licked my lips anxiously. 'Yes. Apple for you and humble for me.'

There was a long moment when I thought I'd played it all wrong. That it was too soon for humour. But then he snorted out a laugh and shook his head almost in disbelief. It gave me a glimmer of hope.

'I hope you intend to pick up the tab,' he said, still maintaining a frosty wall, even though it was slowly starting to melt around the edges.

'For now, and evermore,' I said, not even joking.

Another long moment and then thankfully, remarkably, and with a generosity I didn't deserve, he opened his arms to me. I flew into them.

He brought them into a clasp behind my back and I buried my face into his shirt front, knowing it was going to be damp when we eventually drew apart.

'This doesn't mean you're forgiven,' he said, even while his hand was rhythmically patting my shoulder.

'I know,' I told his shirt buttons.

'I just can't cope with the drama of a feud.' He tightened his hold, and the hug hurt my heart almost as much as it did my ribs.

But I took it as an unspoken reassurance that although we weren't mended yet, this could be fixed over time.

We broke apart when a subtle cough from the teenage waitress announced the arrival of our order. We waited until she'd transferred cups and plates onto our table.

'You really did order pie,' he said in surprise, reaching for a fork and one of the generous slices. 'Damn it, I may have to forgive you even sooner now.'

'Please do,' I said, and although it was meant to be banter, there was no hiding the genuine plea in my eyes.

'So how are things, Ellie? How's the business going?'

'Okay,' I said.

Jackson's eyebrows rose and disappeared into his new shaggier hairstyle. 'That's it? No blow-by-blow account of your latest big sale? No update on the number of Instagram followers you now have, or TikTok engagement?'

His words stung like lemon juice in a cut.

'Was I really that self-absorbed?'

He gave a very Jackson shrug. 'You were very . . . focused,' he said, softening the comment by adding: 'You wanted to make it a success, and kudos to you, you did. I bet your mum's proud.'

The tears were unexpected, and I furiously blinked them away.

'Yeah, she probably is. I think sometimes when you focus so hard on one thing, it stops you seeing whatever else is going on around you.'

'So, how's your vision these days?' Jackson asked, giving me a look.

'It's getting sharper.'

'Good to hear,' he said, lifting the second plate with a flourish and waving it towards me.

I shook my head. 'No thanks. I bought both of them for you.'

He took a large mouthful of the second pie before asking, 'Is the IT system I set up for you still working, or have you found yourself a new computer nerd to fix it when it goes down?'

'I could never find a nerd to replace you,' I said, tentatively dipping my toe back into the ebb and flow of our banter. It felt like putting on a comfortable pair of slippers. 'You're the best geek around.'

'Damn straight,' he said with a wink, running his left hand ostentatiously through his hair.

'I like the new look, by the way,' I said, touching my own chin. Jackson mirrored the movement, deliberately stroking the short facial hair as though petting a small animal.

The penny took a long time to drop, and when it did my cry of surprise had heads turning our way from nearby tables.

'Jackson Winter, what is that?'

My friend's face split into an enormous grin.

'Thank fuck for that. I thought you were never going to notice. Could I have been any more obvious?'

My smile almost matched his as I snatched up his left hand and drew it across the table towards me. I touched the band of gold on his ring finger as though it might be a mirage, but it certainly felt solid beneath my fingertips.

'You're married. You got married. You're a husband,' I said, my head shaking in wonder. 'Who is he? Do I know him?'

Jackson looked momentarily disappointed in me. 'Of course you know him.'

For one dreadful moment my memory was a blank. I could remember a succession of short-lived partners, but no one serious in my friend's life. And then, as though nature had taken pity on me, it threw me a lifeline, parting the fog in my brain.

'It's Lars, isn't it?'

If Jackson's grin got any bigger, someone was going to have to call the Guinness Book of Records.

The tall, handsome Dutchman who was now, incredibly and amazingly, married to one of my best friends, floated back into my memory banks. See, said a small reassuring voice inside my head. The memories aren't lost, after all. They can still be retrieved.

'But didn't the two of you only meet last October? That's so quick.'

Jackson gave the kind of smile that only someone in love can summon.

'When you know, you know.'

'I'm so happy for you.' I scrambled out of my chair and round the table to give him another hug. 'Congratulations to you – to both of you.' I gave the shoulder I was hugging a small shove. 'But I wish you'd invited me to the wedding. Even if I have been the world's shittiest friend.'

'Actually, no one came to the wedding,' he reassured me as I retook my seat. 'Well, apart from Elvis, that is.'

'You got married in Vegas?' My voice had risen to an incredulous squawk.

'We did. It was all a bit of a wild impulse thing. But neither of us wanted to wait. But we'll be doing the big two-white-suits thing later this year. You'll be invited to that . . . unless you're planning on ghosting us all again, of course.'

'Never,' I said with unshakeable certainty.

'It might be a midweek do, so heads up, you'll have to take time off work.'

'That's fine.'

'It might even be in Scotland,' he continued, 'so you'd be away from the business for several days.'

'That's not a problem.'

Jackson leant back in his chair and gave me a long appraising look.

'Who are you and what have you done with the real Ellie Harker?'

'Just doing a little makeover and some long overdue renovations.'

I smiled and there was a wistfulness that I couldn't keep out of my voice. 'But I am really sorry that I wasn't around to see you fall in love. I wish I hadn't missed that.'

'You didn't,' Jackson said. 'You were there in the bar last October on the night we met. That's when it happened. Love at first sight.'

'Is that really a thing?' I asked and there was an intensity to my question that I think surprised me even more than it did him.

'The evidence is right here on my left hand,' Jackson said with a smile.

Two more coffees and half an hour later and I still hadn't found a way to swing the conversation around to my recent near-death experience. It didn't seem to be an appropriate topic for a good-news day, and the relief I felt on deciding to shelve it for another time felt like a boulder rolling off my shoulders.

It was only when Jackson glanced at his watch and declared he really should be getting back to Lars that the question I'd wanted to ask since he first sat down was set free.

'Is Mel very angry with me?'

Jackson paused for a long moment. 'You'd have to ask her that.'

'But you must have spoken to her recently,' I said, surprised at the sudden stab of jealousy that pierced me.

'I have, but to be perfectly blunt, Ellie, we didn't speak about you.'

That stung. A lot. But I let it go.

'It's just that I've rung her, left a voicemail and a WhatsApp, and she hasn't answered any of them.'

'Why the sudden urgency to make contact after all these months? Has something happened?' he asked astutely, leaning forward as though the answer was right there on my face, if he just stared closely enough. Thankfully, unlike Rhys, I bore no visible signs of what I'd experienced.

'Nothing has happened,' I lied. 'I just wanted to make amends, that's all. Do you think she'll let me?'

Jackson gave me a you-should-know-better look. 'She's Mel. Of course she's going to forgive you . . . eventually.'

That made me instantly feel worse rather than better.

Jackson was picking absently at the corner of the menu with his thumbnail, pulling the plastic away from the backing. 'But she's been going through some stuff of her own recently, so maybe give her a bit of time before you launch into another bombardment, eh?'

'Stuff? What stuff? Is she alright? She's not sick or anything, is she?'

I have no idea why illness was my knee-jerk reaction, but the thought of it collided with my heart like a punch that I couldn't dodge.

'No. It's nothing like that. But she and Steve just needed some time away together. They've gone to New York for a bit to get their heads straight.'

I had a million questions, but it was clear Jackson wasn't going to answer any of them.

'It's her news to share, not mine, Ells, you're just going to have to wait until they get back and then see if she wants to see you.'

'Do you think she will?' I asked, sounding more than a little desperate.

His smile was soft. 'She's Mel,' he said, as though that explained everything. And in a way, it did.

Chapter Eight

I closed the office early, which wasn't as surprising as the total lack of guilt felt as I set the alarm and locked the door two hours before quitting time. The high street was still busy with shoppers milling around the stalls set up on both pavements. Friday was market day and the road was closed to traffic, which was why I had arranged for Rhys to pick me up for our 'non-date' at the corner of a nearby residential street.

I was about ten minutes early, so I perched on a convenient bench to wait and lifted my face to the sun. The wooden slats were warm beneath my bare legs, and there wasn't even a whisper of a breeze to stir the leafy trees that lined the road. Behind my sunglasses I could feel my eyes begin to close.

I didn't hear his car pull up. Nor the sound of the driver's door opening as Rhys climbed out. I only woke up when he stood before me, his shadow blocking out the late-afternoon sun.

'Ellie.'

I jolted upright, momentarily thrown to be caught napping in the middle of the day. My sunglasses fell from my nose as I jerked awake and Rhys bent to retrieve them, kneeling at my feet to haul them out from beneath the bench.

A noisy thumping sound filled the air. Still half asleep, I wondered if it was my heart, which had a habit of pounding louder and harder whenever Rhys was around. But it was only an approaching car full of teenagers, the stereo ramped up to a level their eardrums would one day regret. It slowed down as it drove past, and heads leant out of the rolled-down windows.

'Say yes!' one of them called.

'Let's see the ring,' yelled another.

Rhys was grinning as he straightened up with my sunglasses in his hand. I grabbed them and hurriedly slipped them on, wishing they were larger so that my blush had a chance of hiding behind the tinted lenses. I'd wanted to appear so cool and composed today. Unflappable. But just five minutes in and I'd already failed in that mission.

'Well, that was embarrassing. Can we start over?' I asked as he held open the passenger door for me, still smiling.

He gave an easy-going shrug. 'We can if you want. But I think the Sleeping Beauty intro and the proposal bit are going to be hard to beat.'

I gave a reluctant chuckle.

'Mostly, my dates tend to fall asleep at the end of the night, after I've bored them rigid. And I've always been more of a propose-on-the-third-date kind of guy.'

I giggled, caught his eye, and we both burst out laughing, and it felt so right, so easy, like something we'd done a thousand times before, even though we hadn't. It intrigued and scared me.

'This isn't a date,' I reminded him, feeling the need to draw boundary lines in the sand one more time before one of us forgot what they were and did something stupid.

'Whatever you say,' Rhys said amiably, pulling smoothly away from the kerb.

I was still holding the denim jacket which I'd brought but doubted I was going to need.

'You can throw that on the back seat, if you want,' Rhys said, his attention now on the traffic, which was beginning to build up as rush hour approached.

I swivelled around to do as he suggested. The jacket landed on the upholstery, beside a large white paper bag. It was the kind you get from pharmacies when you pick up a prescription. There was a label on it, but I was too far away to read it. And anyway, it was none of my business. But something about the bag bothered me. Even though I laughed at all the appropriate places in an amusing story Rhys related as he drove, the bag kept snagging at my thoughts and tugging at the hemline of my conscience like an impatient toddler.

We stopped just once on the journey for petrol, and my inner Pandora finally got the better of me. When Rhys left the pump to go inside to pay, I twisted around as far as my seat belt would allow. I'm not sure what I was expecting to see on the bag's label, but I don't think it was his daughter's name. I bit my lip worriedly, knowing I was being overly curious – or downright nosy – but that looked like an awful lot of medication for one little girl.

Twenty minutes later we swung onto the gravelled forecourt of a pub I'd never been to before. Despite the hour, the car park and the bar were already busy.

'Shall we try the garden?' Rhys asked, resting one hand at the small of my back to guide me towards a pair of glass doors that led out to the patio and a lawned area beyond.

'Sure.'

His hand fell away the second we emerged into the lingering warmth of one of the hottest June days I could remember. For late afternoon, even the beer garden was surprisingly full. We scoped the area and ended up snagging the only free table, which happened to be next to an enormous lavender bush. From the low hum of bees who were buzzing in and out of the foliage, it was easy to see why this had been the last table to be claimed.

'Would you rather sit inside?' Rhys asked, his eyes following the flight of a bee as it circled my head.

'No, this is fine,' I assured him as I slid onto a wrought-iron chair and repositioned my sunglasses from the top of my head to my nose.

The arresting green of Rhys's eyes was hidden behind dark-tinted shades, but the black t-shirt he'd paired with faded jeans did little to conceal the marks the lightning had left on his body. They appeared, if anything, even more pronounced than the week before. He caught me looking and pulled a rueful expression.

'They're still here,' he said.

I nodded and then stepped over so many boundaries I should have been arrested for trespass. 'They're not unattractive,' I said. 'And they're the mark of a survivor.'

Rhys lowered his sunglasses and looked at me over their rim.

'That's a very glass-half-full way of looking at things.'

'I suppose it is. And if you'd have said that about me a week ago, I'd have told you that wasn't me at all.'

'But now?'

I gave a confused sigh. 'Now everything feels a little different.'

'Different isn't always bad.'

The day was hot but the heat from his eyes was even more intense. I swear I could feel myself about to combust, my sleeveless shift dress too warm and my hair too heavy for the back of my neck. I swept it up in one hand, praying for a breeze. I couldn't tell if his gaze lingered on the curve of my neck longer than it should have before I released the flame-coloured strands or whether the lightning had fried some important circuitry in my brain and I could no longer differentiate fact from fantasy.

I licked my lips, which were suddenly incredibly dry.

'What would you like to drink?'

'A really cold beer,' I said, with so much feeling he laughed.

I tried hard not to let my eyes follow him as he strode back inside to get our drinks, but he pulled my gaze as though it was magnetised to him.

Sitting alone in the sunshine, my thoughts went back to the bag of medication in his car. How rude would it be, on a scale of 'perfectly okay' to 'totally unacceptable', to ask him what the meds were for. Unbidden, my mother popped into my head, like a parental Jiminy Cricket. She was right. Good manners prevented me from asking. But once in my thoughts, Mum proved hard to evict. I'd tried to reach her several times over the last few days but still hadn't been able to make contact.

I glanced towards the pub doors, but there was no tall, dark-haired man standing in their frame. So I reached for my phone and quickly rang my mother's number again.

It wasn't unusual for weeks to pass between our phone calls – sometimes even longer if we'd fallen out over some stupid disagreement. But something was starting to feel wrong about not being able to reach her for the best part of a week.

This time, when I got her voicemail, I did leave a message.

'Hey, Mum, it's me. I was just wondering where you are. Is it your WI day, or the day you go swimming? I can never remember your schedule. Either way, give me a call when you get this, okay?'

I bit my lip as I severed the connection and slid the phone back into my pocket, unable to silence a strange feeling of disquiet at the back of my mind. It felt like something important was hovering there, but each time I tried to grab hold of it, it evaporated away like smoke.

We drank icy-cold beer straight from the bottle, clinking them together in a toast to new friends, which tasted almost as good on my tongue as the Bud Light.

For a man who was so good at keeping a conversation alive, Rhys was equally skilled in the art of maintaining a comfortable silence. So he surprised me when he broke it.

'I've been doing a lot of thinking about what happened to us last week.'

I sat up straighter in my chair.

'Do you think it was something more than just pure luck that we both survived it?' he asked.

I blew out a long breath. 'That sounds like something my friend Mel would say. She's always been way more woo-woo than me.'

The corners of Rhys's eyes crinkled appealingly whenever he smiled. The ever-present grooves there suggested it was something he did a lot.

'She'd probably say it's a sign we're meant to do something big – something important – with our lives from here on.'

'Maybe the universe was giving us a wake-up call?' Rhys suggested.

I tossed the idea from one side of my thoughts to the other, unsure how I felt about it.

'What? Like we're meant to do something spectacular going forward? Because as much as I'd love to find a cure for cancer or solve global warming, I'm actually much better at just selling houses – or at least I used to be.'

He smiled. 'Perhaps the message is more like checking we're on the path we're meant to be travelling. Maybe the lightning has given us a chance to do a system reset.'

'And now you sound more like my other friend, Jackson, who's a computer genius. Are you sure you don't work in tech?'

He shook his head. 'No. Still graphic design,' he said, confirming what he'd previously told me.

There was a long pause, and I honestly thought we were done with the topic when he returned to it in a way that suddenly changed everything.

'The other day, when the lightning struck, I was on my way to meet with Tasha's mum, Annalise.'

Damn it. Even her name was pretty.

The buzzing of bees filled the silence as Rhys appeared to be weighing up whether or not to continue.

'She wants us to try again.'

The words fell like an unexploded bomb between us. The 'we're not together right now' suddenly made sense.

'We've been separated for two years.' There wasn't a cloud in the sky, but Rhys's eyes were suddenly full of them. 'It wasn't a pain-free split. I was on my way to meet her to discuss things when the storm broke and I took shelter beneath the tree.'

'Had you made a decision? If that's not too personal a question to ask.'

It was as personal as hell, but he didn't seem to mind.

'Made it and changed it back again God knows how many times before the rain came down. I guess I was hoping for some kind of sign.'

I gave a humourless laugh. 'You got struck by lightning, Rhys. I think that might have been your sign, right there.'

'Maybe.' He turned away from me then, his green eyes focusing on the sun, which was slowly sinking towards the horizon in an amber ball. 'It's hard to think about walking back into the fire when you've been burnt once before.'

There was a lot to unpack behind his words. Whatever had happened between him and his ex, it had hurt him badly.

'I guess only you can say if the good bits outweigh the bad,' I said, realising I absolutely sucked as an Agony Aunt. Giving relationship advice when I'd yet to have a successful one myself was a joke.

'Every good memory I have of that relationship is tied up in Tasha and being her dad.'

It felt like everything had suddenly gone quiet. As though every customer in the beer garden had fallen silent, the warm summer breeze had stopped rustling the leaves, and even the bees had ceased buzzing. As much as I wanted to join in the silence, my conscience wouldn't let me.

'I'm going to stick my nose in where it doesn't belong, because I know how it feels growing up without a dad.' My throat was getting tighter with every word, making it hard to carry on. 'It was a lot. It always felt like something was missing in my life.' I paused for a second, gathering up the strength to continue. 'Maybe you and Annalise owe it to your daughter to try again.'

Rhys just looked at me for the longest moment.

It's hard to conjure up an encouraging smile when you've just sabotaged something that could have been everything. But I gave it my best shot.

Chapter Nine

As late afternoon tipped into evening and the shadows grew longer, the after-work drinking crowd drifted home and we were surrounded by date-night couples sharing lingering golden-hour kisses or holding hands across tabletops in the twilight. I'd never been one for PDAs – I thought that was just how I was wired – so it was unsettling to realise just how much I wanted to join their ranks. Was it the lightning that had changed me, or was it because I'd never met anyone I wanted to touch as much as I did the man sitting opposite me, despite having virtually advised him to go back to his ex?

I shivered and Rhys sprang to his feet, returning moments later with a soft plaid blanket from a basket the pub made available for garden guests. He draped it around me like a cape, and I managed to hide another shiver as his hand rested briefly on my shoulder. Friends don't do things like that, I reminded myself.

Rhys was two steps towards his own seat when he came to an abrupt halt. 'Ellie, don't move,' he said, his voice urgent. I froze in the act of settling the folds of the blanket more comfortably around me. His tone was calm, but his eyes were staring at my throat, and not in the way he'd done earlier. I twitched the blanket a little tighter around me and that was when I felt the weird tickling sensation beneath the woollen folds.

'Keep absolutely still,' Rhys said quietly, which was impossible now that I could hear an angry buzzing sound coming from beneath the plaid blanket. I jerked, and the enormous bee that had been crawling along my collarbone dropped down inside the scoop neckline of my dress.

'Stay calm,' he instructed, and I tried to, but the bee – realising its predicament – got angry and then got scared. It lashed out at the flesh it was trapped against, which happened to be my right boob.

I winced, unable to stifle a small yelp of pain. Ironically, I think I'd made less fuss when the lightning had struck me.

Rhys was beside me in a second.

'Did it sting you?'

'Yep.' I pulled the fabric of my dress away and peered into the void. 'It's still in there.'

I'd been undressed by others before him, but never with such speed or dexterity. Rhys reached behind me, his hand going unerringly to the zip of my dress, which he slid down as though his fingers had been primed to do so all night. Although probably not in the middle of a pub garden, with every head turned our way. My dress fell open, and the bee tumbled out onto the grass. It wasn't the only thing to spill, as my bra was the half-cup style and so flimsy the outline of my nipples was clearly silhouetted through the lace.

Once again, Rhys's reactions were fast, sweeping up the discarded blanket and throwing it protectively around me.

'Come on,' he said, placing a guiding arm at my back. 'Let's go inside and get some ice for that sting.'

I resisted as he tried to tug me gently towards the warm lights of the pub.

'It's okay, Rhys. I don't want to make a fuss.'

'You're not,' he said. 'We just need some better light to see how bad it is.'

Never before had a man said that he wanted to see my boobs to assess how bad they looked. I could have stayed and argued with him in the middle of the beer garden, but doing so would only draw even more attention our way, so I scooped up my bag and allowed him to lead me towards the main building.

If the pub had been busy before, it was now positively heaving, so Rhys left me standing beside the door as he wove through the crowd towards the bar. It was two-to-three-deep in customers, but somehow he caught the barman's eye as he approached.

'Could we have some ice for a bee sting, please?' I heard him ask, with an apology for queue-jumping to those waiting to be served. The bartender passed him a beer glass filled to the brim with ice cubes and the crowd parted like a biblical sea as he made his way back to me.

'That was impressive,' I said. 'I bet you're great at hailing taxis.'

'Being tall helps.'

It was more than that. It was being him. Being Rhys. But that was taking me back into dangerous waters, so I simply nodded as though that explained everything.

'Shall we find somewhere more private and get you out of that dress.'

I couldn't help a small snort of laughter.

'Has that line ever worked for you in the past?'

I liked the twinkle in his eyes and the way he pretended to seriously consider my question.

'Not so much, now you mention it.'

I had a feeling he was lying.

With his hand cupping my elbow, he steered us towards the Ladies'. I reached to take the glass of ice, but Rhys had already knocked on the door and, getting no response, nudged it open with his shoulder and pulled me inside.

That took the smile from my face.

'You can't be in here,' I said, which was nonsense, as he was very much in there already.

'There are unisex toilets everywhere these days,' he replied easily.

'Yes, but this doesn't happen to be one of them.'

I shot a glance towards the row of cubicles. The open doors revealed they were all empty and there was no one at the hand basins. For now, at least, we had the room to ourselves.

'People will think we're in here for another reason,' I said, seizing on the first objection I could think of.

Rhys's eyebrows rose.

'What reason?'

He was so convincing I almost believed him.

'You know what I'm talking about.' I was a sexually experienced woman in her thirties who had no business blushing like a teenager, but I couldn't seem to help myself. 'They'll think we've ducked in here for a quickie.'

'I don't do quickies,' he said, his words stealing every sassy retort from my head. 'Now, shall we get some ice on that sting?'

I drew in a deep breath before releasing my hold on the blanket, allowing it to fall to the tiled floor. My unzipped dress was hanging from one shoulder, revealing quite a lot of cleavage and a large inflamed area of skin that extended beneath the lace of my bra.

All at once it went very quiet in the Ladies', with only the hum of the fluorescent lighting to mask the fact that one of us was breathing a little raggedly. Maybe we both were. He felt it too. I know he did by the way he took a sudden jerky step backwards as though the bolt of lightning still arced between us.

I could see my breasts rising and falling as my breathing grew shallower.

'Can you see where it stung you?' His voice sounded different now.

I peeled the fabric of the bra cup away. The skin was bright red around an angry puncture mark.

I nodded.

'Is the stinger still in it?'

'I'm not sure. It's hard to see from this angle.'

He'd taken a half step towards me before stopping. 'Do you want me to look?'

It was a question with a hundred different answers, all of them probably wrong.

I nodded, not sure if I could trust my voice.

He stepped forward and I closed my eyes, too scared he'd see things within them that he wasn't meant to know.

He didn't touch me, and I truly don't know if I was relieved or disappointed.

'I think it's fine,' he said, his voice gruff. My eyes flew open, and he was already turning away and reaching for a small hand towel from a basket on the countertop. Taking a handful of ice, he dropped it onto the square, folding it up to make a compress.

'Hold this against you. It should help with the pain and the swelling,' he said, passing me the towel and then turning around again as I slid it onto the inflamed skin of my breast.

'I think it was a bumblebee rather than a honey one,' he told the wall tiles beside the hand drier. 'Which is good because they don't leave their stingers behind.'

'Excellent,' I said, then rashly decided to defuse the moment with humour. 'I'd have hated having to ask anyone to suck out the venom.'

His shoulders twitched. 'I think you'll find that's for snakebites.'

I had another quip at the ready, but it died in my throat when he added, 'But, for the record, I don't think there'd have been a shortage of volunteers to help you out.'

I wanted to ask if he'd have been one of them, but I wasn't that reckless.

Leaving the icy pad inside my bra, I straightened my dress and zipped it back up.

'All decent,' I said.

Rhys turned back to face me. It was hard to be sure in this light, but he looked a little flushed.

'You certainly seem to know a lot about bees.'

He shrugged. 'You have to when your daughter is allergic to their sting and suffers from asthma.'

His words were a much-needed verbal bucket of cold water. There was a physical attraction here, we'd both be stupid to deny it. But it wasn't going anywhere. It couldn't. And if I had to repeat that mantra a thousand times before my traitorous body finally believed me, then so be it.

'Well, that was another really interesting evening.'

I gave a chuff of amusement. 'They do seem to be our speciality,' I said, looking out through his car's windscreen at my flat. I wasn't going to invite him inside and I don't think he expected me to.

We'd left the sexually charged atmosphere behind in the pub bathroom, but if it was haunting him the way it was me, I doubted either of us would get much sleep that night.

'I've had a nice evening, Rhys. Thank you.'

'Me too,' he said, his expression hidden by the shadows of the car.

This was the moment, if it had been a date, where I would lean in or he would pull me towards him for a goodnight kiss. And I was so scared that he would and so scared that he wouldn't that I couldn't get out of the car fast enough. I fumbled with the unfamiliar door catch, but Rhys was already out of the driver's seat and striding to open the door for me.

We stood on the pavement in a pool of light from a streetlamp, like actors on a stage.

His hands came up to rest lightly on my shoulders.

'Take care of yourself, Ellie,' he said, bending to graze a feather-soft kiss on my cheek. 'Watch out for bees.'

'You too,' I said, my voice scarcely more than a whisper.

I turned to walk up my path, knowing his eyes would follow me until I was safely inside. He'd wait for me to unlock the door and slip through it. He probably wouldn't move until he'd seen the lights go on in my flat. That was the kind of man Rhys Davies was. Don't ask me how I knew that about him. I just did.

Chapter Ten

The headache was there when I woke up. A tiny man with a very small hammer had set up shop somewhere at the back of my head and was determined to ruin the first free Saturday morning I'd had in ages.

My bathroom cabinet was well stocked with practically every over-the-counter remedy you could wish for, apart from the painkillers I was looking for. As I rummaged among the packets, my thoughts went back to the large bag of medication on the rear seat of Rhys's car, which I now knew must be for Tasha's asthma. I knew very little about the condition, but I remembered a boy in my primary class being taken to hospital in an ambulance after a severe flare-up in the school playground. I hoped Tasha wasn't as badly affected, although the size of the bag seemed to suggest otherwise.

I eventually found the paracetamols on the top shelf of the cabinet. As I stood on tiptoe to reach them, another box tumbled out, landing face-up on the fluffy bathmat beside me. I stooped to pick it up, a frown already forming. I stared at the packet curiously, willing to swear I'd never seen it before in my life. The medication was for travel sickness, and I was surprised to discover half of the pills inside it were gone.

I wasn't always a good traveller. Cars and trains didn't affect me, but flying wasn't great. And as for water . . . I used to joke that even looking at pictures of the sea made me queasy. I'd actually broken it off with a guy I'd been seeing a while ago because his waterbed made me nauseous. Or maybe that had just been a handy excuse. I'd never needed much of a reason to call it a day once the initial spark of interest had flickered out.

Rhys's face suddenly pushed all other thoughts out of my head. Would it be that way between us if he were free? If he wasn't caught halfway between giving his relationship with his child's mother one last chance or walking away. Was I unnecessarily complicating things for him, or was the undeniable attraction mostly coming from my side?

I sprang two paracetamols from their foil sheet to swallow with my morning orange juice, but for some reason I didn't return the travel pills to the cabinet. Instead, I dropped them into the deep pocket of my towelling robe. They were yet another mystery that was silently pecking away at my consciousness. The other being: why was my mother avoiding my calls? Was she screening them? The thought made me pause halfway through buttering a slice of toast. Had our last squabble been so severe we were no longer speaking at all?

The frustration of not knowing was making me jittery. I pulled the travel pills from one pocket and my mobile phone from the other. There was a connection here, but I just couldn't work out what it was. I glanced at the clock. It was very early. I never phoned her at this hour – at least I didn't think I did, but with a memory as unreliable as mine, who was to say?

I felt sneaky hiding my number so that it wouldn't flash up on her caller ID. Who does that when phoning their own mother?

I poured myself another mug of coffee and sat back down on the breakfast stool, absently toying with the knife on my plate as I waited for the call to connect. I hummed along to the radio, blissfully unaware that in less than ten seconds my whole world was going to be blown apart.

The phone rang, and not just in my ear. I drew it away to check it wasn't on speaker. It wasn't. So why could I still hear it ringing? I looked all around, trying to work out where the sound was coming from. There was something vaguely sinister about the overly cheery default ringtone. I slid off the stool and followed the sound. It was coming from beyond the kitchen. Was my mother here, in my flat? How could she have let herself in without me knowing? She had no key to my home.

Once in the hallway, it was easier to determine where the ringing was coming from. My footsteps were hesitant as I walked towards my bedroom. This had all the makings of a great jump scare scene in a film, and it was far too early in the morning for that kind of fright.

The room was empty, just as I'd left it. The duvet was thrown back, the shutters were opened, and there was no parent standing in a room she'd not set foot in for years. And yet the phone continued to ring.

My eyes scoured the bedroom, trying to pinpoint where the sound was coming from. They settled on the large oak chest of drawers beside the window. I swallowed several times, my palms so sweaty I almost dropped my own phone as I crossed the room.

I pulled open the top drawer of the dresser with unnecessary force, as though trying to derail this particularly unpleasant practical joke. Because that was what it was, wasn't it? Someone was playing a trick on me. And it must have been an incredibly cruel one, because why else would there be tears coursing down my cheeks as I reached for my mother's phone from the place where it had been stored at the back of the drawer.

◆ ◆ ◆

'I forgot. How is that even possible?'

A warm breeze ruffled my hair. Had I brushed it before leaving the flat? It seemed unlikely. I could scarcely even remember pulling on whatever clothes my scrabbling hands had fallen upon and plucking up my car keys.

Clearly, I shouldn't have driven here. No one that distraught should ever get behind the wheel of a car. Luckily it was the weekend, and the roads had been quiet at the early hour. The car park had even been empty, apart from one other vehicle. Maybe it was always empty, who was to say? It wasn't as if all the missing pieces had miraculously fallen into place.

Just the major ones; the ones so devastating I was still reeling from the shock.

'I forgot,' I said again, my voice sadder now. 'I'm so sorry,' I added in a whisper. 'How could I?'

I was still shaking; I had been from the moment I'd plucked my mother's phone from the drawer and immediately staggered backwards as the memories cannoned into me, one after the other.

I still felt dizzy and disorientated, and my knees finally gave up the impossible task of keeping me upright. I sank down onto them, feeling the dew-covered grass immediately seep into the denim of my jeans.

Reaching out, I tentatively touched the black granite headstone with its gold-etched writing. I read the inscription as though I was seeing it for the very first time, which in a way I was. My lower lip began to tremble as I read her name, Elizabeth Louise Harker. But it was the dates beneath it – especially the second one – that wrenched a sob from me. It was six months in the past. My mother had died over half a year ago, and yet for me it was breaking news that I couldn't take in.

She'd been so healthy. So fit. I cast my mind back and couldn't remember a single day she'd ever been off work sick. For most of my childhood, she'd held down at least two jobs, sometimes three. If anyone ever wondered where my fierce independence or unwavering work ethic had come from, they didn't need to look far. This apple hadn't fallen far from the tree.

'What happened, Mum?' It was the voice of the child I hadn't been for a very long time.

More memories found cracks in the wall the lightning had created. And none of them were good. It had been cancer. I remembered that now. It had been horribly and cruelly quick. But she would have welcomed that. She'd never been one for long-drawn-out goodbyes. Had we said ours properly? Had we made peace with all the petty disagreements of the past? I shook my head sadly. Those memories were still locked away from me.

There were flowers on her grave that were borderline past their best. I assumed they must have come from me, because we had no other family. It had always been just her and me. Mum made acquaintances easily, but friends . . . not so much. Those she did have lived far from here. I touched the wilting roses, and a wave of sadness shuddered through me.

I leant forward until my forehead was resting on the cool smooth stone of her marker. It felt familiar, as though I might have done this before. I really hoped that wasn't just my imagination filling in the gaps that still existed.

When had I last visited her in this place? I hoped it hadn't been too long ago. 'Because it looks kind of lonely here,' I said, my voice cracking on the words.

Mum had a solitary plot in a row of doubles, which felt both sad and symbolic. Not that she'd have wanted it any other way. She'd never wanted nor needed anyone beside her in life, so why would she in death? As far as I knew she'd never dated again – not even once – after my father had walked out of our life. 'You can't miss what you never had' was a phrase I grew up hearing. 'Besides, I'm too busy for all that nonsense,' she'd always maintained.

Had she thought it through properly, I wondered? I looked down at the empty space on the grass beside her and ran my fingers through the cool, damp blades. Was spending eternity alone really what she'd wanted, or was it just the hand that life had dealt her?

A bird cawed overhead, and it sounded exactly like the dismissive sound my mother would have made if she knew the direction my thoughts had taken.

I got to my feet and glanced over my shoulder towards an empty bench not far from my mother's plot. Currently its only occupant was a curious robin, who was hopping from seat to armrest. He disappeared into the trees in a flurry of flapping wings when I sat down, only to return moments later as soon as I settled. I wondered if he was a frequent visitor to this spot. I hoped so. It would be nice if Mum had some company.

I sat on the bench until the sun had climbed as high as it could go above the trees and the cemetery began to grow busier. By the time I got to my feet, there were others walking along the footpaths, some carrying flowers, and a young couple carrying a teddy bear.

I spoke to no one as I made my way towards the exit, walking with my head down and studying my feet, which I only now noticed were in mismatched socks. The only interaction I had was when a distinguished-looking older gentleman with sad eyes and a kindly smile nodded my way in unspoken acknowledgement as I passed him at the wrought-iron gates. He looked vaguely familiar, and I wondered if our paths had crossed on one of my previous visits. I had no idea, but then he swept past me without a word, so perhaps we'd never met at all.

Feeling exhausted, I walked slowly back to my car.

Chapter Eleven

There was water all around me. I wasn't swimming in it – it wasn't one of those dreams – but I felt dwarfed by the sheer volume of it and dazzled by its glare. I looked down as though preparing to dive, which even dream-me knew was a bad idea, as I'm only a passable swimmer.

I struggled to pull myself out of the dream, but something was tethering me to it, entangling my limbs as though they were imprisoned in long twists of rope. I woke with a start, my legs still thrashing across the width of the double bed. It took a moment or two for reality to kick in and for me to realise they were tied up in nothing more treacherous than the sheet I'd replaced the duvet with, following the Met Office prediction that tonight would be the hottest in decades.

With an impatient grunt, I freed myself from the sheet and then flopped back on the mattress, waiting for my racing heart to find its usual rhythm. I was covered in a film of sweat; I could feel it greasily sticking the hair to the nape of my neck and trickling unpleasantly down my back. Even the skimpy strappy top and briefs I'd worn to bed were damp with perspiration. It was as if I'd run a marathon in the night, but I hadn't been asleep long enough for one of those. The illuminated screen of the bedside digital clock confirmed it was only a little after two-thirty in the morning.

I'd been asleep for three hours, which was the longest stretch I'd managed to achieve in the seven days since I'd learnt of my mother's death. Those words rolled across my brain like tumbleweed over a prairie, still alien, still incomprehensible. Grief and guilt were as tangled up in my head as the sheets I'd kicked myself free from. It was impossible to separate the strands of loss from the shocking truth that my brain had simply erased her death from my memory. Was that because losing her hadn't hurt? Or because it had hurt too much?

How many times had I charged her phone, just so I could call it and hear her voice one more time? Those were just some of the questions that waited for me in the shadows at the end of the day and in the lonely middle-of-the-night hours when sleep eluded me.

Tonight, in the stifling sultry heat of the bedroom, it had been even harder to slip into the oblivion I craved. Every bedroom window was open, attempting to trap a whisper of a breeze, but the night air was thick and soupy and totally still.

The dream had already lost its potency as it evaporated away, and although I tried to grasp its disintegrating fragments, they were already just wisps of thoughts disappearing from my memory. Like so many other things have done recently, I thought as I flipped over my unpleasantly damp pillow.

As odd as the dream had been, I didn't think it was responsible for jerking me awake. There had been a noise, or a crashing sound. My senses were instantly alert to the possibility of an intruder, but seconds later the room filled with brilliant light as though an invisible hand had momentarily flicked on every lamp in my flat.

I bolted upright, already placing the source of the sound before it came a second time. It roared, louder than a jet engine, from somewhere directly above the rooftops, making the windows rattle in their frames and the entire building shudder.

In pure reflex I drew up my knees, bringing them tightly against my body as though I was trying to make myself so small the lightning couldn't find me. But it did, didn't it, said a voice in my head that refused to be silenced. It found you again.

Those were the words that triggered the third most terrifying thing to happen to me in the last few weeks. Knowing I was spiralling into a panic attack, even though I'd never experienced one before, did nothing to stop my descent into terror so intense it felt as though my heart was surely about to stop. It was pounding against my ribs as though trying to hammer its way out of my chest. My throat was tightening, and every breath became a hoarse gasp that failed to deliver enough oxygen to my lungs. I felt dizzy and light-headed, and there was a weird tingling sensation in my fingers and toes, like pins and needles on overdrive.

A terrified whimper escaped me as the thunder was followed by more forked lightning, so bright I could still see it imprinted on the inside of my eyelids.

You have to get off the bed and close the shutters, I instructed my frozen limbs, and even the voice in my head sounded half hysterical with fear. But I couldn't move. Every joint felt fused together as though I'd been turned into a statue right there in my own bedroom. My eyes went fearfully to the open windows, the nearest one just a metre from where I lay. My obsession with lightning stories on the internet had uncovered numerous accounts of people being struck while inside their homes through open doorways or windows. There'd also been tales of people who'd been struck by lightning more than once. There were theories that these victims had somehow become lightning magnets, which had been crazy enough to make me laugh when I read it. But now, in the middle of the night, with the storm raging right outside my window, it didn't seem nearly as funny. Had the lightning come back to finish what it had started?

With the next flash, I clawed at the sheet, drawing it up to my neck as though the thousand-thread-count fabric could protect me from a second strike. The storm wasn't moving on, and neither was the panic attack.

I'm not sure what would have happened if the lull between the next rumble of thunder hadn't been punctured by a different sound and a light that lit up the area around my bed in a far less threatening way. It was surprisingly hard to persuade myself to let go of the sheet and reach for my phone. My hand felt dead, as though the fingers that were fumbling for the mobile belonged to someone else. But they managed to pluck the device from the bedside cabinet and, after several clumsy stabs at the screen, they answered the call.

As luck would have it, I accidentally turned on the speaker, which was just as well as holding the device steady enough to talk into it would have been beyond me.

'Hello? Ellie?'

It had been over a week since I'd heard his voice, but the relief I felt as it filled the bedroom was so great I immediately began to cry.

'Rhys.' His name was accompanied by a ferocious chattering of my teeth, so violent you'd be forgiven for thinking I was freezing to death instead of sweating more than any sauna could achieve.

'Are you okay?' From the concern in his voice, I think he'd already worked out that I wasn't.

'No. The storm. It woke me. And I can't move. Or breathe properly.'

I don't know if he'd taken a first-aid course in his past, or if he was just so incredibly good in a crisis that his instincts were reliable enough to work out what was happening to me.

'Have you fallen? Are you injured?'

I shook my head fiercely in reply, before realising I needed to somehow summon my vocal cords into action.

'No, but my heart is going so fast I think it's going to stop.'

'It won't,' he said, so reassuringly I almost believed him.

'It feels like I'm going to die,' I said, and even though I knew it was overly dramatic, it felt true in that moment.

'I won't let you,' Rhys reassured me, and for the first time I felt the jackhammering within my chest begin to slow down.

'It's just a panic attack. It'll pass in a minute or so. Just breathe slowly and deeply. In . . . and out.' I did my best to follow the pace of his instructions. 'Keep thinking about every breath and then find something in the room to focus on.'

Still breathing like a beginner, as though inhaling and exhaling was an alien concept, I glanced across the bedroom and saw the white jeans I'd worn that day.

'Okay. Now focus all your senses on whatever it is you're looking at. Think about how it feels when you touch it. Does it make a sound when it's moved? Does it smell?'

'I hope not. It's the clothes I was wearing today.'

His laugh was the best medicine I could have hoped for.

'There you go. You made a joke. You're going to be fine.'

And I realised he was right. My heart rate was slowing down and the weird numbness in my hands and feet had almost gone. I'd been on a precipice, about to tumble into a bottomless abyss, and amazingly he'd talked me back from the edge.

'How do you feel now?'

'Foolish.' It was the most honest answer I could give him.

'Don't be. Not even for a second. Foolish would have been not having a reaction to something that tried its best to kill us a little while ago.'

I really liked that 'us'.

'How did you know to phone me? How did you know I'd be panicking?'

I heard a long exhalation, as though he wasn't altogether satisfied with the answer he was about to give.

'To be honest, I don't know. The storm woke me too, and I lay here for a few minutes, telling myself I was being irrational, but something kept compelling me to call you, to check you were okay. I just hoped I wasn't going to get an earful of abuse for waking you up in the middle of the night.'

'I'm so glad you called,' I said, flinching as yet another strobe of lightning flickered beyond the open window.

'Is it still bad outside?'

I looked at the rain teeming down like bullets from artillery fire.

'Yes, it's wild here. And the lightning still hasn't passed.'

'On a scale of "slightly bothered" to "really terrified", where are you right now?'

'Is there a "paralysed with fear" option?'

The terror must have still been there in my voice, because I heard the rustle of bedcovers, as though they'd been hastily tossed aside.

'Just hang tight. I can be there in about twenty minutes.'

'What?' I said, and I knew I must have been feeling better when my first thought was of my sweaty body and perspiration-drenched hair. 'No. You don't need to do that. The roads will be treacherous in this rain.'

'That's not important,' he said, and I heard the sound of a zip being hastily pulled up. A totally different kind of heat flooded into my cheeks, because I knew it belonged to his trousers.

'Honestly, Rhys, please stay where you are. I couldn't bear the thought of anything happening to you on the road because you were on your way to me.'

There was a jingle that I guessed was probably his car keys, and I found myself holding my breath for what felt like an eternity before they clattered back down.

'Are you absolutely sure, Ellie? I hate the thought of you being there all alone and terrified.'

For just a second or two I wondered if some of the reason he'd offered to come over was because he too was scared. But that idea couldn't find a foothold. I truly couldn't imagine Rhys being frightened of anything.

'I can't have you racing over to comfort me every time there's thunder and lightning or it rains. We live in the UK. You'd be dashing over every five minutes.'

I could hear the smile in his voice. 'Well, I didn't say I'd do it every time.'

My lips curved in response and then I heard the sound of the zip again, this time being tugged back down. That took the grin from my face and made swallowing suddenly difficult.

'Will you stay on the line though, for just a minute or two longer?' I asked, wincing at another roll of thunder.

'Of course I will,' he said, and although I couldn't hear it, I imagined the sound of bed springs taking his weight as he lay back down.

'So, what do you want to chat about?' he asked, before adding on a lighter note, 'Now that the good old English standby of the weather is off the menu.'

I laughed nervously. Rhys's ability to defuse what had been an explosion of fear within me was nothing short of miraculous. On one level I knew I could probably tell him that I'd unbelievably forgotten the death of my only living relative, and he wouldn't judge me. But it still felt too soon, too raw to share that confession with anyone. Even him.

'I don't know. Anything. What did you do today? What did you have for dinner? What kind of music do you like?'

'I designed a book jacket. Spaghetti carbonara. And country.'

'I'm going to need more background on answers one and three. The spaghetti one we can ignore.'

'Ah, but that's the one worth talking about. It's my signature dish. I'll have to make it for you sometime.'

'I'd like that.'

Friends could cook for each other, couldn't they? That wasn't stepping over any line, was it? My conscience must have been feeling kindly towards me following the panic attack, because it offered no argument.

We talked for hours, long after the storm had passed and the rain had died down to a very non-terrifying drizzle. Rhys's voice had soothed and relaxed me like a fine wine flowing through my veins. At some point I'd lain back down on the bed, curling onto my side, with the phone now off speaker and nestled against my ear, because it felt more intimate to hear his voice that way. My eyes were growing heavy, and it was getting harder to disguise the yawns that were punctuating my side of the conversation. But Rhys never said he was tired or that he wanted to hang up. I think he was regaling me with a story about a trip to Alaska that he'd taken in his twenties when my eyes eventually fluttered to a close.

I don't remember drifting off to sleep and have no idea how long he kept talking to me after I'd fallen silent. But when I woke up in the morning, my mobile was still in my hand and sunlight was streaming in through the open windows. I looked down at the phone screen. There was a new message that I clicked on even before I lifted my head off the pillow.

Goodnight. Sweet dreams. R

Oh God, I was in so much trouble.

Chapter Twelve

The sun was surprisingly strong. Despite the heavy canopy of leaves, the dappled rays felt warm on my bare legs as I wriggled my feet off the blanket I'd remembered to bring and let the blades of grass tickle my toes. Discarded a few feet away were the shoes I'd worn to the office that morning; bright red kitten-heeled sandals that had screamed at me to buy them from the shoe shop window. They made me feel like Dorothy in The Wizard of Oz, perhaps because she'd also survived a devastating storm.

My taste in footwear was just one of the countless changes I kept noticing. Before the accident, I couldn't ever have imagined flipping the Open sign to Closed halfway through the workday and taking off to the park with my laptop and a meal deal sandwich. Both were currently lying open on the blanket beside me. In fairness, I wasn't exactly skiving off. I'd already answered several emails and was now working my way through an alarmingly full inbox, ruthlessly deleting messages like a gardener on a weed purge.

'Junk. Junk. Junk,' I muttered, shaking my head at the amount of rubbish that found its way into my account. There were cold canvassing emails from companies I'd never heard of, determined to sell me products I'd never buy, as well as an inordinate number from cruise companies trying to sell a holiday to someone who hadn't taken one in years. And as I got seasick just thinking about water, that definitely wouldn't be the type I'd go for, if by some miracle I ever managed to take some time off. Something snagged briefly at my memory as I clicked on the link from an exclusive ocean liner company and hit the Unsubscribe button. It felt as though something important had drifted tantalisingly close but frustratingly remained outside the periphery of what I could remember.

A scurrying sound in the long grass derailed my train of thought as a particularly bold squirrel, who clearly had his eye on the uneaten half of my sandwich, darted a little closer and then froze. I tore off a sizeable piece of crust and threw it towards him. He dived for the treat and sped up the tree trunk faster than my eyes could follow, disappearing into the foliage. My gaze travelled the route he'd taken, and then stopped when it came to the ugly charred scar scored deep into the bark where the oak had taken the brunt of the lightning.

I could have chosen to sit anywhere in the park. There were plenty of vacant benches and shady areas to have picked, but I'd been pulled back to the tree, in much the same way as I was continually drawn to Rhys. It was as though something primal and unfathomable had connected us in the moment the lightning struck. Something that still had a hold on us even now.

It had been an interesting and frustrating time since the night of the storm and even though I'd never admit it, I was a little disappointed not to have heard anything from Rhys. *I will not contact him first*, I promised myself . . . and I hadn't. *It's up to fate if our paths cross again.* But nine days later, I was starting to realise our reconnection might be very low down on fate's to-do list.

Ignoring the new listing I'd intended to work on, I reached instead for a buff-coloured folder that had lived in my desk drawer long enough to have dog-eared corners. I flipped over the cover and leafed through the sheaf of papers within it. I'd read them all before, but where I'd previously dismissed the proposal as time-consuming and unwieldy, I felt a strange and unexpected spark of interest for an idea I'd initially dismissed.

When Florrie, the elderly owner of Ripping Yarns, the small craft and textile shop at the end of the high street, had passed away, many of the local business owners had wondered what her daughter planned to do with the property. My hopes of adding it to my books had been raised when she'd walked into my office with the same folder in her hands that was now in mine.

But selling the property was the last thing on her mind. Ripping Yarns scarcely made enough to cover the overheads, but it was well known locally for its open-door policy that Florrie had established. What had begun as afternoon sewing classes had quickly expanded to become a place for the lonely, bereaved, or simply those who were a little down on their luck to gather, chat, and maybe even do a little needlework. It wasn't unusual to walk past and see an eclectic group of OAPs, residents from the local hostel, or even the occasional homeless person sitting around the craft table, enjoying a slice of cake and the chance to talk with someone, possibly for the only time that day.

'Mum was so passionate about helping people and giving back to the community. She really wanted the doors to stay open after she was gone, and I want to respect her wishes.'

'So, you won't be selling the building?' I'd asked, trying to disguise my disappointment.

Florrie's daughter had shaken her head emphatically.

'Definitely not. But I do need someone to oversee the project. Mum told me to ask the other shop owners if they'd be willing to help, and she specifically said I should speak to you.'

'Me?' There'd been no hiding my surprise. I'd cast my mind back, trying to remember any conversation I'd ever had with Florrie that could have led her to think this was something I'd like to be involved in. It was completely out of my wheelhouse. The only thing I could recollect talking about with her was a random memory of my own mother teaching me how to knit, a hobby she'd loved but one I hadn't touched in years. I was at a loss to work out how a throwaway conversation about such an old memory could have made her think I was the right person to oversee this project.

I'd politely told Florrie's daughter it wasn't something I could help her with, but she'd been oddly reluctant to take no for an answer. 'Mum thought you'd probably not say yes straightaway. But she said I should leave the idea with you.'

And she had, for months now, and every so often something would make me pull the folder out, read through the vague, ill-planned ideas, and shake my head in bemusement that this file had ended up in my desk. My eyes fell again, as they always did, to the list of local businesses who'd already offered some means of support should the project go ahead. Beth's name was there, with a solid tick beside her shop Crazy Daisy, as well as several of my fellow business owners. Surprisingly there was an appetite to continue what Florrie had started and for the first time I could feel a stir of interest that had me reaching for my pen as I began scribbling down notes.

Four pages of scrawled thoughts later, I set the folder aside, feeling a strange fizz of excitement that I usually only experienced when finalising a sale or securing a tenancy. It was strange, a little unsettling, but also incredibly satisfying.

Still buzzing with ideas, I lay down on the soft fleecy blanket and stared up into the tree that had simultaneously almost killed me and possibly saved my life. I could no longer decide which. Either way, coming here today had felt curiously healing, which given what had happened on this spot made no sense whatsoever.

My eyes were closed, but I heard the patter of footsteps coming from behind the thick girth of the oak's trunk.

'Is this it? Is this the one, Daddy?'

Behind the concealing tint of my sunglasses, my eyes sprang open. Even before he answered, I knew exactly whose voice I would hear in reply.

'Yes, sweetheart, this is the oak tree,' Rhys said.

I gave a nervous swallow and wondered if there was any chance at all that they'd stay on the opposite side of the tree and not notice me or my blanket. Having spent over a week feeling disappointed to have not accidentally run into Rhys, I was suddenly thrown by the prospect of encountering him now, here, with his daughter. My breath caught in my throat as I realised she might not be the only one who'd accompanied him to the park today. His ex, the all too perfect Annalise, might be here too.

Very slowly I inched myself upright. My belongings were too widely scattered for me to make a quick getaway, and I realised there was no easy escape when a slender young arm snaked around the enormous tree trunk, hugging the gnarled bark.

'Thank you, tree, for looking after my daddy. I'm sorry you got hurt too.'

This was getting embarrassing. I was going to have to reveal myself or else it would look like I was deliberately trying to hide, which I absolutely would have done if I'd thought for a moment that I could get away with it.

But before I could work out how to casually pretend that I'd only just noticed them, a shadow fell across the foot of my blanket.

'Ellie?' Rhys asked, even before he'd emerged from behind the tree. 'Is that you?'

'Yes,' I said, scrabbling to my feet and tugging down on the hem of my dress to make sure my legs weren't on display. *He saw more of you than just a pair of naked legs the last time you met*, I reminded myself, which did nothing to stop the heat of a blush from creeping onto my cheeks.

Rhys pulled off his sunglasses, and I was momentarily distracted by the brilliant green of his eyes. Seriously, how did people ever concentrate when he looked at them the way he was looking at me right now?

'This is a happy coincidence, running into you,' I said, smiling wide enough so the young girl knew I was including her in the greeting.

Even so, she seemed a little wary, hanging back behind the protective shield of the tree. Rhys extended his hand, and she slid her small one into it.

'Tasha, this is my friend, Ellie.'

'Hello, Tasha. It's very nice to meet you,' I said, extending my own hand for a second before catching the confused look on the child's face and hastily dropping my arm. Idiot. From Rhys's hastily smothered smile, I knew he'd seen my rookie error.

'Are we interrupting your work?' Rhys asked, inclining his head towards my laptop and folder. I wrinkled my nose in reply.

'Not really, I was just . . .' I gave a small shrug, wondering if he would understand if I attempted to explain why I'd felt the need to come here.

'I get it. I've been here a couple of times myself since it happened.'

That made me feel a great deal better, or was it just that I always felt a little bit better in his company? These were definitely not the kind of thoughts I should be having around his daughter – nor anybody, come to that.

'My daddy was here when the tree was hit by a huge bolt of lightning,' Tasha told me earnestly, as though sharing a secret.

'Ellie knows that, sweetheart,' Rhys said, pulling the little girl to his side and giving her a brief cuddle. 'She was here on that day as well. It got her too.'

Tasha's eyes widened in awe, and she gave me a very slow head-to-toe appraisal.

'Did you get the magic marks on you too?'

I realised then what she'd been looking for, and in the same breath realised the Lichtenberg figures Rhys had acquired when the lightning had struck were fainter but still there.

I turned to study him with the same kind of scrutiny his daughter had just given me.

'They're starting to fade,' he confirmed, but I saw that wasn't entirely true. Although in places the figures were now faint and insipid, as though he'd been tattooed with invisible ink, where they disappeared beneath the collar of his shirt, the marks still looked as vivid as ever.

Tasha's interest in me was quickly overtaken when she caught sight of a large ginger cat, who I recognised as one of the park's most regular visitors.

'Can I go and see the cat, Dad? I promise I won't touch him.'

'You can. Just stay where I can see you.'

Tasha immediately took off at a run, two blonde bunches flying like streamers through the air behind her.

'I think he's okay for her to pet. He's not vicious or anything.'

Rhys's eyes were still on his daughter, who had caught up with the moggy who was now lying on his side in one of the park flowerbeds.

'It's not that,' he said, his eyes narrowing as Tasha dropped to a crouch in front of the cat but made no move to reach out and stroke him. 'Sometimes animal fur can set off an asthma flare-up.'

In a move I suspected he'd done a thousand times before, Rhys reached into the back pocket of his jeans and pulled out a small inhaler. It lay in his palm for a moment, as though he'd needed visual confirmation that it was close at hand, before he slipped it back into his pocket.

'She has her own on her,' he explained, his eyes never leaving his daughter. 'But I like to be certain that I do too.'

I felt more than a little ignorant.

'It must be hard, having to be so vigilant.'

He gave an easy shrug. 'You get used to it. And Tasha is very good at knowing how to avoid her triggers.' He gave a sigh. 'The worst of it is that she absolutely adores animals. She wants to be a vet,' he said with a rueful expression.

His eyes took on a new gentleness as they settled on his daughter, now engaged in a deep conversation with the sunbathing feline.

Seeing Rhys in this new light was like discovering a secret room in a house you thought you knew. It had happened to me once, professionally, and had been really thrilling . . . but this was even better. It shone a spotlight on a whole new side of him and touched something in me that I hadn't even known was there.

Feeling a little unsettled, I quickly scooped up the blanket and stuffed it, along with my laptop and folder, into the large canvas tote I'd brought to the park. The sandwich remains I took to the base of the tree and made a low clicking noise, which I hoped the squirrel would understand meant I left this for you.

When I straightened up, Rhys was watching me with an intrigued smile on his face. In one hand he was carrying the tote and in the other he had my shoes.

'Looks like Tasha isn't the only Doctor Dolittle in the park today.'

I gave a half-embarrassed grin and reached out to relieve him of my belongings, but he just shook his head. 'That's okay. I'll carry them. Unless you need these back, Shoe Girl,' he said, his eyes going to my bare feet.

I shook my head, secretly loving the nonsense nickname he'd given me. Our footsteps fell naturally in sync as we walked towards the park cat and its newest number-one fan.

'Do you think he has a home?' Tasha asked Rhys wistfully as we approached.

'I think he belongs to the lady who runs the café,' I said gently, not wanting to disappoint Tasha, nor be part of a catnapping plot.

'That's good to know,' Rhys said, dropping to a crouch to scratch the feline between his eyes.

I was going to have to look an awful lot harder to find some flaws in this man, because thus far I hadn't stumbled across a single one.

'I wish we could change Mummy's mind about getting a cat. I could take my allergy pills every day.'

And there you have it. There's the flaw, the fly in the ointment. This man has commitments and a partner who wants him back. He isn't even remotely unattached. Why is it so hard to keep remembering that?

'I wanted a cat too when I was your age,' I said, joining them on the ground beside the loudly purring feline. 'But I never got to own one.'

'Why not?' Tasha was now staring at me, as though sensing a kindred spirit.

'My mum was allergic.' Was that really true? It was a fact I'd never actually questioned until that moment.

'Do you still live with your mum?'

I swallowed the lump of grief that threatened to lock my throat.

'No, sweetheart, I don't, not anymore.'

'So why don't you have a cat now?'

I'd had job interviews that hadn't felt as probing. I think Rhys must have sensed my discomfort, for he ruffled his daughter's hair. 'Come on, you. That's enough interrogating for one day. Let's go and get that ice cream I promised you.'

We all got to our feet, but before I could make my excuses to leave, a small soft hand curled its way into mine.

'Can Ellie come with us?'

I threw a surprised glance Rhys's way. 'Oh no, that's fine. I don't want to intrude—'

'You wouldn't be,' Rhys replied. 'If you can spare the time, we'd love you to join us.'

There were probably a great many excuses I could have made, should have made, but every single one escaped me as I stood there in the sunshine with Rhys and his daughter.

As we headed towards the park gates, Tasha tugged on my arm, bringing me down to her level and allowing her to whisper softly into my ear.

'I'm sorry you never got a cat, Ellie.'

I'd thought my greatest challenge was going to be how not to fall in love with Rhys, but I realised in that moment that it might be just as hard not to fall for his daughter too.

There were smears of chocolate around her lips. They made me reach for a serviette in case I also wore traces of the most decadent ice cream I'd ever eaten. It had been big enough to feed a family of four, and I'd ended up admitting defeat long before the plate was even half cleared.

The ice cream parlour had only recently opened, and with its 1950s American décor and queue that snaked out of the door, it looked to be a huge success. We were surrounded on every side by families seated at gingham cloth-covered tables. I shifted a little on my milk churn stool, wondering if it was as apparent as it felt that I was an imposter here. We might look like a family, but a beautiful blonde-haired woman was meant to be sitting in my place.

Tasha, with the determination of a pint-sized politician, had successfully managed to steer the conversation back to cats once again. And somehow, before my dessert was gone, I found myself agreeing to only get a cat from a shelter, and if I needed help selecting one, she would happily accompany me.

Rhys waited until she had jumped down from her stool to visit the Ladies' before saying quietly, 'She likes you.'

His words ignited a warm glow inside me.

'It's one hundred per cent mutual. She's a lovely little girl.' I gave a small laugh. 'And very persuasive.'

He smiled. 'Don't worry. I don't think anything you've agreed to is legally binding. You don't have to get a cat.'

I gave a small shrug. 'I don't know. Maybe I will. It'd be nice not to come home to an empty house all the time.'

I saw a dark cloud scud across his features and could have bitten my tongue for being so insensitive. My home was empty out of choice. His was empty because his partner had left him for another man. It was a fact I still found as astonishing as I had when he'd revealed it on the night of the last storm.

Fortunately, at that moment Tasha reappeared, changing the expression on her father's face in a heartbeat. The truth was glaringly obvious: Rhys wanted nothing more than to be able to see his daughter on a daily basis again. And I'd be willing to bet that was exactly what Tasha wanted too. The sweet taste of ice cream suddenly turned sour in my mouth. I shouldn't be here. I shouldn't be allowing myself to become a potential obstacle, getting in the way of this family reuniting. I should step away; that's the advice I'd give anyone in this situation. What I needed was some straight-talking guidance, and I knew exactly who I should ask. The only problem was she wasn't answering my calls.

Chapter Thirteen

The fact it took me four attempts to parallel park in her street indicated just how nervous I was because I was usually pretty good at parking in tight spaces. I could feel a vague tremor in my fingers as I switched off the engine. The spot I'd found was only a short distance down the road from the three-bedroom semi that Mel and Steve called home.

Her car was in the driveway, and I gave a sigh of relief as I climbed out of my own and reached for the items on the back seat. I'd taken a chance that Mel's work schedule was the same and that she still worked from home on Fridays. I'd taken an even greater chance that she'd be willing to see me.

I'd decided to leave it four weeks before contacting Mel again – I'd lasted just over three. Maybe I'd caught her when she was still jet-lagged from her return from New York. Or maybe she was simply a much nicer person than me – which was probably closer to the truth. For whatever reason, when I'd messaged to say I'd really like to see her again, she hadn't told me no. Admittedly, she hadn't said yes either. But that was how I chose to interpret her somewhat lukewarm reply of 'Sometime soon, perhaps.'

What was the worst she could do, I wondered, as I adjusted the cumbersome object in my arms to get a better hold? Slam the door in your face? Throw a bucket of water on you from an upstairs window? Simply not answer the door? There were no end of possibilities, none of which I liked. This was Mel, for God's sake. She was my person, and I was hers. Or at least I used to be.

The container I was carrying was heavy and digging painfully into the flesh of my forearms. Perhaps I should have gone with a bouquet of flowers after all. There'd certainly been plenty to choose from in the florists that morning.

'Hi, Ellie,' Beth, the shop's owner, had said with a welcoming smile. 'Another client arrangement?' Her pen had been poised, waiting for the details and a delivery address.

'Actually, I'm looking for something different today. Something that says I'm sorry.' That was when I'd spotted the ceramic pot standing in the corner of Crazy Daisy.

'What kind of plant is that?' I'd asked, already sure I knew the answer.

'It's an olive tree.'

I'd smiled and reached for my purse.

'Perfect. I'll take it. Can you tie a fancy ribbon around it?'

Repositioning the tree in my arms as I walked towards my friend's front door, I wasn't holding out an olive branch . . . I was extending the whole damn tree. I just hoped it was enough for Mel to forgive me for being a truly awful and neglectful friend.

I rang the doorbell and resisted the impulse to duck back out of range of the wall-mounted camera so she couldn't see who was there. She took a worryingly long time answering. Long enough for me to wonder if I should have tied a white flag to the olive tree instead of a big old red ribbon.

I'd been straining my ears for the sound of footsteps on the wooden boards of her hallway, but Mel was barefoot when she answered the door, catching me by surprise when it suddenly swung open.

The first emotion that hit me was a wave of love for my old friend. How could I not have realised how much I'd missed her until that very second when she was standing there in front of me? The second emotion came fast on the heels of the first: shock. She looked different. Mel had always had the kind of curves that filled a pair of skinny jeans far better than mine ever did and boobs that made me feel like I'd only just graduated from a training bra. But today she looked so much thinner, and not in the way you did after a healthier eating regime. She looked gaunt and tired. It's probably just jet lag, I told myself, even though I was already afraid it was something way worse than the results of an exhausting trip.

Her hair had escaped from its usual crocodile clip restraint and the wild curls were taking advantage of the freedom by swamping her face. They made her cheekbones look even more prominent and her eyes appear enormous. Although, to be fair, finding me on her doorstep for the first time in goodness-only-knows-how-long might have been another reason for that.

'Ellie,' she said. Despite straining my ears for a clue, I couldn't decipher how she felt about this ambush from the way she said my name.

'Hello, Mel,' I said. Feeling suddenly shy in front of the person who knows you better than anyone else in the world is both a lonely and a terrifying experience.

Guilt pierced me like a poisoned dart. I had squandered something precious. What right did I have to think some stupid olive tree gift was all it would take to make things right again?

'I'm sorry for dropping in unannounced like this,' I began, intending to tag on the lie but I was in the area. So, I was almost as surprised as I imagine she was when my voice cracked. ' . . . but I was so scared to call first in case you wouldn't agree to see me.'

I followed her down the hallway and into her bright, friendly, chaotic kitchen that was bathed in late-morning sunlight. I'd clearly interrupted her workday, for her laptop was open on the kitchen table and was surrounded by a sea of paperwork and pamphlets. Mel worked for a charity who redistributed unused food from supermarkets to shelters and the homeless. Even the career she'd chosen illustrated exactly why everyone who met Mel immediately fell in love with her. She was a good person, who worked hard to make life better for people in need. What did my choice of job, with its veneer of perfectly staged homes and aspirational lifestyles, say about me?

'So, is that tree for me, or is it just something you carry around with you these days?'

She had done it again, made me laugh even when I was on the cliff edge of crying. No one did that better than her.

She plucked up a box of tissues from a nearby countertop and plonked them down on the table in front of me. 'Just in cases,' she said, quoting a line from one of our favourite films, and for some stupid reason that made me want to cry even more, remembering all the late-night popcorn and movie sessions we'd shared. Pulling out a chair painted in a particularly cheerful shade of buttercup yellow, she motioned for me to sit.

I made use of both the seat and the box of Kleenex while Mel scooped up the papers strewn across the table into a haphazard bundle that immediately made me want to volunteer to sort them out. Sensibly, I quashed the impulse.

Mel had taken the olive tree from my arms and set it down in the corner of her delightfully messy kitchen beside a jumbled heap of shoes. The pile was topped with a pair of fluorescent green Crocs that I bet Mel wore even when she wasn't gardening. They were very her.

Our taste in clothes had always been very different. She was boho through and through, favouring long flowing skirts and floaty tops. She wore a collection of silver rings on every finger and so many bangles on her slender wrists I used to wonder how she found the strength to lift her arms. She wasn't wearing any today, which was just as well because her wrists looked too thin and her forearms too delicate to bear their weight. The fear that she was sick, seriously sick, muscled its way back into my head, despite Jackson's assurance that illness wasn't the issue.

'I was just about to make a coffee. Do you want one?'

'Yes please,' I said, looking around the kitchen I could remember so well, even though I couldn't remember when I'd last been here.

I waited until she'd brought the coffees over to the table, along with a jar of honey, the same brand she'd always used in drinks instead of refined sugar. She spooned a sizeable amount into her mug and then cocked her head on one side in a question that I answered with a nod. The taste of it took me back to countless nights spent in either her room or mine, cramming for tests or exams, moaning about boys, or binge-watching box sets of the Gilmore Girls, a series I'd enjoyed with a bewildered fascination. Were there really mothers and daughters who got on that well? I gave a small sigh as I remembered how Mel had always said the show reminded her of her own mum, who'd passed away when she was only a teenager.

The fear that something was really wrong with my friend was like a whole herd of elephants in the room. They might trample me to death for interfering, but there was no way I could ignore them.

'How are you, Mel?'

'I'm fine.'

I shook my head. 'No, you're not.'

It was a tricky card to have laid so early in the game. It could have seen me back outside her front door in a heartbeat. But that wasn't her.

'Okay. Well, I'm pretty pissed off with you. Is that better? Is that what you wanted to hear?'

I gave a helpless shrug. 'I think it's more honest than "fine". Pissed off I can deal with. Pissed off I deserve. Because I've been a bad friend.'

'Yes, you have.'

I swallowed uncomfortably, every word of the speech I'd carefully prepared fleeing from my brain.

'What are you doing here, Ellie?' She looked pointedly at the watch on her slender wrist. 'Shouldn't you be at work?'

I shook my head. 'Some things are more important than work.'

Her eyebrows rose. 'Easy to say; harder to prove.'

I flinched like a boxer taking a blow in the ring. I'd been expecting this. I was prepared for it to be way harder than just buying coffee and cake had been. Mel wasn't Jackson and she had clearly taken my abandonment much harder than he had.

'So where exactly have you been for the last nine months or so?'

I gave a helpless shrug. It wasn't that I didn't want to answer, it was just that a great deal of that time period was still a hazy mystery.

'Because to be perfectly honest, nothing short of an alien abduction is going to work for me.'

'I got lost,' I said, my voice small. 'I strayed so far into my own head, into what I thought I wanted to achieve, I forgot what was really important.' I gave a small laugh that threatened to break into a sob. 'I stupidly thought a thousand friends online was just as important as my real-life ones.'

She stared at me for a long moment, almost without blinking.

'I was wrong. So wrong. I was a bloody idiot.'

There was a weighty silence, filled only with the hum of the fridge.

'Sorry. Was I meant to contradict you there?' Mel eventually asked.

'Not at all.'

She looked out of the window into the neat garden, which was bathed in morning sunlight.

'You really hurt me, Ellie. I hadn't done anything to deserve the ghosting.'

I wanted so badly to grab hold of her hand but was terrified she'd snatch it away, which would undo me.

'There was no fault on your part. Or on Jackson's. You both tried, I know you did.' That much at least I could remember, even though I wished the lightning had robbed me of that too. 'I think I just got so overwhelmed with the fear of failing that I gave everything I had to the business. It became my baby.'

She flinched at that.

'So, you chose to win at being an estate agent and fail at being a friend?'

I got to my feet, not sure how much longer I could hold back the tears.

'Maybe it's just too soon for this,' I said, turning away from the table and pushing my chair back in.

'Maybe it's just too late,' she countered, and that would have felled me to my knees if it hadn't been for the crack I heard in her voice.

I was almost at the door before she stopped me. 'You might as well stay and finish your coffee. I hate seeing anything good go to waste.'

I turned around slowly, hoping I wasn't imagining the potential double meaning in her words. Did she mean us? Our friendship? She kicked my chair away from the table with her foot. It was all the encouragement I needed and I dropped back gratefully onto it.

I picked up my coffee cup and was mid-sip when my friend sighed.

'Jackson warned me you'd probably do something like this.'

I wondered what she meant. Turn up and grovel? Beg for forgiveness? Or ask for her help? Because I couldn't imagine her anticipating the last, but it was the ace up my sleeve, and I was desperate enough to play it.

'I'm going to keep apologising as many times as you need to hear it,' I assured her.

She shook her head. 'I'm going to be honest, Ellie. I still don't know if that'll be enough to mend this.'

She was putting me through the wringer. And I deserved every last excruciating minute of it.

'I understand. But apologising and making amends isn't the only reason I'm here today.'

She immediately sat up straighter in her seat. 'What did Jackson say to you?'

I'd inadvertently walked straight into a minefield. One wrong step and I could blow up our friendship even more cataclysmically than I'd already done.

'Nothing. He said nothing. Except that I should give you some space and that you'd been through a bit of a rough time.'

I was used to seeing those eyes laughing at me, not narrowing in suspicion like they were doing right now.

'I caved before it got to four weeks,' I said, biting my lower lip, which was starting to tremble. 'That felt like long enough.'

'You always did have appalling willpower.'

I risked just the tiniest smile, because it was the first time she had referenced the way she knew me better than anyone else did.

'And although it's not the main reason I'm here today – far from it – I do have a favour to ask of you.'

'Ballsy,' she said with a shake of her head. 'Asking me for something when I'm still spitting feathers.'

I let my eyes stray to the buff-coloured folder that I'd set down on her kitchen table.

'The favour isn't for me. It's for a really worthy cause. And I want to get involved but I need help, and even though I know you're still mad at me, you're the best person – the only person – I know who can guide me on what I should do next.'

Her eyes strayed to the folder and then back to my face.

'Damn it. Now I'm curious,' she said, reaching out a hand to slide the folder towards her. She paused with one finger on the corner. 'If this thing erupts with a load of "I'm sorry" confetti, you and I might be done for good.' It wasn't a big smile, but it was a glimmer of one, and right now that was way more than I deserved.

'It won't,' I assured her.

'You're going to need to appoint trustees – at least three of them,' Mel said, nibbling absent-mindedly on the end of a biro as she scanned the sheet of paper in her hands.

I added Trustees to my to-do list that already covered half a sheet of A4.

'But not if you decide it will be a social enterprise rather than a registered charity. You won't need them if it is.'

I added an oversized question mark beside Trustees and then three exclamation marks for good measure.

'And how do I work out which one it should be?'

Mel shook her head, not quite in despair but more in resignation. She pulled her own notepad closer and scribbled rapidly upon it.

'I'll do it. It can be a minefield if you don't know what you're doing and it's quicker and easier than trying to explain it to you.'

I wasn't stupid, but I took the veiled insult on the chin.

Leaning back against the slats of the wooden garden bench, I resisted the urge to slip on my sunglasses. True, they'd shield me from the midday glare, but they'd also hide the gratitude and admiration in my eyes. And it felt important that Mel saw just how much it meant that she was willing to help me. Except it wasn't really for me, I knew that. It was for all the potential visitors to the old yarn shop, who would now hopefully still have somewhere warm and comforting to go where they could enjoy a drink, a bite to eat, but more importantly some much-needed companionship.

'I knew you'd be the right person to help me with all this,' I said, daring a tentative smile.

'Please don't blow smoke up my arse. You'll set off the detectors in the kitchen.'

I just about managed to smother a laugh, even though we were out of range of the alarms. We'd moved from the house to the garden and Mel had generously spent the last hour going through the contents of the buff folder, sometimes nodding wisely, sometimes shaking her head at whatever she read.

'It's a good idea. But it needs quite a bit of fine tuning to make sure you're doing everything legitimately and by the book. Have you given any thought to who'll staff the place? How many days it will be open, and the general running costs?'

'Not in great detail,' I answered truthfully. 'I think all the shop owners who've said they'll contribute financially are also willing to volunteer a few hours each week to run the place.'

Mel's eyebrows had risen at that.

'Even you?' The incredulity in her voice had stung.

'Yes, even me.'

This time it was Mel's turn to lean back in her chair and eye me speculatively.

'Something's different about you.'

I didn't bother pretending that she was referring to the way I currently wore my hair or did my make-up.

'Yes. I feel different.' In a thousand ways and for a great many reasons, but this wasn't the time to share any of them.

The biro found its way back into her mouth as she bent to the next item on the list she was compiling, but not before I heard her murmur: 'You remind me of someone I used to know, someone I've not seen for a really long time.'

My eyes were overbright, and while I could have pretended it was the glare of the sun, we both knew that wasn't true.

Once Mel had grasped the size of the proposed project, she'd wordlessly disappeared into the kitchen, returning five minutes later with a plate of hastily constructed sandwiches.

From the outside peering in, we probably looked like two old friends enjoying a lazy al fresco lunch in the sunshine. But not every picture tells the full story. We were wallpapering over the cracks for now, but that didn't mean they weren't still there.

'Have you decided what you're going to call this place?' Mel asked, tapping the point of her pen on the notepad as she waited for my reply. 'Ripping Yarns doesn't really work if you're going to drop the crafting element.'

As I scarcely knew one end of a needle from the other, she made a good point. The answer came so easily to mind it was as though the decision had already been made a long time ago.

'Florrie's,' I said decisively.

Mel nodded in agreement. 'Florrie's it is then.'

I left a short while later, taking back the folder which Mel had already photocopied. I leafed through the papers when she handed it back to me, making sure I had them all, and almost dropped them in her hallway when I saw the chart of volunteers we'd drawn up to manage the shop. Among the names of my neighbouring shop owners was one that took me completely by surprise. Mel Gooding.

She must have seen my shocked expression that was quickly followed by one of thanks.

'I'm not doing it for you. It's a really good cause, and this kind of thing is right up my street.'

I successfully bit back both 'I know' and 'That's why I'm here' because our truce was built on gossamer wings and could be crushed by a single thoughtless comment.

'You're a good person, Mel, and even though I know I'm still in the doghouse, I want to say again how sorry I am for how I behaved. And that if you let me back in, I won't ever do anything to hurt this friendship again.'

'Let's just concentrate on Florrie's for now,' she said, not meeting my eyes or the wistful expression in them.

'Agreed,' I said, not sure if I should offer her my hand to shake or my cheek to kiss. In the end I did neither.

She closed the front door behind me with a click that wasn't quite loud enough to hide her sigh. At least she hadn't slammed it in my face.

It wasn't a big win, but it felt like the world to me.

Chapter Fourteen

There ought to be some sort of rule about sneaking up on people in cemeteries. My heart was robust, I didn't spook easily. But when you hear a voice in a supposedly deserted graveyard, it's hard not to overreact. My pulse rate went sky-high and I gave a squawk of alarm. The trowel slipped from my fingers and I lost my balance, wobbling from my crouched position to land heavily on my backside, directly on top of the pile of soil I'd just removed from the hole I was digging.

I'd got there ridiculously early, still not entirely sure if I was breaking the rules, because to be honest the website hadn't been at all clear on what was and what wasn't permissible planting. I'd seen other graves with flowering shrubs beside them, and it had made me sad that everything I laid beside my mother's plot was destined to wither and die. I wanted something there that would grow and flourish.

'Peonies.'

That was what the man had said, in a totally non-threatening, non-scary way, but it had still thrown me into a mini panic.

'Oh, my goodness, I'm so sorry,' he apologised, stepping off the pathway and walking across the dew-damp grass to reach me. 'Did I startle you?'

'No. Not at all,' I lied, trying to pretend it was always my intention to end up with damp soil smeared all over the back of my jeans.

'Please, allow me to help you up,' he said, holding out his hand. I saw neatly trimmed nails, and palms covered in callouses. If I had to guess his age, I would probably say early seventies, but his hand didn't look frail, despite the smattering of age spots across the back of his knuckles. Even so, I declined his offer of assistance, holding up both my hands as though I was surrendering to arrest. My palms were smeared with dirt. My gel polish French manicure, only two days old, was ruined. These weren't hands fit for touching anyone.

'That's okay,' I said. 'I'm a bit grubby.'

That was an understatement. Filthy was closer to the mark. If evidence was needed of my rookie status as a gardener, it was right there in the tools that were so new they all still had their price labels on them, and the fact that I hadn't thought to pick up a pair of gardening gloves when buying the rest of my supplies at the DIY store.

I scrabbled to my feet, scattering displaced soil in all directions as I straightened up.

'Peonies are an excellent choice,' the man said, nodding slowly in approval and stepping back out of the danger zone. His shoes, I noted, were black brogues, polished so well they practically reflected the early morning sunlight in their gleaming leather.

'They were my mother's favourite flower,' I admitted, surprising myself by sharing that information. I rarely spoke about my mum, even to people I knew well, so to do so now with a total stranger was more than a little unusual.

I bent to retrieve my dropped trowel, expecting the man to be on his way. Instead, I saw him turn towards the wooden bench nearby and lower himself onto it.

'You don't mind if I sit here for a moment or two, do you? Just to catch my breath.'

It would have been downright rude to point out there were probably a dozen other empty benches throughout the cemetery he could have picked. It would have been even more inappropriate to add that he didn't look the least bit breathless or in need of a rest. The woman lying six feet beneath the soil beside me would have been mortified if I'd voiced a single objection. So, I didn't.

I turned back to the area I'd been digging before the man had interrupted me. It was a bit late to realise I should probably have paid closer attention to the advice Beth had offered about planting the peonies I'd bought from her store when I'd purchased the olive tree. She'd definitely said something specific about the depth of the hole I should dig, or was it the distance between each plant?

I freed the first peony from its plastic pot and dropped it into the hole. I had a feeling that the man sitting on the bench was watching me. When I'd finished refilling the hole around the vibrant pink plant, I chanced a glance over my shoulder. The man's face was tilted up towards the sun and his eyes appeared to be closed. I assumed he'd gone to sleep, and after a moment of hesitation, I began digging a second hole.

I was only two shovelfuls in when the man on the bench cleared his throat. I paused, then resumed digging. He cleared it again. I turned around, but he still appeared to be in exactly the same position; his eyes were still closed.

Even so, I abandoned the hole and began to dig a new one a little farther away from the first. I paused with the tip of my trowel in the soil. The man didn't make a sound, although for a split second I thought I saw his lips curve in what could have been a smile.

I'd brought eight plants to the cemetery, and there was a great deal more throat clearing and unspoken gardening guidance as one by one they were set into the ground beside my mother's grave. I got to my feet when I was done, brushing the soil from my hands and turning to face him. I gave him a quizzical look, not sure if

I should be thanking him for his help or buying him a box of Strepsils. 'Thank you,' I said softly, taking a seat at the far end of the bench not looking at him but at the row of neatly spaced-out, vibrant-coloured plants that my mother would have loved. 'I'm not really much of a gardener.'

'They look pretty good to me,' the man said.

'Thanks to your advice.'

He gave a charming shrug. 'I don't know what you mean. You did all the hard work.'

I smiled, turning more fully towards him. There was definitely something familiar about him which I couldn't pin down. It came to me a moment later when he inclined his head politely towards another early morning visitor who had passed by our bench. He was the man who I'd seen at the gates on my last visit . . . when I'd first remembered that my mother had died.

Those words still felt like a kick to the stomach, and it was hard to hide my instinctive flinch.

'Are you alright? You suddenly look a little queasy.'

He was certainly observant; I'd give him that. But I found his interest kind, rather than intrusive.

'Just a little overwarm,' I said, gathering up a handful of my auburn hair and lifting it free from the back of my neck.

For a moment the old man's eyes flickered strangely. Then he blinked and the bland, friendly expression was back, making me wonder if I'd imagined it.

'Have you brought water with you?'

'I've got a can of cola in the car,' I told him. 'I'll be fine with that.'

He chuckled softly. 'Actually, I meant for the plants. You need to water them in.'

I flushed in embarrassment.

'Oh. No. I didn't think.' I glanced around the rows of neatly maintained graves. 'Is there a tap or something nearby?'

'Not that I've seen. But don't worry. I can bring in a five-litre container with me tomorrow and water them for you.'

I'm sure my cheeks were still more pink than the peonies I'd planted when I swivelled to fully face him.

'That's very kind of you, but I can't ask you to do that.'

'You didn't ask, I volunteered. There's a difference.' His voice was firm and in a blinding flash of intuition I felt certain that this man had once been a teacher, because he reminded me of every good one I'd ever had.

'It really is no problem, Miss . . .'

He paused for me to fill in the missing surname. I skipped past it.

'Ellie. My name is Ellie Harker.' And then, before I could stop to think why I did it, I nodded towards the black granite gravestone beside us. 'And this is my mother, Elizabeth Harker.'

His eyes softened with sympathy as he nodded slowly. 'It's a pleasure to meet you both.'

His name was Henry. He was seventy-two years old and a widower. And apparently, he visited the cemetery on a daily basis.

'You're here every single day?' I repeated, as though there might have been some different interpretation to those words.

He nodded.

'Who is it that you come to visit?'

His eyes were faded blue, but they darkened at my question until they looked even deeper than mine in colour.

'I'm sorry,' I said hurriedly, realising I'd probably broken every rule of cemetery etiquette. 'That's far too personal a question to ask a stranger.'

'Well, we're not exactly strangers now, seeing as we've introduced ourselves,' Henry said reasonably. 'And all the visitors you encounter here, the regulars and the not-so-frequent ones, are all here to talk to the people we've loved and lost. We have so much in common it feels like we're all already connected, already friends.'

It was a very romanticised way of looking at it, but strangely I rather liked it.

'But to answer your question, Ellie, I come here each day to be close to the only woman I ever loved. My Bee.' He turned in his seat and his gaze focused on a row of gravestones on the other side of the path beneath the shade of several willow trees.

'I'm sorry for your loss,' I said.

'As am I, for yours,' Henry replied, his eyes going back to Mum's plot. 'It's very recent for you,' he observed, no doubt having noticed the dates engraved on the granite plinth.

'Newer than you can imagine,' I said.

His eyebrows were white and bushy, in the way older men's often are. They were currently raised on his forehead, like albino caterpillars.

I bit my lip. Was I really about to confess my failings as a daughter to a total stranger, when I hadn't even found the courage to do so to either my friends, or to Rhys? Apparently, I was.

'I . . . I had an accident a short while ago.'

Henry sat up straighter, his face full of concern. What an incredibly nice man he was.

'I'm fine now. Well, almost fine. But it did some strange things to my memory.' I could feel my eyes filling with tears. They were literally one blink away from coursing down my face. My voice dropped to a hoarse confessional box whisper.

'I forgot my own mother had died.'

His lips parted, closed, and then parted again, as though he kept finding a suitable response and just as quickly discarding it. I didn't blame him. It was hardly something you heard every day.

'So, for me it's been more like a few days to get my head around losing her. I mean, I can now remember bits and pieces of what happened. I remember her getting sick, and that it all went to shit very soon after that. Sorry,' I said, apologising for swearing.

He gave a wry smile. 'I was a schoolteacher for forty-five years, my dear. I don't think there's anything you could say that I haven't heard a thousand times before.'

I knew it.

'Do you know what's the worst thing about forgetting?'

Henry inclined his head, encouraging me to continue. 'It's not knowing if I came here to visit her during the last six months.'

'Why would you think that you hadn't?'

He really did ask excellent questions.

'My mother and I didn't always have the best of relationships. She and I clashed . . . a lot. I don't think either of us found the other very easy to get along with.'

'That seems hard to believe,' Henry said gently. 'I mean I've only known you for . . .' He consulted his watch. ' . . . less than half an hour, and I find you extremely easy to get on with.'

I smiled at that before my eyes went to my mother's plot. 'I don't think you'd have said the same thing about her, sadly.' Up went his eyebrows again. 'She was always very critical, very prickly.'

'I'm so sorry, my dear,' Henry said sadly. And it really sounded as though he meant it.

Chapter Fifteen

'You don't mind taking him again, do you?'

Actually, I sort of did mind, but before I could voice my objection, the eight-month-old baby was thrust back into my arms again.

'We just want one last quick peek at the bedroom,' the woman explained as her partner began pulling a tape measure from his pocket.

'Hello again,' I said to the infant, who was looking at me suspiciously as his parents disappeared back inside the house I was showing them. If I was bad at talking to seven-year-olds, then my chat with those not yet able to speak had to be heard to be believed.

The clients were clearly the most laid-back parents ever. They appeared to have absolutely no qualms about passing their baby into the arms of someone who was patently not qualified for child-minding. They'd done it the first time when I'd been showing them the bathroom with its double-size shower enclosure.

'Could you hold him for a sec?' the husband had asked, unclipping the infant from the carrier on his chest and passing him to me. 'We'd just like to check out the shower.' For a worrying moment, as they'd both kicked off their shoes, I'd thought they were about to strip off and give it a test run. Thankfully they'd stepped into the enclosure still fully clothed.

The viewing continued to be a contender for one of my weirdest ever, when they'd once again passed me their baby as they both insisted on scaling the loft ladder to examine the attic for possible conversion.

I'd waited in the hallway below, bouncing the infant – whose name I believe was George – on my hip, because that's how I'd seen it done in films. It didn't feel exactly natural, and George certainly wasn't shy in making his feelings known about being left with a total amateur in the baby-rearing department.

'I bet Mel would know how to do this,' I muttered as the little boy began to cry, growing redder and redder in the face until it looked like I was holding a human beetroot instead of a tiny person.

He looked hot, thirsty, and incredibly angry, and yet despite the fact his indignant wails were now filling the street, his parents didn't seem to be in any hurry to reappear.

'Come on, George. They'll be out soon,' I told the distraught infant, feeling terrible when I saw there were genuine tears rolling down his overheated chubby cheeks.

'I'm so sorry. I don't know what you want,' I apologised, my eyes going once again to the bedroom window of the property, which George's parents probably weren't even going to buy anyway. 'Two more minutes,' I promised him. 'If they're not out by then, we're going in to get them. Okay?'

It was mid-afternoon on another uncommonly hot day, and the shade on the pavement was practically non-existent. A tall fern in the front garden afforded a narrow pocket of shadow, which I manoeuvred us both into. The quiet residential street was deserted, or so I thought until I heard the rhythmic slap of rubber on concrete when George paused to take a breath. I peered out from beneath the leafy fronds and spotted a man in shorts and sports vest who'd emerged at speed from a side street.

'Hush, hush,' I urged George, not wanting the stranger to think I was kidnapping the baby, or totally inept at calming him. The first was unlikely, the second was undeniably true.

I heard the steady tempo of the runner's feet as they approached, and focused my attention on George, blowing raspberries into his face, which for some reason made him bawl even harder.

I saw a pair of expensive running shoes jog past me and then come to a stop. I rearranged my features into those of someone who doesn't look like they haven't got a clue what they're doing.

'That's not a happy face.'

I wasn't sure if the stranger meant George or me. To be honest, it could have been either of us. But mine changed almost instantly when I recognised the man standing before me, bouncing lightly on the balls of his feet.

'Rhys, hi,' I said, my voice sounding equal parts delighted and embarrassed. 'This is a weird coincidence.'

'Isn't it? And it's one that keeps happening to us.'

He smiled and his eyes dropped to the screaming baby in my arms.

'And this is . . . ?'

'This is George. He hates me.'

Rhys chuckled softly and gave the baby the kind of smile that was guaranteed to make anyone stop crying. It almost succeeded, as George peered up at the tall man who'd joined us on the pavement.

'I've been showing the house behind us to his parents, and they've gone back in for one last quick look and left me – quite literally – holding the baby.'

Rhys reached out a finger and gently touched the tip of George's nose, making a soft beeping sound as he did. The crying stopped like a switch had been flipped. Rhys repeated the action and George, who I'd started to think might be possessed by the devil, actually giggled.

I looked at Rhys in total awe. 'How did you do that?'

He gave an easy shrug. 'It always used to work with Tasha. I thought it was worth a try.'

'You're a genius.'

'No. You just pick up a few tricks along the way,' he said.

'Well, thank you.' I shot a look over my shoulder at the open front door of the house. There was still no sign of George's parents.

'Are you in a hurry to be somewhere?' I asked.

'Do you ask that because I was running?' he teased.

I felt my cheeks turn every bit as scarlet as George's had done.

'Sorry,' Rhys said, smiling at the baby when he reached out a pudgy hand and grabbed hold of Rhys's finger. Something inside me, something that I didn't even know lived there, melted.

'It's just that George seems to like you, and I wondered if you could hang about for a minute or two until his parents get out.'

'Of course I can,' he said, and I liked the way he hadn't hesitated for a single second.

One of Rhys's hands was still being firmly held by George, but with his free one Rhys reached for a water bottle.

'I've not drunk from it yet,' he said, offering me the container. Despite my raging thirst, I was about to decline when he added. 'You look a little hot and bothered.'

That was perhaps more to do with him than George. There was a sheen of perspiration that glistened on his arms and broad shoulders like a sprinkling of fool's gold. His running vest, with its university logo, was sticking to him like a second skin that I very much wanted to peel away. I was suddenly incredibly glad my arms were full of baby.

'Ahh, Georgie, have you been a good boy for Ellie?' crooned a voice from behind me.

I summoned a smile for my charge's mother. It grew when she plucked her offspring from me. George looked far more distressed at losing his hold on Rhys's finger than he did at leaving me.

'This is Rhys. He's a friend of mine,' I explained as George's dad slammed shut the door of the house they'd been viewing.

'We really like the place,' he said. 'We just need to go home and do our sums and then we'll get back to you.'

I nodded slowly, making sure the smile on my face didn't slip.

The couple didn't quite manage to hide their relief when I politely declined their offer of a lift back into town, even though we'd all travelled to the property together. As they fastened a newly calm and chirpy George into his car seat and drove away, I knew without a shadow of a doubt that that would be the last time I ever saw them.

'They're not going to buy the house?' Rhys asked, as though I'd just displayed psychic abilities.

I shook my head.

'How do you know that?' he asked, clearly fascinated.

I gave a small shrug. 'You just get a feeling for how these things are going when you've done this job for a while. I used to think it was all about TikTok engagement and selling the best house in a street at the highest price, but actually it's more about matching the right property to the right person. That's the bit I now realise I like best.'

'Perhaps you're just particularly insightful?' Rhys suggested as he lifted the loose hem of his running vest and absently used it as a makeshift towel to wipe his face, which was still streaked with perspiration from his run.

I lost my train of thought and then all ability to think straight as the action briefly exposed the taut flat planes of his stomach. I saw exactly what he'd meant about the marks left by the lightning. The curious fern-like patterns, the Lichtenberg figures, that had almost faded from his arm were still clearly visible on one side of his torso, running across his chest in a diagonal swathe that bleached into thin tendrils before disappearing beneath the waistband of his running shorts.

'I'm sorry,' Rhys apologised. 'I don't think I'm the most fragrant of company right now.'

He smelled just fine to me.

'Are you heading back to town on foot?' he asked, his head tilted to one side with a look that was pure adorable Labrador. The decision I'd made to get an Uber back was suddenly the last thing on my mind.

'Yes, I am,' I said, conveniently forgetting that I actually had no idea of the route back.

'Well, if I promise to stay downwind of you, do you fancy some company?'

My entire day just got exponentially better.

'I won't have to run, will I?' I joked.

His smile was on maximum wattage. 'No. You can set the pace,' he said.

Sadly, the speed at which we walked was probably the only thing in my control as far as Rhys was concerned, because everything else felt like it was totally out of my hands.

We walked in companionable silence as the sun shifted lower in the sky, throwing some much-needed slices of shade onto the pavements and pathways. I didn't know the streets he was taking me down, but I felt nothing but safe in his company. I always did.

We eventually emerged at a crossroads. There was a sprawling business park on one side of the road, a post office delivery depot on the other, and several utilitarian apartment blocks right in front of us.

I was looking around as we walked, trying to orientate myself, when the door of the centre block of flats opened and a middle-aged man exited. He spotted us, raised a hand, and called out a greeting to Rhys before heading towards a row of parking spaces.

All the pennies dropped at once. 'Is this your place?'

'It is,' Rhys said, looking vaguely uncomfortable, especially when he realised I'd come to a halt.

'Were you just about to walk past your own home without saying you lived here?' I questioned.

His discomfort appeared to be growing.

'Yes, I was.'

'Why?'

He dug his hands into his pockets and all at once lost about twenty-five years. He looked like a sheepish little boy in the headmaster's office.

'Because I didn't want you to think I'd engineered it so that we'd end up at my place and you'd feel coerced into coming inside, if you hadn't wanted to.'

There was a lot to unpack in his explanation, and I took my time doing it.

'Is it possible that maybe you're a bit of an overthinker?' I said carefully.

'It has been said.'

I looked around at the deserted area. I suppose if he was an entirely different kind of man, maybe this situation might have made me nervous or twitchy. But I felt as relaxed with Rhys as I always did.

'I'm not easily coercible,' I said at last. His face still looked serious. 'Is that even a word?' That, at last, released a smile. 'Nothing about this,' I said, wafting my hand in the air to encompass where we were, 'or our friendship makes me feel anything except completely comfortable.'

Rhys nodded and the lingering traces of concern left his face.

'To be honest, I can't remember the last time a man was this worried that I'd misinterpret his actions. Probably because it's never happened to me before.'

'Then you've been mixing with all the wrong men,' he said, finally extracting one hand from his pocket, along with his door key.

'You might be right there,' I murmured low enough that he couldn't hear. He had already turned towards the entrance to his building.

'So now that we've sorted that out, can I interest you in coming up for a beer or some wine?'

My nod came with a smile that seemed to live permanently on my lips in his company.

I followed him into the deliciously cool air-conditioned hallway and towards a bank of lifts. A tiny thrill of anticipation thrummed through me as we waited for the carriage to arrive. My desire to see inside his home was more than just estate agent nosiness. Seeing how a person lived was one of the most illuminating ways to understand them better. And Rhys was a puzzle I was still trying to figure out.

His flat was on the middle floor of the five-storey building. It was everything he'd said: modern, airy, functional, and impersonal. It escaped being bland only by scattered splashes of colour from a handful of brightly patterned cushions and a huge Aztec-style rug on the floor.

The layout was open plan, and I followed him into the kitchen area, where he went straight to the fridge. I pulled up a stool at the breakfast bar. It was the kind that resembles a chip basket and was just about as comfortable. To protect my bare legs, I tugged on the skirt of my dress, making the neckline dip lower and display more cleavage than I would have liked. I knew Rhys had already seen more than that, but that had been a medical emergency – or at least that was how I liked to categorise it.

'White or pink?' he asked, straightening from the fridge with a bottle in each hand.

'Pink, please.'

He pulled two glasses from a cupboard and filled them generously. The wine was deliciously cold and refreshing and Rhys took a generous swig before wrinkling his nose.

I took a subtle sniff of the wine in my own glass, which had tasted just fine to me.

'At the risk of putting you on sleaze alert again, would you mind if I left you for five minutes so I can jump in the shower? I promise you it's not my usual routine with visitors, but one of us doesn't smell that great, and it's definitely not you.'

'That's okay. I mean, you're perfectly fine as you are, but I'm happy to entertain myself for a bit.'

Rhys took another sip then set his wine glass back down on the counter beside mine.

'I won't be long. Make yourself at home.'

For someone who is very used to being alone in other people's homes, I felt strangely wrong-footed to be on my own in Rhys's. I waited until he left the room before gingerly extracting myself from the stool. With my wine glass still in hand, I wandered back into the living area, taking my time to focus on the room's layout and the furniture he'd chosen. It told me very little about the man himself . . . but the walls yielded far more information. The plain white expanses were decorated with an eclectic accumulation of artwork.

Modern abstracts sat beside watercolours. Monochrome paintings beside framed prints so vibrant I almost felt the need to pull out my sunglasses. I perused each one, walking around the lounge as though I was visiting an art gallery. The styles were too diverse to identify his preferences. But they did tell me that the man loved art, although as he was a graphic designer, that was hardly breaking news.

There was just one wall I'd yet to examine, bare of all artwork except for two drawings in matching black frames. That was their only similarity. The first one I instantly recognised. I saw it in my dreams every night. It was burnt into the retina of my memory. Rhys had perfectly captured the dignity of the majestic old oak. I stepped closer, awed by the intricate detail that so clearly depicted the grainy bark and the individual leaves of the tree. This was no ordinary sketch; it was a piece that exuded so much emotion I could feel my throat tightening in response. This was how art was meant to make you feel, I acknowledged, as my eyes were drawn to the gouge marks the lightning had left in its wake. I lifted a hand and gently ran my fingers over the glass of the frame.

The second picture was just as powerful, but in a totally different way. The subject was a newborn infant, held in a pair of slender feminine arms. I immediately recognised what I was looking at. The baby was staring upwards towards its mother, whose face wasn't visible in the sketch. But it didn't have to be. I knew the strands of hair that fell down like curtains towards the infant were blonde. I knew the fingers lovingly touching the soft skin of the child's cheek belonged to Annalise. I just knew it. I didn't need to look at the lower right-hand corner of the frame . . . but I did anyway. Rhys's name was there.

He was barefoot following his shower, so I didn't hear him enter the lounge. I was alerted to his return by a kind of sixth sense that seemed to go into overdrive whenever I was near him. One of my regular senses also kicked in as my nose captured the aroma of cedar and apple from whatever products he used in the shower.

I turned around to find him much closer behind me than I'd realised. I jumped and he immediately stepped back.

'Sorry. I didn't mean to startle you.'

I turned back to the two pictures again. 'These are amazing.'

He gave a small gracious nod of thanks.

'The one of Tasha is obviously quite old.' I wondered if he knew how his expression softened when his gaze fell on the sketch of his daughter and his partner. Ex or otherwise, there had been love there when he'd drawn that portrait. It was visible in every line of his pencil.

A totally different expression slid onto his features as his eyes then went to the oak tree.

'This one is – obviously – more recent.'

I gave a slow nod, stepping even closer to the picture of the tree.

'I've got an entire sketch book full of similar drawings,' Rhys admitted, looking a little rueful. 'I was starting to worry that I was getting obsessed. I was afraid that tree would be the only thing I'd ever draw again.' He gave a dry laugh. 'Which would have been very bad for my career prospects.'

It was surprisingly hard to tear my eyes away from the image of the oak tree. 'I ignorantly thought you just created book covers and stuff like that. I had no idea you were such a talented artist.'

He gave a small shrug and stepped away from the drawings to sit at one end of the black leather sofa. I took a place at the opposite end.

'The book covers pay the rent and the bills. The other stuff is just for me, at least for now.'

'Well, if those two examples are anything to go by, you need to get a gallery interested enough to show your work. You're that good.'

He looked modestly embarrassed but also a little bit pleased, which made me feel like I'd done something right today.

An idea was whispering in the back of my head, refusing to be silenced. It was sharpening and crystallising, even as I began to speak.

'Do you paint houses?' I said with absolutely no preamble.

It's no wonder he got the wrong end of the stick.

'Do you mean like decorating them?'

I spluttered inelegantly into my wine and narrowly escaped a coughing fit.

'No. I mean like drawing houses. In ink or charcoal or some other medium.'

Rhys gave a casual shrug. 'I guess I'm what they call a pen for hire. I could do any of those.'

'Then I'd like to hire you.'

His head tilted again, less adorable puppy this time, more curious collie.

'I'm always looking for new ways to make my business stand out from the competition,' I explained. 'And I wanted to have something unique to give my clients when a deal is completed, be it a house sale, or letting a property.' I nodded, as much to myself as him, as the idea grew larger and sharper in my mind. 'If you're interested, I'd like to commission you to do sketches of the properties my clients are leaving behind, as a keepsake gift for them.'

There was something very warm in those green eyes as they looked back at me.

'That's a really nice idea. It's way more personal than simply sending a bunch of flowers.'

'Oh well, I'll still do that too,' I said, knowing my conscience wouldn't allow me to withdraw my custom from Beth and her flower shop. 'I just thought this could be a really nice addition.'

'It would be,' he agreed.

'And you'd be okay with it? I mean, you'd have to tell me what a fair price would be for your work.' My nose crinkled as I wondered if my suggestion was going to alter the dynamic of our relationship in any way.

But it's a really great way of keeping him in your life, isn't it? Ellie of old chose to point out. To be fair, this time at least, she wasn't wrong.

'So,' Rhys said, drawing out the word with clear amusement. 'Does this mean you'd be my boss?'

'No. I mean, not really. Well, kind of. Maybe just a little bit.'

His grin lit up his face, the room, and a place in my heart where it really had no business setting up home. 'I think we could give it a try.'

Chapter Sixteen

I blinked like a mole as I descended the short flight of steps and left the dwindling light of early evening to slip into an interior that felt like midnight in contrast. I paused by the doorway to allow my eyes to adjust and wished my pulse would do the same. I was nervous, and I had no idea why.

I'd spent countless evenings in bars, pubs, and clubs with Jackson, although admittedly Mel had usually been present too. Tonight, it would be just Jackson and me, a fact he'd been very clear about when he'd messaged to invite me out for a drink. I could only assume Mel had filled him in on my unexpected visit to her home two weeks ago and that she still didn't want to see me socially. Even though I'd heard from her several times in the interim, it had only been in connection with the Florrie's project, when she'd needed a question answered or more information about something.

'Mel's definitely not coming?' I'd asked Jackson, hoping the wistful note in my voice wasn't as noticeable to him as it was to me.

'No, Ells. It'll just be you and me. That's okay, isn't it?'

'Absolutely fine,' I'd assured him. At least fifty per cent of my friends were willing to forgive me for ignoring them. I was just going to have to work harder to win the other half over. All I could do was hope I'd banked enough good friend credits in the years before I checked out of the group.

I straightened my spine and stole a quick glance in the enormous smoked glass mirror by the doorway. My hair was loosely styled in beachy waves and my make-up freshly applied after work. The jeans I was wearing were so new they still crunched when I sat down, but they went well with the black halter top I'd teamed them with. I drew in a steadying breath and headed into the main bar.

One of the servers directed me towards the booth at the back of the bar which Jackson had reserved.

'The other member of your party is already there,' the waitress told me with a wave of her hand.

I zigzagged through tables to reach the booth, a smile and a greeting already on my lips. Both froze as the shadowy shape waiting for me in the booth looked up at my approach. It's hard to say which one of us looked the most surprised.

'Jackson,' Mel said, her voice practically a growl.

I was just as quick to put the pieces together. 'He's not here, is he?' Though it wasn't really a question.

'Of course he isn't,' Mel said, squeezing out the words through lips pursed tight in irritation.

I held up my hands in defence. 'I knew nothing about this, Mel. He told me it was just going to be him and me.'

'Ditto,' Mel said. If she was a cartoon drawing, there would be steam coming out of her ears right now.

I was still wondering what to say next when both of our phones pinged simultaneously.

'Don't be mad.' Mel read the words on her screen out loud, even though the exact same message was on mine.

'It was the only way I could think of to get you both on neutral territory,' I completed.

Our eyes met and locked.

'Interfering, meddling little busybody,' Mel muttered furiously, setting her phone down on the table.

'I couldn't agree more,' I said, unthinkingly sliding into the seat opposite her.

Both our mobiles chimed again. Mel glared at hers as I read our incoming message.

'So now you can both bitch about what a pain in the backside I am, and then, when you're done with that, for fuck's sake get over yourselves and kiss and make up. This nonsense has gone on for long enough.'

'Un-be-liev-a-ble,' Mel said, dragging all five syllables out of the word.

I huffed out a laugh. 'He's not changed much over the years, has he?'

'He never could stand conflict,' Mel agreed with a sigh.

I looked up when a shadow fell across the table as a waitress carrying a tray of cocktails came to a stop beside our booth.

'These are from Jackson,' she said, sounding a little bemused. She frowned as though trying to remember her next line. 'He said, "Don't throw them at each other."' She set two margaritas down in front of us.

'As if,' Mel said, sliding a glass closer. 'I hope he's left a sizeable amount on the bar tab.' The waitress backed away with a slightly nervous smile.

'So, what do we do now?' I asked, still unsure if Mel intended to get to her feet and leave.

'I guess we stay,' she said, lifting her glass from the table as her phone pinged.

She read the screen and her eyes flickered with an expression that looked troubled.

'What did he say?' I asked, as my own phone had remained silent.

'Talk to Ellie. Tell her what's been going on with you.'

My eyes probably held a thousand questions as they searched her clearly distraught face.

My phone dragged my attention away.

Mel looked up, waiting to hear the latest missive.

'Don't screw this up, Harker,' I read in a deadpan tone.

'What did Jackson mean? What is it that you're not telling me? Because whatever it is, I want to help.'

Mel was biting her lip, drawing the sensitive skin back and forth until it began to look painful.

'Not having you around to talk to was always going to hurt, but you unknowingly picked the worst time ever to go AWOL.' Her chest gave a tiny hitch, and I could see how close she was to tears. 'And that's been hard, because I could have really done with you being around these last six months.'

I wanted to get out of my seat and put my arms around her, but had I lost the right to offer that kind of support? Wasn't that reserved for friends who know what you've been dealing with, because they've been right there beside you, helping you through it? Whatever the hell 'it' was.

Throwing caution to the wind, I reached across the table and gripped her hand. She didn't pull away.

'I don't know what's happened. I don't know what you're having to deal with, but please, Mel, let me help you.'

There were tears running slowly down her cheeks as she looked up at me. She looked tragic and ethereal and incredibly beautiful.

'Whatever is wrong, let me try to fix it.'

'You can't,' she said softly, her lips managing to summon up a sad smile.

I was frantically rifling through ideas of what was troubling her. Was Steve the one who was sick? Were they in financial trouble? Had he lost his job? Was he cheating on her? The last seemed almost as ludicrous as imagining anyone ever cheating on Rhys. Steve and Mel were one of the most well-matched and in-love couples I'd ever met.

'At least let me try to help,' I implored.

'It's not possible,' she said, reaching up to wipe away her tears with the back of her hand. 'Unless you're willing to have a baby for me. Because it turns out that's something I can't do myself.'

It took half an hour and another round of margaritas for her to tell me everything I would have known if I hadn't dropped off the radar and devoted all my time to nurturing my business instead of my friends. How could I have got my priorities so badly screwed up?

'As far back as two years ago we suspected there might be a problem,' Mel confided. 'We'd always been a bit hit-and-miss with birth control and when we abandoned it completely, I imagined I'd fall straight away.'

That would have been my worst nightmare, but Mel was different; for her it was a perfect fit. She would glow throughout pregnancy, she would blossom, she was a natural-born earth mother. But it seemed nature had no intention of making it that easy. Mel and Steve hadn't got pregnant. 'And let me tell you, it wasn't for want of trying,' she said, colouring in a way that brought some much-needed pink back to her cheeks.

'I tried homeopathic remedies, crystals, herbal therapies, anything I could think of to work with my body in a natural and healing way.' She looked across at me, one eyebrow half raised. I knew what she was waiting for, some reaction of cynicism or disbelief. I showed nothing.

'Wow, you really do feel bad about ghosting me, don't you? That was great bait, and you didn't even take a nibble.'

'I'm a changed woman,' I said, but now wasn't the moment to tell her why or how. 'And besides, I know absolutely nothing about fertility. If dancing naked in a meadow under a full moon helps . . . then you should definitely give it a try.'

Mel's lips twitched and I was so grateful to have made her smile I almost cheered.

'Obviously we did try that. But nothing,' she joked, before her face sobered again. 'So, then we turned to conventional medicine.'

I drew in a deep breath. I knew how Mel felt about doctors, hospitals, and medical technology. It was a hang-up from losing her mum so young, but hospitals terrified her. For Mel and Steve to embark on the kind of journey they'd been on – were still on – spoke volumes about just how much they wanted this.

I should have been there, giving her whatever support she'd needed. But instead, I'd taken my eye off the ball for so long the game had gone on without me.

'We've had two failed attempts at IVF now,' she admitted sadly, telling the fabric of her skirt rather than meet my eyes. 'And that's all we're allowed on the NHS. From hereon we'll have to save up and go private.'

'Oh, Mel, I'm so sorry.'

'I wanted to cancel our trip to New York, cash in the tickets, but Steve insisted we needed some time away from doctors' appointments, hormone injections, and temperature charts.'

I nodded wisely as though I knew exactly what they'd been going through, but she was speaking the language of a country I'd never visited, nor one I'd ever particularly wanted to see.

'It's wearing. It takes it out of you. And it was starting to become all we ever spoke about. That's not healthy.'

I shook my head and squeezed her hand. 'No. It's far better to obsess about how many likes your latest TikTok got, or how many properties you currently have listed on your books.' I gave a humourless laugh. 'That's way healthier.'

My eyes went to hers and I tried to convey the depth of just how sorry I was that I'd failed her. It was the first time our friendship had ever been tested, and I'd flunked the exam.

'I could have reached out to you,' Mel said, with a graciousness she didn't need to show me. 'I guess I just didn't want to admit I was so rubbish at doing the one thing my stupid body was built to do.'

'I won't have you speaking about my friend like that,' I said, injecting a small dose of humour into my words. I sobered for a second and bit my lip uncertainly. 'That's if I'm still allowed to call you that.'

In answer she looked up at me through tear-spiked lashes. 'Who else would put up with you? Who else would stay up all night talking to you when you have a problem?'

I was glad my face was partly in shadow so she couldn't read the expression on it. If she had, she'd have known about Rhys. Don't ask me how . . . but she'd have known.

Chapter Seventeen

'Well, well, well. What a surprise. Who'd have thought I'd run into the two of you here,' declared Jackson. His acting was appalling, but you couldn't fault his timing, nor the fact that he was carrying a tray bearing a fresh round of cocktails.

'Budge up,' he said, getting Mel to scoot along the bench. He set down the tray and then took a seat, beaming widely at both of us. 'I see no blood, nor contusions. I take it my cunning plan went well.'

'We thought we'd save the GBH until you got here,' I said sweetly.

Jackson frowned. 'You knew I'd turn up?'

'Your meddling is infamous,' Mel said, rewarding him with a none too gentle jab in the ribs. 'You're like a criminal who can't resist returning to the scene of his crime.'

Jackson hammed another overly dramatic sigh. 'Is this the thanks I get for finally getting you two talking again?' His voice sobered as his eyes went first to me and then to Mel. 'You are talking again, aren't you? Is everything going to be alright?'

There was an almost boyish anxiety in his voice. Jackson never spoke much about his own younger years, but from the little he'd mentioned, I didn't think his home life had been particularly harmonious. It explained why he'd always shied away from conflict.

I often wondered if that was part of the glue that had held us together over the years; that we'd all had less than perfect childhoods. Mel's had been destroyed by losing her mum, Jackson's had been filled with arguments, and mine . . . well, mine had been a mixed bag, spent with a woman I'd always loved but had never properly understood.

'We're good. Or we will be,' I said, double-checking my reply with Mel, who gave me a gentle nod.

'Thank the Lord. No, thank me,' Jackson cried delightedly. 'Because I have a secret ulterior motive and a very good reason why I didn't want the two of you at each other's throats.'

'We were never that,' Mel said softly.

The thread I'd carelessly allowed to fray was still strong enough to bind us into something stronger than just friends. It had withstood challenges before: new relationships, lost jobs, and unexpected detours in life plans. But what bound us together was constructed out of something like elastic. You might pull against it, or stretch it so tight you nearly broke it, but when the tension was as its greatest it still held, and then it pinged you right back in again.

Thank God.

I will not let these people down again, I silently vowed. Not ever.

'Are you caught up on Mel's news?' Jackson asked, his eyes going in concern to the woman sitting beside him.

'She is,' Mel confirmed, her eyes overbright.

'Great,' Jackson exclaimed. 'Then are you ready to hear mine?'

He was fidgeting on his seat, which probably should have alerted me to the fact he had big news to share.

'Soooo . . .' he said, drawing out the word for maximum impact. 'Lars and I have locked down the wedding venue. But there's still one important detail outstanding.'

He waited until we were both looking his way.

'I want you to be my Groom's Woman.'

My eyes went to Mel's, because misinterpreting this was going to be embarrassing.

'Which one of us?' Mel asked, which was so much better coming from her than me.

Jackson flopped back against the velvet banquette as though he'd been shot.

'Both of you, of course. I'm not having a best man. Why would I when I have two of the best women ever in my life already?'

His eyes danced happily between us, clearly waiting for a reaction. I'm not sure he got the one he was expecting when we both burst into tears.

'I'm sorry, it's these bloody hormones,' Mel declared, grabbing a wodge of serviettes from the table and passing half to me.

I couldn't borrow that excuse, and I think we all knew why I, the friend who never cried, was suddenly teary-eyed.

'I don't deserve this,' I whispered in Jackson's ear as I got up and hugged him tightly.

'Yeah, you do,' he said, before releasing me to embrace Mel.

'So, what's going on with you, Ells?' he asked. 'Given that we have about nine months of news to catch up on, perhaps you'd better lead with the headlines.'

A burst of laughter from the other side of the bar momentarily distracted me, or perhaps I was looking for anything to delay the moment when I stepped out of my comfort zone and straight into Mel's wheelhouse. I determinedly pulled my focus away from the far end of the bar and back to the booth where my two friends were looking at me expectantly.

'I guess the most notable event was being struck by lightning.'

A pause, slightly uncomfortable, as though they were both waiting for the punchline of a joke which was sure to follow. Only it didn't.

'You mean metaphorically?' asked Mel, with a slightly nervous laugh.

Very slowly I shook my head.

'No. Literally.'

Mel's expression was a hazy fog of doubt, but Jackson's showed a slow-dawning shock.

'Oh, my God,' he said, his voice scarcely more than a whisper.

Mel's eyes flashed his way before settling back on my face.

'Are you one of the Park People?' Jackson asked. It was an expression some of the local media had coined when they hadn't been able to uncover our identities. I didn't much like it. But in answer, I simply nodded.

'Fuck me.'

Mel was staring at us both; Jackson, with his frankly astounded expression, and me with my vaguely uncomfortable one.

The intrusive sound of a champagne cork popping seemed incongruous when you were telling people you cared about that you'd almost died.

'Will one of you please explain what you're talking about. What Park People? What's going on?'

Jackson blew out a long breath, and although he answered Mel, he didn't take his eyes off me. 'Of course, you were in New York when it happened. I guess it wasn't big enough news to travel that far.'

'I think it happens over there more than it does here, anyway,' I said.

'What happens?' Mel asked, so obviously frustrated that I wished I'd found a different way, place, or time to tell her. But Jackson had already picked up his phone and after a moment or two of rapid scrolling, he passed it to Mel. The familiar video of two figures lying on the grass, receiving life-saving emergency treatment beneath the oak, began to play.

Mel's eyes grew wider and wider until I felt sure the skin could stretch no farther. She zoomed in on the video, enlarging the grainy image. 'It's you,' she said, her lower lip trembling as her fingers expanded the footage as far as it would go. 'Those are your red stilettos.' I'm not sure why that brought tears to her eyes – perhaps because she'd been with me when I'd bought them. 'Oh my God, Ellie,' Mel breathed. 'Why didn't you tell us?'

I gave what I hoped looked like a casual shrug, which is hard when there's a yoke of guilt weighing down on your shoulders.

'I'm telling you now.'

'Weeks after it happened.'

'Well, this was the first opportunity to tell you both together.'

'That's a rubbish excuse,' Jackson said. 'Total BS.'

He wasn't wrong, but I was running low on courage by this point and wasn't sure if I had enough left to say, Actually I wasn't sure you'd even have cared.

The fact that I'd been so wrong about their reaction was almost a cause to celebrate. They cared. They still cared about me.

I answered all their questions, including the obvious ones that I knew everyone wanted to know. What did it feel like? How much did it hurt? Have you made a full recovery? That last was from Mel. And Has it left you with any superpowers? which could only ever have come from Jackson.

'Apart from some pretty serious memory loss issues, I was lucky. I came out of it fairly unscathed,' I said. The relief on both of their faces was heartwarming. I almost wished I could stop right there, but then the story would only be half told. 'Except for some weird stuff that defies any logical explanation.'

I know I didn't imagine the flare of interest in Mel's eyes. We were venturing right into her home territory here.

'What kind of stuff?' Jackson asked, leaning forward, elbows resting on his knees as though craning closer would make me reveal the answer even quicker.

'There's a really powerful connection between me and the other survivor that I can't explain. At first, I thought it was just because we both understood what we'd been through in a way that other people never could. But it goes deeper than that.'

'Weird,' said Jackson.

I licked my lips nervously. 'I just can't seem to get this guy out of my head.'

Mel's neatly plucked eyebrows rose in perfect unison.

'And our paths keep crossing, and there's something really potent there, like the electrical current in the lightning is still arcing between us.' It was a nonsense explanation but neither of my friends laughed.

'This man,' Mel began.

'Rhys,' I supplied.

Mel's focus didn't falter. 'Is he tall and good-looking? In his late thirties or thereabouts? And does he have really piercing bright green eyes?'

I shook my head in amazement. How had she seen all of that from the shaky bystander video?

'Because if he does,' Mel continued, her voice dropping a little lower, 'he's making his way over to our table right now.'

'Ellie?' The voice I secretly yearned to hear whisper good morning to me every day, from now until forever, was right behind me. 'I thought it was you.'

I swivelled on my seat, and he was standing beside our booth, looking truly devastating in a formal suit. It couldn't have been more different from the jeans and t-shirt he'd changed into yesterday, but it affected me just as viscerally.

I looked back across the room towards the party he'd left. They were the champagne-drinking group whose arrival had set off a silent proximity alert in my head.

'What are the chances of us both turning up in the same bar?'

'About the same as being hit by lightning,' I said, adding – because it felt like it needed to be said – 'I've actually never been in here before.'

'Me neither.' Rhys's green eyes darkened in puzzlement. 'The work colleagues I'm with suggested dropping in.'

I stole a quick glance past him to the people he'd come with. Two women in sharp business dresses – the kind I used to favour – were perched on bar stools. Three other men in smart suits were clustered around them. One of the women laughed, really loudly, and it sounded like fingernails running down a blackboard.

I was slow to realise I was being rude, and that behind me Mel and Jackson were practically champing at the bit to be introduced.

'These are my friends, Jackson and Mel,' I said, trying to ignore the appreciative ooh well done expression in Mel's eyes. 'Mel, Jackson, this is Rhys Davies.'

Rhys extended a hand first to Jackson, who shook it politely, and then to Mel, who totally ignored it and instead sprang to her feet to give the man she'd only just met a brief and totally unexpected hug.

Rhys good-naturedly hugged her back and did a fairly decent job of pretending that her impulsive behaviour was entirely normal.

'Forgive her. She's drunk,' I said, perfectly aware that she wasn't.

Rhys didn't stay for more than a minute or two. One of his male companions pantomimed tapping the watch on his wrist, and Rhys turned to me with an apologetic smile.

'I'm sorry. We've got early dinner reservations.'

'Go,' I urged, and yet he still didn't move.

'I'd love to have stayed and chatted,' he apologised to my friends, his manners as ever impeccable. 'But we're meeting up with some other colleagues at the restaurant.'

'Looks like you're celebrating,' Jackson said, referring to the two upside-down bottles of champagne in the ice bucket on the bar.

'Something like that,' Rhys said, looking genuinely torn that he had to leave, which was rather pleasing.

'I'll speak to you soon,' he said, bending down to me.

I schooled my features not to react to the kiss I felt sure he was going to leave on my cheek. Mel would read way too much into my reaction if I did.

But as Rhys bent lower, his lips didn't graze my skin at all. But he did whisper in my ear, so quietly I had to strain to catch his words.

'You look really lovely tonight.'

No one said anything as Rhys rejoined his group and the women slid off their stools, picked up bags and jackets, and headed en masse for the door. They began to file out, with Rhys bringing up the rear.

Turn around. If this thing I feel is there for you too, even just a tiny fraction, then turn around before you leave.

'Why on earth did you hug that guy?' I heard Jackson ask Mel.

Even though it was a wrench, I pulled my eyes away from the exiting group to glance back at my friends, because I was curious to know the answer to that one too.

Mel looked unperturbed and a little smug, in an I know more than you ever will kind of way.

'Because I predict he's going to be in our lives for a very long time, and I wanted to make a welcoming first impression.'

Jackson mimed a swirling finger beside his own temple and said knowingly, 'Ignore her. It's the hormones again.' That earned him a shove that almost made him lose his balance, but I scarcely noticed because I was staring at the door once more as the last person was about to leave the bar.

I was holding my breath, and I truly had no idea why.

And then Rhys turned around, his eyes finding mine across the room.

And I knew.

Chapter Eighteen

'Was this the kind of thing you had in mind?'

I tore my eyes from the intricate pen and ink drawing in my hands. Even though he'd only had a couple of photographs to go on, Rhys had managed to perfectly capture the lines of the house and had even included small details, like the bird's nest in the tree beside the front door and the trailing wisteria that spilled from the garden wall onto the driveway. The Dexters, the couple who'd lived in the house for over thirty years, were going to love it.

'You've absolutely nailed it,' I said, looking up at him with admiration.

'Great. I'm glad you like it.'

I still wasn't certain if inserting a business element into our friendship was wise, but it clearly didn't seem to worry him.

'I'll transfer the money to your bank account this afternoon. But I still don't think you're charging me enough.'

Rhys half perched on the corner of my desk. 'Are you sure you're good at this negotiating stuff, because I'm pretty certain you're not supposed to persuade me to ask for more money.'

'I just want to keep this professional.' I softened my words with a smile. 'That way I can call on you to do more of these without feeling guilty.'

‘There’s no need for you to feel guilty, Ellie. Not about anything.’

I swallowed uncomfortably, uncertain if we were still talking about commissioning him as an artist, or something else altogether.

I’d been thrown off-kilter ever since he’d walked into my office that morning, carrying two cups of coffee and a bag of pastries.

I’d been midway through what was turning out to be a very tricky conversation with a new client, who wanted every single clause of a boilerplate tenancy agreement explained to them ‘as though I was five years old’. Frankly, it would have been easier getting a classroom of primary school children to understand it than the man on the end of the line.

I mouthed a silent ‘Sorry’ to Rhys, followed by a less easy to lip-read ‘This might take a while.’

He mimed, ‘That’s okay. Take your time.’ At least I think that’s what he said. Staring at his lips had a way of making me lose focus, and I needed all my concentration on the call.

Setting the takeout cup and the pastries in front of me, Rhys had taken himself off to the opposite side of my office with his coffee, settled onto the client sofa, and begun leafing through one of the glossy magazines fanned out on the table beside him.

Half of my brain was engaged with soothing the nervous new landlord on the phone, but there were more than enough cells left to appreciate just how good Rhys looked that morning. He was wearing a pale chambray shirt with the cuffs rolled up, and casual trousers teamed with boots that looked worn enough to be comfortable. It was a good look on him.

The sunlight filtering through the stained-glass window above him brought out midnight blue highlights in his dark hair. It would have made for a stunning photograph, but if Rhys caught me secretly snapping one, I wouldn’t blame him for taking out a restraining order.

When my new client had asked every last question known to man, I was finally able to end the call.

Rhys set aside the magazine and gave me a smile that made my stomach flip.

'You're really very good at this, aren't you?' he asked.

'Don't let one half of a phone call fool you. I've made more than my fair share of mistakes since setting up in business.'

'I don't fool easily,' Rhys said. 'And as for mistakes, well, everyone makes them. It's how you move on, it's the things they teach us, that's what's important.'

'Well, I think I'm very much a work in progress,' I said, willing myself to keep this light and breezy, which was becoming increasingly hard with those green eyes studying me the way they were doing right now.

And how is that, exactly? Old Ellie popped up to ask. *Just out of interest.*

As though he likes what he sees?

It wasn't hard to imagine her shaking her head in disbelief. It was troubling to realise that former me was starting to sound increasingly like my mother in her critiques, as though a vacancy had opened up and she'd slipped right into the role.

A ringtone that wasn't mine interrupted the moment, which perhaps was no bad thing. Rhys pulled his phone from his pocket and glanced down at the screen. Whatever he saw there brought his brows closer together and made frown lines appear on his normally unmarked forehead.

'It's fine if you need to take that,' I assured him.

He shook his head and silenced the ringing. 'It's not important,' he said and some feminine instinct that was buried deep inside my psyche told me that the caller had been Annalise. I knew it with a certainty that defied all reason. Perhaps I was becoming more like Mel than I realised.

'But I do have to go,' he said. 'I've a meeting I need to attend in about an hour.'

'With the people you were with at the bar the other night?' I've no idea why I assumed that, or why I thought it was any of my business.

'Yes,' Rhys said. He got to his feet, and I came out from behind my desk which I was beginning to think I'd been using as a safety barrier – not to keep him away, but more to keep me from getting inappropriately close.

'Actually, that's one of the reasons I wanted to drop the sketch off in person this morning.'

For some reason he suddenly appeared a little less self-assured. There was a look of hesitancy on his face that I couldn't remember seeing there before.

'Those people are part of a design team I worked with on a huge campaign before I went freelance.'

I nodded, wondering where he was going with this.

'Anyway, we did quite well, and the campaign has been short-listed for this prestigious industry award.'

'Oh, well done. Congratulations.'

His smile was like quicksilver, there one second and gone the next.

'Anyway, there's a big ceremony thing next week. Black tie, red carpet, that kind of thing.'

He paused and I nodded, unsure what I was meant to add here. I decided to play it safe. 'Wow. Again, congratulations.'

'Will you come with me?'

My lips parted, but nothing came out.

Yes, I'd love to was right there on my tongue, but for the life of me I couldn't find the trigger to release it.

Rhys gave a disarming shrug. 'I realise it might not be your kind of thing, and it's perfectly okay if you don't fancy it. It'll probably be terribly dull, lots of stuffed shirts and endless clapping.'

'I love stuffed shirts,' I said, perfectly aware I was talking nonsense. 'And I'm excellent at clapping.'

'I could tell you had skills.'

His grin landed about a second before mine did.

'Okay then. I'll message you with the details.'

'Great!' I was already mentally rifling through my wardrobe and knowing a shopping trip was on the horizon.

We were about to take the next step on this curious journey we were on, moving us in a direction I hadn't expected. Was it wise? Probably not. Was I going to do it anyway? Absolutely.

'Well, if you want my opinion, the blue one makes your boobs look amazing, and your cleavage in the red one could take someone's eye out.'

I turned away from my reflection in the changing room mirror and shook my head despairingly at my friend.

'Could we possibly focus more on the dresses and less on how my breasts fit into them?'

Mel tutted, like a plumber confronted by some tricky pipework. 'I dunno, Ellie. I mean they're just kind of . . . there, in your face.'

'Then we keep looking,' I said, turning to my shopping companion and scooping up a handful of hair to give her easy access to the zip.

Mel obligingly released me from the red dress with a muttered, 'I can't help thinking you're making a mistake here.'

'It's just not the impression I want to make.'

Mel nodded sagely. 'So, just to clarify. You don't want to look drop-dead gorgeous and sexy as hell on this date?'

I pulled a face. 'Well, yes . . . but not in a "look at my chest" kind of way. And besides, it's not a date.'

'He's going to a fancy awards ceremony, and he's asked you to go with him?'

I nodded.

'Then it's a date.'

'No, it's not,' I muttered, falling into step behind her. I'd spoken so low she wasn't meant to have heard, but when she spun on her heel to face me, I knew she had.

'Why are you scared of admitting that you like this guy?'

'I'm not scared of anything.' That was a blatant lie. You only had to see me cowering indoors any time lightning speared the skies to know that.

'Okay, not scared then. But you certainly seem reluctant to acknowledge the attraction between the two of you.'

'Because it only came about because of the lightning. It did something to us.'

For a woman who enjoyed walking in the twilight zone as much as Mel, the last thing I'd expected was to hear her scoff of laughter.

'And that is scientifically proven, is it?'

I felt like a bug on a pin under her uncompromising stare.

'We're just not compatible in about a hundred different ways.'

'Name them.'

'What? All of them?'

Mel gave an easy shrug. 'I've got all day.'

I blew out a long breath.

'Well, for a start he's very family orientated. His daughter means the absolute world to him.'

'That just sounds like a great big tick in his favour rather than a negative,' Mel said.

'It is, or rather it would be if I was the kind of person who'd ever seen themselves as having a kid. But I've never been able to visualise myself wanting that kind of life.'

'Maybe that's because you've never met anyone until now that you could see yourself having a baby with.'

The intensity in Mel's eyes burnt through my defences. That was her dream, not mine . . . wasn't it?

'And then there's his work. He's basically an artist. Or at least that's what he'd love to be if he could make it pay the bills. Not that there's anything wrong with that – don't get me wrong – but the men I've always been attracted to were more high-flyer, high-achieving types.'

'Hmmm . . .' said Mel, nodding wisely. 'And how did that work out for you, by the way?' I opened my mouth to reply, but she jumped in before I had the chance. 'In case your faulty memory has lost the details, let me tell you that the answer to that one was "disastrously".'

'Rhys isn't the type of man I would ever have been drawn towards.'

'Kind, gentle, supportive and last – but definitely not least – incredibly good-looking. Yeah, I can see why you'd have a problem with all of that.'

It was a relief to find ourselves back on the concourse of the busy shopping centre, where further probing conversation that felt more like a cross-examination was impossible.

Having tried almost every chain store and high street outlet, I was still no closer to finding a dress for Rhys's event. And with only two days left, time was rapidly running out.

'What do you say we stop for a coffee and then try some of the smaller shops in the side streets?' Mel suggested.

'I think most of them are going to be outside my price bracket.' I pulled a rueful face. 'But I'm definitely up for a coffee.' I linked my arm with hers, still marvelling that I could. Slowly but surely, we were beginning to mend the relationship I'd very nearly broken.

The heat hit like a blast wave as we left the air-conditioned mall. By the time we'd meandered down a few cobblestoned streets in search of a café with outdoor seating, I was feeling uncomfortably sticky. Just the thought of having to try on more dresses was exhausting.

'Maybe I could make do with something I already own.' I paused to flash a smile at the waitress as she placed two iced coffees in front of us. 'I mean, you can't go wrong with a little black dress, can you?' I asked Mel, or rather the back of her head, for her attention was firmly focused in the opposite direction. 'What do you think?'

'Hmmm. Yes,' she said distractedly.

I peered around her, trying to work out what had snagged her attention, but could see nothing unusual. Just an ordinary street on an ordinary day, busier than usual perhaps, but we were in the middle of the school holidays so that was to be expected.

'Of course. If I really wanted to make a memorable impression, I suppose I could rock up wearing nothing but a big smile and a sparkly G-string.'

Mel nodded in agreement.

'Yes, definitely,' she murmured, before my words pierced whatever bubble she'd floated off in. 'You what?'

'Oh, so you were listening. Sort of.'

She bit her lip guiltily and that made me feel bad. Especially as there was a new expression in her eyes, one I'd never seen there before.

'Mel?' I reached across and folded my hand around hers. 'What is it? Is something wrong?' I was right to be concerned when my innocent question caused her bottom lip to tremble.

'It's nothing,' she said, shaking her head.

'It's something,' I countered. My eyes went once again to the street, searching for whatever it was that had upset her. I scanned the crowds but could see no obvious culprit among the mums pushing prams, or those corralling little children who'd clearly rather be anywhere but shopping on a sunny summer's day.

'How did they all do it?' Mel asked, her voice not entirely steady. But then neither was her hand as she reached for her iced coffee.

'How did who do what?' I asked, inarticulately.

'Her,' Mel said, her voice low as she nodded at a woman disappearing down the road, her right hand firmly clasping that of a little girl skipping along beside her.

'Or her,' Mel said, this time her gaze going to a young woman who was trying to stop her small boy from chasing the street pigeons scavenging on the pavement.

'Or her,' Mel whispered, her voice almost fracturing as a heavily pregnant woman crossed the road at the nearby pedestrian lights.

I should have been quicker to recognise that the everyday sights I scarcely even noticed were real triggers for her. Guilt took a nip at my heels as I realised just how deeply Mel was affected by her desire for a child and the difficulty she was having getting pregnant.

I sat back in my uncomfortable metal foldaway chair, looking at her and wondering how long I'd been this blind. Admittedly, there was a lot about the last year I still didn't remember. But this pain, the one I could now see so clearly in my friend's eyes, was obviously not new. The longing must have been there for a very long time before the despair found a foothold.

'Last week I found myself counting how many pregnant women I saw walking around Sainsbury's. That can't be healthy, can it?'

I shook my head sadly.

'I just wish I knew how it seems to be so easy for everyone else and so impossibly hard for us.'

'I don't know, hon. I wish I could give you an answer. But the truth is, you never really know what anyone is going through. Maybe each one of those women experienced something similar before it worked out for them.'

'Maybe,' she said, sounding far from convinced.

I dug deep, trying to find something that didn't sound like a meaningless platitude. It was ironic that we'd spent our twenties desperately trying not to get pregnant. And now, when I hadn't been paying attention, someone had moved all the goalposts – or at least they had as far as Mel was concerned. Now the very thing that would derail my life was the only thing she could think about.

'Even though you know how I feel about all that woo-woo stuff, I really do have a feeling that it's going to happen for you,' I said, leaning across the table, uncaring about the sticky spills from previous customers on its surface. 'I've met loads of couples over the years, and I've yet to find one that would make better parents than you and Steve, and I refuse to believe the universe doesn't know that too.'

'It's just such an uphill battle,' she said on a sad sigh.

I bit my lip worriedly, wondering if this was the right moment to say what had been on my mind since the night in the bar.

'I don't know much about how these things work,' I said, walking on the thinnest ice imaginable. 'But I do know that IVF is expensive, and I just wanted to say that if money is tight, or if worrying about funds is holding you back . . .' I cleared my throat, feeling weirdly nervous. 'Well, the business hasn't been doing too badly recently and I'm sure I could—'

'Absolutely not,' Mel interjected emphatically, her curls bouncing in protest. 'That's very generous of you, Ellie, but this is our problem, not yours.'

I knew better than to push it. Mel had always been a little prickly about money.

'Okay. But if you should change your mind . . .'

She squeezed my hand. 'Just the fact that you've offered means more to me than you could know.' She gave me a slow smile.

'What?' I asked, feeling self-conscious under her scrutiny.

'It's just good to have you back again.'

We looked at each other, and suddenly we were the same two girls who'd met on the first day of university, who'd known in that moment that they'd found a friend for life.

'Okay,' Mel declared, her sunny disposition firmly back in place. 'Let's go get you a knock-out dress that'll make that gorgeous man – the one who isn't taking you on a date – reconsider this whole "just good friends" thing.'

We found it in the very next shop. It was a small boutique tucked away at the far end of a cobbled alleyway. Stepping beneath the wrought-iron archway felt like entering a secret passageway. There were two exclusive jewellery shops, an art gallery with a single ceramic vase in its window, and a shop with designer shoes that could easily have drained my entire bank account.

'You know that scene in Pretty Woman?' I murmured to Mel, who was insistently tugging me towards the dress shop tucked away in the corner. 'The one where she's looked down on by the shop assistant?' Mel pushed open the door of the shop and a bell chimed above our heads. 'Prepare to watch it re-enacted in real life,' I whispered.

'Shh,' Mel hissed, smiling widely at the woman behind the counter. 'I have a good feeling about this place.'

'Another one?' I teased, but I allowed her to propel me farther into the shop.

I'd been right. Every price tag made me wince. I was about to suggest a hasty exit when I spotted a solitary rail at the back of the shop with a Sale sign.

The dress was in the middle of the rack, its sequins catching the sunlight shafting through the shop window. I followed a sunbeam to the rail while Mel continued to browse by the door. I was smiling as I plucked the hanger from the rail. Even before I released the garment from its neighbours or checked the size on the label, I knew this was the dress I'd be wearing on my 'definitely not a date' with Rhys.

The changing room was nothing more than a tiny curtained-off section at the back of the shop. There wasn't even a mirror, but I didn't need one to know the dress was a perfect fit. From the front it was decorous, almost modest, with a halter neckline that came up to my throat in a collared band. But the back . . . well, basically there wasn't one. I'd slipped off my bra to get a better idea of just how risqué it was. Pretty daring, as it turned out, with the material falling in a loose swathe at the small of my back, almost – but not quite – revealing the colour of the briefs I'd put on that morning. The fabric fell to the ground like a sparkling waterfall, close-fitting and slinky. Without the slit that ran from the hem up to the back of my knees, walking would have been a real challenge. There was something about the blue-black sequins that reminded me of the highlights the sun picked out in Rhys's dark hair. They shimmered as I walked, making me look like a mermaid.

'Oh my God, Ellie. That dress could have been made for you. You look amazing.'

Mel's enthusiastic response made me forget my limited budget or even try to cheekily bargain over the price. Estate agents are known for their love of haggling – it's practically in our DNA – but buying this dress had been a foregone conclusion even before I'd known how incredible it would look on my body.

I was proud of the way I didn't even grimace when I slid my credit card across the counter five minutes later. I'd have to sell an extraordinary number of properties in the next few months to justify this extravagance, but when the glossy cardboard carrier was passed to me, I knew it was worth it.

Chapter Nineteen

I thought at first that someone had fallen over or collapsed in the heat of the day. Then it occurred to me that the figure I could see slumped and immobile in the distance was horribly still and might not be conscious. My heart began to pound as I quickened my pace and broke into a run, already pulling my mobile from my pocket to summon help. It sounded like the punchline from a very tasteless joke, but I guess, by the law of averages, some people really did pass away in cemeteries.

But thankfully not today.

With the pounding of my Nikes announcing my arrival, I approached the figure and realised with relief that they weren't actually face-down in the dirt but were hunched over beside my mother's grave. On hearing me, they straightened up and sat back onto their knees.

A hand, protected by a gardening glove, lifted to the man's eyes to shield them from the afternoon sunlight. In the other he held a handful of weeds.

'Henry? What are you doing?'

The older man looked truly thrown at seeing me, as though I was the interloper at my mother's resting place and not him. He looked so confused, as though he didn't know who I was, and I took a step to one side so he didn't have to stare directly into the glare of sunlight to see me.

'Oh, Ellie, it's you.'

I'm not exactly sure who else he might have been expecting. The hand that was grasping the weeds let them fall to the ground and he peeled off the glove. His fingers were trembling.

'Are you alright, Henry? You look a little pasty.'

I hoped he'd forgive the impertinence, but in truth his complexion looked decidedly waxy and was now the colour of rancid butter.

'No. I'm absolutely fine,' he said, getting to his feet with an ease that belied his years. 'You just startled me for a moment.'

'That seems to happen a lot on this spot,' I said, remembering this was exactly how I'd met him several weeks earlier.

'I thought, as you usually visit the cemetery in the mornings, the afternoon would be a good time to have a quick tidy-up of your mum's plot.'

I did usually visit earlier in the day, and it worried me a little that he sounded so familiar with my movements. Was there an upper age limit to being a stalker? I dismissed the thought as ridiculous.

'You came here just to tend to my mother's plants?'

The waxy grey of his cheeks was replaced by a raspberry-coloured flush. Shame on you, my mother chided from somewhere very close by. Embarrassing a nice old man like that.

'No, no,' refuted Henry, looking flustered. 'I was tidying up Bee's plot today,' he explained, nodding in the direction of the rows of graves on the other side of the path. 'And once I was done with that, I thought I'd just have a quick tidy-up over here too.' He inclined his head towards a collection of gardening paraphernalia that I now noticed was neatly lined up beside Mum's headstone.

'That's really kind of you,' I said, looking at the peonies, which seemed to have almost doubled in size since I planted them. They all looked remarkably healthy.

'They're looking good, aren't they?' Henry said, and there was something about the pride in his voice that told me that wasn't just a happy accident.

'You've been watering them?'

He seemed to have regained his composure now. 'Now and then,' he admitted. 'And I've given them the odd drop of plant food too.' He smiled, and for a fleeting moment I caught a glimpse of what a handsome man he must have been in his youth. Not quite as good-looking as Rhys, admittedly, but even so, I could imagine how easily his wife Bee's head must have been turned when they met.

'Well, it's very nice of you to help keep the flowers I planted alive, but truly, you don't have to split your time here doing garden maintenance on two plots.'

Henry gave a small shrug and began gathering up his tools and dropping them into a canvas bag. 'It really is no trouble, Ellie. I like to keep busy, and if I'm being totally honest, I really miss the big garden I used to have at my bungalow.'

With the tools now packed away, Henry moved to the bench, and it felt totally natural to take a seat beside him.

'Have you moved house recently?'

He gave a nod. 'Yes. After my wife passed away, I didn't need such a big place anymore. So, I've moved into one of those retirement village places.' He gave a small regretful expression, his nose wrinkling.

'You don't like it?'

His eyes twinkled and I sensed that buried somewhere beneath the passage of the years was a wicked sense of humour.

'It's full of old people.'

I'm not sure if it's considered bad manners to laugh quite so heartily in a graveyard, but I couldn't help it.

'I think that's the general idea, isn't it?'

He gave a sad smile. 'Also, there are more elderly couples there than I'd been expecting.' He gave an old man's sigh. 'Perhaps I'd have liked it a whole lot more if my Bee could have been there with me.'

My heart ached a little for him, despite knowing next to nothing about him and his late wife.

'And I miss gardening,' he added, taking us back in a circuit to where our conversation had begun. 'Which is why I like to tidy up the odd weed or two that I might spot on other people's plots.' He gave a little chuckle. 'It's the first time I've been caught red-handed, though.'

I'm not usually a very touchy-feely kind of person, so I totally surprised myself by leaning across the bench and gently patting his age-spotted hand. 'Well, you can tidy up my mother's plot anytime you feel like it. I don't mind at all.'

He smiled as though I'd bestowed a gift on him, and I felt a sudden pang for his loneliness.

'You're a very kind young lady, Ellie. Very thoughtful.'

It was my turn to smile, but mine had a wry twist to it. 'You only say that because you don't know me very well.' I looked across at the black granite headstone. 'I don't think I was terribly good at being a daughter.'

That seemed to really trouble him for some reason.

'Did you and your wife have any children?' I asked.

I was going to have to stop asking him questions, because the ones I was posing seemed to put too much regret on his face.

'Sadly, we weren't able to have any,' he said. The pain of that fact must have been thirty or forty years old, and yet it still looked fresh in his eyes. 'There wasn't so much help available for couples like us who were struggling back in those days.' A sudden image of

Mel flashed into my thoughts, with her injections, hospital visits, and constant aching grief for something she'd never had and might never get to experience. It made me wonder why those same yearnings didn't run through my own veins and I couldn't help looking towards the plot beside us.

'Get yourself a career. Become financially stable. You won't regret the hours you studied harder and worked longer than everyone else when you're in control of your own destiny and never have to rely on anyone.'

I swallowed several times because the old memory had left a sour taste in my mouth. That was how it had always been with my mum. I did well at school, but every achievement had been tainted by her needing to know who'd scored higher than me. With the benefit of hindsight and the wisdom of age, I eventually came to realise that her drive for me to succeed was tangled up in her own struggle as a single parent after my father had left us. But however well-intentioned she'd been, the takeaway had always been that however great my achievement, it was never quite enough.

'Ellie? Ellie?'

I jumped out of the reverie to find Henry looking at me with obvious concern.

'I'm sorry. Did you say something? I was miles away.' Years away would have been more accurate, but Mum had always been big on never showing emotional vulnerability. It seemed like that particular apple hadn't fallen very far from the tree.

'I was just asking if I could interest you in a glass of chilled lemonade.' He reached into another compartment of the canvas bag and pulled out an old-fashioned thermos flask. 'I make it myself. It was my wife's recipe, and I have to admit, it's exceedingly good.'

'Go on then,' I said, smiling at this kindly elderly gentleman who seemed to be my newest and most surprising friend.

He pulled off the thermos cap, revealing a second beaker beneath it, and poured out two drinks.

'Cheers,' he said, holding up his white plastic cup and clinking it against the one he'd just passed to me.

It was incongruous and kind of crazy, but also funny and charming. I glanced over at the headstone and realised that Mum would actually have found it really amusing. She might have had high, often unrealistic, expectations of me, and life hadn't always dealt her the kindest of hands, but her sense of humour had miraculously remained intact.

Henry saw the direction of my gaze and tilted his own cup towards the black granite headstone in a salute. 'And cheers to you too, Elizabeth.'

That was the moment when I knew that Henry was exactly the friend I needed in my life right then.

Chapter Twenty

He wasn't late. It was more that I was ridiculously early. I'd left work two hours before I actually needed to – as though I'd somehow forgotten how long it took to shower and wash my hair. And for someone who'd been wearing make-up for over twenty years, my confidence in applying it this evening had been decidedly shaky. As had my hand, which meant my first two attempts at eyeliner had ended very badly indeed.

I refused to accept I was nervous, despite the irrefutable evidence that I clearly was. I'd been all fingers and thumbs when pinning up my hair into the loose-tendril updo style I'd chosen to showcase the backless dress. When I was eventually ready, the woman staring back at me in the full-length bedroom mirror didn't look entirely like me. She was more sultry and sexier than the person who normally lived behind the glass, or was that just the dress?

My phone pinged with an incoming message, and I felt my stomach drop away like floors in a plummeting lift as I snatched it up from the bedside table. He's cancelling. I have no idea where that thought had come from, or why. It certainly hadn't been from Rhys's last message, sent earlier that afternoon, when he'd let me know what time the cab taking us to the event would get here.

Anyone would think this is your first date, ever, Old Ellie – who knew perfectly well that it wasn't – interjected scornfully. Terrific, now even my subconscious was calling it a date.

I felt a rush of pure relief when I saw Mel's name on my phone screen and not Rhys's.

Are you dressed and ready? Send me a photo.

I shook my head, laughing softly. Mel was taking way too much interest in my evening plans. 'That's just what old married people do,' she'd said, 'we live vicariously through our single mates' love lives.'

I could have wasted my breath yet again by reminding her that I currently didn't have a love life, but I knew this was more about her finding something to distract herself from her fertility struggle. It really wasn't about Rhys and me at all.

I rattled off a couple of quick selfies and sent them to her and her reply came back almost instantly.

Poor guy. He doesn't stand a chance. Have fun xx

I was still smiling when the sound of an engine idling in the street below had me hurrying to the window. Or moving as fast as I could manage in the ridiculously high shoes I'd teamed with my dress. It was surprising how quickly I'd forgotten how to walk in heels. And my feet had already warned me they'd be doing some serious protesting over my choice of footwear before the night was over.

I peered through my bedroom window, but my view was hindered by the old sprawling elm in the front garden. Some of the residents claimed it blocked out too much light and wanted it cut down, but I'd always rather liked the way its branches threw lacy shadows into the flat.

The sound of the front door buzzer made me jump and I hurried to the intercom to answer it.

'It's me. I'm early. I'm sorry, we can circle the streets for a while, if you want.'

'No, that's okay. Come on up,' I said, pressing the door release and using the sixty seconds or so it would take Rhys to climb the three flights of stairs to erase the stupid grin off my face.

I used to be so much better at playing it cool, I told my reflection in the hallway mirror. Perhaps that was the problem. It was an interesting thought to explore, but not now. Not when I could hear his footsteps on the last few stairs and my heart was already beating way faster than necessary.

'The traffic was non-existent, and every light was green,' Rhys led with, before breaking off as I opened the door wider and his eyes took me in. I couldn't help the frisson of pleasure at the expression I caught in them.

'You look incredible,' he said, in a voice that sounded a little huskier than usual.

'Thank you,' I said softly.

Something was preventing me from moving, and whatever it was it seemed to be affecting him too, because several seconds ticked by and neither of us said a word or moved away from my open door.

If my appearance had caught him by surprise, then his was just as arresting. Almost every man looks good in a dinner suit, but Rhys took it to another level. It's just the power of a tux, I told myself, not sure if I entirely believed that.

'We've got plenty of time, but if you're ready to go?'

I nodded and turned on my heel to pluck up the shimmery wrap I'd left on the hallway table. As I did, I heard a small, stifled sound, as though Rhys's next indrawn breath had suddenly got caught in his throat. Between the tuxedo and the backless dress, we could both be in trouble here. The thought stayed with me as I followed him down the stairs to the waiting cab.

◆ ◆ ◆

The venue was impressive and far more grand than I'd been expecting. I'd imagined our destination would be a typical city hotel, so the elite former private members' club took me by surprise. The sun was low in the sky, its rays bouncing off the building's many windows, making it look as though a score of fires blazed from within.

While Rhys paid the cab, I stood on the pavement, admiring the building's exterior. I was pretty good at dating architecture, and I put this one to be somewhere around the late 1800s. I was eager to see inside, yet part of me wanted to freeze the moment. The night had yet to unfold; we were poised on its threshold, and a feeling of anticipation was already fizzing inside me.

The orange light from the sunlit windows reflected for a moment in Rhys's eyes. Amber flames burning in fathomless green pools. I shook my head, but the fanciful imagery refused to be evicted.

'All set?' Rhys asked, offering me his arm. I took it gratefully. Cobblestones and heels are a dangerous combo at the best of times, and tonight absolutely nothing about me felt steady or sure-footed, literally or metaphorically.

The entrance foyer was as breathtaking as the exterior. A small table had been set up to one side of an enormous, sweeping flight of red-carpeted stairs. It was the kind Cinderella ran down at midnight or Rhett climbed with Scarlett in his arms. After giving his name to the woman at the welcome table, we were directed to a huge reception room bordered on each side by enormous columns covered in gold leaf. Crystal chandeliers hung from the ceiling, redundant for now as golden sunlight still flooded through the room's floor-to-ceiling French windows.

We were so early the guests were outnumbered by the catering staff, who immediately swooped on us with trays of champagne and canapés.

'Thank you for a wonderful evening, Rhys,' I said, clinking my long-stemmed flute against his in a toast.

His eyebrows rose in amusement. 'Aren't you meant to say that at the end of the night?'

I gave an easy shrug. 'Well, you know what my memory is like these days. I might forget.'

He smiled. 'Then you're welcome.'

My eyes toured the room, which was still empty enough to appreciate the intricately decorated panelling. 'It's spectacular, isn't it?' I murmured.

'Wait until you see the library where they present the awards – it's even more impressive.'

'You've been here before?'

'Yes. We were shortlisted a couple of years ago but lost out to a much bigger company. Maybe this time you'll bring us luck.'

'Never thought of myself as particularly lucky. I grew up being told you had to make your own luck.'

His frown spoke volumes.

I wondered if Annalise had been standing in my place on that previous awards night, but I think I already knew the answer to that one. Just when I thought I recognised the ground we were standing on, it slipped away again beneath my feet.

'Does it feel strange being back in the corporate world?' I asked, surveying the rapidly filling room. 'Do you miss it?'

If Rhys was surprised that I'd steered us back onto neutral territory, he hid it well.

'I've always liked being part of a team.' His words were careful, as though he wasn't entirely sure if he was being secretly tested.

'When you're with the right people, it can be really fulfilling and inspiring.'

More double meanings.

'I'm not sure I agree with you there. I kind of like being a lone wolf.'

Rhys gave a quick smile. 'That's something I'd already guessed about you. But even wolves need a pack, Ellie.' Were we still talking about business, or something more personal? He held my gaze with his kryptonite green eyes, and I've never been so happy to be interrupted in my whole life.

'Rhys. You beat us here.' I looked up to see the watch-tapping colleague from the bar standing beside us. He clapped a weighty hand on Rhys's shoulder.

'Charlie, this is Ellie. Ellie, Charlie.'

A large damp hand was held out for me to shake, which I did, proud of the way I didn't grimace or wipe my now decidedly sticky palm on the side of my dress.

'Charlie and I have worked together on several projects,' Rhys explained.

Charlie, who was busily scanning the room for new arrivals, had his head turned away from us, and Rhys used the moment to subtly pass me a couple of serviettes from one of the canapé trays to dry my hand. His eyes were dancing with amusement and mine couldn't help but join in. The look we shared felt so easy, so right, as though out of all the pairs of eyes in the world, his were the only ones I ever wanted to look into, to laugh with. And just like that, we were back in the game of emotional snakes and ladders, and I'd slithered right back down to square one all over again.

Rhys hadn't been exaggerating about the library, which we adjourned to some forty-five minutes later. It was a booklover's paradise with spectacular double-height floor-to-ceiling bookshelves lining every wall. The room had been lavishly decked out for tonight's gala, with round white-clothed tables bearing towering candelabras and exotic floral centrepieces.

One by one we'd been joined by the rest of Rhys's colleagues, who were his fellow award nominees. I was usually good with names, but the only ones that stuck belonged to the two women, who I recognised from the bar: Nina and Helen. Nina gave me a warm smile, but the one from Helen looked less genuine. It stayed on the lower half of her face and never reached her eyes.

Interestingly, both women appeared surprised and a little intrigued by my presence. I couldn't work out why, until we wandered over to the seating plan by the doorway. Then it made sense. No one else at our table had brought a partner to the awards. I was the only plus-one. I shot Rhys a sideways glance, but he clearly hadn't picked up on the anomaly.

Our table was on the far side of the library, and there was a lot of weaving and swerving to avoid other guests still hunting for their seats, as well as avoiding the circulating wait staff, who were busily serving drinks from overloaded trays.

When a waiter suddenly stepped backwards, directly in my path, Rhys's reactions were as quick as a cat's. His hand shot out and circled my waist, pulling me to one side and saving me from wearing whatever had been in the glasses on the waiter's tray. The poor man looked mortified and went the same shade of red as the velvet covering on the chairs as he righted the fallen glasses on his tray, and he wasn't the only one. The touch of Rhys's hand on my naked back when he'd pulled me out of the way was something I clearly hadn't thought through when buying the dress. The sensation of his skin against mine was electrifying – and for two people who'd been through what we had, that wasn't a term I used lightly. I found myself unconsciously holding my breath for the remainder of the time it took us to cross the room. When we reached our table and his hand fell away, I was practically gasping for air.

We were the last to take our seats. There were only two unoccupied chairs left, on opposite sides of the table from each other. It didn't occur to me that someone might have deliberately engineered it so that we weren't sitting together until I noticed a flash of satisfaction in Helen's eyes. In any other situation I'd probably have responded with an eloquently arched eyebrow, but these weren't my people, they were Rhys's, and I wasn't about to make a scene. I was a grown woman who was perfectly capable of sitting alone for an hour or two. I stepped towards one of the vacant seats, but Rhys stopped me, his eyes going to the second empty chair on the far side of the table.

'Do you mind if we rearrange the seating?' He put the question to the whole group, but Helen was the only one who looked irritated enough to allow an audible sigh to escape. Was there some history between them? Something that predated his relationship with Annalise? Because his former work colleague certainly seemed put out by his request.

'Here, you can have my place,' volunteered Charlie, jumping out of his chair which was next to one of the vacant seats. He picked up his drink and switched places, and I immediately forgave him for having the sweatiest handshake in the world.

It felt like six pairs of eyes were on us as Rhys pulled out the chair for me before slipping into the one on my right.

His friends were amusing and exuberant and possibly a little tipsy from the overflowing glasses of champagne, which the waiters ensured were never empty. They spoke quickly, out-quipping each other and finishing every anecdote with peals of laughter. Their stories went back over the years, and I quickly realised the Rhys of old was a very different man from the one I knew. The word workaholic was used to describe him more than once. The old him and the old me would have been an excellent match if he'd been free back then. But the jury was still out as to whether the newer versions stood a chance.

There wasn't much opportunity for private conversation, but I was happy to sit back and take it all in. So, when the focus abruptly swivelled our way, I wasn't ready for it.

'So, how did the two of you meet?' asked a man sitting on Charlie's right-hand side, who may or may not have been called Hugh.

'We didn't even know he was seeing anyone,' Nina said, her eyes going reproachfully to the man beside me.

I was glad the lighting in the library was more atmospheric than illuminating, because I think my cheeks had turned an interesting shade of pink. I shot a quick sideways glance at Rhys, who didn't seem as thrown by their interest as I was.

'Ellie and I met in a park, actually,' he said easily.

Perhaps I wasn't quick enough to disguise my surprise at the pared-down version of the truth, because I felt Helen's radar had immediately been activated. She craned forward on her chair, clearly anxious not to miss a single word.

'Although we're not—' I began and then guillotined the rest of that sentence when, beneath the table, Rhys's hand captured mine and squeezed it tightly. I pasted a big smile on my face and didn't glance his way at all.

'We're not sure what made either of us go to the park that day.' I turned to face the man beside me, who still had my hand clasped in his own. 'Just fate, I guess.' His eyes were molten green, full of silent admiration and gratitude, and something inside me melted. I could lie compulsively for the rest of my days to earn that look over and over again.

The arrival of the first course couldn't have been better timed. The service was like a well-choreographed ballet, with plates arriving and being whisked away with uncommon speed, leaving little opportunity for anything beyond surface-level conversation.

When a microphone and stand were brought onto the stage, I excused myself for a quick trip to the Ladies' before the presentation ceremony began. I couldn't have been more than halfway across the room when I got the feeling that someone was following me.

Helen entered the washroom about fifteen seconds behind me. It could have been a coincidence. But I didn't think it was. It was clear Rhys didn't want his colleagues to know how we'd met, or that our relationship was very much in the friend zone. What would have been useful to know in advance was why.

I could certainly have done with a heads up, because when I emerged from the cubicle, Helen was already at the bank of basins. She was washing her hands thoroughly enough to perform surgery or simply stalling and waiting for me to join her. Unfortunately, the only free basin was beside hers.

'I didn't realise Rhys was bringing a plus-one tonight.'

I would have loved to ask why that was any of her business, but I was at a disadvantage here. I didn't know the nature of their relationship. They could be long-term best friends or former lovers for all I knew. Although either, in my opinion, represented extremely poor judgement on Rhys's part. I felt totally wrong-footed and silently cursed Rhys for not giving me at least a sketchy backstory to work with.

'It was a last-minute decision to come,' I said. That, at least, was true.

'You and he are . . . ?' Helen left the rest of the question dangling in the air, like a puppeteer's marionette.

'Together,' I said succinctly, smiling at her reflection in the washroom mirror. 'A force of nature, you could say.' That, at least, amused me, although obviously it sailed straight over her head.

I stepped aside for someone else to use the basin, but Helen followed me to a dressing table area set up for hair and make-up repairs.

'I'm not sure if you're aware of this,' she said, pausing to slick blood-red lipstick onto her pursed lips, 'but Annalise is actually one of my best friends.'

Well, that explained everything. It was no wonder she was practically feral now that the others were no longer around. I drew in a deep and steadying breath. I couldn't fault her for her loyalty. I'd probably be exactly the same if anyone was threatening Mel's happiness. But it meant I had to tread even more carefully on a tightrope that I couldn't see above an abyss I was probably going to tumble into anyway.

Rescue came in a timely and unexpected manner when a middle-aged woman holding a clipboard burst into the bathroom, declaring importantly: 'We're about to start presenting the awards. If I could ask any nominees to please retake your seats.'

I gave Helen a look that I hoped said Oh, what a shame we can't stay and chat and reached for my bag.

It was only half a dozen strides to reach the exit, but just far enough for me to feel each one of the invisible daggers Helen threw at my exposed back.

'Is everything okay?' Rhys whispered as I took my place beside him.

'Sort of,' I whispered back, under cover of the MC's welcoming speech. 'Although a heads up that Helen and your ex are BFFs would have been useful.'

Rhys reached for my hand again, only this time he didn't hide doing so beneath the table.

'I'm sorry. I didn't think she'd say anything. Can I explain later?'

I nodded.

The award Rhys and his colleagues were nominated for was the last of the night to be presented. The cycle of envelope opening, applause, and acceptance speeches made further conversation almost impossible. But in a gap between awards, I leant into the space between Rhys's chair and mine. The warm, spicy aroma of his cologne almost derailed me, making it hard to concentrate.

'Why am I here tonight, Rhys?' I whispered in his ear. 'Why did you ask me to come?'

He turned in his chair to face me, looking so thrown by my question that I almost let him off the hook. But I had to know. The moment stretched on, and just when I felt sure he was about to explain, Charlie suddenly materialised beside us. Once again, he enthusiastically clapped Rhys on the back.

'We're next,' he declared excitedly.

Rhys, in contrast, appeared outwardly calm, although his fingers were drumming lightly on the white-clothed table in a revealing tell. It was the first time, since witnessing him being resuscitated in the park, that I'd seen him look like this. Vulnerable. Was this my doing? I acted purely on instinct, laying my hand on top of his, and was rewarded with a look of gratitude that I found difficult to look away from.

'And the winner is . . .'

My thoughts had been wandering, and it took a moment to realise that chairs were being pushed back from our table as Rhys and his colleagues got to their feet. They'd won.

Applause ricocheted from every corner of the room, snapping me out of my own head, with its jumble of conflicting emotions. I joined in enthusiastically. I may even have allowed a totally inappropriate whoop to escape as my fellow table members approached the stage to accept their trophies. Rhys flashed a quick smile my way as he climbed the steps to the waiting MC. I clamped my lips, silencing any further embarrassing exclamations of delight, but there was no stopping me from clapping so hard my palms would probably be scarlet by the end of the evening.

Rhys gave the best acceptance speech of the night, bar none. It was easy to see why the group had chosen him as their spokesman. He was funny, humble, and generous in praise, both for his colleagues and the other nominees. Before stepping away from the mic, he paused and looked down at the trophy in his hands. 'This award is a testimony to teamwork but also to friendship,' he said, aiming a smile at his fellow prize-winners, who were all beaming with pride and champagne.

And then he looked directly at me. 'Because when you have the right people beside you, anything is possible.'

Internal organs aren't capable of actually melting, but mine felt decidedly less than solid as his words slipped over and under every single one of my barriers. My eyes remained fixed on his as he descended the steps from the stage and returned to the table with the others. Everyone was talking at once, but their words flowed past us, as though we were an island in the sea of noise.

'That was a great speech.' I paused, teetering on the edge of bravery before taking a leap of faith. 'I especially liked the last bit.'

'Thank you, Ellie.' His voice was low as he leant even closer towards me. 'I meant every word of it.'

The moment was ripped out of our hands when someone suddenly called out 'Smile' as a phone was pointed towards us and a photograph taken. I flinched at the flash. It was something I was still struggling to control since the lightning strike. Rhys threw up a protective hand, shielding my face as Helen attempted to take a second snap. She frowned, clearly unhappy at being thwarted.

'Just trying to capture the moment, guys,' she said sulkily before turning away.

Rhys reached for his chair and set it down at an angle, with his back to the rest of the table.

'I'm sorry about Helen.'

'I'm sorry about whooping when you won. It was very uncool of me,' I counter-apologised.

Rhys was at his most endearing when he was trying not to smile. 'Really? It was my favourite part of the night so far.'

His face suddenly sobered. 'You asked earlier why I invited you tonight.'

I nodded.

His eyes closed for a moment, and I wondered if the memory of me acting like an over-enthusiastic cheerleader was playing silently behind his lids. I prayed he wasn't imagining pompoms.

'Tonight is probably the last time I'll attend an event like this. I've stepped off the corporate treadmill, which makes this evening feel like a landmark moment. And it just felt right to share it with someone who'd been beside me for another recent landmark moment.' He smiled. 'Besides, I knew that if we won, you'd be genuinely excited and happy for me. And you were.'

'I have to say, you set a fairly low bar for picking your dates.' I shook my head as though I wasn't sure I believed him.

'Actually, I don't. It's just that you blow everyone else out of the water.'

We were sailing straight into dangerous uncharted seas, and it was with both relief and regret that I saw the woman with the clipboard approaching the table.

'Could I steal all the prize-winners away for some official photographs.'

Rhys got to his feet with a look of obvious reluctance. 'We'll continue this later,' he promised, his breath warm on the shell of my ear as he whispered the words.

Chapter Twenty-One

'Where's that gorgeous blonde he's usually with? Anna-something-or-other.'

I stiffened, freezing like a statue on the deserted balcony in the warm night air.

'Rhys? You're well behind the times, mate. I don't think they've been together since that messy business with Marco,' a second man replied. 'Personally, I prefer the upgrade.'

I lost whatever was said next as a bus rumbled over the cobblestoned street below me. Many years ago, my mother had warned me eavesdroppers seldom hear anything good about themselves. I had a horrible suspicion she was about to be proved right. Half of me wanted the two gossiping men to move away from the French windows, which were open just far enough to allow their voices to reach me on the balcony. The other half hoped they'd stay right where they were.

'It's always the redheads you need to watch out for. They're all fire and passion.'

The only fire right now was the one setting my cheeks alight, and as for passion . . . well, that was a word that had practically dropped out of my vocabulary over the last three years.

With the presentations over, people had left their tables to mingle, and after a minute, I too got to my feet. I could have circled the room; it would certainly have been a great opportunity to do some networking, and there were more than enough business cards in my bag to pass around. But that's exactly where they stayed. After one circuit of the room, I'd spotted a temptingly ajar French window and slipped out onto the stone-balustraded sanctuary.

The night air hit my lungs like an antidote from the clashing cocktail of three hundred different perfumes and aftershaves in the library. It was still warm enough to not regret leaving my wrap draped over the back of my chair. I stepped to the edge of the balcony, resting my hands on the worn Georgian stonework, which still retained the heat of the day.

The lights of the city were laid out before me, a twinkling panorama of trapped fireflies that would look totally different when daylight changed them back into buildings, traffic signals, and streetlamps. The hum of traffic from the street below was in competition with the strains of a saxophone played by a busker at the crossroads several floors below me. His repertoire seemed to consist entirely of love songs.

I looked up into the star-studded sky, wondering why the universe was determined to keep giving me so many reasons to make this night into a memory that wasn't mine for the taking.

Not when there were other forces in play with the exact opposite agenda. Helen's poorly disguised venom and the overheard conversation were just the tip of the iceberg. There were people here, people who'd known Rhys far longer than I had, who obviously believed he and Annalise were still unfinished business.

Was I in danger of becoming the one thing I'd always sworn I would never be? Was I the obstacle in someone else's path? The fly in the ointment? I shook my head, refusing to hide behind euphemisms. If I didn't halt whatever this was right now, was I in danger of becoming the other woman? I didn't do triangles; never had, never would. They were the worst kind of relationship geometry. I might not be able to recall my mother ever reading me a fairy story, but her cautionary tale of never allowing yourself to become involved with a man whose heart was committed elsewhere, that I could definitely remember.

I kept telling myself – and anyone else who would listen – that Rhys and I were friends, and a friend would want to help him make the right decision and support him whatever he chose to do.

A friend wouldn't be spending her nights wondering what his lips would feel like crushing her mouth. Or imagining his body pressed hard upon hers, reminding them that miraculously they were both still amazingly and incredibly alive, and that the best way to celebrate that would be to —

'There you are.'

A slice of warm yellow light from the library grew wider as Rhys nudged open the French window and stepped out onto the balcony to join me. He pushed the door shut behind him, blocking out the noise of the gathering.

'I'm sorry. I had no idea that would take so long. I hope you weren't bored.'

'Not at all. It's been an interesting night. I've liked meeting your friends.' Helen's face flashed into my thoughts. 'Well, most of them,' I corrected on a wry laugh that I knew he'd understand.

'They're not bad people. It's not a bad life. It's just not a life I want to live anymore. I don't want to be working until midnight, chasing deadlines or neglecting the people I love, just so I can spend more time at work. Who wants to live like that?'

I had. I did. I shivered as I recognised the old me in so many of the things he was saying. I'd needed thousands of volts of electricity to question whether I was living life the wrong way, but Rhys had figured it out all by himself. I admired him more than he'd ever know for that.

'Well, even though you're too polite to admit it, I apologise for taking you on the dullest date you've probably ever had.'

'Clearly you have no idea how many tragic dates I've been on.'

'Aha, so we are calling this a date now?' he said in mock triumph.

I'd been tricked into walking straight into that one.

'No. I didn't say that. In fact, I think tonight would be a really good time to draw some lines in the sand. Just so we know where we are.'

He moved to stand beside me and I shivered, wondering why all the cells in my body went haywire whenever he entered my personal space. Surely that had to be something chemical? Something to do with the lightning? He noticed the raised goosebumps on my arms and wordlessly slipped off his jacket.

There were at least a hundred good reasons why I should object to him draping it around my shoulders, but I forgot all of them when he enveloped me in the garment still warm from the heat of his body. I breathed him in from the fabric, like a drug I was taking one final hit from before I quit it forever.

'I know exactly where we are, and where I hope we'll go,' Rhys said.

Damn my heart for lurching within me at his words, for racing at the warmth in his voice. I had the most rebellious internal organs known to man. Not one of them knew how to behave when this man got close.

'What would have happened if I hadn't agreed to come with you tonight?' I asked.

He turned to me.

'Then I probably wouldn't have spent half of the afternoon in a state of excitement that even teenage me would have been embarrassed to admit to. I wouldn't have been holding my breath in anticipation until the moment you opened your door and smiled at me.'

I was trembling, and it wasn't because I was cold. My hands were visibly shaking, and I balled them tightly into fists on the stone wall so he couldn't see.

'I also wouldn't have spent the entire evening wondering if this would be the night when I'd finally get to hold you in my arms and kiss you. And I also wouldn't be worrying right now that you're about to say something that's going to stop this thing in its tracks for no good reason, except that you're scared of where it might go.'

'I'll give you a good reason. Two in fact. You have a partner and a child.'

Had my voice ever sounded so small? So sad?

'I have an ex-partner, who I haven't loved for a very long time, and a daughter who I'm going to love forever,' he corrected gently.

'You should be with Tasha, Rhys. Little girls need their daddies.'

He lifted one hand and gently cupped my cheek. The pad of his thumb ran across my skin and came away wet. How had I not known that I was crying?

'Where is this coming from? Tasha has me. She'll always have me. But I don't think she's the little girl who's making you cry right now, is she?'

I was losing ground, losing my focus in an argument I'd thought was watertight and now realised – too late – was leaking like a sieve.

'This isn't real. Feelings like this, connections this strong don't just spring up out of nowhere. I think something weird, something electrical, happened to us when the lightning struck. It's done something, hotwired us into thinking this attraction between us is real.'

'So, you're willing to admit there is an attraction?'

Damn, I'd walked straight into that one. Denying it would make me a liar – we both knew it was there.

'Yes. Of course I do. But I don't think that just because the lightning has affected us on a molecular level that we have to act on it.'

He looked down at me, shaking his head sadly.

'That's not it. That's just how we met. It could have been in a lift, or in a sandwich shop, or crashing trolleys in a supermarket aisle. I could have met you anywhere and still felt like this.'

'Well, I disagree,' I said, my chin jutting out obstinately. It was a gesture anyone who'd known me in my argumentative teenage years would easily recognise.

'So, if you think none of this is real, what do you suggest we do about it?'

'We should probably ignore it,' I said decisively.

'What if I can't?' Rhys said.

I lost the ability to breathe for a second and that had a lot to do with the expression on his face as he looked down at me. We were now just one reckless footstep apart. My heart rate kicked up a gear.

'Well, we have to,' I said, aware I was nervously chewing on my lower lip. 'Because it's just lust.' I was grasping at straws and plucked the one that seemed most logical.

He shook his head again, but there was a glimmer of humour on his lips. Magnetic humour, because suddenly I couldn't tear my eyes away from them.

'Okay,' he said, as though we'd been haggling in a marketplace and a deal had just been struck. 'I'll take lust then, even though I know that's not what this is. But I'll take it and then show you that no one feels this way because all they want is to get the other person into bed.'

Those words alone almost undid me. I felt a fuse light somewhere low inside and travel down to the place between my legs which was suddenly on fire with need.

He brought his other hand up, cupping my face.

'Let me prove to you that I'm right.'

'I'll prove to you that you're not,' I said, looking up at him with eyelashes still spiky from my tears.

'Are you done arguing with me for now?' Rhys asked, as his fingers slid gently into my hair, freeing it from its pins to spill like a molten waterfall over his hands. 'Because we've got the moon, starlight, and some guy somewhere playing love songs, and I really can't think of a better place or time for our first kiss.'

The lips he was about to claim curved into a reluctant smile. 'You're way too cocky. You know that, don't you?'

'That one we can discuss later,' Rhys said, his voice gruff.

And then he kissed me.

Chapter Twenty-Two

The moment his lips touched mine was like being hit by lightning all over again. The kiss was filled with the same electricity as a storm, only stronger, so much stronger. There was no holding back, and my mouth opened under his, allowing his tongue to find mine. One of us groaned.

The kiss was confident but not overpowering. He allowed me to give as much as I took. And I did, running my tongue along the fulness of his lower lip until I felt him shudder, and then deepen the kiss until my knees threatened to give way. But I couldn't fall, because he'd moved one hand from my hair and slid it slowly down my naked back, stopping where the material of my dress began. His splayed fingers supported me and pulled me tightly against him.

I gave a small moan of protest when his lips left mine and then shivered as he laid a trail of featherlight kisses down my neck before running his tongue teasingly along my collarbone. It was an area that had never featured in foreplay before, which was clearly a huge oversight. Drunk on his touch, his taste, on him, my grip on his shoulders tightened. Beneath the fine linen of his white shirt, I could feel the strong muscles of his shoulders and the trembling he was unable to control. If it hadn't been for the fact that there was a room full of his associates directly behind us, I would have been tearing the buttons off the fabric barrier, relishing the sound of them ripping free and hitting the stonework beneath our feet.

Rhys's lips returned to mine, and the kiss that I already knew would claim the title as the best of my entire life once again threatened to turn me into a molten mess of desire.

I like to think we had enough control and good sense to have stopped on our own accord and that we hadn't needed the interruption of another guest coming out onto the balcony to make us spring apart like guilty teenagers who'd just been caught by one of their parents.

But I was so lost in the moment I didn't even identify if the intruder was a man or a woman from their hasty apology and rapid disappearance back into the library. Rhys had instinctively moved his body to protect me from view when the French window opened, and I'd remained behind him in a hidden pocket of anonymity. It was a chivalrous and probably unnecessary gesture because no one here knew me. Rhys was the one who could potentially be embarrassed by our actions.

But he didn't look that way. He looked hot, sexy as hell, and still very much lost in the same red mist of desire that had enveloped me. His breathing remained uneven, and there was just enough moonlight for me to see that his green eyes were all dilated pupils. Desire looked good on him.

'I don't think I've ever felt so close to losing control,' he admitted, running a hand through the hair that I'd already messed up with my fingers. He gave a shaky laugh. 'At least not in public.'

'Me neither,' I said, my chest still rising and falling as though I'd run for miles but still hadn't left the starting line.

'That kiss was . . .' He paused as his eyes went to my lips and he seemed to lose his train of thought.

'Yes, it was,' I agreed.

He lifted a hand and ran his thumb tenderly over my swollen lower lip.

'All I can think about is wanting to do it again . . . and again . . . and again.'

'Ditto,' I said, which was about as articulate as I was capable of being right then.

'Do you want to get out of here?' he asked, and I loved the way there was still a flicker of doubt in his eyes. As though he couldn't quite believe the fire that was burning him up was incinerating me too.

'Oh, yes.' My reply sounded almost like a plea.

'Then let's go.' He looped an arm around my bare shoulders and scooped up his jacket that had fallen to the ground, in the way I hoped my own clothes were about to do before too much longer.

It was emptier now inside the library. Quite a few people must have already left, and the evening was clearly winding up. However, a few tables, occupied by diehard party animals, were still going strong, and ours was one of them. There were several new bottles of champagne in ice buckets, and everyone looked just a little more tipsy than they had the last time I'd seen them.

'Rhys. There you are. We've been looking all over for you,' exclaimed Charlie. If he had been engaged in a manhunt, it was a very relaxed one, because Charlie appeared well ensconced on his seat, with one arm thrown companionably over Helen's shoulder. 'We were just deciding where to go on to next.'

'Not us, thanks,' Rhys said smoothly, reaching across and retrieving my bag and wrap from the chair. 'Ellie has work in the morning.'

That was news to me, but I did a very good job of not showing my surprise.

I addressed the table with what was meant to be a regretful smile. 'Sorry, everyone, but Saturday is one of my busiest days of the week. But I hope you all enjoy the rest of the night. It's been great meeting you, and congratulations again on the win.'

Rhys had his arm firmly planted around my waist and was gently steering us away from the table when Charlie got to his feet with a visible sway. He rounded the table to envelop us both in a champagne-infused embrace.

'Look, if you want to join us after you've dropped Ellie off, we'll probably wind up at that place on Baldock Street that we used to go to back in the day.'

Before Rhys could politely refuse, Helen's voice cut across the table.

'Don't be an idiot, Charlie.' She swept her eyes over us, and I felt like a bug on a microscope slide. 'They've got other plans.' The men at the table might not have noticed that my hair was now freed from its clips, or that my lips were pinker and more swollen than they'd been before, but Helen hadn't missed a thing.

'Do you think they all know why we didn't want to join them?' I asked Rhys as we began our descent of the sweeping staircase back to the foyer.

He reached for my hand and folded it within his. 'I don't know, and I don't care.' He shot me a smile that made me glad he had a firm hold of me because the stairs were steep and when he looked at me the way he was doing right now, my equilibrium disappeared. *It's MIA along with your good sense.* I had to hand it to my conscience; it wasn't going down without a fight.

Rhys must have messaged the cab that we were ready to be picked up, because I could see the vehicle already idling by the kerb through the building's double glass doors.

I slid onto the back seat and realised I was in trouble when my fingers were incapable of fastening the seat belt. After two abortive attempts, Rhys leant closer and took the buckle from my hand.

'I've got it,' he said, his face intoxicatingly close as he bent to slide the metal fastener home. The fire within me hadn't been extinguished, just tamped down, and when he looked up at me through his long black lashes, I blinked back at him through eyes heavy with desire.

I'd have happily tipped the driver extra to go faster, but he must have been in a hurry to get home too, for he somehow managed to shave fifteen minutes off our journey time.

'Are we still doing two drop-offs?' he asked, his eyes going to the rearview mirror as he waited for our reply.

Rhys looked at me for a long moment and I loved how he was allowing me to take the reins. If I wanted to change my mind and derail the rest of the night, he was willing to let me. Except that was the last thing I wanted to do.

I shook my head. 'No, just one stop,' I said as we swung into my road.

The main door was a challenge. I was stone-cold sober, yet it took several attempts to insert the Yale key into the lock. Hopefully my inability to open locked doors was only a temporary glitch, because that could be a real hindrance in my line of work.

We shut the street door behind us with a soft click, and it was as though a spring had been released. Rhys reached blindly for me, and all the restraint we'd had to put in place in the taxi was suddenly set free. My arms wrapped around his neck as we half fell back against the door. His mouth was on mine, hungrily making up for every single minute we'd been separated since the balcony. Mid-kiss he reached up to find my hands, removing them from his shoulders and lifting them up above my head, gently pinioning me against my own front door.

I thrust my hips towards him and gasped at just how hard and ready he was. There were still three flights of stairs to climb before we reached the privacy of my flat, and I was beginning to doubt either of us was capable of holding out until we got there.

Rhys lowered his head and gently bit the sensitive skin at the juncture of my neck and shoulder, and I arched my throat to give him further access. There wasn't going to be any holding back once we hit the mattress of my king-size bed. We were standing in the path of a tsunami of emotions, and neither of us was making even a token effort at getting out of the way.

'Upstairs,' I murmured into his mouth. He raised his head, his eyes clouded with lust, and nodded. Lust. It's just lust. I repeated the words like a mantra as he took my hand and we climbed the steps to my flat. It felt important that one of us kept in mind that we were simply obeying a carnal impulse that had the ability to override good sense.

Once the fire is put out, we'll be able to think clearly, I told myself, my hands already roving over him as Rhys took my flat key from my hands and unlocked the door.

I don't remember how my shoes came off, but they began a trail of discarded clothing that led from the door and into the hallway. Rhys's tie was already loosened and it fell by my stilettos, quickly followed by his jacket. I pulled impatiently on his shirt, freeing it from the waistband of his black trousers as his mouth ravaged mine. I could feel the faint and delicious rasp of stubble on his cheek. Tomorrow there'd be a rash wherever he'd grazed me, and as his hands ran over my body, I didn't think my face would be the only area affected.

'Which way?' he asked.

I nodded in the direction of my bedroom door and then gasped as he lifted me off the ground, his hands firmly planted on my bottom. Thankful for the deep split in my dress, I brought my legs up, locking them tightly around his hips. We moved like a single entity as he strode into my bedroom. The room was bathed in moonlight, with the tree outside my window casting intriguing shadows on the walls. Our silhouettes joined them in an X-rated shadow-play.

My fingers worked furiously on the buttons of his shirt and it's a miracle that I didn't rip a single one off as I finally undid the garment and slid my hands onto his hard, warm, torso. The marks left by the lightning were still there, visible in the light of the moon, and my hands and then my lips caressed them. They were the reason we were here. They were why his body was just moments away from joining with mine and satisfying a desire so intense that I already knew he was going to ruin me for any other lover.

'How do I get you out of this?' he groaned, his hands searching for the zip on my dress. For a second I felt an ancient power thrumming through me, hearing how badly he wanted me. But as I guided his hand to the fastening, I knew that he held just as much power over me.

The zip slid down and his hands found every inch of skin it revealed as it fell open. My back was still to him as the dress tumbled past my knees and then to my ankles. I stepped out of it. His hands slid around my ribcage and then travelled slowly upwards until his palms covered my naked breasts. I fell back against him, groaning in pleasure as his fingers and thumbs found my nipples and began teasing them. I wriggled back against him and felt a hardness that I couldn't wait to reveal and release. I reached behind me, my fingers already fumbling with the hook at his waistband, when I felt a vibration thrum against my arm. I sprang the clip free and my hand dipped into the opening. Beneath my fingertips I felt the arrow of hair that I was planning to follow, but then the vibration came again and this time we both froze.

His hands fell away from my boobs, and I looked down sadly at the way my erect nipples still stupidly thought this was going to continue, because the rest of me already realised that it wouldn't.

'I'm so sorry,' Rhys whispered hoarsely into my ear. 'I should take this.'

I swallowed hard. 'I know. I understand.'

I stepped away as he pulled the mobile from his pocket. The room was warm, but despite slipping on the robe I plucked from its hook on my door, I felt cold. I burrowed deeper into the soft velour folds as though they were a shield against the inevitable.

Rhys had turned away to face the window as he took the call. I'm not sure why, because I could obviously hear every word of his side of the conversation.

'What's wrong?'

I don't know what Annalise said in reply, but my own response would have been 'everything'.

Shame made my legs give way and I sank down onto the mattress that we'd never quite made it to as he asked, 'How bad was it? Did you need to call for an ambulance?'

I could see his face from where I sat. The passion had been erased by criss-cross etch marks of concern. 'Did you phone 111?'

His jaw tightened to whatever the response had been to that one. The shadows from the moon and the tree branches decorated his face with moving tattoos. I focused on them as Rhys continued to ask questions.

'How is her breathing now?' His shoulders relaxed at whatever his ex said, and for the first time, he looked my way. His eyes were full of regret.

I shook my head, letting him know that it was fine. It didn't matter.

'Yes. Yes. Alright,' he said before lifting his wrist to check his watch.

'About half an hour, or so. Tell her I'm on my way.'

By the time he'd hung up, I'd rearranged my features into the right expression.

'Tasha?'

He sighed. 'She's had an asthma attack. It wasn't a major flare-up, so Annalise decided it didn't warrant a trip to A and E.' He shook his head, and I saw on his face the toll that each episode like this must have on him . . . on all of them.

'I'm sorry, Ellie, I need to go and see her. Annalise says she's asking for me.'

'Of course you must go,' I said, scrabbling off the bed and searching on the floor for his abandoned clothes. I kept my face averted as I hunted for the items that I'd been so eager to remove, while Rhys summoned an Uber.

'It will be here in four minutes,' he said, slipping the phone back into his pocket.

'Still plenty of time for a quickie, then,' I said, hoping that the joke would land the way I wanted it to.

He gave the first smile I'd seen since the phone call had interrupted us.

'I told you before, I don't do quickies.' But even while he was saying the right words, I knew his thoughts were already flying across town towards his daughter. Which is exactly as it should be, I told myself, and for once my conscience completely agreed with me.

I hated that his daughter was sick. I hated seeing the anxiety on his face. But most of all I hated his torn expression when he looked at me.

'The car's here,' Rhys said, glancing down to the street below to verify what his phone had already confirmed. 'I have to go, but I'll call you tomorrow.'

He brought his hand to the back of my neck and pulled me in before pressing a hard parting kiss onto my mouth. It tasted like regret.

He stopped just once at the door, to look back at me.

'I really hate this.'

I nodded and waited until I could hear his footsteps descending the stairs before saying softly,

'Which is why it will never happen again.'

Chapter Twenty-Three

'So, it wasn't a full-blown asthma attack?'

'They call the less serious ones flare-ups,' I corrected. I was a brand-new expert on the condition, having spent a large part of the previous night following every online link I could find relating to childhood asthma. I'd probably only scratched the surface of available information, and yet it had still been enough to frighten the life out of me. How did anyone ever manage to navigate being a parent without living in a constant state of panic?

I looked across the room at my friend and added a footnote to that thought: unless they were like Mel, of course. There were some people who were born to nurture and care for others. Unfortunately, I didn't think I was one of them.

'Tell me again exactly what Rhys said when he phoned this morning,' Mel questioned, swapping out my empty coffee mug for a fresh one. She paused on her way to the dishwasher to wave at Steve, who was walking up and down their lawn pushing a mower. He waved back and they both looked so happy that I immediately regretted bringing down the mood of their happy home by intruding on their Saturday morning routine.

‘He said that by the time he got to Annalise’s, Tasha was fast asleep in bed and was breathing okay. Thankfully the flare-up had subsided.’

Mel made a face like she was sucking lemons.

‘Did his ex say what had triggered it?’

I shook my head, but I knew that triggers could come from anywhere. ‘Maybe it was pollen, dust, or pollution. Or perhaps she just has a nasty cold. They’re often the cause,’ I said, quoting Dr Google. ‘Lots of kids suffer really badly in winter.’

‘It’s summer,’ Mel said, nodding towards the rays of sunlight slanting in through her open kitchen windows.

‘A summer cold then,’ I said, wondering where she was going with this. Mel loved nothing more than a good crime thriller. Film, TV, or book, she adored them all. She could sniff out a red herring faster than a bloodhound and left most fictional detectives in the dust when solving clues.

‘Just hypothesising here, but how sure are we that Rhys’s little girl—’

‘—Tasha. Her name is Tasha,’ I supplied.

‘How sure are we that Tasha was as bad as her mum made out last night?’

There were a great many thoughts that had run through my head since Rhys had left my flat the night before, but that one hadn’t even occurred to me. I was so shocked that the full cup of coffee wobbled in my hand as I set it back down on the kitchen table.

‘Are you suggesting that Annalise made it up?’

Mel gave an eloquent shrug.

‘What kind of mother would do something like that?’ My own had certainly had some questionable parenting skills, but I also knew she would never have feigned an illness.

I shook my head vehemently and the ponytail I’d gathered my hair into swung from side to side like a red warning flag.

'No. I can't imagine Rhys ever falling in love with someone capable of lying about their own kid's health.'

Mel gave a you-could-be-right shrug. 'Although I bet if you'd asked him a few years ago if she'd sleep with another man in their bed, he'd probably have said she wouldn't do that either.' I felt a sudden stab of guilt at having shared Annalise's betrayal with my friend, because it hadn't been my secret to tell.

'This is different,' I insisted. 'This is a step too far. If you had a sick child, you wouldn't tempt fate like that.'

Mel gave a twisted smile. 'Listen to you, talking about fate as though it's something you actually believe in. Where's that career-driven woman who always said you make your own destiny?'

'I killed her off,' I said, reaching for a second brownie before my conscience told me it was a bad idea. 'In a lightning flash.'

'Just think about it for a moment,' Mel urged. 'You and Rhys bump into wicked best friend at your awards do—'

'We can't say for sure that Helen is wicked,' I said, determined to play devil's advocate.

'Okay. Well, Helen is none too pleased to see her bestie's ex turn up with a new girlfriend.'

'Whoa. Back up there. I'm not Rhys's girlfriend,' I protested.

Mel shook her hand as though batting away an annoying wasp. 'It's just a word. Anyway, she sees that the two of you are looking pretty cosy together, plus Rhys seems happy to let them all think that you're an item.'

She was right there, so I nodded.

'She is obviously going to report all of that back to Annalise. That's just standard best-friend protocol. It wouldn't surprise me if she even took some covert photos of you to pass on.'

I remembered the camera flash and realised Mel could well be on the right track.

'Then you both emerge from making out on the balcony.'

'Do people in this country call it making out?'

'Stop interrupting me. Helen obviously knew exactly why you and Rhys were leaving the event early and what you were planning on getting up to afterwards.'

'You're making this all sound really sordid and dirty.'

Mel reached across the table and squeezed my hand. 'Sorry, hon. But I actually think you're long overdue some dirty sex. Unless you've been at it like a rabbit during the months of radio silence.

'Anyway, the obvious thing for Helen to do is call her friend the moment you left the event. And then the obvious thing for Annalise to do is to find a reason to pull Rhys right back in again. And nothing was more likely to do that than a phone call saying that their little girl was sick.'

I shook my head. 'I don't think so.'

'But it could have happened. At best, she could have been exaggerating the symptoms. In half an hour the kid was miraculously well enough to be fast asleep again. And Annalise had the man who was meant to be giving you the best sex you've ever had in her house instead of yours.'

She made a compelling case.

Mel got to her feet, miming a letter T through the window and a very hot and sweaty-looking Steve nodded gratefully. While Mel started to make her husband a drink, I stared at the whirls in the wood of her kitchen table as though they held the secret to the mystery of life.

'It doesn't really matter if Annalise fabricated, exaggerated, or plain-out lied about Tasha's condition last night,' I said, with iron-clad conviction.

Mel paused at the open fridge door. 'Why is that?'

'Because it could have happened, even if it didn't last night. One night there will be an emergency, and Rhys needs to be there when it does. He needs to be on hand to soothe Tasha, help her calm down, use her inhaler properly, and take charge if things get worse and it turns into an emergency.'

'He doesn't need to live under the same roof as them to do any of those things,' Mel pointed out reasonably.

'Well, I think he does. Fathers who love their children as much as he does shouldn't have to live apart from them.'

Mel shook her head and bit her lip. Half of me really wanted to know what it was she was refusing to allow to escape. The other half of me was too scared that I already knew.

'That's not what he has ever said to you though, is it? That he has to move back?'

'Not in so many words,' I admitted, starting to feel cornered.

Mel abandoned the tea and crossed the kitchen again and gave me a hug.

'The only person using those excuses isn't Rhys, hon, it's you. You're the one setting up these roadblocks. You really need to get out of your own way, Ellie, or you're going to miss the chance to see where this thing could actually go.'

◆ ◆ ◆

There were three missed calls from Rhys on my phone when I finally checked it. I'd put my mobile on silent as I'd stood on Mel's doorstep that morning, carrying a bag of brownies still warm from the bakery, and was quite proud of how I'd kept my phone tucked away in my pocket throughout my visit. But each time it had vibrated soundlessly against my hip bone, I could feel my resolve weakening.

When Rhys had called that morning, I hadn't been entirely honest with him. After confirming Tasha's flare-up hadn't been serious, he'd asked if he could come and see me, but in a knee-jerk reaction that took me by surprise, I said I'd already made plans for the day. Had he believed me? Perhaps not, because we both knew that just twelve hours earlier the only plan in my head had been to wake up in his arms.

But things change. They have to when life sends you the kind of reminder that it had done so effectively the night before.

I stared at his name now on my phone screen and felt a tug of longing. You're doing the right thing, I told myself determinedly. You're stepping aside to let a family find its way back together again. That was a good thing. So why did it make me feel so terrible?

'How about after you've been to Mel?' Rhys had asked, with a persistence that would have given me a warm glow if only things had been different.

'Sorry, Rhys, I'm visiting family after that.' It was a plausible lie to have plucked from thin air.

There'd been a long pause on the line, during which I could almost hear him trying to rearrange his life around mine. Don't do that, I silently pleaded. Just let me go.

'I have Tasha all day tomorrow, so that wipes out the rest of the weekend,' Rhys said, his voice full of regret.

'That's okay.'

'No, Ellie, none of this is okay,' he said, sounding genuinely concerned. 'But I don't know how to fix it over the phone. I need to see you. I need to convince you that there's something special here – or at least there could be.'

In the end I'd suggested that we grab a quick lunch in the week, which had been the least romantic scenario I could come up with.

'I'll take whatever time you can spare. I'll fit in around you.'

Everything he did, everything he said, made it almost impossible to remember that we were a lost cause. There was no point trying to fight for us, because we weren't meant to be.

It was something I should try telling my feet, because as much as I wanted them to walk away, all they wanted to do was run straight back to him.

◆ ◆ ◆

I could smell the flowers even before I'd pushed open the street door. Their scent filled the communal hallway. One of my neighbours must have propped them up on the narrow table where we left the mail, and they lifted and brightened both the entrance hall and me.

There was a card stapled to the cellophane wrapping, but there was no need to tear it open straight away, because I already knew who they were from. No one else in the world called me 'Shoe Girl'. It must have confused the hell out of whoever had taken in the delivery, but it made perfect sense to me and was an advance warning that there'd be no sappy message inside the small square envelope. The flowers had been sent to make me smile, something they'd already achieved, I realised, as I bent to burrow my face in the exotic blooms. I regularly bought flowers and plants for clients, but there were several stems in this bouquet I'd never seen before.

As I filled the biggest vase I owned with water, I finally tugged the small white envelope from the cellophane. There was a quote on the card, one I'd never heard before, despite having studied American Literature at university.

'Thunder is good, thunder is impressive; but it is lightning that does the work.'

Mark Twain.

Every time I tried to convince myself that there was nothing special about this man, he revealed yet another facet of his personality that drew me right back to him all over again. On a whim, I used the app on my phone to identify the unfamiliar flowers in the arrangement. I couldn't help smiling as my phone recognised them as Thunder Roses and Lightning Bolt Jewel Orchids. Who took that much time, put that much effort into preparing such a perfect gift? And what kind of fool walks away from a man like that?

Chapter Twenty-Four

I'd told Rhys I would be visiting family that afternoon, and suddenly it felt important to turn the lie into truth.

There'd been too many flowers in the bouquet to fit in the vase, so I bundled the remainder up in their cellophane wrapper. They were tucked beneath my arm as my feet followed the familiar pathway that led to the only family I had in the world.

'Hey, Mum,' I said, no longer feeling self-conscious saying the words out loud as my fingertips grazed along the cool, smooth black granite headstone.

I adjusted my sunglasses more comfortably on my nose and scanned the immediate vicinity. It was a sunny Saturday afternoon, and the cemetery was much busier than usual, but I could see no distinguished-looking silver-haired gentleman among the clusters of visitors.

What I did see, however, was evidence that Henry had been there since my last visit. Discreetly positioned behind my mother's headstone was a brand-new bright red watering can. It was a thoughtful gesture and said a lot about the man who had left it there.

The can was conveniently full of water, so after giving the peonies a generous drink, I dropped the flowers inside it and positioned it beneath the gold engraving of Mum's name.

She'd always been house-proud, even when the homes we'd lived in hadn't been the kind of place anyone would be proud of. She'd made the best of even the shabbiest one-room accommodation, working endless hours of overtime until she could upgrade us to something better. Having one of the most attractive plots in the cemetery would definitely have met with her approval. It was very her.

'Ahh, I see you found the watering can.'

My eyes flew open behind my sunglasses. I hadn't heard him approach, but the sun was warm and the bench had been surprisingly comfortable. It wasn't like me to take an afternoon nap, but then a lot of things in my life weren't like me these days.

'Hello, Henry. It's nice to see you again.'

'And you, my dear,' he said, taking a seat on what I was fast coming to think of as his end of the bench.

'Those are very exotic,' Henry observed, his gaze going to the flowers in the red watering can.

'Someone sent me a bouquet, so I thought I'd share it with Mum.'

'That's a nice thing to do. I'm sure she would have liked that.'

It was a sweet thing to say, and even though he hadn't known her, he was one hundred per cent on the money. Mum would have liked it.

'Are they from an admirer?'

I think he was teasing me, but I rather liked that.

'No, just a friend,' I said firmly.

'Orchids speak the language of love, you know,' Henry said, his voice still playful.

I shook my head. 'These ones don't.'

My response must have sounded more abrupt than I'd intended, because my new friend looked instantly contrite. 'I'm sorry, Ellie. I didn't mean to offend you.'

I gave him a reassuring smile. 'You didn't. I don't think anything you say could ever do that.'

For a micro-second I thought he looked troubled, but then I blinked, and his usual affable expression was back in place.

For two people who hardly knew each other, we got on remarkably well. Henry was a good conversationalist and had a host of amusing stories about his days as a teacher, which I swapped with some about being an estate agent. He was a really good listener, asked excellent questions about the industry and how I'd set up my own business. He seemed genuinely fascinated by every aspect of my job and was either incredibly polite or a very good actor.

'Your mother must have been very proud of all that you've achieved,' he said, his head inclining gently towards the woman who I'd tried so hard to please yet somehow had never quite managed to do so.

'I'm not sure. Mum wasn't one for handing out praise.'

Henry's brow furrowed as though I'd said something quite unexpected. But then he hadn't known her. He'd look far less surprised if he had.

'She gave me the drive to succeed,' I conceded thoughtfully. 'I just think I took things a little too far and dropped too many balls along the way.' I glanced towards the granite headstone. 'But I can't blame her for that. That one's on me.'

'Perhaps the fault doesn't lie with either of you,' Henry said thoughtfully. 'Perhaps there are other mitigating factors.'

I shook my head. 'None that I know of.'

We chatted until the sun slipped lower in the sky and the shadows on the grass grew longer. There hadn't been a single awkward silence or conversational lull as we hopped seamlessly from one topic to another and I could happily have stayed talking to him for hours, but it was growing late and I got the feeling he wanted to be on his way.

'I should go now and let you have a little alone time to chat to your mother,' he said, getting to his feet.

'Is that what you do when you come to visit Bee? Do you talk to her?'

'Always.'

Something deep inside my heart stirred at the sadness in his voice.

'You see, there's still so much I have to say to her. So many things I want to share. I know I could talk to her anywhere – and of course I do – but there's something special about speaking to her here. It feels more meaningful.'

'Have you told her about meeting me?'

I had no idea what made me ask that question, or why its answer suddenly felt important.

'It was one of the first things we spoke about after I met you.'

I liked that, and yet I had no idea why.

'You should try talking to your mother.'

'I will,' I said. 'Although I doubt if she'll be any more forthcoming with her answers than she was when she was alive.'

I came very close to slapping a hand over my mouth, as though those words should never have been spoken.

'There are questions you never asked her when she was alive?'

I smiled wryly. 'Oh, I asked the questions. Many, many times. I just never got any straight answers.'

'What were you enquiring about – if that's not too personal a question.'

It was way too personal, but I'd been the one to unlock this normally secure vault. I had no one to blame except myself for his curiosity.

'Mainly about my father.'

Henry's eyes looked troubled, and I suspected he might be regretting following me down this road.

'What did you want to know?'

'Oh, you know, the usual kind of things. Who the hell he was? What did he do that was so terrible it made my mother send him away.' The lump was right there in my throat, making it almost impossible to finish. 'And why he never came back to see me. Not once. Not ever.'

The kind, compassionate expression on Henry's face froze, as though he didn't quite know what to do with so much honesty.

'All she ever said was that we were better off without him.'

'That must have been very hard to hear,' Henry said.

I gave a shrug that failed miserably at appearing nonchalant.

'Mum said you couldn't miss what you never had.'

I looked towards the grave as though we were once again in the middle of the same old argument we'd had so many times during my adolescence.

'No disrespect to your mother, but I think she was wrong,' Henry said firmly. I turned towards him and was surprised to see the raw emotion on his face. 'You can, most definitely, miss things you've never had. I certainly do.'

His words stayed with me long after he had said farewell and headed off in the direction of Bee's resting place. I cursed myself for having spoken without thinking. It was obvious my words had torn open a wound in my new friend. The absence of children in the life he shared with Bee was a cruel blow, and even though she was no longer at his side, it was easy to see that it still cut deep.

Chapter Twenty-Five

It had been six days since I'd seen Rhys and yet the heat between us was still intense. I'd felt it in the hand he placed on my shoulder, alerting me to his arrival, and it raged like a furnace when he bent down and lightly kissed my cheek. There was a gentle summer breeze in the air, ruffling the strands of my hair and rustling the leaves on the trees, but it wasn't enough to cool the flames that still flickered between Rhys and me. It was ridiculous – even molten lava would have cooled by now, but we were still burning.

'I'm sorry I'm late. Have you been waiting long?' he asked, pulling out one of the ornate wrought-iron chairs on the park café's patio.

'No. My viewing overran, so I've only just got here.'

Rhys leant back in his chair, slipping off his sunglasses – even though the midday sun was still high in the sky.

'It's good to see you again. You look nice,' he said, his eyes warm.

'Nice' had actually taken three outfit changes and twice as long as I usually spent on my hair and make-up to achieve. I really wanted to say he looked good too, but that wasn't the direction I was intending things to go today. But privately, I couldn't help notice how well his black t-shirt fitted the contours of his chest, reminding me a little too vividly of what lay beneath it. It didn't quite meet the waistband of his jeans, which were riding low on his hips. He'd been at the café less than two minutes, and I'd already caught several glimpses of skin as he reached for the chair, then the pitcher of water on the table, pouring us both out a glass.

I drained half of mine in a single nervous gulp.

He caught me off guard by capturing my hand when I thought he was reaching for the menu. Every nerve ending in my body screamed out in protest when after only a second or two I gently extricated my fingers from his.

His emerald-green eyes went straight to mine with a hundred questions.

Ellie?

I blinked twice. I don't want to talk about this, mine silently replied.

What is it? Is something wrong?

Nothing is wrong, mine lied.

At least, that was my interpretation of our silent exchange. It's possible Rhys had an entirely different transcript. Either way, he didn't try to hold my hand again, which should have made me happy but actually had the exact opposite effect.

I switched my attention to the specials board and rambled on for a good two minutes about the merits of the café's excellent BLT over their quiche in a voice that sounded like a parody of mine. I could see Rhys looking at me curiously across the width of the table, and I could hardly blame him. This wasn't the same Ellie he'd left semi-naked in her bedroom just under a week ago.

'I get the feeling I'm missing something here,' he said, a troubled expression on his face as he got to his feet to place our order at the café's outdoor counter.

I allowed my eyes to follow him as he wove past the tables to the till, wondering how it was possible to be so entranced by everything a person did. From his easy loping stride, to the way he chatted amiably to another queuing customer, to the smile he gave the woman at the cash register. There was nothing about Rhys that I didn't like. And that was the problem.

I reached for my sunglasses and slipped them on, because either the pollen count had suddenly shot through the roof or I was dangerously close to changing my mind, or crying. At this point it really could go either way.

The park café had been a convenient meeting point, situated as it was halfway between my morning appointment and the property outside town that I was visiting later that afternoon. It was only now, when I looked across the expanse of grass and saw the lightning-struck oak in the distance, that I questioned whether this had been the best location for us to meet. It was as though I kept dropping lighted matches into a box of dynamite, waiting to see how many it was going to take before everything blew up in my face.

Rhys was making his way back to the table, carrying two cans of chilled soda, and behind the privacy of my darkly tinted glasses, my eyes softened as he paused and bent to stroke the park cat. It was the same one his daughter had been fascinated by on our last visit, and a timely reminder of what was important here.

Rhys returned to the table and set down the cans of Coke.

'How is Tasha?'

It was a good opener, because I wanted his daughter to be front and centre in our thoughts throughout this conversation.

'She's doing great.'

I already knew from his text messages that Tasha had recovered quickly from the flare-up on the night of the award ceremony. If it really was a flare-up, said a suspicious voice in my head, which sounded remarkably like Mel's.

'She doesn't appear to have any after-effects at all.'

He looked down, as though pulling the ring free from his drink can required all his concentration. 'It's strange though, because normally the summer months are the best ones for her. It's not until the colder weather gets here that she tends to suffer most. That's when things can sometimes get dicey.

'I think,' he continued, picking out his words carefully, as though the wrong ones could be dangerous, 'Annalise might have jumped the gun a little the other night.'

'I imagine that would be very easy to do. It must be terrifying watching your child struggling to breathe.'

'It is. But we're usually better at not panicking.'

The 'we' hurt. There was no point in hiding it. But it was probably exactly what I needed to hear.

'Are we going to talk about what happened on that night, Ellie?'

I was mid-gulp, and it took all my concentration not to splutter a mouthful of fizzy drink all over myself.

'Yes. I think we should.'

His eyes were on me, and I already knew this was going to be so much harder than it had been when I'd practised it in front of my bedroom mirror. 'I think, maybe, getting interrupted on Friday might have been the best thing that could have happened,' I said.

His frown told me he didn't agree. 'I think you and I must have vastly different opinions on the best way for a night to end.' He shook his head. 'Walking away from you was torture. Seeing the look in your eyes. It's haunted me all week. If it had been anything else, anyone else, nothing on earth could have made me leave you like that.'

'I think we were about to make a huge mistake.'

'I don't see how something that felt so right can be called a mistake.'

With just one sentence he'd conjured up the memories I'd spent six days trying my best to suppress. Once again I could feel his hands on my body and my own travelling down the planes of his stomach, inching closer to freeing him from his clothes. I shook my head, but the images refused to budge.

'What worries me most, what I can't get out of my head, is that when Tasha needed you the other night, you were with me. I'm afraid that I'm getting in the way of where you ought to be. I never want to be the reason that you're not going back to Annalise,' I said firmly.

'Annalise is the reason I'm not going back to Annalise. If I'd thought there was even the slightest possibility of getting back together with her, I'd never have let anything happen between us that night.'

'But you do want to be with your daughter. And she wants to be with you.'

I wasn't playing fair, but none of the usual rules applied here.

'She has me,' Rhys said, leaning forward until our faces were tantalisingly close. 'She'll always have me. I loved that little girl before I even met her, before I held her in my arms for the very first time. For as long as I live, until the last beat of my heart, I will love her.' He took a moment. 'But the last two years have shown me that I don't need to share her address to share my heart with her, and that maybe a dad who is happy elsewhere is better than one who is miserable right there beside her.'

It felt like he'd reached into my chest, found every secret hope that I'd hidden away, and exposed them all. The love a father might feel for his daughter was a mystery that I'd never been given the chance to unravel. After thirty-five years it shouldn't still hurt this much, but damn it, it did.

'What are we doing here, Rhys? What exactly is this?'

It was hard watching some of the light slowly dim in his eyes.

'Us?' he asked.

I nodded.

'We're getting to know each other.'

'And then what?' I was pushing, I knew that, and I could see him bristling a little uncomfortably.

'I don't know, Ellie. Does it have to be labelled and categorised upfront?'

'For me, yes, I think it does.'

A stave of frown lines appeared on his brow.

'I don't want to pigeonhole this. I'd rather just take things slowly and see where it goes.'

I shook my head sadly. 'That could be a problem, because I'm a big fan of pigeons and the holes they live in.' I gave an unhappy sigh. 'We are so different in so many ways.'

'That's meant to be a good thing, isn't it? Opposites attract.'

'Not always.' I chewed anxiously on my lower lip.

He was quiet for a long moment, his face unreadable.

'Something inside me changed two years ago.'

My mouth felt suddenly dry. 'When you and Annalise broke up?'

'When I came home and found her in our bed with Marco. When the person you trust most, the person you thought you'd grow old with, does something like that, it breaks you. And I hadn't seen it coming. I was totally blindsided. I swore I'd never allow myself to get hurt like that again.'

'I get that.'

'I convinced myself that being a good father to Tasha was the only role I was interested in. Perhaps, in hindsight, I should have listened to Olly and gone to see someone professionally and talk it all through. But I thought I was coping just fine.'

'And now you're not?'

His lips tightened as though he wasn't sure if he could hold back the truth behind them. 'When you asked for a label just now, a definition of what we were, my knee-jerk reaction was to get up and walk away.'

I swallowed audibly.

'So perhaps I'm not as well adjusted as I thought I was.'

'At least you didn't say it's not you, it's me.'

'Don't do that. Don't make this into something flippant and unimportant. Because that isn't how it feels to me. I know you still believe it can all be explained away by science; that it's simply something chemical, an after-effect of both getting struck by the same bolt of lightning. It's obvious you think that whatever this is, it won't last, just like the marks it left on my body.'

My eyes went to his t-shirt as though I had X-ray vision and could see through the fabric. 'Nothing ever does.'

My words seemed to make him sad.

'But those marks are still there, even though everything we've both read says they should be gone by now.' I wasn't sure where he was going with this. 'So maybe what we feel isn't going to disappear either.'

'What are you saying? That we keep seeing each other until the Lichtenberg figures disappear?'

Something flickered in his eyes. 'I wasn't going to say that, but I'm happy to go along with your suggestion.'

'I . . . what? I wasn't suggesting that. It was just a crazy throw-away remark.'

'Well,' Rhys said, settling back more comfortably in his chair. 'I actually think it's too good a plan to discard. Maybe we're the exception to the rule. I'll have marks that never fade and the connection you're so determined to dismiss will actually turn out to be something that was meant to last. Stop thinking about what could go wrong here, Ellie . . . think about what could go right.'

Despite the voice screaming in my head that this was crazy, he must have seen I was wavering.

'Let's just relax, forget about giving this a label, enjoy the rest of the summer and see what happens,' he said gently. 'We can take the physical side of things out of the equation if that makes it easier. In fact,' he lowered his voice to a whisper, 'even if you got down on your knees and begged me to take you to bed, I would have to respectfully decline.'

That brought out my smile.

He held out his hand as though we'd just negotiated a tricky contract. I looked at it for a long moment before placing my palm against his.

'One condition,' I said, before allowing us to seal our words with a handshake.

'Go on.'

'Tasha comes first. You have to promise you'll put her before me, every single time.'

There were so many questions in his eyes, but I wasn't ready to answer any of them.

He nodded slowly and solemnly. 'Tasha comes first.'

Finally, I smiled. 'Okay then. You've got yourself a deal.'

Chapter Twenty-Six

'I'm sorry, Ellie. Whichever way you slice it, it sounds like a red flag to me.'

'I thought you liked Rhys.'

Mel set down her paintbrush, dripping a few drops of emulsion onto the plastic sheeting that covered the floor. 'I did. I do. And I admire him for being honest and upfront with you. But it's hard to hear that he might only see this as a summer fling.'

'Maybe a fling is all I want too. And to be fair, that wasn't exactly how he phrased it.' It wasn't easy defending Rhys when I privately agreed with everything Mel said.

She reached for a rag to wipe her paint-stained fingers. The look on her face needed no caption.

'Well, I want more for you. You deserve more. I want you to be somebody's everything. And as much as I like what you've told me about Rhys, I'm not convinced that ex of his will ever accept that he's moved on. Or hasn't damaged him so much that he never can.' Her voice softened. 'I want someone who'll look at you the way Steve looks at me. Even when I'm feeling grotty, pumped full of hormones, and tearful 24-7.'

'I think they broke the mould when they made your husband.'

Mel's eyes lit up the way I could remember them doing after her very first date with Steve, when she'd come home and woken me up at two a.m. to tell me she'd just met 'the one'.

'Not everyone gets the fairy tale, you know.'

'No. Some people have to be zapped with a gazillion volts of electricity to find their man,' teased Jackson, carefully descending the stepladder with a paint roller in his hand and specks of emulsion in his hair.

He paused on the bottom rung and surveyed his handiwork. 'I told you we were going to run out of paint.'

I frowned and glanced at my watch. 'I could make a quick dash to the DIY store.'

Jackson came up between us and threw an arm around both our shoulders. 'It's okay. I'll go. There's a cake shop near the one on the industrial estate that I want to scope out for our wedding cake. Cupcakes and Rainbows, or something like that.'

I looked at both of my oldest friends and felt overwhelmed with a wave of love. Jackson was busy with wedding plans, Mel with her fertility journey, and yet neither had hesitated for a second when I'd asked them if they were interested in helping me decorate the old wool shop.

'This is kind of like old times, isn't it?' Jackson said, his eyes going to me. I think we'd all been sucked back into memories of evenings and weekends spent decorating my office three years earlier. 'Or did the lightning wipe those memories out too?'

My smile was warm. 'No. They stuck. Maybe because they're some of my favourites.'

Jackson inhaled deeply. 'Nothing like the smell of paint and white spirit to make you all dewy-eyed and nostalgic.'

I looked around the empty shop that had once sold wool and crafting goods and would soon be up and running as an official charitable enterprise. We were just weeks away from opening the doors to the public and that was due – in no small part – to Mel's tireless efforts in pushing the paperwork through.

'It's actually been good for me to have something to take my mind off everything else that's going on,' she'd said when I thanked her yet again for all her hard work.

Her eyes had clouded a little and it was easy to see that she was counting the days until they began their next round of IVF.

'My lovely mother-in-law has gifted Steve and me the money for one more round,' she'd told me hesitantly. 'I know you offered to help, Ellie, and I turned you down, but accepting the money from Sylvia feels different. She wants grandchildren almost as much as we want to be parents. And she'd do absolutely anything for Steve.'

I hugged her and tried to ignore a fleeting sting of regret that I'd never known that kind of relationship with my own mother.

Of course, there were no guarantees that their third attempt at IVF would be successful, but the hope that had been missing from my friend's eyes was back there again. I could cope with a lot of things in life, but seeing my eternally optimistic friend robbed of that emotion had been beyond cruel.

'I'll be back in about half an hour,' promised Jackson, pressing a possibly paint-stained kiss onto my cheek and then Mel's.

The shop seemed strangely empty once he was gone. Jackson had always had the kind of personality that filled every corner of a room and left you missing him almost instantly.

'Let's take a breather,' I suggested, moving to a relatively clean section of the plastic sheeting in the far corner of Florrie's.

Mel dropped down to the floor beside me, and we both surveyed the almost completed room.

'You did it,' she said with obvious admiration.

'We did it,' I corrected gently. Mel might not be one of the participating shop owners but she'd thrown herself wholeheartedly into the project with a gusto that suggested she welcomed every moment of thinking time it had consumed.

'How are things?' I asked now, tentatively stepping on ground where only an old friend dared to tread.

'They're okay,' Mel replied, but there was a glimmer of something in her smile that tripped an instant alarm in my head.

'Do you have some news?'

'No. No. No,' Mel said, shaking her head hard enough for a few curls to spring free from the crocodile clip.

'That's an awful lot of nos,' I observed, my eyes trained on hers. There was an undeniable glint in them. Her lips parted, clamped shut, and then parted again.

'Mel?'

She bit her lower lip. 'I'm three days late.'

I swivelled towards her so hard I heard the tiny bones in my neck crick in protest.

'You are?'

She nodded.

'I mean, it's really too early to test. And it's probably nothing. My cycle is all over the place.' She reached for my hand and squeezed it excitedly. 'But how crazy would it be if after all those failed IVF attempts, we actually got pregnant the good old-fashioned way?'

'It would be wonderful,' I said, feeling the unexpected sting of tears.

'I know the odds are stacked against it. That it would be nothing short of a miracle if I was.'

'Firm believer in miracles over here.'

Mel's eyes were overbright as she turned them to me. 'Can you imagine Steve's face if I told him we didn't need to take up his mum's offer after all.'

'Steve doesn't know you're late?'

Mel shook her head. 'I didn't want to get his hopes up. I think he takes each negative test result even harder than I do. I thought this time it would be wonderful if I could – just maybe – surprise him with some great news.'

I nodded, not sure if getting too excited at this point was the right way to go but unable to rein it back.

'Is he still away at that conference?'

Mel nodded. 'Yes, until tomorrow night. I should know one way or the other by the time he gets back.'

I lifted my hands, revealing four sets of crossed fingers. 'Well, here's hoping I'm finally going to be an honorary auntie – not that I'll have a clue what that involves, mind you, but I already know it'll be the best damn job I'll ever have.'

Mel looked at the quadruple symbols of good luck and covered them with her paint-stained hands.

'No way are you going to be an auntie to any future child we have,' she declared.

She sounded emphatic, and I could hardly blame her. What I knew about young children could be written on the back of a very small Post-it note.

'Steve and I have already decided you're going to be his or her godmother.'

Now it was my turn to grow misty-eyed. I wanted to say thank you, that it was an honour I didn't deserve, but the words were locked down in my throat. Mel smiled and gently nodded. She'd heard them anyway.

'Will you do a test tomorrow?'

'If I can hold out that long.'

'Well, if you need any help. I could . . .' My voice trailed away. 'I was going to say hold the stick while you pee on it, but that sounded kind of gross.'

'It is,' Mel said, wrinkling her nose prettily. There was a look of excitement on her face. 'I could do one of the tests now.'

'You have more than one?' Her eyebrows rose halfway up her forehead. 'Of course you have more than one,' I said, knowing her in a way that still filled me with gratitude. 'How many exactly?'

'Four,' she replied with an impish smile.

It was the longest three minutes of my entire life. And the most nerve-wracking. I knew the answer the second the shop's bathroom door opened. She'd walked into that room with so much hope and expectation, but there was none left when she lifted her face to mine.

She was dry-eyed. She'd been through this moment many times before. My face, however, was awash with tears.

'Oh, Mel, I'm so sorry,' I said, folding her into my arms. She felt so small. So fragile. So lost.

She sniffed. 'It was always a long shot. A million-to-one chance.'

'Maybe it's a false negative?' I was torn between raising her hopes and clutching at straws.

She shook her head sadly. 'Unlikely. None of the other negatives have ever been wrong.'

I wanted to sob, to howl out at the injustice of a world where the one thing, the only thing, my friend wanted was denied her. But my tears weren't going to help her, and so I just held her, as she stood upright but broken in my arms.

'It will happen for you. One day it will happen.'

She nodded mutely against my shoulder.

'At least I spared Steve from having to go through yet another disappointment.'

Even from the depths of her sadness, the love she felt for him was uppermost in her thoughts.

And for the first time, I envied her that. Because that was what I wanted too . . . from a man who didn't want to commit.

Chapter Twenty-Seven

'Ellie?'

I looked up from the bottle of Rioja I was about to put in my basket and glanced up and down the supermarket aisle. I could see no one I knew.

I hesitated for a moment before reaching for a second bottle. I didn't know how many people Mel had invited this evening, but one bottle wasn't going to go very far.

'Ellie?' The voice sounded closer this time. 'It is you. I thought it was.'

A tall man with shaggy hair and the most lurid board shorts I'd ever seen was striding towards me, his flip-flops smacking on the tiled floor of the supermarket.

Not being able to immediately place someone still sent me into a mini panic. It made me afraid that the memory loss I'd experienced after the lightning strike had returned with a vengeance. Most of the gaps I'd experienced had slowly filled in over the last three months, but some still remained, as did the fear.

I was still struggling to recognise the man who'd hailed me in the wine aisle, but it wasn't the lightning to blame. It was the perfectly normal confusion you get when you bump into someone totally out of context. The pieces slotted into place a millisecond before his 'G'day' gave him away. Admittedly, the last time I'd seen Olly he'd been in hospital scrubs and hadn't looked like he'd just wandered straight off the set of Baywatch.

'Olly. What a surprise,' I said, unsure whether I was referring to finding him in my local Tesco, or the huge bear hug he enveloped me in. He released me just as I was beginning to worry whether my ribs were strong enough to withstand such an exuberant embrace. I'd forgotten that everything about Rhys's Aussie friend was somewhat larger than life.

'You're looking way better than you did the last time I saw you,' Olly said with a grin.

'Thanks. Turns out getting shocked with high-voltage electricity isn't for everyone.'

It wasn't my best quip ever, but Olly laughed out loud. 'Rhys said you've got a good sense of humour.'

If I were a dog, that would have been the moment when my ears pricked up to attention. It had only been a week since I'd last seen him, but there was a big Rhys-shaped hole in my life which I had totally not been expecting when he'd taken Tasha away for a beach break holiday.

Without me even realising it, I'd become addicted to his presence. It's not that I saw him every day. But since we'd struck that agreement in the park café four weeks ago, he'd been a feature of my daily life. Whether it was turning up unexpectedly at my office with takeaway coffees (which always reminded me of our first encounter), delivering a client's sketch I'd commissioned from him, or just a random WhatsApp to say hi or share something amusing he'd seen on the internet.

I understood him so much better than I had before. I knew about his passion for art, American sitcoms, and his love of silly puns. I knew he adored mustard but hated ketchup, and how he voted. I knew he phoned his parents every week and had cried unashamedly when their family dog had died while he was away at university. On many levels it felt like I knew him intimately. But we'd never been intimate. And behind all this new knowledge was the niggling concern that I'd somehow got myself so firmly entrenched in the friend zone there was no way I was ever getting out of it.

Because there'd been no dating per se; we'd had café lunches, park picnics, and drinks after work, but nothing that could be deemed romantic. It would be ridiculous to blame him for following the guidelines I'd set out so exactly, but Rhys was sticking to them as though they were commandments set in stone.

I was desperate to ask Olly what else Rhys might have said about me, but that was a line I knew better than to cross. He glanced down into the shopping basket at my feet and gave a cheeky wink. 'That's his favourite wine, you know.'

Actually, I hadn't known that, and I felt my cheeks grow instantly warmer for no good reason at all.

'It's for a barbecue my friend is hosting tonight,' I said, the words bubbling out too fast, like water over rapids. 'But Rhys isn't coming.'

'Still knackered after his week away with Tasha, is he?'

I bit my lip and wondered how I'd fallen into this potential pitfall of a conversation on a simple shopping trip.

'No. It's not that. I didn't ask him.'

'Why's that then?' Maybe it was an Australian thing, or possibly just an Olly thing, but I'd definitely not been expecting that question. And could I even answer it? Why I hadn't invited Rhys, when Mel had practically insisted that I should, was a big old can of worms that I really didn't want to open right now in the middle of the supermarket.

'Oh, you know. We're still taking things very slowly. We're more just friends, you know. That works best for us right now.'

The laid-back surfer-dude persona, the one that fitted so perfectly with his current attire, melted away and I was left with what I assumed was Olly's serious medical-professional face.

'You do know he's crazy about you, don't you?'

'I . . . I what? No. I mean there's an attraction there – on both sides, that's no big secret but—'

Olly held up a stalling finger, as though I was talking in class and about to get into a whole heap of trouble.

'That's bullshit, Ellie. I've known the guy for years and I know when it's a casual thing for him and when it's something more meaningful.'

I swallowed, not sure what to do or say with that information.

'Well, you know, it's not that straightforward. There's Annalise and—'

Olly suddenly looked remarkably angry.

'Please don't tell me that's what has been holding you back. I don't like speaking ill of a fellow Aussie, but that woman does not deserve him. Not after what she did to him.' He tapped his own chest forcefully. 'I was there when the pieces all got broken. I was there when he finally picked them up again. Do not let her be the reason that nothing has moved on between you two. I've seen him get involved with people, I've even seen him fall in love . . . but I've never seen him like he is about you. Not ever.' He shook his head as though he still found it an entirely incredible phenomenon that needed further investigation. 'This means something to him, Ellie. You mean something.'

'But he's never said anything. The one time I asked where we were heading, he practically did a runner—'

Another warning finger felled me into silence.

'The fact that he's said nothing doesn't mean it isn't how he feels. And remember, he's been burnt before, so it's perfectly understandable that he wants to take things slow. Plus, he probably doesn't want to scare you off. What that says to me is that he's putting your needs ahead of his.'

Olly gave a very Antipodean shrug, as though such a concept was unheard of where he came from.

'Now, do I go for the easy cliché and buy a box of Foster's, or pretend that I've acquired a taste for British-brewed beer?' he asked, in the most abrupt conversational one-eighty I'd ever known. He winked as he reached for an enormous box.

Olly's opinion of how Rhys felt about our situation was just that: Olly's opinion. It didn't mean he was necessarily right. But it certainly cast enough seeds of doubt to make me suddenly wonder if our curious agreement was coming to the end of its natural lifespan.

I'd missed him, not just on his week's holiday with Tasha. I missed him constantly, even in places where he'd never been: on nights out with my friends; sitting beside me on the couch watching TV; in my bed. He was in my head all the time, but that wasn't enough anymore. Maybe it never had been.

'You'd better not tell him I said anything,' Olly said, suddenly realising that he might just have put his size thirteen foot in his mouth. 'He'll have my balls for earrings if I've gone and screwed this up for him.'

This time the hug was of my making. 'Don't worry. You haven't done anything wrong. Far from it, in fact.'

'Bonzer,' Olly said, reaching again for the box of amber nectar. 'Well, I ought to get going. Don't want to miss the last of the rays. It's a lovely evening for a barbie.'

I watched him head towards the checkout and on impulse placed a third bottle of Rhys's favourite wine into my basket. 'It certainly is,' I said softly.

I didn't wait until I got home to make the phone call. I called right there in the supermarket car park, my hands sweaty with nerves as I held my mobile.

'Are you doing anything tonight? Do you have any plans?'

'No.' Rhys's voice felt like a caress in my ear.

We didn't do this. We didn't see each other in the evenings. It was as though there was an unspoken hidden agreement within our original one that meeting after darkness had fallen would be too dangerous, too much of a challenge for our self-control. And from the state of my palms and the tingling excitement that was already thrumming through me, perhaps it had been just as well. But something had happened today, something I hadn't been expecting. The tide had turned, not gently, but with a tsunami-like velocity.

'Mel and Steve are having a barbecue tonight, and I wondered if you'd like to come with me.'

'What time shall I pick you up?'

Chapter Twenty-Eight

The delicious aroma of barbecue was on the wind. Even if I hadn't known the way to Mel's front door like the back of my hand, I would only have had to follow the tantalising airborne trail to find their house.

'This would be a really bad time to tell me you've gone vegan,' I teased, knowing perfectly well that he had not.

'You don't have to worry on that score. I'm still very much a caveman carnivore.'

An image of a Stone Age Rhys popped into my head and my reaction was purely primal. I had no idea why suddenly everything seemed to have sexual undertones, but I was hearing double meanings and hidden innuendoes all over the place. I really hoped Mel had plenty of ice-cold drink on hand, because I definitely needed to cool down.

We walked side by side along the pavement until we reached Mel's house, our shoulders occasionally colliding. It made me miss the guiding hand he usually placed against my back whenever we walked together. But Rhys's arms were filled with flowers for Mel and beers for Steve, while mine carried the bottles of Rioja.

'This is it,' I said unnecessarily, as the noise of the party drifted over the rooftops from the back garden.

'Nice area,' Rhys said, his eyes travelling up and down the street, where every other front lawn seemed to have a child's bike, a swing set, or a football net. 'It looks like a great place to raise a family.' For once I found myself looking at the rows of houses not through the eyes of an estate agent, but through those of a best friend. I crossed my fingers superstitiously and hoped that Mel and Steve's front garden would one day soon match their neighbours'.

As I juggled the bottles of wine in my arms to ring the doorbell, I noticed the speculative expression on Rhys's face had been replaced by one that I hardly ever saw. If I didn't know better, I would have labelled it trepidation.

The familiar Ring chime echoed in the hallway beyond, and out of the corner of my eye I saw Rhys shift his weight from one leg to the other. He was nervous.

'Are you okay?'

He gave a small half laugh. 'I kind of feel like I've been brought home to meet the parents.' He shook his head as though even he couldn't believe he was anxious. 'It feels strange.' He bit his lower lip, which immediately made me want to do exactly the same thing – in a totally different context.

'I guess I just want to make a good impression. I want them to think I'm good enough for you.'

I freed up one hand to give his arm a reassuring squeeze. 'They'll probably end up saying I'm not good enough for you,' I said, only half joking.

It was a conversation I would really have liked to explore further, but I could already hear the heavy tread of footsteps approaching the door. It was flung open with such force it practically bounced on its hinges.

'Ellie,' declared Steve, who was looking decidedly harried and uptight for someone who was meant to be in party mode.

'Hey, Steve,' I said leaning in and giving his cheek a kiss. He smiled vaguely and I saw then that his attention was focused primarily on Rhys.

'You must be Ellie's new bloke,' he said artlessly.

I was too busy feeling mortified to leap in with a correction, and I probably wouldn't have had a chance, because our stressed-out host reached for my date and practically hauled him over the threshold. 'What do you know about gas barbecues, mate? And please don't say "nothing" because I've got thirty hungry neighbours who are about to turn feral if I can't get ours going again.'

More than anything, I loved how Rhys never seemed fazed by the unexpected.

'I know a bit,' he said, allowing himself to be dragged farther into the hallway. 'My friend has one that I've helped him fix a couple of times.'

'Thank God,' said Steve, raising his eyes to the Artex ceiling as though that was where he was most likely to be found. 'I knew Ellie would have a boyfriend with home maintenance skills.'

'He's not my boyfriend,' I said, but I was already talking to their retreating backs.

'I'm stealing him anyway,' Steve sang out as he instructed Rhys to dump the beer and the flowers and follow him.

Before he allowed himself to be press-ganged into action, Rhys turned around and gave me a look that managed to say, Don't worry, I've got this. I don't mind helping. I won't be too long. And I really want to kiss you right now. Okay, maybe the last one was a bit of a stretch, but it didn't hurt to dream, did it?

'You're here!' declared Mel dramatically, as though she'd been about to send out a search party for me. She looked at the empty space beside me and her face fell.

'Didn't Rhys come with you?'

I couldn't help but smile. The people I'd known for years were far more interested in my plus-one than me. Rhys had clearly been worrying about nothing.

'Your husband already kidnapped him at the doorstep,' I said, picking up the flowers that Rhys had left in the hallway. 'These are for you, from him.'

Mel reached for the bouquet with one hand while rummaging in a cupboard for a vase. 'I knew I was going to like him. And if he manages to fix the bloody barbecue, Steve will probably adopt him.'

'What happened to it?' I asked, peering through the open kitchen doors where a group of men were all standing around the broken barbecue, scratching their heads, some literally.

'Halfway through cooking the first load of chicken, it curled up and died. So if Rhys can't figure out what's wrong, I'm about to give half the street salmonella.'

She looked flushed and kind of glowing, with what I assumed was the heat in the kitchen, where Plan B, 'we'll have to cook it in the oven', was about to go into operation.

I glanced once more in the direction of the men in the garden and felt my heart skitter in my chest as I saw Rhys in their midst. He was taller, broader, and altogether more gorgeous than any other male in the group. It was, of course, not an exactly objective opinion, but I was sticking with it.

As if sensing my eyes on him, Rhys suddenly looked my way as he began rolling up the sleeves of his shirt. I gave a totally ridiculous wave and he returned it with a huge grin.

Mel was clearly distracted and doing a piss-poor job of arranging the flowers, so I took them from her. 'Why don't you take a breather? I'll do these for you and then you can put me to work. You look kind of hot and bothered.'

Mel took hold of the neckline of her floaty boho dress and flapped it in an attempt to fan her cleavage, which was looking particularly impressive and in danger of spilling out of the low scooped neck. 'It is rather warm in here.'

With the degree of comfort that you only really know in the homes of your very good friends, I went to her fridge and extracted a can of ice-cold lemonade.

'Sit,' I commanded, proffering the drink, then quickly popping the remaining flowers into what looked like the right gaps. I stepped back to admire my handiwork. It wasn't exactly up to Beth's standard, but it was a pretty good effort for an amateur.

'So why are you and Steve so convinced that Rhys will be able to fix the barbecue?'

Mel looked at me as though out of all the ridiculous questions I had ever asked, that one might pip all the others to be top of the list.

'Because he's an engineer.'

'No, he's not.'

Mel's expression froze somewhere between disbelief and horror.

'Yes, he is.'

I was trying very hard not to laugh, but it was getting harder by the second.

'He's a graphic designer and a pretty amazing artist, but he's definitely not an engineer.'

'Shit!' Mel cried, leaping to her feet. 'Why did he volunteer to fix it then?'

This time there was no holding back my laughter. 'I don't think he did. He was kind of pounced on by your other half.' I threw another look into the garden, where people were passing Rhys various tools. It looked for all the world like a surgical operation. 'But apparently his Australian mate has a fancy barbie, and if he's willing to have a go at fixing yours . . .'

Mel plonked back down on the stool. 'I feel like such an idiot. I don't know how I muddled up engineer with designer. I guess I'm distracted at the moment.' She must have sensed my gaze sharpening. 'You know, what with having this many neighbours round for a party. We've not done it before. I just want everything to go right.'

'It will,' I said, my eyes going to the kitchen table which was overflowing with bottles of wine, Prosecco, and beer. 'You've got enough alcohol to make everything run smoothly, and if all else fails, we'll just get takeaway pizza for everyone.'

Mel looked at me as though I'd just found a cure for cancer. 'I knew you'd come to the rescue.' This time she looked out into the garden. 'Was he that hot the night we met him in the bar?'

I smiled. 'He sure was.'

'Then I commend your excellent taste.'

'Pwah. I didn't get to choose him. The lightning did that.'

Mel rolled her eyes expressively. 'However he came into your life, perhaps this one is worth hanging on to.'

'I worry we're too different. He's nothing like any of the men I've dated before.'

'To use your estate agent language, I think that might be his biggest USP,' Mel said, with best-friend candour. 'He might have some issues . . . but, hon – and I say this with love – you do too. If you both want to make this thing work, don't let him be the one who got away.'

I wanted to tell her that I wouldn't, but nothing about Rhys and me was a foregone conclusion. We were about a million miles away from a happy-ever-after ending, but for the first time I was willing to take that journey.

'I bloody love your boyfriend.' I'm not sure if it was enthusiastic gratitude, or several cans from a six-pack talking, but fifteen minutes later Steve came charging into the kitchen in search of the tray of sausages and burgers. 'He's only gone and fixed it.'

I gave a secret smile. 'Artists do that,' I said, enjoying the private joke that flew straight over Steve's head.

'Now the celebrations can get going properly,' Steve declared, throwing a tea towel over one shoulder with more panache than accuracy. As he bent to pick it up off the floor, I turned my curious gaze to Mel.

'What is it that we're celebrating?'

Her eyes flickered for a moment. 'Oh, nothing in particular,' she said, and I caught a glimpse of the look she shot her husband. 'Just having a party to celebrate summer, you know. Like you do.'

'As long as we all don't have to get naked and dance around some standing stones,' said a voice that was always guaranteed to make me smile.

I leapt to my feet and quickly crossed the room to throw my arms around Jackson's neck.

'That only happens in September,' Mel quipped, smiling at us both. 'We've still got almost a week to go before then.'

'Shame,' Jackson said, releasing me just enough so that he could wind an arm around my waist. 'I think that tall drink of water of a boyfriend you've snagged might look pretty good disrobed.'

'Tall drink of water?' I said, spluttering in the glass of Prosecco that Mel had just poured me. It didn't surprise me at all that she was sticking to lemonade. 'Just what era did you steal that one from? And as for how he looks disrobed, I really wouldn't know.'

In a contest of whose eyebrows rose highest, I think it was a photo finish between Jackson and Steve.

'Honestly, can we all stop thinking about my boyfriend being naked.'

'I thought he wasn't your boyfriend,' all three of them chorused in perfect unison.

'Oh, shut up,' I said, laughing in a way that sounded giddy and light-headed and had absolutely nothing to do with the Prosecco.

'Is my fiancé getting out of hand again?' asked a deep, accented voice.

I looked up and met Lars's amused face. He laid a hand on Jackson's shoulder and my old friend, who had always been practically allergic to PDAs, brushed his cheek against his partner's fingers.

My heart swelled at their happiness. I slipped out of Jackson's arms so that Lars could take my place. Picking up my glass of fizz, I headed towards the doors that led into the garden. I paused before stepping onto the deck and saw Steve come up behind Mel and gently, as though acting with supreme caution, slide his arms around her waist.

I stepped out into the early evening sunshine with a feeling that maybe, just maybe, all of us might be about to get our happy ever after.

'I can't believe they've got you on chef duties,' I said, slipping in beside Rhys at the now fully functioning barbecue. 'How did that happen?'

He gave an easy-going, good-humoured shrug. 'Not entirely sure. Steve was going inside to get the food and asked me to keep an eye on things . . . and here we are.'

Where we were certainly looked impressive, with plates of cooked sausages, drumsticks, and burgers piled up high.

'Would you like me to take over?' I offered.

'Nah, don't worry. I already smell of smoke and cooked pork,' he joked.

'Two of my favourite aromas,' I said, which was meant to be a quip, but came out kind of sexier than I'd intended.

'I'll bear that in mind.'

He patted the low garden wall beside him. 'You can stay and keep me company though, if you like.' I didn't need asking twice and hopped up onto the sun-warmed bricks, feeling their heat beneath the lace of my red sundress. It was a new purchase that had an elaborate cat's cradle of shoestring straps that ran across my shoulders and back. Doing it up was a nightmare, but it was super flattering, and I was defiantly disobeying the rule that redheads shouldn't wear scarlet.

When the cooking was finally done and Mel and Steve had wheeled out half a dozen desserts, Rhys switched off the barbecue.

'It was good of you to do this for them,' I said, getting down from the wall and feeling the third glass of Prosecco affect my balance.

Rhys's arm was there in an instant, his hand going to my waist to steady me.

'I didn't do it for them,' he said, his voice low as he bent down, resting his forehead against mine. 'I did it for you.'

I swallowed and licked my lips nervously. His eyes followed the passage of my tongue and suddenly it wasn't just the wine making me feel unsteady.

Someone had brought out some speakers and hooked them up to a phone. The garden was twinkling with fairy lights which Steve and his friends must have spent hours draping over every tree and bush. It looked like Christmas but felt like summer, and now that the sun had finally slipped below the horizon, there was an air of magic in the garden that was almost palpable.

'Will you dance with me?' Rhys asked as the romantic strains of a popular love song filtered out from the speakers. There were already a few couples on the lawn with a similar idea, but it wouldn't have mattered if we were the only ones there. It certainly felt as if we were when Rhys clasped my hand in his and drew me gently onto the lawn. He was backlit by the moon, the stars, and about a thousand fairy lights as he stared down at me. It was one of those moments that you know you're going to remember forever, regardless of what might happen from this point onwards. And as he pulled me against him and into his arms, that was good enough for now.

Chapter Twenty-Nine

The temperature had been slowly dropping for hours, but I hadn't felt it. Wrapped in Rhys's arms, slow dancing in the moonlight, the cool night air had been incapable of chilling me. We moved in slow circles, swaying against each other, oblivious to the change in tempo when the music got livelier. We probably looked ridiculous slow dancing when everyone around us was doing the Macarena, but we didn't care.

Even when the music had been silenced and the dancing had ended, Rhys still held me close. I was tucked into a me-shaped space at his side as we chatted with Mel's neighbours. When Jackson regaled everyone with an amusing story about his wedding planner, Rhys's hand had been palmed against my hip. When Steve thanked him for his help with the barbecue, Rhys's thumb had traced lazy circles against my pulse point, sending it into overdrive.

Wherever Rhys touched me, my skin felt warmed. If I lived with him, I'd probably never have to pay a single heating bill for the rest of my life. That thought pulled me out of a dangerous fantasy I could easily have spiralled into. My brain was racing ahead into territory it had no business visiting. No one was talking about living together – we weren't even dating. And as for 'forever', well that felt about as distant as the Milky Way.

We said our goodbyes to my friends with a round of hugs, kisses, and handshakes.

'Definitely a keeper,' Mel whispered into my ear as she pulled me in and squeezed me tightly against her. It was something I really hoped we wouldn't be able to do for very much longer.

I pulled away just far enough to let my eyes ask the question that had been on my mind all evening.

She grinned and silently mouthed my two new favourite words in the entire English language.

'False negative.'

I was still beaming when Jackson enveloped me in a hug. His comment, unsurprisingly, was more earthy than Mel's had been. 'Don't fuck this one up, Harker.'

We fell into step as we walked back to his car, Rhys's arm looped casually around my shoulders. It felt so easy, so natural, as though we had walked like this, laughed and danced together, a thousand times before. It made no sense, but then nothing about us ever had. We felt right, meant to be, in a way I'd never experienced or comprehended before. Was this how Henry had felt when he'd first met Bee? If so, I could better understand the lingering sadness I saw in his eyes. The thought of losing someone who made you feel this way was almost too awful to contemplate.

'Do you think I passed the meet the parents test?' Rhys asked, slipping into the driver's seat beside me.

'With flying colours.' I turned towards him with a grin. 'In fact, I think they like you even more than they do me.'

His soft chuckle resonated around the car.

'Only because I flip a mean burger.'

I smiled in the green glow of the dashboard lights.

'Well, that definitely helped, but it was more than that. My friends really like you. I knew they would.'

We were paused at a set of traffic lights on red. It wasn't the place or the time that I'd envisaged dropping my guard, but sometimes you don't pick the moment. The moment picks you.

An amber light clicked on beneath the red.

'I like you too,' I said.

His smile could have melted polar ice caps. It certainly dissolved away the last of my hesitation.

The lights turned green, but Rhys was still looking at me and not the road.

'A lot,' I added softly.

'That's good to know, because I've more-than-liked-you a lot for a long time now.'

It was a special moment, or it would have been if it hadn't been pierced by the strident blare of a car horn from the driver behind us.

Rhys swore softly, put the car in gear, and pulled away with a raised hand of apology. He didn't return it to the steering wheel but captured mine within his grip. We were probably breaking innumerable Highway Code rules as he drove one-handed through the surprisingly busy late-night traffic. I knew the ball was still firmly in my court. He'd given me the power weeks ago to set the pace and the direction of where we were going, and it felt like tonight we'd reached an important fork in the road.

Cars were flashing past us on both sides. His concentration was on the traffic. I probably should have waited, but the words were right there in the back of my throat. I had to set them free or risk losing my nerve.

'I don't want to go slowly.'

His eyes dropped to the speedometer. 'I'm already on the limit for this road.'

'I'm not talking about driving. I mean us.'

He took his eyes off the highway briefly, and I really hoped my face was saying all the things that my voice seemed incapable of doing.

'I know it's late, but I don't want tonight to end yet.'

I saw in silhouette the way he swallowed at that.

'Are you sure, Ellie? We don't need to rush things if you're not ready.'

'Oh God, I'm so ready,' I said on a shaky laugh.

It was good to see him smile even while he was shaking his head in slight disbelief.

'You had to tell me at a time when I can't pull you into my arms and show you exactly how much I've been waiting and dreaming of hearing you say that.'

'Sorry,' I said, not sorry at all because anticipation was fizzing through me more potently than one hundred per cent proof alcohol.

'Should I be driving towards your place or mine?' he asked. We were at the point in the road where we had to decide which way to go, in more ways than one.

'Yours. It's closer,' I said decisively.

My legs felt as though someone had replaced the bones with rubber. And there was a kaleidoscope of butterflies in my stomach, frantically swirling around as though caught in a tornado. This was far from being my first time. I shouldn't be this jittery. I knew what turned-on felt like, but this excitement was raw and primal and unlike anything I'd experienced before.

Outwardly Rhys appeared as calm and controlled as ever as he took my hand and led me across the residents' car park towards his home. But he'd had to jog back to the car to switch off the headlights he'd accidentally left on and had needed three attempts to key in the correct passcode to access the building.

'I've never been this nervous,' Rhys confessed as we waited for the lift to join us in the foyer. 'Not even back when I didn't know what I was doing.'

'It feels different,' I said, so quietly I wasn't even sure he had heard me.

His eyes met mine and there was a fire burning in them that made the breath catch in my throat.

We held out longer than I thought we would. We waited until the doors of the lift had slid to a close before we let the flames consume us. We came together like magnets and his mouth hungrily sought mine, his tongue searching and finding its mate. I pressed up against him, moulding my body to his as his hands gripped my hips, holding me against him in a way that told me exactly how much he wanted me.

He stole the gasp I gave, smuggling it into his mouth as though it was treasure that was his for the taking. Which it was. All of me was.

There was too much of everything. Too many floors to reach his flat, too many steps from the lift to his front door. Too many items to be discarded: his keys, my bag, our shoes. And there were way too many clothes on his body and too many fiddly clasps on mine. I groaned as he kissed me, greedy and impatient for the feel of his skin on mine.

'We should slow this down,' Rhys said, his voice a feral growl.

'No,' I said as my fingers released the second and then the third button of his shirt. 'We can do slow later.' I pressed a kiss on every inch of chest that I exposed, revelling when I felt the pounding of his heart beneath my lips.

He shuddered when I trailed the tip of my tongue down his torso and tried to stop me from going lower, but I resisted the tug as he tried to bring me back to his mouth. Instead, I allowed my knees to do what they'd been in danger of doing since the moment we'd arrived and buckle beneath me.

'Ellie,' Rhys ground out, his voice half warning me to stop, half urging me onwards. His fingers threaded through my hair. Was he holding me there, or hanging on for dear life? I was beyond knowing or caring.

We hadn't made it to his bedroom and were still only in the hallway. The light was dim, coming from a single table lamp he'd left burning, but it was bright enough for me to see the look on his face as my hands went to his zip.

I looked up at him and could no longer tell if the trembling I felt came from him or me. It didn't matter because we were just moments away from being one, and nothing had ever felt so good, so right.

The sound of the zip sliding down was lost beneath his moan. He tightened his fingers in the long strands of my hair, winding the auburn curls around them. He said my name like it was a prayer and it was all I could do not to cry.

'You said you wouldn't take me to bed even if I was down on my knees begging you,' I reminded him, my voice a husky replica of the one I usually used. 'Well, I'm on my knees now. And I'm begging you. I really hope you've changed your mind. Please, Rhys, let me do this.'

His silent nod was all the permission I needed. Later he would take the lead – I knew that, and I didn't doubt for a minute that he would show me a whole new level of pleasure. But this was him at his most vulnerable, most open, allowing me to take control. And as my lips found him and he pressed into me, I knew beyond all doubt that I was ruined for anyone else.

Chapter Thirty

It could have been the morning sunlight that woke me, because no one had spared a thought to closing the shutters when we'd moved from the hallway to his bed. But it was more likely to be the lazy passage of his finger travelling slowly down my spine and then detouring for a pit stop on my hip bone. I smiled into his pillow, which smelled deliciously of him and which I might try to smuggle out of his flat. One night: that was all it had taken for me to become so addicted to Rhys that I was already worrying about how to cope with separation.

I rolled over onto my back, unencumbered by the sheets that were still tangled in a ball by our feet.

I smiled up into the face that was looking down at me with an expression so open, so tender, that I wanted to photograph it and save it forever.

'I woke you,' he said, trying to sound regretful but failing miserably.

'It's a nice way to start the day,' I said, my voice low.

The finger left my hip and journeyed north, skating over every rib it passed and then pausing as it reached the underside of my breast. I drew in a sharp breath.

'I can think of a better way,' Rhys said, his fingers travelling upwards over the soft curve and finding my nipple, which was already erect and waiting for him.

'Again?' I teased softly, seconds before his mouth silenced me with a long, slow kiss.

'I can't seem to get enough of you,' he said, biting gently on my lower lip. 'It could be quite a problem.'

I ran my hands down his back and gripped his hips, pulling him closer.

'No problem here.'

Much later, sated and sleepy, I burrowed my face into the hollow of his shoulder, trying to stifle a yawn, but he saw it and smiled.

'Tired or bored?'

I looked up, my eyes straying to his lips as a kaleidoscope of memories from the previous night flashed through my head. It was no wonder I was tired.

'Definitely not bored,' I said, pressing a kiss against his throat and enjoying the raspy feel of his stubble against my lips. 'And we didn't get much sleep last night.' There wasn't even a hint of complaint in my voice.

'I feel like I ought to apologise,' he said, running his thumb gently across my lips, which were still swollen from his kisses. 'But there's not a single thing about last night that I'd change.'

His fingers left my face and moved into my hair, which was spread out across his pillow. He picked up a strand, winding it over and through his fingers and held it up like a skein of silk. It caught the sunlight, turning the usual russet red into an amber flame.

'I've looked through so many colour charts, trying to find one that matches this,' he said, talking more to himself than me.

'Farrow and Ball probably have one,' I joked.

'I was thinking more of oil paints than emulsion.' He switched his gaze from my hair to my face. 'I'd really like to paint you, Ellie.'

‘Do you mean “like one of your French girls”?’ I said, not sure why I’d gone for a sassy retort rather than a serious one. ‘That’s a line from—’

‘I know where it’s from,’ Rhys said with a smile. ‘And for what it’s worth, there was definitely room for both of them on that door.’

I dissolved into giggles that I tried to smother in his shoulder. I’d never had anyone so in tune with me before that we even shared the same sense of humour. There were differences between us, undoubtedly, but I took comfort in the fact that there were also many areas where we were well matched. I gave a secret smile, knowing I could now add ‘sexually’ to that list. Was that enough? Or was it just enough for now?

‘I suppose if the painting was for your eyes only, that would be okay.’

He tilted my chin with one hand while the other ran down my body, making every nerve ending tingle and my legs want to part.

‘I don’t want to share this with anyone,’ he said.

‘Me neither,’ I said, grazing my fingertips over the Lichtenberg figures on his chest.

‘They’re still there,’ he said reassuringly.

‘And now we’re here . . . sharing your bed.’

He pulled me closer towards him.

‘Finally,’ he said, his voice a husky burr. It was a beautiful moment that I somehow managed to ruin as my stomach growled noisily.

‘Hungry?’

‘Ravenous,’ I said with so much feeling that he laughed.

‘Okay. The fridge is embarrassingly empty, but if you can hold on for twenty minutes, I’ll go out and pick us up some breakfast.’

He was already swinging his legs out of bed and striding across the room. It was rude to stare, but my eyes couldn’t be torn away from the perfection of his body. If anybody deserved to be immortalised in a painting or a sculpture, it was definitely him, rather than me.

'If you keep looking at me like that, I'm going to break my promise to feed you and end up climbing back into bed,' he warned.

'Wouldn't be the worst thing in the world,' I said, trying so hard to sound sultry and totally blowing it when once again my stomach rumbled.

He pulled on joggers and a t-shirt from the drawers of a pine dresser before either of us derailed the plan. After stepping into trainers, Rhys returned to the bed and pressed a quick hard kiss on my mouth.

'Why don't you try to get some sleep while I'm gone?'

I shook my head. 'I think maybe I'll have a shower, if that's okay?'

'Of course it is. There are clean towels in the bathroom cabinet and help yourself to anything you need.' He inclined his head towards the dresser. 'There are some of my t-shirts in the top drawer, if you want to wear something other than your dress.' His eyebrows waggled comically. 'Or you could wear absolutely nothing at all. That would be good too.'

We were both still laughing as he left the room, and moments later I heard the click of the front door closing.

The shower was double size – big enough for two, I couldn't help noticing. I lifted my face to the enormous rainforest head and let the water pour down on me. It seemed like Rhys wasn't the only one who couldn't get enough of us. Maybe I should turn the thermostat down to cold, I wondered, as my fingers worked a thick sudsy lather of shampoo into my hair. It was tantalising to recognise the fragrances he used on my own skin. It felt almost – but not quite – as good as having him in there with me.

You'd think you'd never had sex before, my reflection scathingly pointed out when I cleared a space in the steamed-up bathroom mirror to comb my hair.

I smiled into the glass. It kind of feels like I haven't, or that I've spent the last fifteen years not doing it right.

I looked younger and fresher now the previous night's make-up had been washed away and with my hair hanging in a damp cloak down my back. There was mascara and lip gloss in my bag, but I didn't apply them. I couldn't remember ever wanting someone to see the real me, know the real me, the way I did with him.

With the towel wrapped around me like a sarong, I padded back into Rhys's bedroom and headed for the chest of drawers to borrow something to wear. I let the towel drop to my ankles as I reached for a pale blue t-shirt that looked large enough for me to wear as a dress. The fabric was soft and loose-fitting, and I burrowed my face into its folds, hoping to catch a trace of its owner, but all I could smell was fabric conditioner. My underwear was still scattered somewhere I'd yet to discover, so I slipped the t-shirt on without it. It hung loosely on me and threatened to slip off my shoulder every time I moved, but at least it covered everything that needed covering.

I made my way to the kitchen with the intention of making a much-needed cup of coffee. I'd already opened three wrong cabinets and was no closer to finding where he kept the coffee or mugs when I heard the sound of a key in the front door.

I glanced at the kitchen clock – Rhys had made it back faster than expected. The idea that perhaps he'd wanted to hurry back to me made me smile. It also made me reckless. With a mischievous smile, I went to pull the t-shirt off, already imagining his look of surprise when he found me naked in his kitchen. I don't know what instinct stopped me at the last moment, but I'm eternally grateful for it.

The lightness of the tread gave me a millisecond of warning, but not enough to wipe the look of shock off my face.

'Who the hell are you?' demanded the woman glaring at me.

It was a question I had no need to ask her. Standing before me was Rhys's very beautiful and very angry-looking ex, dangling a set of door keys from her fingers.

In that second every tender memory from the previous night was swept away. Annalise was glaring furiously at the interloper who was standing in what I was suddenly afraid was her kitchen. Had he lied to me about going back to her? People talk about the bottom falling out of their world and it had always sounded overly dramatic, but that is exactly what it felt like as her icy blue eyes raked me from head to bare feet.

Told you he was too good to be true, crowed Old Ellie, whose presence in my head was almost as unwelcome as Annalise's was in the kitchen.

The photographs I'd seen of her hadn't done her justice, and it threw me totally when she said the same of me.

'You're prettier in real life than I thought you'd be.' The way she said the words told me no thank you was required. It wasn't a compliment. 'So, you're Ally,' she said, her voice still glacial.

I almost didn't correct her. 'Ellie, actually.' I cleared my throat uncomfortably. 'I can explain . . .'

She dropped the door keys on the worktop and leant back against it as though this wasn't the most awkward encounter in the world.

'Go on then. This should be interesting.'

'Look, I'm sorry. I never would have . . . It was never my intention to . . . I didn't know that . . .'

Her pretty mouth twisted in a sneer at my inability to finish a sentence.

'English not your first language?' She was like a sniper, picking off easy prey.

'I wouldn't be here if I'd known for a moment that you and Rhys were still—'

'I can't find it anywhere, Mummy.'

It felt like a scene in a farce as yet another member of Rhys's family rushed into the kitchen. But this one I knew.

'Ellie,' cried Tasha with delight, barrelling straight into the toxic situation with blissful innocence.

It certainly didn't help when she ran straight past her mother and launched herself at me, flinging her spindly arms around my waist. Instinctively I hugged her back, which earned me the deadliest stare yet from her mother. If looks could kill, I should be booking the plot alongside my mother.

'You've met my daughter? Rhys actually did that?' Annalise sounded incredulous.

'It wasn't planned. We accidentally bumped into each other in the park,' I told her, not sure if anything I said could make this conversation any better.

'And then we went for ice creams,' added Tasha, which succeeded in making things a great deal worse.

'We have rules about that,' Annalise said, each word dipped in fury.

I frowned. Something wasn't adding up here. If Rhys and Annalise were back together, why weren't any of her clothes in his bedroom, or toiletries in the bathroom? Relief hit me like a hurricane as I realised I'd jumped to the wrong conclusion, something she must surely have known. She just hadn't chosen to correct me.

'You don't live here, do you? You and Rhys aren't back together.' It was a statement rather than a question.

Annalise's mouth tightened. Like a cat with a mouse, she had clearly hoped to toy with me for longer.

'I bought him the t-shirt you're wearing.'

Touché. It was a good comeback.

Tasha, who was currently standing between us like a pint-size referee, was clearly growing bored.

'Have you seen my ballet bag anywhere, Ellie?'

I looked at the smaller, infinitely nicer version of Annalise and gave her a regretful smile. 'I haven't, sweetheart. But I can certainly help you look for it.'

'That won't be necessary,' her mother cut in. 'Why don't you look under the bed in your room, Tash,' she said in an entirely different voice.

My eyes went to her set of keys on the countertop. She and Rhys might not be together, but she still had a key to his home. She obviously felt entitled to come and go whenever she wanted to, and he'd certainly never bothered telling me that. It made me wonder what else I didn't know.

'Look, I know this is all kinds of awkward,' I said, wishing I was wearing something that had less of me on display, and that I hadn't decided to skip on the make-up. 'But I really don't want to make things uncomfortable for Tasha.'

She softened infinitesimally at that. 'At least we're in agreement about that, although I doubt we'll be about much else.'

Beneath the anger, for the first time I glimpsed the hurt. She might not be back with her ex – Rhys had been truthful about that – but that didn't mean she'd given up on hoping it would still happen. I was the fly in the ointment. A big ugly bluebottle standing semi-naked in the kitchen of the man she wanted back.

I surprised her and myself even more when I said, 'Look, I was just about to make myself a coffee. Do you want a cup?'

It wasn't a hard question, but she took a long time before answering it.

'Alright.'

She took way too much pleasure in watching me try yet another two incorrect cupboards before directing me to the right ones. It was a little galling to realise that she was here often enough to know where he kept everything.

'I take it this is something new?' Annalise asked as I placed a cup of coffee in front of her. I wasn't ready to talk about my fledgling relationship with Rhys with anyone, much less his last partner.

'I think that's probably something you should discuss with Rhys.'

'Oh, don't worry,' Annalise said darkly. 'I will.'

We were standing on either side of the breakfast bar, neither of us comfortable enough to pull up a stool and sit down. Annalise eyed me over the rim of her coffee cup, and I wondered what Helen had told her and how that description compared to the reality.

'You're never going to be the most important person in his life; you know that, don't you?'

Her words pierced my flimsy armour, and for a moment I thought she was talking about herself, before her eyes flew down the hallway.

'Tasha will always come first,' she said as though laying down an ace.

'That is absolutely as it should be.' It was good to finally gain a foothold in the confrontation, and I could see my answer had shaken her. 'That was always a given.'

I could see her mentally trying to regroup, perhaps looking for another angle of assault, but she didn't get the chance because at that moment the sound of a key slotting into the door lock was heard again.

'I'm so sorry, the traffic was heavier than I expected,' Rhys said, striding into the kitchen with the biggest smile I'd ever seen. It took less than a second to disappear when he saw I wasn't alone.

'Annalise. What the hell are you doing here?'

'Daddy!' cried Tasha, who'd run back into the kitchen proudly holding the missing ballet bag.

'Hello, pickle,' Rhys said, sweeping his daughter up with one arm and giving her a huge hug.

'I left my ballet bag here and I need it for my lesson tomorrow,' Tasha explained in a delightful lisp that I couldn't remember noticing before. She grinned and I saw that a missing tooth was responsible.

'And you didn't think of calling first?' Rhys asked, his question directed to Annalise. 'You just decided to barge in?'

She had the grace to look uncomfortable. 'Look, we were passing, and I saw your car was missing so I knew you were out. I thought we'd just pop in, get the bag, and be gone. It certainly hadn't been my intention to catch you in flagrante delicto with your latest bit on the side.'

Rhys's expression darkened. 'You're way out of line and you know it.'

'What does "grante-deli" mean?' asked Tasha innocently from her spot in his arms.

No one enlightened her.

Rhys looked down pointedly at the bunch of keys on the worktop. 'This wasn't why I gave you a key. And you know that.'

Annalise bit her lip.

'Well, we have the ballet bag now, so everything is fine,' she said breezily. 'Come on, Tash, say goodbye to Daddy and let's go.'

'Oh, can't we stay and have breakfast with Daddy and Ellie?'

It's hard to know which of the three adults looked most horrified at the suggestion.

'Maybe another time,' Rhys said, giving his daughter a kiss.

'Come on, honey, let's go to the swings like we planned.'

Tasha smiled, easily mollified. The speed with which Annalise had flipped from bunny boiler to kindly mum was fast enough to make my head spin.

Neither Rhys nor I said a word until Annalise and his daughter had left. For a long moment we didn't move. We were so new, so fragile, this could easily destroy everything. He opened his arms, and it would be a long time before I forgot the look of uncertainty in his eyes as he waited to see what I would do next.

I stepped into them like it was the only place I belonged.

'That was not meant to happen. Not ever,' he said, his words whispered into my hair. 'That key was for emergencies.'

'I guessed that,' I said into the fabric of his t-shirt.

He leant back, creating enough space between us so that he could see my face. 'I've only ever been honest with you, Ellie.'

I nodded. I knew that now. I just wished my first instinct hadn't been to mistrust him. He'd been honest about his own trust issues, but it appeared there were still some fairly major ones on my side too.

Chapter Thirty-One

'Those are supposed to be for the customers.'

Jackson paused in the act of biting into an icing-topped cupcake. With a look of pained reluctance, he lowered the confectionery, which now bore a neat indentation of his teeth, and gave a charming shrug that I was willing to bet was one of the reasons Lars had fallen for him. He was kind of hard to resist or stay mad at.

'Well, you might as well have it now,' I said, my eyes going to the counter where several platters of cakes and pastries were set out. I glanced at the clock. Just ten minutes until we officially opened the doors of Florrie's. Flyers had been sent out. There were posters in practically every shop window in the high street, as well as a large ad in the local paper. But there was still every chance that Jackson could end up eating more cake today than he'd ever be able to devour. What if no one showed up?

With that uncanny way she'd always had of knowing exactly what was troubling me, Mel came up and threw an arm around my shoulders and pulled me in for a hug.

'Stop worrying.'

'Who said I was worrying?'

She gave a humph of laughter. 'You're kidding, right? You look as tautly strung as a violin string.'

'And your forehead looks like a before ad for Botox,' added Jackson around a mouthful of sponge cake.

'Not helping,' Mel said, shoving him off towards the counter, which was currently being manned by Beth from Crazy Daisy.

'I'll just go and pay for my cake, shall I?' he said, glancing back over his shoulder. 'What does it cost anyway? There are no prices on anything.'

I exchanged a smile with Mel. It was something we'd discussed almost from our very first conversation about Florrie's. I wanted people to come and spend time here without having to worry about the cost or whether they could afford it. That was why there was a collection tin, rather than a cash register, on the counter.

'Just pay whatever you think it was worth or whatever you can spare,' I said.

Jackson raised his eyebrows and sauntered away.

The shop was ready and as I looked around the premises I wondered if any of the high street establishments were open for business today, because almost every shop owner who'd agreed to be involved in Florrie's was here for its inaugural opening.

Also present was our guest of honour, Christina, Florrie's daughter, who was now on her second round of the room, effusively hugging and thanking everyone for helping to make her mother's dream come true. She'd finally stopped crying when she did so, although seeing the framed photograph of her mum that I'd hung on the wall had set us both off.

'Where on earth did you find this photo?' she'd asked in wonder.

'Rosemary from the tea shop had it on her phone,' I'd told her with a smile, 'and John from the art shop got it framed.'

She'd struggled with her lower lip on hearing that. 'You've all been so incredibly generous, so kind. This is exactly what Mum wanted. I just know it is.'

That had made me happy, because this wasn't my project, it was everyone's. And even though I might have taken on the lion's share of the admin – with a lot of help from Mel – it was a community effort that we were committed to make a success. There was no profit or gain for any of us, except the satisfaction of knowing we were doing a really good thing. And that meant more to me than any commission I could ever have earned from selling the property.

'The artwork looks really cool,' Mel said, stepping up to one of half a dozen framed originals that I'd hung on the freshly painted walls. She studied a charcoal drawing of a windswept beach, one of my personal favourites. 'Rhys is really talented, isn't he?'

'That's what I keep telling him.'

Mel waggled her eyebrows suggestively.

'I meant as an artist,' I said, unable to stop a flush from flooding my cheeks.

'Ellie Harker, are you blushing?'

'No. Well, maybe a little,' I admitted, suddenly flustered. I focused my gaze back to the drawings on the wall. 'One day his pieces will be hung on the walls of a proper gallery, and then everyone will get to see how good he is.'

Another surprised look from Mel.

'What? Now what have I said?'

'Nothing,' Mel replied, trying to button down a smile and failing miserably. 'It's just been a long time since I've seen you giddy about anyone.'

'I'm not giddy,' I denied, turning to straighten up a stack of board games that were positioned on a table. 'I have my feet firmly planted on the floor. See, rock-steady,' I said, and then lost my own argument when I caught sight of a tall dark-haired man with brilliant green eyes striding up to the door and promptly walked straight into a stand of donated paperbacks.

'Sure you are,' said Mel on a laugh, turning away to answer a question from one of the volunteers as I hurried towards the door to let Rhys in.

When I passed the counter, I caught Beth's incredulous face as she looked down at the donation tin, into which Jackson had just dropped two fifty-pound notes.

Perhaps that's why my eyes were sparkling with tears when I slid back the bolt on the door to let Rhys in.

'I thought you weren't going to be able to make it today? That you had meetings this morning?'

'I rescheduled them,' he said, bending down to drop a kiss on my cheek. 'I couldn't miss your big opening.'

'Not just mine,' I said, peering beyond him at the empty street and pulling a worried face. 'But you might have wasted your time as I don't think anyone is going to show up.'

Rhys gave a knowing smile. 'Well, I just passed about a dozen people who were patiently queuing around the corner and most of them were clutching flyers in their hands. So, I don't think that's something you need to worry about.'

I lit up. And yes, some of that was down to Rhys and the way he was looking at me right then, but perhaps even more was because I was so proud of what we'd all achieved.

I looked around the room, smiling at everyone present.

'Everyone ready?' A chorus of yesses and an overly loud whoop and a 'hell yeah' which could only have come from Jackson was the reply.

I turned to the door and flipped the Closed sign to Open.

'Okay then. Let's do this.'

* * *

'How many good memories do you have of Bee?'

Henry paused in the act of deadheading the flowers in front of him and turned to me with a quizzical look. 'Someone once told me that any relationship worth having should have at least four good memories,' I explained. 'I was just wondering how many you had of Bee.'

His face softened, the way I'd noticed it always did whenever he spoke about the woman he loved.

'Four thousand, four million, four to infinity,' he said. He gave a twisted smile. 'I do realise that's not a very scientific answer for a former mathematics teacher, but every memory with her was one to treasure. Every single second.'

I sighed, revealing a longing that I was trying very hard to suppress.

'How many do you have of you and your mother?' Henry asked, flipping the question right back at me.

I drew in a long breath, like a builder who'd been asked to give an estimate for a particularly tricky job.

'Hard to say, really. None that come immediately to mind.'

A glint of steel that I don't think I'd ever seen before flashed momentarily in his eyes.

'Try harder,' he urged. 'There must have been some, even if you have to go way back in the past.'

I was a little taken aback by the unexpected dose of tough love. I could see what he was trying to do here, I just wasn't sure I liked it. Plus, I didn't think that reframing the past was going to be enough to undo too many years of emotional erosion. But I didn't want to refuse, so I cast my mind back, like a fisherman throwing out a net without any hopes of catching anything.

But surprisingly, after a few moments of contemplation, I did.

'Nicholas Pritchard,' I said, in the same tone of voice that I imagine Archimedes employed when he cried out 'Eureka'.

'Nicholas Pritchard. The boy in Year Nine who everybody wanted to go out with, who asked me out on a date, and then stood me up outside the Empire Cinema.'

'Thoughtless swine,' Henry said in mock outrage. 'I'd have given him a week of detention just for being stupid. And then another for being blind.'

I laughed. 'I think he'd done it as a dare. I was kind of geeky back then: train track braces, bad skin, and glasses. Not one of the popular girls.'

'I don't care. It still shows appalling lack of judgement. I bet he'd regret it if he saw you now.'

'You're very kind,' I said, passing him one of the two chilled bottles of water I'd brought with me. It was becoming almost an automatic habit to double up on whatever I was bringing with me to the cemetery. I plucked two apples from the fruit bowl instead of one, ordered two lattes to go from the coffee shop, and picked up two sandwiches from the supermarket shelf. Somehow, without me even realising it, spending time with Henry had become an intrinsic part of visiting my mother's grave. When I looked back on this summer, I knew these memories would be just as strong as those of Rhys and the lightning.

'So where does your mother fit into the Nicholas Pritchard story?' Henry asked.

It felt good to smile when I thought of something my mother had done, and I realised how little I must have done that over the years.

'She didn't tell me I was being stupid when I eventually gave up waiting and walked back home in floods of tears. She was the fiercest feminist I've ever met and yet on that night, when my fragile teenage heart had its first knock, she didn't dismiss the pain of being rejected by a boy I was really into. It was one of the rare moments when I felt she truly understood me.

'She let me cry it out, and I can remember that after I'd got into my pyjamas and crawled into bed, she'd sat down on the armchair in the corner of my room. I asked her if she'd stay with me until I fell asleep.'

'And did she?' Henry asked, his voice hushed as though he was truly invested in this old tale.

I smiled sadly as the memory came back to me with crystal-clear clarity.

'She was still there when I woke up in the morning.'

The tears caught me by surprise, but they weren't ones of sadness.

'That was a good memory,' I said.

Chapter Thirty-Two

'So, you finally told him. It was about time,' Mel said, reaching for the last choux bun on the plate. She shot me a reluctant Do you want this? expression, and I shook my head. I had a feeling if I'd gone for it, I could have ended up with a fork in the back of my hand.

We'd both taken time off work that morning to attend the second fitting for the outfits Jackson had chosen for us to wear at his wedding, which was fast approaching.

'If that dressmaker could only see you now,' I teased.

'I did warn her she'd need to let out the seams again,' Mel said around a mouthful of pastry and cream.

My eyes dropped to the small bump of her belly, and I smiled, loving the person behind it before I'd even met them.

Having demolished the final pastry, Mel delicately patted her lips with a napkin. 'Don't think I didn't notice that you avoided answering me, by the way. How did Rhys take it when you told him about your mum?'

'Better than you did,' I said. 'There was no melodramatic gasping or clutching of the chest in shock.'

'In my defence, I was extremely hormonal when you told me. I still am. You have no idea what this pregnancy business does to you. And as for libido, it's just about off the charts. Steve has started to look very scared at bedtime.'

I laughed.

Mel settled herself more comfortably on the wooden bench in the café booth where we'd stopped for a quick coffee before going back to our respective jobs.

'It went okay with Rhys, though?' Mel asked, returning to the topic like a bloodhound on the scent.

I closed my eyes and the scene from the previous night began playing in my head like a movie reel.

I'd waited over four weeks before telling Rhys, and I still wasn't entirely sure why.

'You'll feel better when there are no secrets between you,' Henry had told me with a look in his eyes that suggested he knew what he was talking about.

'It's just so hard to admit that you haven't been entirely truthful with someone who you lo—' I'd broken off, shocking myself far more than I had my elderly friend, who I suspected knew me quite well by this point. 'Someone who you care about,' I'd amended.

'Secrets can fester,' Henry had told me. 'Nothing you tell that man of yours will make him change his mind about you, but the longer you leave it, the harder it will get.'

Both Jackson and Mel had said exactly the same thing. They'd both been shocked that I'd hidden my mother's death from them for so long, but it hadn't damaged our friendship. So why was I so worried that it might do so with Rhys, that I'd let all of September slip by before I finally found the courage to tell him?

We were having dinner at my place. We alternated between his home and mine on the evenings when we chose not to go out. And

I'd wanted to be on home turf when we had the conversation I had been putting off for far too long.

Perhaps I should have told him all those weeks ago, after Annalise had barged into his flat. But we'd been so new, so caught up in the whirlwind of burgeoning feelings that I hadn't wanted to bring us down. Is lying by omission as bad as just flat-out lying? It was a question I asked myself repeatedly, usually in the middle of the night on the occasions when we didn't share a bed. They were becoming fewer and fewer. Some of my clothes and toiletries had migrated to his flat, and I'd cleared out a drawer for him in my closet. I liked where we were going. I liked the time we spent together, both in and out of bed. I liked the way he spoke about future us, as though it was something that might actually happen.

And I really, really liked the memory of the night when he'd gathered me into his arms, our bodies still hot and sated from making love, when he'd quietly confessed, 'For so long I was scared of ever letting anyone get close enough to hurt me again, but now I know the only thing I should have been scared of was letting the wrong person in.' His voice had dropped until I had to strain to hear the words. 'Thank God it was you I found.'

There was only one thing I didn't like about us, and that was the fact I'd been hiding something from him, lying to cover up something I should have come clean about a long time ago.

'Do you usually spend Christmas with your mother?'

It was a reasonable question for him to ask, but it had come out of nowhere. I dropped the serving spoon onto the table, leaving a trail of pasta sauce. I bought myself a few seconds' thinking time as I retrieved a cloth. It was time. It was past time. Part of me felt terrified, the other part felt relieved.

I cleared up the spill slowly, before lifting my eyes to his.

'We do. There have been times when it was a bit strained, but it always felt wrong not to see her over the holidays.'

He nodded understandingly, an emotion I was afraid was shortly going to evaporate.

'I probably will visit her this Christmas,' I said, choosing my words carefully. 'In fact, I've been visiting her fairly regularly for quite a while now.'

He put down his drink and looked at me with obvious surprise. 'You have? I thought you hadn't heard from her for ages.'

I nodded sadly. 'That too is true.'

I could almost see the wheels turning in his head as he tried to make sense of my conflicting remarks. My lips were suddenly really, really dry. I licked them nervously.

'Isn't her home quite some distance from here?'

I nodded, my thoughts going to the house that I still hadn't been able to bring myself to sell.

'Then how have you been able to visit regularly?'

I drew in a deep breath, readying myself for the disappointment I was convinced I'd see in his eyes. What I'd done wasn't normal, and continuing to lie about it was downright dishonest. And that spoke to my character. I didn't want him to think less of me; I didn't want to dim the warmth I'd got used to seeing in his eyes whenever he looked at me. And I was terribly afraid that when I revealed the truth about my lie, he'd never entirely trust me again.

'My mother is dead, Rhys.'

Whatever answer he'd been expecting, I could tell this wasn't it.

'What? I'm so sorry, Ellie. When did this happen?'

'She got sick last year and passed away after a short battle with cancer . . . nine months ago.'

'What? Why didn't you tell me this before?' His eyes were green pools of confusion.

'Because, I forgot she had died,' I said. The tears I hadn't expected had found the one sentence guaranteed to release them.

'When the lightning struck me, it took away all memory of her illness, her death, the funeral, everything.'

'Oh, Ellie,' Rhys said, pulling me to my feet and gathering me into his arms.

'What kind of shitty, ungrateful daughter forgets that her own mother has died?' I sobbed.

'Hush, hush,' Rhys soothed, his hand running down the back of my head as though settling a petrified animal. 'You are none of those things,' he said. 'Your memory was affected by the lightning, everyone knows that. That wasn't something you could have prevented.'

His arm was around my shoulders, holding me gently against him. But I couldn't relax until he'd heard it all. It was the next most obvious question to ask, and I was ready for it.

'When did you finally remember what had happened?'

I leant back, my eyes still wet as I studied his face, wondering if this was the last moment he would ever look at me with one hundred per cent trust.

'Very soon after the lightning strike. Months and months ago.'

'Why didn't you say anything back then? Why did you continue to talk about her as though she was still alive?'

That was the sixty-four-thousand-dollar question, and I still wasn't sure I knew the answer. Not all of it, anyway.

'Because I blamed myself for the rifts that I had allowed to deepen, for all the times when I could have said, "Hey, Mum, you know what, it doesn't matter." "It's all water under the bridge." And "I still love you."'

I looked up at him sadly. 'I don't think I said any of those things. I can only recall bits and pieces. But I can remember being determined to restore her faith in me. She'd been a tough one to impress, and I really wanted to do that in the time we had left. That's why I started working even harder to make my business a success. I was desperate for her to be proud of me before she died. But I can't remember if she ever said that she was.'

His arms tightened around me. 'I'm sure she was. How could she not be?'

'I was a horrible teenager, Rhys. I blamed her for sending my father away. I was furious with her for not even telling me his name, as though who he was could never be important to me. I didn't see all the things she did for me; I just focused on all the things she didn't.'

'I know I never met your mum,' he said sadly, 'but I do know what it's like to be a parent. There's no rule book to follow. Most of the time you're just winging it. Sometimes you'll get it right, sometimes you won't. But I'm sure that even when you and she were at odds with each other, even when you argued, the love was still there.'

'I felt like I couldn't tell anyone how sad I felt when I eventually remembered losing her, because I'd spent so long acting as though I never really cared. I felt like I'd forfeited the right to grieve for her. So, I hid behind a lie.'

'She would always have known that you cared. Trust me,' Rhys said tenderly.

I gave an inelegant sniff. 'That's what Henry says.'

'Who's Henry?'

'He's a man I met in the cemetery. We've grown quite close over the last few months.'

He took a beat as his trust in me took a second knock in as many minutes.

'Close? As in friends, or is this something I should be worrying about?'

I didn't expect to laugh during this conversation, but I did then.

‘Henry is a lonely old man in his seventies who visits his dead wife Bee’s grave practically every day. He’s kind of taken me under his wing.’

Rhys pulled me close and kissed my forehead. ‘Then I’m very glad you had someone looking out for you while you went through this. I wish it had been me, that you’d felt able to tell me, but I’m glad you found this old chap.’

‘Me too,’ I said solemnly.

Chapter Thirty-Three

It was later than I usually visited, so I wasn't particularly concerned when I didn't run into Henry at the cemetery that afternoon. I'd been playing catch-up for most of the day, trying to recoup the time I'd lost at the dress fitting that morning. And it wasn't as if I saw Henry every time I came, although he was there frequently enough for it to feel strange when our paths didn't cross.

I was probably one of the last visitors of the day and could have had my pick of spaces in the car park, but I swung into the one I'd come to think of as mine. I followed the familiar pathway to my mother's section of the burial grounds, feeling a little disappointed when I didn't see a tall silver-haired septuagenarian somewhere nearby. Although in fairness, I couldn't see anyone else around either.

That didn't bother me in the way it might once have done. If you'd told teenage me, who'd been an avid fan of horror films and Buffy episodes, that one day I'd find a graveyard a comforting and peaceful place, I'd never have believed you. But there was something special about this one. Perhaps because this was where I was learning to look back on so many memories from my past and see them from a different perspective.

The shift in my viewpoint started small. You would have thought hearing snippets of my childhood recollections would have been boring to Henry, but he was far too polite for that. The story of when I'd told Mum, the night before a school play, that I needed a fairy costume for the next day was hardly riveting, but Henry listened with rapt attention. He grinned broadly when I revealed there'd been a gorgeous sparkly dress on the foot of my bed the following morning, in a fabric very much like my mother's one and only good dress . . . a dress I'd actually never seen again after that day.

It was strange how even the things that had once made me cringe now made me smile.

'She embarrassed the hell out of me by running in both the mothers' and the fathers' race on my last junior school sports day.'

Henry chuckled softly at that. 'Oh, I do like the sound of your mother. What a character she must have been. Tell me, did she win either of them?'

'Came first in the mums' race and second in the dads',' I said, feeling suddenly guilty, twenty-five years too late, that I'd been so mortified by her actions I hadn't spoken to her for days.

She'd never been like the other mothers and all I'd ever wanted was to have a normal family like everyone else seemed to, and to fit in.

I was only now starting to realise that I'd spent so much of my youth focusing on every time she hadn't shown up at a school event or parents' evening that I hadn't appreciated how she'd shown up for me in a myriad of other ways.

Of course, there were incidents that still stung, but with the benefit of age, hindsight, and some guiding prompts from a kindly stranger, who'd now become a friend, I realised that neither Mum nor I had been totally right, or totally wrong. I'd been stubborn and unwilling to listen to any viewpoint other than mine . . . but so had she. I gave a sad smile. I'd always thought our similarities were only physical, but as I unlocked the doors to the past, I realised they ran deeper than that.

Sometimes I wondered if I'd ever have made those discoveries alone, without Henry's quiet influence. Maybe, but he'd undoubtedly made it easier. Which was why it was disappointing to have missed him today, because I wanted to let him know that I was no longer hiding from the truth of losing her. Now that Rhys had been told, everyone important to me knew what had happened.

'Hi, Mum,' I said, crouching down beside her plot. A cool breeze rustled through the surrounding trees and I looked up into their branches, fancifully imagining that she was greeting me too.

It was colder today, and I was glad I'd grabbed the thick-knit cardigan from the back seat of my car. September had slipped into October, and it was inevitable the warm weather we'd enjoyed wouldn't last much longer. Would I continue to visit the cemetery this often when the seasons changed? I didn't mind the cold, but I still had issues with storms, and a tendency to panic whenever the TV weather map showed dark grey clouds and lightning bolts. But if I wasn't going to be trapped indoors every time the weather turned squally, that was something I really needed to address.

'I finally told Rhys about you,' I said out loud as I reached for a handful of fallen leaves and twigs that had blown onto Mum's plot and dropped them into the rubbish bag I'd brought with me. There seemed to be more foliage and scraps of litter to clear away than usual, and as I plucked them from between the peonies I'd planted, I noticed the soil was bone-dry. There'd been no rain for weeks, but thanks to Henry and his regular watering regime, everything had been flourishing. Until now.

I cast my mind back, trying to remember how long it had been since my last visit. It had to be at least five days ago, possibly longer, and now that I thought about it, Henry hadn't been here then, either. In fact, when was the last time I'd seen him?

Concern prickled down my spine like a rash.

Looking more closely at Mum's headstone, I noticed there were several weeds poking through the soil. It wasn't Henry's responsibility to keep things tidy for me; he was here for his wife, after all. But whenever I'd tried to dissuade him from helping, he'd always assured me it was no trouble.

'Perhaps he'd just run out of time,' I suggested to Mum, who had no comment to offer.

I filled the watering can from a nearby tap Henry had discovered, but the niggling feeling that something was wrong refused to leave as I watered the peonies. It was still there when I pulled up the handful of weeds, and I couldn't help but wonder if Bee's plot was similarly neglected. Now that would be worrying.

I got to my feet, rubbing the soil and dirt from my hands, and turned my gaze in the direction where Henry always headed when we parted. Shielding my eyes against the last rays of the day, I scanned a seemingly endless horizon of gravestones. Thinking with my feet rather than my head, I strode across the pathway towards the other section of the cemetery. Luckily good sense kicked in before I stepped onto the turf. I'd never accompanied Henry to his wife's plot and had no idea which block was Bee's. I could literally search the rows for hours and still not find it.

'Gates will be closing soon, love,' declared a voice directly behind me, making me jump out of my skin and taking at least ten years off my life expectancy. I spun around to face its owner.

'We lock 'em at dusk,' a ruddy-featured groundsman informed me.

'Oh, okay. Thank you. I'm just going,' I said hurriedly.

'Wouldn't want you to get accidentally locked in.'

'No. Absolutely,' I said, turning to scan the tombstones as though expecting Henry to miraculously pop up from behind one. Although if he had, it would probably have lopped another decade off my life.

'Lost someone, have you?' the groundsman asked intuitively.

'Kind of.'

The groundsman smiled, revealing the gaps where several teeth should have been. 'They'll turn up. Sooner or later we all turn up here.'

◆ ◆ ◆

'It was the creepiest thing ever,' I told Mel, who happened to call me on the drive home, when the incident was still fresh in my head.

'I tell you what is even more spooky,' Mel said. 'What if this Henry guy of yours isn't real?'

'What do you mean, not real? The man carries a bag of Werther's Originals in his pocket and drinks Starbucks coffee when I bring it in.'

'Apparitions can do stuff like that,' said Mel, taking a quantum leap into the twilight zone, her old stomping ground.

'Apparitions? Do you mean like ghosts? Is that what you're saying? That Henry is a ghost?'

'I'm just offering up a perfectly plausible explanation,' Mel said, settling comfortably into the kind of argument that used to occupy us for hours in our student days. 'Think about it. He's always there when you are. He doesn't interact with anyone else. He helped you resolve your feelings about your mum and now that you have, he's mysteriously disappeared. Maybe he's not a ghost at all. Maybe he's an angel.'

'Okay. Hanging up now,' I said, just about managing to stifle my amusement.

'The truth is out there,' Mel said, trying very hard not to laugh herself.

'Sure it is,' I said, as I severed our connection.

'What exactly are you looking for?' Rhys asked me later that evening, shifting slightly on the settee so that I could position my laptop more comfortably on my legs.

'I'm trying to track someone down.'

'Intriguing.' Rhys leant forward to rest his chin on my shoulder, the better to see my screen, where my search bar was still visible.

Retirement homes near me.

'Mel thinks the person I'm looking for is a ghost.'

'Okay. I'm officially hooked now. Do you need the internet or a Ouija board?'

I glanced back over my shoulder and gave him a quick kiss.

'I think the web should do it.'

It would have been all too easy to allow myself to get distracted by Rhys. Lord knows, it never took much for him to take me from nought to sixty. But whatever it was that had ignited the first embers of concern in the cemetery was still quietly smouldering away several hours later.

'Henry, the man I've made friends with at the cemetery, hasn't been there on the last two or three times I've visited.'

'And that's worrying you?' It was a perfectly reasonable question.

I wrinkled my nose. 'I don't know why, exactly. Maybe because he's old and doesn't appear to have any family to worry about him. And after months of seeing him there practically every time I go, it's strange when suddenly he isn't.'

'But he's only been missing a couple of times?'

Rhys was playing the part of devil's advocate extremely well.

'I know. I'm being ridiculous for worrying. I mean, there's probably a hundred good reasons why I haven't seen him. He could be on holiday or have gone somewhere else for a while.'

'Like another astral plane?' Rhys asked, his eyes twinkling.

I gave his shoulder a gentle shove, but he captured my hand and didn't release it.

'You're really concerned about this old chap, aren't you?'

I nodded.

'Okay,' Rhys said, as though he wasn't talking to someone who was making absolutely no sense. He gave my hand a reassuring squeeze before releasing it to pull his mobile from his pocket.

'How can I help? What are we searching for?'

When stripped down like that, I realised how little I knew about Henry or how to find him. I blew out a long breath. 'Well, I know that his name is Henry, although I don't know his surname.'

'Anything else?'

'I know he's a retired mathematics teacher; that he used to live in a bungalow before moving to the retirement place – which he doesn't particularly like. I know he loves gardening and that his wife's name was Bee and that she was the love of his life.'

'That's all we have to go on?'

Rhys would never know how much that 'we' meant to me.

''Fraid so. I don't even know when Bee passed away, although I've always felt it must be quite recent because he still looks and sounds so sad when he talks about losing her.'

'I don't think we can use that as evidence,' Rhys said, running one finger gently down my cheek. 'I don't think I would ever get over losing you.'

For a moment all thoughts of trying to find Henry were set aside as I lost myself in his eyes. We'd grown so much closer over the last few weeks, but we kept dancing around the L word. No one had said it, but there had been times, like now, when it seemed close enough to touch.

Just remember, L is for lightning as well as love, Old Ellie materialised long enough to point out. I did my best to ignore her.

'That's a lovely thing to say,' I whispered.

'It's true,' Rhys said, his eyes turning momentarily sad for something that hadn't even happened. 'Some things are too painful to even think about,' he said softly.

'Well, I'm not planning on going anywhere anytime soon.'

'Ditto,' he said before pulling me in for a kiss, a longer one this time. It was the kind that could easily have spilled over into something more, and I could already feel a very familiar stirring deep inside me. Ironically, it was Rhys who pulled away first.

'Enough of this. We have some cyberstalking to do.'

We split our searches, with me taking the retirement homes and Rhys looking into the gardening and horticultural connection. It took over an hour of scrolling and I think I fell a little bit more in love with Rhys with every passing minute as he trawled through his phone, never once complaining or moaning about searching for someone who probably didn't need to be found anyway.

In the end we located him almost simultaneously.

'I think this might be him,' declared Rhys at almost the same moment as I cried out 'Got him!'

We swapped devices. On Rhys's was an archived article from a local paper about an amateur gardening competition, where first prize had gone to someone called Henry Thatcher, who'd won with his hybrid rose called Bee's Delight.

'I mean, it could be the kind of bee that found its way inside your bra,' Rhys said with a twinkle in his eye. 'But equally, it could be his wife's name. What did you find?'

I'd also found a local newspaper article, but mine concerned the expansion of an exclusive retirement village. Accompanying the article was a grainy photograph showing a ribbon strung across an archway, about to be cut by an official wielding an impossibly large pair of scissors. Behind the satin barrier were a handful of the new wing's occupants, and among them, standing a little to one side and alone, was a familiar silver-haired figure with a smile on his face that looked like it was only going to be there until the camera had flashed.

Chapter Thirty-Four

'Friend or family?' asked the woman behind the reception desk.

For a bizarre moment it reminded me of being asked if you were 'bride or groom?' at a wedding. For an even more bizarre moment I considered lying and saying I was family, in case that made it easier to get in.

To say Freeman Manor was exclusive would be an understatement. The grounds alone explained why Henry chose this as his new home. They were truly spectacular. It was a gardener's paradise. I'd taken a shortcut across the lawn from the car park, panicking halfway across in case I was breaking the rules. It looked like that kind of place. Beneath my feet the grass had been deep and springy, as though below the turf someone had planted a layer of memory foam. I found myself tottering as I walked on the balls of my feet, fearful that my kitten heels would damage Freeman Manor's immaculate lawns and I'd be evicted before I'd even made it to the reception.

'Friend,' I said decisively.

I knew from the home's website that visitors were welcome at any time, but I still felt like an imposter as the woman reached for a sign-in book and visitor's pass.

'Would someone be able to direct me to Henry's apartment? I've not been here before.'

'I know. I've an excellent memory for faces . . . although there is something very familiar about yours.' She lifted a single eyebrow curiously. It was an impressive facial manoeuvre that looked like it must have taken a great deal of practice to perfect. I was a little envious of it, to be honest.

'Actually, I believe you'll find Henry in the conservatory at this time of day. I'll ask one of the carers to show you the way. If you'd just take a seat over there for a moment, someone will be with you shortly.'

I dutifully crossed the foyer to sit on one of the velvet-covered armchairs I'd been directed towards. As the minutes ticked past, I was beginning to regret turning down Rhys's offer to come with me.

'I can easily rearrange my morning,' he assured me, buttering slices of toast for both of us. I liked seeing him in my kitchen on the mornings when he stayed over. It was a novelty that I really didn't think was ever going to wear off.

'That's lovely of you, but I'll be fine on my own.'

He'd abandoned the butter knife and come around the kitchen island to slide his arms around my waist.

'I know that. You're the most capable woman I've ever met. I just wanted you to know that you don't have to do everything alone if you don't want to. If you need someone to lean on, you can lean on me.'

'Same,' I said.

He gave me a kiss that tasted of butter, marmalade, and a promise of tomorrow. It was a sweetly intoxicating combination. My hands slid to his shoulders, revelling in the solidity of him. It was hard to imagine a time when Rhys would ever need to lean on me, but it was a lovely sentiment.

◆ ◆ ◆

After ten minutes a young, cheery-faced carer bounced into the reception to escort me to Henry. I'd spent the intervening time studying my surroundings, noting with interest that everything around me looked expensive. I'd seen enough furniture in my job to recognise the difference between antique and reproduction, and these were definitely the real deal. I knew nothing of Henry's personal circumstances, but clearly being a maths teacher was far more lucrative than I realised, because this place must cost a fortune.

What I hadn't allowed myself time to consider, I realised as I fell into step beside the carer, was how to explain to Henry why I was there. I wanted to make sure you were alright was almost as ludicrous as I wanted to make sure you weren't a guardian angel. Before I could find a solution, the young girl turned one last corner and we came to a stop before the doors of an enormous conservatory. Beyond the glass I could see a room filled with ferns and palms and dotted among them were comfortable armchairs and settees.

My first sweep of the room failed to spot its single occupant, but the girl beside me gave a smile and inclined her head towards the far end of the room, where someone was sitting in a wing armchair reading a newspaper. Protruding above the top of the broadsheet were tufts of silver-coloured hair.

'There he is. In his favourite spot,' she said, frowning as the pager clipped to her uniform suddenly trilled and flashed red. 'Sorry, I need to answer this.'

'That's okay,' I said, my hand already reaching for the door handle. I fixed a smile on my face and made my way across the gleamingly polished wooden floor towards my friend.

'Hello, Henry.'

I'm not sure which of us was the most startled. He dropped his newspaper at the sound of my voice, and my jaw dropped just as fast when I saw the large wound dressing on his forehead. Creeping out from beneath it was a yellow-tinged bruise that didn't stop until it reached his cheekbone.

'Ellie, what are you doing here?' Henry exclaimed, immediately moving as though to stand up.

My eyes took in the tremor in his hands and the walking stick beside his chair.

'Please don't get up,' I said, taking a step towards him, aware that my heart was thudding in my chest. I'd been right. There had been a reason to be concerned. But how on earth had I known it?

'What happened to you, Henry?'

'Gravity,' he said with a rueful smile. 'Well, that and a tiny altercation with a rug and a slippery floor.'

'Oh my God, did you break anything?'

'Bone-wise, happily no,' he replied with his usual acerbic wit. 'But there was a vase on a nearby table that didn't fare so well.' He raised a hand and tapped the covered head wound with his index finger. 'I got this from the table. It's all so silly, really. Just a big fuss over nothing.'

'It looks a little more serious than that, if you don't mind me saying,' I said, my eyes going from the dressing to the bruise, and then to the stick. 'But I'm glad it wasn't any worse.'

Henry nodded sagely. 'It's nowhere near as dramatic as being struck by lightning. You still win with that one.'

I shook my head, but my smile made its first tentative appearance. 'I don't think it's a competition.' I could still vividly remember the look of absolute horror on Henry's face when I'd told him what had happened to Rhys and me.

Without waiting to be asked, I slipped onto the chintz-covered armchair beside him.

'Well, I've answered your question, Ellie, but you still haven't replied to mine. What are you doing here?'

'I came to check you were okay, obviously,' I said, still covertly scanning him for further signs of injury. 'I realised I hadn't seen you at the cemetery for quite a while, and I started to worry that something might have happened. With good cause, as it turns out.'

'You came all this way for a casual acquaintance who you sometimes see at the cemetery?'

I leant closer and placed my hand over his.

'No, I came all this way for a friend who was worryingly absent.'

Something happened then on Henry's face. His eyes grew a little brighter and for just a moment I thought his lower lip might be trembling. But his voice was as measured and calm as ever.

'You are an exceptionally kind and thoughtful young woman, Ellie.' He turned his hand, and just for a moment his fingers gripped mine. 'You are a credit to the woman who raised you. Elizabeth would be very proud of you.'

For once I didn't try to deflect his words or deny them. 'I really hope that's true.'

'I'm absolutely sure of it,' Henry said in a voice that brooked no argument.

This time it was my lip that was in danger of trembling. I drew in a steadying breath and turned my attention to the room we were sitting in.

'This is a beautiful place to come and relax.'

'Hardly any of the residents seem to use it,' Henry said sadly. 'But I like to come here in the morning with a cup of coffee and read the newspaper.'

It sounded like a delightful way to spend his time, and not at all the kind of thing someone who hated living here would say.

'The flowers are amazing,' I said, noticing that on practically every side table a vase was positioned holding a gorgeous display of blooms.

'Ah, those are left over from a recent wedding in the home. Two of our lady residents got married quite recently. It was my first same-sex wedding, and it was really rather beautiful. We all had to wear hats.'

I smiled. No, it definitely didn't sound as though Henry hated it here. A knot of concern that I hadn't even known I was harbouring slowly began to unwind.

'I am so sorry to have worried you and not to have been around to keep an eye on your mother's plot for you. I hope it hasn't grown too unwieldy.'

'That's not something you should be worrying about,' I reminded him for what had to be at least the twentieth time.

'Still, I don't like to leave a job half done.'

'You've taught me well,' I said, extending my hands. 'These fingers are practically green now.' Henry, who could remember when I scarcely knew one end of a trowel from the other, simply smiled.

We spent a very pleasant hour in the conservatory. A woman pushing a trolley came around with tea and coffee, and it was with genuine reluctance that I eventually got to my feet. I would have liked to have stayed longer, but I had afternoon viewings scheduled and needed to go back to work.

'I'll see you at the cemetery as soon as the doctors give me a green light,' Henry promised.

'Don't rush back. Bee will understand why you haven't been able to visit her, I'm sure of it.' I'd heard so many stories about Henry's other half that I felt like I knew her myself.

'As I said before, Ellie, you are a very kind and thoughtful person.'

Impulsively, I bent down and pressed a brief kiss on his cheek. I wasn't sure if that was appropriate, but the softening in Henry's expression made me think it had been a good call.

'I'll take care of things at the cemetery until I see you there again,' I assured him, never knowing that I was going to be seeing him much sooner than that.

Chapter Thirty-Five

It was unusual for me to visit the cemetery twice in quick succession, but there was a special purpose behind my next visit. In a large canvas bag were my gardening tools, gloves, and an exquisite bunch of pale pink roses.

The plan had come to me in the middle of the night, where sometimes bad ideas can seem astonishingly wise. I tested this one out again as dawn broke, and it still seemed sound.

I'd been intending to send Henry a bouquet of flowers as a get-well gift. But my subconscious had conjured up something I thought he'd appreciate even more. I would find his wife's plot, tidy it up if that was needed, and lay some new flowers for her. Then I would photograph it to show Henry, so that he didn't have to worry about it being neglected in his absence. I might even have a little chat with Bee and let her know – in case she was in any doubt – what a lovely man her husband was. I felt sure she'd be pleased to know he'd made a new friend.

A surprisingly full work diary meant I had to wait several days before I could put my plan into action. I often worked on Saturdays, but this week I was letting go of the reins and allowing my new assistant to manage the office without me. Taking on a member of staff had felt like a huge but totally logical move, and Simon was such an easy hire I knew it would have been crazy not to have given him the job. I wasn't the old Ellie anymore, the one who believed she had to do everything alone, that asking or accepting help was a sign of weakness. Sometimes I truly believed getting struck by lightning had been the best thing that had ever happened to me.

'Not only is Simon passionate about learning the estate agency business, but he's super smart at all the technical stuff,' I told Jackson. 'I mean, he's obviously not as good as you,' I backtracked, as I saw my old friend bristle slightly. 'But he's shit-hot on the social media side, which has always been our USP.'

Jackson had nodded wisely. 'That's why I make sure I stay current. It's important to be "down with the kids".'

I tried admirably to silence my snort of laughter, but it got away from me.

'Do they still use that phrase, Grandpa?' I said, giving my old friend an affectionate squeeze.

'Fuck knows,' he replied with a grin. 'Although if you were looking for someone to help you out with the business, I'm a little hurt you didn't ask me.'

Jackson had mentioned weeks ago that when he and Lars sold their respective flats and bought their first home together, he'd like to invest some of his money and time in a growing business. I just hadn't realised he'd been serious.

'Can you imagine you and I working together?' I said, covering up my guilt with a nervous laugh.

'Very easily, actually.'

It wasn't the answer I'd expected, and it had stuck in my head for days.

◆ ◆ ◆

I carefully checked the weather forecast, the way I always did now, before leaving my flat. Rain was predicted for late afternoon, but for now the sun was still valiantly trying to prove the meteorologists wrong.

'Here. Let me take that,' Rhys said, reaching for my bag of gardening tools. I passed him the jute carrier, which he slipped over his shoulder before placing a guiding hand at my back as we walked to his car.

His offer to accompany me to the cemetery had been a surprise. 'Two pairs of eyes are better than one,' he reasoned. 'And you got me intrigued with all that cyber sleuthing the other day.'

He blipped open the car and the boot obediently rose. He stowed my bag in the back beside another bunch of flowers. The roses I'd bought for Bee looked quintessentially British; beautiful but refined. The other bouquet was all exotic tropical blooms in a riot of colours.

'I thought it was only right to bring your mum some flowers the first time I meet her,' Rhys said.

I didn't think it was possible to keep falling in love with the same person over and over again, and yet somehow that was what kept happening to me.

'She'll adore them,' I said softly.

I could feel Rhys's eyes watching me carefully on the walk from the cemetery car park to my mother's plot. It didn't matter how many times I visited – I knew my demeanour changed during my time here. My stride was slower, my eyes more thoughtful, and my smile a little harder to locate.

Rhys held out his hand and as I felt his fingers curl around mine, some of the usual tension began to fade. His own parents were happily still alive, but he was so in tune with me he appeared to know – without me having to say a word – that this bit, before I reached her, was always the hardest.

'Are you okay?'

I gave him a quick nod and a smile that couldn't find my eyes if it was given a map. He took our joined hands and lifted them to his lips, grazing my knuckles with a kiss.

'Thank you for coming today,' I said in a voice that wasn't entirely steady. 'It's been a long time since I introduced a boyfriend to my mum.'

His smile eased the knot in my chest. 'Boyfriend. I don't think I've heard you call me that before.'

For a moment I wondered if I'd taken a huge misstep, crossed a line I hadn't seen, and made him uncomfortable. But then I saw the way his eyes were crinkling at the edges.

'Do you mind?' I asked, feeling tentative.

Another kiss, this one brief and firm on my lips. 'Not at all. Boyfriend is fine for now, until we decide to find another title.'

That one was going to be stuck in my head for the rest of the day, but thinking about its implications would have to wait until later, for we were already at my mother's grave.

I released my hand from Rhys's, and he stayed back as I crossed the grass to bend down beside the granite headstone.

'Hi, Mum,' I said, running my fingertips over the engraving of her name, the way I often did when talking to her. 'I've brought someone with me today. They wanted to meet you.'

I looked back over my shoulder at Rhys, who was waiting patiently to one side, holding the flowers he'd brought for a woman who could no longer smell their exquisite fragrance.

I hadn't really thought through what this moment would be like, but what I hadn't anticipated was how natural and right it felt to introduce the man I loved to the only family I'd ever had.

'It's a pleasure to meet you, Mrs Harker,' Rhys said, not sounding the least bit embarrassed or self-conscious to be having a conversation with a slab of granite.

How did I ever get so lucky to find a man like this? I glanced back at my mother's headstone. She would have loved him in real life, I knew that instinctively.

Rhys bent down beside me, and still sounding completely natural, he laid the flowers he'd brought at the base of Mum's headstone. 'These are for you, Mrs Harker.'

'I think it's probably okay to call her Elizabeth,' I said with a gentle smile.

'Not Liz, or Lizzy?'

I gave a mock shudder. 'God no. She hated it when anyone abbreviated her name. It was one of her pet peeves.'

'Then Elizabeth it is.'

Dark clouds had been slowly building on the drive to the cemetery and were now starting to buddy up in the sky. I glanced up. It looked like the Met Office had been right. Rain was clearly on the way.

'I should probably start searching for Bee's plot before it rains,' I said.

'Do you mind if I take a moment or two with your mum before I join you?' Rhys asked. He must have read the questions in my eyes. 'I can't expect her to approve of me just on your say-so.' His eyes swivelled to my mother's name. 'She needs to form her own opinion as to whether I'm worthy of her daughter.'

'You are,' I said, my voice no more than a whisper. 'Just saying what you did proves it.'

I got to my feet, fumbling a little when I bent to pick up the bag with Bee's roses. As I headed towards the other side of the path, I strained my ears and just managed to hear Rhys's voice carried by the wind.

'Before I say anything else, Elizabeth, it's only right that I tell you that what I feel for Ellie is like nothing I've ever known before.'

◆ ◆ ◆

We'd agreed to search separate sections of the graveyard to maximise our chance of success, messaging each other every fifteen minutes or so to see if either of us had found Bee's plot yet.

I walked up and down the first few rows, trying not to let myself get distracted by the poignant memorials that I couldn't help but read in passing. There were many that could easily have moved me to tears: *Adam, husband and best friend* hit a chord, as did *My beloved Grandmother*.

Had my mother ever secretly longed to be a grandparent? It was a question that simply hadn't occurred to me before now. I tried to summon up an image of her cradling the grandchild she'd never get to know in her arms and was shocked by an unexpected ache of longing for something I'd never wanted. The image haunted me as I went up and down several farther rows of graves.

Grey clouds continued to gather overhead, and when a strong breeze began whipping through the trees and foliage, I knew the rain wouldn't be far behind. The first drops were thick and fat, decorating the concrete walkways with polka-dot splatters.

'Do you want to take a break until it passes?'

It was a perfectly reasonable suggestion, and the fact that I'd had to wipe my phone screen clear of raindrops to read it should have made my answer an easy yes.

Think I'll keep going, I rapidly typed. *But I can meet you back at the car if you like?*

Rhys didn't reply.

The grass had become slippery underfoot, and my trainers skidded more than once as I trudged through puddles. I glanced back across the sea of black and white headstones and saw how far from my mother's plot I'd travelled. Did Henry really walk this far between his wife's resting place and Mum's? It seemed unlikely. A niggling doubt that I'd been trying to ignore was starting to grow more insistent.

The rain began falling with a vengeance and it didn't take long for it to plaster the hair to my head and stick the clothes to my body like a second skin. The moment when I should have abandoned the search for today had clearly been and gone. It was now raining so hard it was difficult to read the names on the grave markers; I could easily miss the one I was searching for.

I straightened at the end of a row, on the point of messaging Rhys, only to see there was no need. Blurred by the deluge, he looked like a mirage as he strode towards me. But the hug as he drew me into his arms certainly felt real enough. He was every bit as wet as me, but whereas I was giving out drowned-rat vibes, he was definitely more Mr-Darcy-coming-out-of-the-lake.

I felt a pang of guilt, knowing he'd only stayed out in the rain because I had.

'I'm done,' I said, looking up into his face and seeing something that looked an awful lot like concern in his eyes.

'Come on, let's get back to the car.' I was right. Something was definitely troubling him. I could hear it in his voice.

With his arm still around me, we ran through the rain to the car park. Raindrops had found a gap between the back of my neck and my hoodie and were trickling down my spine, making me shiver. At least I think that was the reason.

We fell into his car, and I sent a silent apology to his upholstery for my sodden jeans and saturated sweatshirt. The latter at least I could remove, or at least I tried to, until I got stuck in the wet fabric and needed Rhys to tug it over my head. Once done, his hands rested on my ribcage. I could feel the heat of his palms through the thin fabric of my t-shirt. Inches above his fingers, my nipples were sharply outlined from the chill. The fact that his hands never strayed northwards should have alerted me that something was distracting him.

There was a towel on the back seat that he insisted I use first. It wicked most of the water from my hair, even if it did leave me looking more like a scarecrow than a person.

'I don't think we're going to find Bee's grave,' Rhys said carefully.

I nodded. 'No, I think you're right. It's too hard in all this rain.'

He shook his head, and I caught again a strained look on his face before he buried it in the towel that I passed him.

'In fact,' Rhys said, his eyes fixing on mine, 'I know we're not going to find it.'

'How? How do you know that?' My voice sounded hollow in the steamed-up car.

'Because she's not buried here, Ellie. There's no one in the cemetery by the name of Bee Thatcher, or Beatrice Thatcher, or even Beatrix Thatcher.'

'How can you be so sure?'

'I looked on the cemetery website. One of the groundsmen saw me searching and told me that was the easiest way to find anyone buried here. Every single grave is logged. The records go back hundreds of years. I'm sorry, Ellie, but there's no one here by that name.'

It felt like there were wheels in my head, not turning, but spinning on mud trying to find traction.

'There's a record of every single plot?'

Rhys nodded sadly, allowing me to put all the pieces together. I felt stupid and gullible. Why on earth hadn't I thought to check the website? But more importantly, had Henry been lying to me for months? And if so, why?

Rhys was already way ahead of me on that score. 'Has he ever asked you for money?'

Shock bleached all colour from my face.

'You think I'm being scammed?'

Rhys gave a sympathetic but regretful smile. 'It's possible.'

I shook my head. 'No, it can't be that. The place where he lives is ridiculously expensive. He's clearly got money.'

I could tell Rhys was treading carefully. He knew how attached I'd grown to my senior friend and how painful it was to suddenly wonder if I'd been taken for a ride.

'He might be confused,' he suggested generously. 'Perhaps he's suffering from some kind of dementia and genuinely believes everything he has told you.'

It was a solution, but I couldn't fit it comfortably with the man I knew, who had always seemed as sharp as a tack. And if Henry was scamming me, he was very good at it. I'd believed every single story he'd told me about Bee, and yet now that I thought about it, he'd never once shown me a photograph of her. Even if he didn't have a camera on his phone, surely he'd carry pictures of his late wife in his wallet? Why had I never asked to see one?

'I feel really stupid,' I said. 'I thought I was smarter than this.'

'You don't know the whole story yet,' Rhys said, pulling me in for a hug that I really needed right then. 'There might still be a perfectly logical explanation.'

My lips tightened. 'Maybe. But you don't think there is, do you?'

Rhys was very cautious in his choice of words. 'I think Henry Thatcher has some explaining to do.'

He'd wanted to come with me. That hadn't surprised me. But what did was my insistence that I needed to do this alone. I'd bared my soul to Henry, told him things about my mother and me and our troubled history that even Mel didn't know. He'd been a wise and sympathetic sounding board, and even though I no longer understood his motives, I couldn't deny that meeting him, knowing him, had helped me in a way that maybe even years of therapy might never have done.

'Go back to your place. Get some dry clothes,' I said, my hand already on the door handle of his car as soon as he pulled up outside my flat.

'I could come with you. Even if I just stayed in the car?'

I leant across the centre console and pressed a kiss on his lips.

'I'll be fine. Henry might not have been honest with me, but I still believe he's as fond of me as I am of him. I'm not in any danger here. Besides, I think I could take down an injured guy in his seventies if I had to.'

It was totally too soon to have gone for humour. I knew that from the look of concern that flashed through Rhys's green eyes.

One more kiss seemed to help. 'Honestly, Rhys, I'll be okay.'

But now, freshly showered and dressed in dry clothes, I wondered if I was as prepared for this encounter as I'd made out.

As luck would have it, the same receptionist sat behind the desk at Freeman Manor.

'Hello again, Miss Harker,' she said with a cheery smile.

She must have seen my surprise and tapped her temple with a forefinger. 'Never forget a name, never forget a face.'

For one moment I almost asked her if she knew anyone called Bee Thatcher but then thought better of it. The person who had all the answers I needed was just minutes away from telling me what the hell had been going on for the last few months.

Henry was in his apartment, or so the receptionist told me. I must have clearly passed some kind of test, because she simply gave me directions on how to find it, rather than get someone to escort me.

The new apartments were in a different block, but easy enough to find. Henry's was on the second floor and I took my time climbing the stairs, ignoring the lift that would have got me there faster. I still had no idea what I was going to say, but perhaps it was better if I simply let him do the talking.

I heard his voice through the thickness of his apartment door as he responded to my knock.

'I'm coming,' he called out. 'Give me a moment.'

I used the time it took him to reach the door to concentrate on my breathing. By the time I heard the Yale lock being opened, I was almost in control of my nerves.

'Ellie. What an unexpected delight.'

He looked so genuinely happy to see me that I immediately felt guilty that I was being every bit as deceitful as I feared he'd been with me.

'You're walking better,' I said, noting he'd made it to the door without needing to use the stick.

'It was never as bad as it looked,' he said, taking a step backwards into his hallway and beckoning me in. 'Please come in.'

I stepped across the threshold, feeling unsettled. He really didn't seem any different than usual.

'Can I get you something to drink? I could make us both a coffee, although it won't be a patch on the ones you bring to the cemetery.'

I was glad he'd said that, because it brought my focus back to the place where we knew each other best. Or at least I'd thought we had.

'No thanks, Henry.'

Perhaps I wasn't as good at concealing my emotions as I thought, because he was looking at me with a curiosity that hadn't been there when he'd found me on his doorstep.

'Shall we sit down?' I directed, as though I was the host here.

Something stirred in his eyes. Was that guilt or nerves? It was hard to say for sure.

I waited until he was safely seated before I began. I didn't want to be responsible for him tumbling to the ground in shock. I might have been taken for a ride, but the fondness I felt for him hadn't disappeared.

'I bought some pink roses today,' I began.

Henry nodded, encouraging me to continue.

'I asked the florist if she knew of ones called Bee's Delight. But sadly, she didn't.'

All the muscles in Henry's face seemed to have frozen.

'I thought I'd surprise you by laying them on your wife's grave. But guess what? I couldn't find it.'

There was such an expression of regret in Henry's eyes that I hesitated then, unsure if I had the stomach to finish this.

'It turns out there isn't anyone buried in the cemetery called Bee Thatcher. Why is that, Henry? Why couldn't I find your wife's grave?'

The room was silent except for the ticking of a carriage clock on the mantelpiece.

Henry sat up straighter in his chair and carefully folded his hands in his lap. Today they weren't trembling. But mine were.

'Because my wife was never buried. She was cremated and her ashes were scattered on the beach near where she grew up. Caroline always loved the sea.'

'Caroline?' It felt like the room was a fairground ride and what I'd thought was up was suddenly and inexplicably down. 'Who is Caroline?'

His smile looked sad and full of nostalgia. 'Caroline was my wife. We were married for thirty-three years.'

My eyes were darting everywhere as though searching for hidden cameras, because it certainly felt as though I had just been pranked. Big time.

'Then who is—?' I broke off as my eyes travelled past something on an ornate dresser and were then yanked back towards it.

'Why the hell do you have a photograph of my mother? What is going on here?'

◆ ◆ ◆

The picture frame was still in my hands. Henry hadn't asked for it back. He might have had a tug of war on his hands if he had. Beside me on a side table was an empty glass of whiskey. It was a spirit I never drank, but I'd knocked it back when he'd pressed it into my hand. It had burnt all the way down, searing the questions in my throat. At least for now.

I couldn't tear my eyes away from the picture in my hands. It was one I'd never seen before. Mum couldn't have been much older than her early twenties when it was taken. But her youth wasn't the thing that shocked me the most. It was the dancing laughter in her eyes and the unmistakable expression of love that was solely for the person who'd taken the photograph.

'That's the only one I have of her,' Henry said sadly. 'But it captures her perfectly.'

My eyes scoured the image, trying to see any trace of the person I'd known in the features of the carefree young woman. I could find none.

I had so many questions; there was so much that made absolutely no sense, I had no idea where to begin.

'So, if your wife was called Caroline, and you have a photograph of my mother in your possession, where the hell does Bee come into this?'

I didn't apologise for cursing, and I could see he hadn't expected me to.

'That is Bee in your hands,' Henry said, his features softening as his eyes went to the photograph I was holding. 'The only woman I have ever truly loved.'

I doubted that was something his late wife would ever have wanted to hear.

'Bee?' I said, grappling with the first of a thousand questions. 'Why do you call her that?'

His smile wasn't that of an old man, it was that of a man who was so in love – was still so in love – that just the mention of her name could warm his heart.

'She introduced herself as Beth, the very first time we met,' he said, his eyes faraway as though that first meeting was a video that played on a loop through his memories. 'That's what she used to call herself. "Elizabeth isn't me at all," she said. "There's no fun in that name." But in the end, I never called her Beth. She was always Bee to me. It was my nickname for her, and she loved it.'

I had no idea who the person he was describing might be, but she certainly didn't sound like the woman I knew.

'Mum hated nicknames. She never let anyone shorten her name. She said it was lazy; it made her angry.'

Henry looked sad enough to cry. 'I think a great many of the things you've told me about her, the sharp edges, the anger, and the bitterness weren't really her fault.' A single tear escaped, running down his lined cheek. 'They were down to me. There's a place in hell for people like me. I found an angel and then broke her wings. I'm the one who made her the way she was.'

The glass of whiskey had been replaced by a cup of sweet tea that I told him I didn't want, but which, curiously, I appeared to have drained.

'Tell me,' I said, my voice not entirely steady. 'Tell me everything.'

Chapter Thirty-Six

'Let's walk,' said Henry, already getting to his feet and reaching for his stick before I could reply. 'This may take some time, and I think the fresh air will do us both good.'

We rode the lift down to the ground floor in silence while I replayed every single conversation Henry and I had ever had in my head. I was searching for missed clues or dropped hints that this man had known my mother and effectively spent months fooling me into believing a lie.

I wanted to be angry with him. I was angry with him. But there was a new level of sadness in his eyes, as though I'd ripped off a vital protective layer and left him exposed and vulnerable to the power of his memories. He looked like a man facing a firing squad.

There were double doors that led out to the home's expansive grounds and Henry went through them, leaning a little on his stick.

'Are you up to this?' I asked, meaning the walk. The ground was still damp from the rain, and the grass was certain to be slippery.

'Probably not,' he said, deliberately misreading me. We stepped off the paved walkway and onto the damp lawn.

The rain had cleared the air. It felt fresh and cleansing and Henry breathed it in deeply, as though stockpiling its restorative powers.

'Before I say anything, and before you ask the many questions you have every right to do, it's important you know the one thing I have never misled you about is my fondness for you, Ellie. Your friendship has been a highlight I never expected to find this late in my life and if I have damaged that, if I have made you mistrust me, then it will be the second biggest regret in my life.'

It was a question that begged to be asked.

'What is the first?'

'Breaking your mother's heart,' he said simply.

I swallowed uncomfortably.

'I told you the story some weeks ago about how Bee and I had met?'

I nodded, still struggling to superimpose my mother into every story of Bee that Henry had shared with me. He gave a long sigh and his eyes grew nostalgic, and I could almost feel the past tugging him back through the years.

'There were many reasons why Bee and I should never have met.'

'Because you were older than her?' I'd already done the maths and knew he must have been almost twelve years her senior.

Henry inclined his head. 'Yes. There was that too. But that wasn't what I meant. I wasn't supposed to be on the road where I found Bee with a punctured bicycle tyre that day. I was running late for a meeting with the man who was going to employ me for the summer. But I'd taken a wrong turn on the unfamiliar roads and was lost. Like I said, it was fate, pure chance that I was on the wrong road, at the wrong time, and came upon the one woman I was always meant to find.'

There was something in his story that reminded me very much of how Rhys and I had met. Fate had a way of intervening in the most peculiar ways when it wanted two people's paths to cross.

'As you know, Bee flagged me down and within minutes of meeting her, I realised I wasn't lost anymore. I was exactly where I was always meant to be.

'There have been some very difficult moments in my life, Ellie. But falling in love with your mother was one of the easiest things I have ever done.' He turned to me, and there was something different in his face. It was as though the years were melting away and I was now seeing the handsome man my mother had met on a deserted country road on a sunny summer morning.

'Of course, she should never have agreed to get in a car with a total stranger, but she did.' He shook his head. 'That's just the way she was.'

It was absolutely not the way she was when she'd belonged to me and not him, but I was already sucked into his story now. I needed to hear what had happened to them.

'She directed me to the place where I was meeting my new employer. But before hopping out of my car she pressed a folded square of paper into my hand with her address on it. "So you can drop my bike off later".' He tutted softly. 'So foolish to give a man you don't know your home address, but that was your mother. She always looked for the best in everyone. She only saw the good, never the bad.'

Not for the first time I wondered if he had actually muddled up the Elizabeth Harker I knew with someone else. If it hadn't been for the irrefutable evidence of the photograph, I truly wouldn't have believed we were talking about the same person.

'After I was done with my meeting, I drove to her home, that piece of paper clutched in my hand.' His smile emerged. 'I still have it, you know. The ink is faded, you can hardly read it now, but I've carried it with me forever, along with your mother's memory.

'She was waiting for me. She'd packed a picnic lunch for us.'

Mum always hated picnics. She claimed there were too many flies and ants. Apparently, she hadn't always thought that way.

'I think I fell in love with her on that very first day,' Henry said, his eyes looking a little misty. 'She was a whirlwind of fun, laughter, and joy. A unique and remarkable gift of a person.'

'If everything was so perfect, why did you break up?'

Henry had steered us across the immaculate lawns towards a rose garden. We passed beneath an arbour into a secret garden of fragrance and exotic blooms. There were several benches set around a small bubbling fountain.

'Shall we sit?' he asked, sounding suddenly tired, and if I hadn't been so absorbed in his tale, I might have noticed sooner that he was now leaning more heavily on his stick.

We sat at opposite ends of one of the benches.

'I told you there were a great many reasons why I should never have allowed myself to fall in love with Bee. But the greatest is that when I met her, I wasn't a free man.'

'You were already married?' I didn't bother disguising my shock.

'No. Nor was I engaged, but I had known Caroline for almost all my life. Her family and mine were very close. We'd been nudged towards each other by them for years, and we'd eventually settled into a kind of understanding. I'd never proposed, but there was an expectation that was where we were heading.'

'So you led my mother on?' I couldn't keep the icy disapproval from my voice.

Henry's eyes flared wide. 'Absolutely not. I told your mother about Caroline on that very first date. I told her that my life had somehow been heading in the wrong direction, but that I didn't know how to find my way back.

'"If you give me the summer, I'll show you the way," she told me. "Neither you nor Caroline should be with someone who doesn't love you the way you both deserve to be loved."'

Give me the summer. Wasn't that exactly what Rhys had asked of me? The similarities between our two stories were astonishing.

And I was so lost in their love story now, I stopped wondering who the woman was that Henry was describing. I liked her spirit, her unstoppable enthusiasm to grasp happiness wherever you could.

'Long before the summer was over, I knew I was going to break things off with Caroline as soon as she returned from her travels. She'd gone away for the summer, touring with a friend across Europe and beyond. No one had mobiles in those days, and even if we had, I owed it to Caroline to tell her face to face that I'd met someone else.'

'You were going to choose Bee?' Somehow it was easier to keep referring to her like that, rather than calling her Mum.

'I was. Absolutely and emphatically. She was all I ever wanted. That's as true now as it was then.'

'Then what happened?'

'At the end of the best summer of my life, I told your mother I was going back to Devon. I wanted to be there when Caroline got home and to break things off as kindly and gently as I could.'

I looked down and saw that his hands were clenched in his lap, the knuckles showing white through the thin skin.

'There was an accident on the way back from the airport. Caroline's taxi was hit by a huge lorry. Her friend died on impact.' He swallowed several times before he was able to continue. 'Caroline's back was broken, along with virtually every bone in her lower body.'

Suddenly it wasn't just Henry who was finding it difficult to swallow.

'I spent that night and the next by her bedside, and we almost lost her three times. No one was certain if she was going to wake up. But she did. She squeezed my fingers that were wrapped around hers and opened her eyes, and the first words she said to me were: "Thank God you are here. I only came back for you."

'She was paralysed from the waist down, and we knew then that she would spend the rest of her life in a wheelchair. How could I abandon her?'

There were tears streaming down his face and mine too. I was crying for a woman I never knew, and a man who'd been placed in an impossible situation, and lastly for another woman whose heart was going to get broken.

'What did Bee say when you told her what had happened to Caroline?' I asked.

I'd never seen anyone tortured by guilt the way Henry looked as he turned to me then in the peaceful rose garden.

'I never told her.'

I knew my eyes were saucers of disbelief, but I couldn't help it.

'Why on earth not?'

Henry took his time answering, as though the words were scurrying creatures that kept getting away from him.

'I made a judgement call. I wanted your mother to forget all about me, to go on with her life and meet someone new, and I foolishly believed the best and easiest way to achieve that was to tell her that I'd made a mistake; that Caroline was the person I wanted to spend my life with. I thought Bee would recover quicker and less painfully if I severed everything between us, and that hate would be an easier emotion for her to live with than love.'

'You destroyed her with that,' I said, fighting my mother's corner because she no longer could and hadn't been given the chance to when it could have changed everything.

'I made a terrible mistake. I thought I was doing what was best for everyone. But it's a decision I will regret until the day I die.'

I fell silent, my eyes unseeing as I tried to imagine the devastation of losing the man you loved, of feeling that you'd been betrayed by the person you trusted most in the world. Pieces of my mother, the parts I'd never really understood, were now beginning to make sense.

'She must have been heartbroken. She'd been alone, and she'd been—' The truth hurtled towards me out of nowhere, like a train I hadn't seen approaching while I stood on the tracks.

'When was this? What year did this happen?' My words were like bullets fired from a gun.

And there it was on Henry's face; the moment he had been steering this story towards. I didn't need to hear the date. I already knew it.

'Oh my God.'

He nodded slowly, a world of uncertainty in his eyes.

'You're my father, aren't you?'

Chapter Thirty-Seven

'It's like one of those long-lost-family TV shows,' Mel said, blowing her nose so loudly I was glad we were the only ones in the waiting room.

'You're not crying again, are you?' I asked, amazed that the story of discovering Henry was my father still made her teary every single time we spoke about it.

'It's my hormones,' Mel said, which was her go-to reply to everything these days. She lifted the water bottle to her lips and took another enormous swig. 'I swear if they don't call us soon, my bladder is literally going to explode . . . and it won't be pretty.'

She checked her watch for what had to be the tenth time in the last five minutes. 'And if Steve doesn't get here soon, he's going to miss our appointment, for which I will literally kill him.'

'I had no idea pregnancy would bring out such a dark side of your personality,' I teased, trying to distract her from her currently missing husband. 'It's all exploding body parts and homicide with you these days.'

Mel snorted into her water bottle.

'Steve will be here soon,' I reassured her. 'He's probably just got held up in traffic. We'll ask them to wait if he hasn't arrived when they call us in.'

I'd been incredibly touched when Mel had asked if I'd like to go with them for the private 4D pregnancy scan. 'This one is just for fun,' she'd told me, reaching for my hand and squeezing it warmly. 'And I'd really love you to be there when we see his or her face for the first time.'

Mel gave her watch one last scowl.

'Tell me again what happened after you realised Henry was your dad. I love that bit.'

I shook my head, but in a loving rather than despairing way. Mel's expanding waistline made it hard to deny her anything, something she wasn't above exploiting.

'Well, for several minutes I couldn't say anything at all . . .'

◆ ◆ ◆

'You're my father, aren't you?'

The silence stretched, until reality felt gossamer thin. I kept grappling for the right words, but they were as slippery as eels, slithering away before I could formulate a sentence.

And then, while I was still reeling from the revelation, something powerful barrelled through the debris of my memory. Something so immense, so shocking, that if I hadn't been sitting down, it would have knocked me over in its wake.

'Oh my God, we've had this conversation before.'

It wasn't a question; it was an accusation. The lightning was a capricious thief and sometimes it threw back the memories it had stolen from me with absolutely no warning. This was one of those times.

'I found you by her grave, the day after the funeral.' My voice sounded shrill and strident in the quiet beauty of the rose garden.

I smacked my hand against my forehead in a way I didn't think people did in real life. Henry's watery gaze locked with mine, full of regret but also, strangely, with relief.

I closed my eyes as the past unfolded behind them . . .

I'd gone back to work the day after the funeral, because it had always been my sanctuary. But I'd closed the office early and found myself driving to the cemetery. Without a headstone the grave hadn't been easy to find, but eventually I located the neat raw rectangle of flattened soil covered by the flowers I'd asked the funeral director to leave. Mum had always liked flowers.

I must have stood there for half an hour as the sky grew darker and swirling specks of snow began to fall. It was freezing and desolate and I remember thinking how cold Mum must be, lying there in the icy ground. Acting on impulse, I removed my coat and shrugged out of the thick cardigan I was wearing beneath it. I laid it gently onto the earth that covered her.

'Here you go, Mum,' I said, my voice threatening to break.

I strode back to the car park, not sure if the swirling snow or my tears were the reason it was so hard to see. Beside my vehicle once more, I delved into my coat pocket for my keys, only to find it empty. I checked the other pocket. Nothing. Damn it. They must have fallen out when I'd taken my coat off. Snow stung my cheeks like a thousand tiny needles as I hurried back to the graveside to search for my lost car keys.

With my head bowed against the falling snow, I was close to the plot before I noticed someone else was now there. I blinked icy crystals from my lashes, unable to believe what I was seeing. A man was kneeling on the snow-speckled ground beside my mother's grave . . . and cradled in his hands was my cardigan.

Anger like I'd never known before coursed through me. What was this stranger doing? The film of snow on the ground muffled the sound of my heels on the pathway, masking my approach.

'Excuse me,' I said, sounding very British, the way I always did when I was furious.

Perhaps the 'thief' was a homeless person, who needed the warmth of my cardigan even more than my mother did. But I rapidly revised that opinion when the figure on the ground finally realised he was no longer alone. He jumped guiltily to his feet and turned to face me. He was old and distinguished-looking, with silvery white hair. Dressed in an expensive wool coat, with a scarf that looked like cashmere around his neck, he certainly didn't appear homeless. I was so busy cataloguing his appearance it took longer than it should have done for me to notice the man was crying.

The realisation knocked my anger off the boil, and I cleared my throat, trying to remember the manners the woman who lay between us had instilled in me.

'Do you mind if I ask what exactly it is you're doing?'

The old man's eyes were fixed on my face in a way that made me uncomfortable.

'I'm talking to the woman I loved,' he said unguardedly.

I took a step backwards, unsure if I'd made a colossal mistake and had returned to the wrong grave. Except that was my cardigan right there in his hands. One of us might be at the wrong graveside, but it certainly wasn't me.

'I'm sorry, but I think you must be at the wrong plot. This is my mother's grave. Elizabeth Harker. I'm sure she isn't the person you're looking for.'

The old man stared at me for a long moment. He looked weary and worried at the same time. He cleared his throat several times before speaking.

'Actually, she is,' he said carefully, before turning what I'd thought was an innocent mistake into a live grenade. 'Your mother was the love of my life; the woman I should have married, but who I stupidly walked away from.'

For several moments I just stood there, staring back at him in horror and disbelief, shaking my head in denial.

'I'm afraid you've made a terrible mistake. This is my mother's plot, and she is most definitely not the Elizabeth Harker you are looking for.'

Whatever reaction I'd been expecting, it wasn't to see his features soften as he studied my face.

'You look just like her.'

My mouth opened and closed. For the first time in my life, I fully understood the expression lost for words.

The man took advantage of my silence and took a step towards me.

'Your mother is the person I came here to see. And you, of course.'

'Me? Why do you want to see me?' My voice, when I finally found it, sounded about an octave higher than usual.

'Because you are my daughter.'

The words hung in the air, and I was back to shaking my head again, but there was something in his voice that cut through any hope that this man was lying.

'You?' I said, my voice quivering with emotion. 'You're the man who walked away from us thirty-five years ago? Who abandoned us for someone else, someone better?'

The man flinched from my words as though they were knives.

'It was never like that.'

'Then how was it?' I spat back before shaking my head vehemently. 'Do you know what, I don't care. You're over three decades too late. You didn't want either of us back then and we don't want you now.'

The old man staggered backwards as though I'd struck him, and for a moment the red mist cleared enough for me to realise I wasn't acting rationally. Grief and shock were making me behave totally out of character, but I was too far down that road to detour now.

'Whatever it is you're looking for – redemption, forgiveness, or a family reunion, it isn't going to happen. Not now. Not ever.' I'd spent so much of my life longing to know my father, and yet when the moment finally arrived, all I felt was incandescent rage. I spun on my heel and began walking away in angry, scissor-sharp steps.

The man called out to my retreating back. 'I see now this is all too soon. Your grief is still too raw. Please believe me, I never intended for you to find out like this, Ellie.'

I swirled back to face him.

'Don't you dare call me by my name. That was a right you gave up a long time ago.'

◆ ◆ ◆

'Ellie?'

Henry's voice was tentative as it pulled me out of the memory. He'd been crying in the past and was doing so again now.

'You remember,' he said sadly.

For a moment my vision blurred and doubled, superimposing the stranger in the winter coat in the snowy cemetery over the man I knew and cared for. Henry. My friend. My father.

'All these months. All those conversations. You've had a thousand opportunities to tell me who you really were. But you never did.'

'I couldn't.'

My expression hardened. 'Why not? Didn't I deserve the truth? Were you ever going to tell me?'

'Of course I was. I just needed more time.'

'Not good enough, Henry. You had months.'

His head bowed. He looked as though he'd aged twenty years since he opened the door to me earlier.

'You're absolutely right. The truth is, I was scared. It had gone so badly the first time. And your parting words made it perfectly clear you never wanted to see me again.'

Henry gave an old man's humourless laugh. 'Which, ironically, was the exact sentiment of what your mother said to me thirty-five years earlier: "Just know that when you walk away from me now, you lose all right to speak to me ever again." I thought I'd lost all chance of ever making amends with you, Ellie. But I couldn't stay away from Bee. So, I continued to visit the cemetery; I just got to learn your schedule and made sure you never saw me again. And then one Saturday morning I passed you by the gates, and you looked straight at me and just smiled politely. And I knew immediately that you didn't recognise me. You didn't remember who I was. It was as though fate had given me a second chance to do better. To allow you to get to know me, the kind of man I was, and then decide if you want me to be a part of your life.'

I remembered the day he was talking about. 'That's why I thought you looked vaguely familiar the first time our paths crossed. It was because I'd met you before.'

'The lightning didn't just give you another chance . . . it gave me one too,' Henry said, his voice low. 'And I'm ashamed to say I took it.'

A silence fell between us as the wheels in my head spun, looking for traction. Was this the end for us? Or was it a new beginning? If this was the last time I'd ever speak to him, if the betrayal was simply too large to get over, there were still questions I needed answering.

'When did you know about me? When did Mum tell you she was having your baby?'

Henry's face twisted into a mask of pain and regret. 'She never did, Ellie. Bee never let me know.'

'But she always said my father hadn't wanted us. That he'd walked away.'

'That's partly true. I did walk away, but I had no idea what I was leaving behind.' He sounded broken.

'Telling Bee I was going to marry Caroline broke my heart and if I'd have known you were on the way, I think it would have destroyed me.'

'Would it have made a difference?'

It was all so many years ago, it shouldn't still matter, but God help me, it did.

'It would have made all the difference in the world. I would have found a way to be there for you.'

I met his eyes.

'Something changed in Mum when you told her you were choosing Caroline.'

Henry nodded sadly.

'I believe you're right. But I don't blame her. I wish with all my heart I could rewind time and do everything differently.' He hesitated as though uncertain if the ground he was standing on was strong enough to hold him. 'I would have loved to have been your dad. But I think what I've done might have ruined that now.'

Time seemed to slow down. We had reached a pivotal moment in both of our lives.

'Let's just take things one step at a time,' I said hesitantly.

Very slowly, Henry's hand reached out to bridge the gap between us on the bench. In the split second before I allowed mine to be folded in his, I noticed something amazing. For months I'd watched those hands pull up weeds, tend to plants, or wrap themselves around takeaway cups, and I'd never once noticed our hands were practically identical. We shared the same long, tapering fingers – even the nails were similar. I have my father's hands. I let the sentence spool through my head several times, amazed at the comfort it gave me.

The sun had almost slipped beneath the horizon, and the temperature had dropped a further few degrees. We should probably have returned to Henry's apartment long before now, but I think we were both reluctant to leave the sanctuary of the rose garden.

'Your mother made me promise she'd never hear from me again, but there were many times over the years when I almost weakened. If I had, it wouldn't have taken me until now to realise there was a you in this world.'

He gave a sad sigh, and I wondered again why he still didn't appear angry with my mother for not telling him. Because quite frankly, I was still furious with both of them for the lies they'd told each other and for the ones they'd told me.

'It was sheer chance that I came across Bee's obituary in the newspaper.' He gave a twisted smile. 'Or maybe chance had nothing to do with it. Maybe it was fate dealing out one last round of cards. Whatever the reason, I was devastated to learn she had passed away. And then when I read that she'd never married and was survived by a thirty-four-year-old daughter . . .' He gave a shrug that in any other circumstance would have made me smile. 'I'm a maths teacher. I did the sums and knew you were mine.'

He licked his lips, looking suddenly nervous. 'Maybe this is where our journey to get to know each other could actually begin?'

'Maybe it is.'

◆ ◆ ◆

'That's my favourite bit of the story,' Mel declared, reaching for one last tissue.

'Please tell me I haven't missed it.' Steve barrelled through the door of the waiting room, scarlet-faced and sweating profusely. 'I've just run the entire length of the high street after leaping from the bus like a stuntman.'

'Don't panic, Dad,' assured a technician, who with perfect timing had appeared in the waiting room doorway to call us in.

'Dad,' Steve repeated in a kind of dazed wonder. 'No one has ever called me that before.'

'It's kind of amazing, isn't it?' I said, catching Mel's eye and almost tearing up myself.

'Let's go meet your godchild,' she said with a Madonna-like smile.

Chapter Thirty-Eight

I closed the fridge door, pausing the way I did every single time to look at the ultrasound photograph held there with a pineapple-shaped fridge magnet.

'Hello, little one, remember me? I'm your God-mummy,' I said, kissing my fingertips and gently pressing them onto the sepia-coloured face in the photo. 'We're going to have such fun together, you and me.'

I startled guiltily at a sound from the doorway which had made me jump. I looked over my shoulder to find Rhys standing there, leaning against the doorframe with an expression on his face I'd never seen before.

'Okay. I know. I'm officially crazy, talking to my fridge.'

He shook his head, a smile slowly covering his face like a sunrise.

'Not at all. I love how much you already love that little baby.'

I returned his smile. 'You do? I still find it vaguely shocking.'

Rhys shook his head. 'I don't.'

I returned my attention to the contents of my freezer cabinet, grateful for the sudden waft of cool air against my heated cheeks. If Rhys thought me talking to my fridge was peculiar, goodness only knows what he'd have thought if he'd been present at the cemetery the day after Henry's shocking revelation.

But no one had been. I'd deliberately made sure I was at the gates the moment they were unlocked, knowing the conversation I was about to have was best held without an audience.

I walked with purpose towards her plot, my pace only slowing when I was close enough to read the inscription on her headstone.

'Hello, Mum,' I said. 'Or would you prefer it if I called you Bee?'

A frantic fluttering from a nearby tree was followed by a pigeon's hasty exit. I think it was the tone of my voice that had startled it. I don't expect many people sound quite as pissed off as I did right then when they're talking to the people they've lost.

I crouched down beside her marker. 'You've got some explaining to do, young lady.' That at least made me smile, because it was a phrase I'd heard innumerable times during my angry and rebellious teenage years, and it was kind of amusing to be flipping it back to its originator.

'Trust you,' I said with a sigh, 'to make sure I'm still left guessing as to what you were thinking back then.'

A breeze whipped up from nowhere, ruffling my hair and brushing my cheek like a caress. I raised wondering fingers to the skin there and even looked skywards for a second.

'Oh, so now you're sorry, are you?' I shook my head despairingly.

'Honestly, Mum. How can a person be so sharp, so clued-up about practically everything and yet still have got it all so spectacularly wrong?'

There was a long silence, which I fractured with a broken laugh. 'Okay, I guess that one could apply to either of us, now I think about it.'

I ran my fingers over her name etched in the granite.

'So, you never liked being called Elizabeth? Who knew?' My lips twisted into a smile. 'Well, someone did, that's for sure.' I shook my head slowly. 'He really loved you, Mum. He still does. I know Henry broke your heart, but he broke his own too when he left you.'

I lowered myself onto the grass so I was sitting on the dew-damp turf. 'He did a really bad thing all those years ago, but he believed he was doing it for a good reason. You did a bad thing too, not telling him about me, or me about him, but I guess you had our best interests at heart.'

I stroked the icy-cool granite. 'I wish you would at least have trusted me with the truth. Maybe when I first started asking about my father, I was too young to understand, but when I was older it would have helped to explain so much about why you were the way you were. Maybe we'd still have clashed the way we always have done – maybe that's just the way you and I were made. We always were like petrol and flames.' I touched the red of my hair. 'There's a good reason why people like to call us fiery.

'I could spend every day from now until forever being angry with Henry for what he did to you and for having withheld his identity from me for so long. But I think not knowing who he was has actually helped me to see more of the man you fell in love with all those years ago.' A single tear ran down my cheek and plopped soundlessly into my lap. 'I really hope you've been listening in on every conversation he and I have had here, because if you have, you'll know for sure that you found the right man to spend your life with, the right man to be a father to your child. It's fate that's to blame for taking him away from both of us.

'Part of me likes to think that deep down you always knew he was the right one. And maybe you never stopped hoping that one day he'd come back to us.'

Another breeze whistled through the cemetery, and I stopped wondering if I was being fanciful. I just went with it.

'I'll take that as a yes, shall I, Mum?'

I leant closer to the slab of granite and ridiculously lowered my voice to a whisper. 'I understand so much more now. You were hurting for years and years, and without the armour you pulled on every day you'd never have been able to get through life. I understand how much pain you were in and how determined you were to protect me from ever experiencing anything like it. Your methods might have been questionable, but I know you were just trying to make me strong enough to get through life without you.'

More tears coursed down my cheeks. 'I just wish now, when I finally know the truth, that I didn't have to.'

I brushed the tears from my eyes, focusing my gaze on the golden lettering beneath her name.

'I'm not angry anymore. I want you to know that. I spent too much of my life being furious with you; neither of us need for that to carry on in the afterlife as well.

'Thank you, for being my mother and for always wanting the best for me. You did a good job.' I leant in and gently kissed the chilled granite. 'I love you, Mum.'

The trees beside me rustled. That's how I knew she'd heard me.

Things were slowly slotting into place – they had been for weeks. It was as though a puzzle I never thought I would figure out was finally about to be finished. Mel was healthy and happy and positively blooming in pregnancy. Jackson was about to marry the man he adored, and Henry and I were taking the first tentative steps in our new relationship as father and daughter. I gave a satisfied sigh. And then there was Rhys. Always Rhys. The summer was over, the lingering marks left by the lightning had almost faded into oblivion, and yet we were still together. I kept waiting for one of us to point out we'd sailed straight past our expiration date . . . and yet neither of us did.

It had been a practically perfect evening. Later that somehow made it worse. It exacerbated my guilt, so heaven knows what it did to Rhys's. When had things begun to go so tragically wrong?

Had it been when we'd been preparing our evening meal in my kitchen, enjoying the simple pleasure of doing so together? The thought that the drama had been unfolding while I'd been standing at the worktop, wearing only Rhys's t-shirt, while he found one more reason to brush up behind me, was like a spear to my conscience.

'If I lose a finger chopping this carrot, you're going to be one hundred per cent to blame,' I said, arching my neck as he nipped gently at the place where it joined my shoulder, playing havoc with my ability to do anything except melt back against him. The warmth of his bare chest against my back was tantalising, and I knew if I turned in his arms, it would only be minutes before his jeans and the borrowed t-shirt were tugged off again and we'd be stumbling back towards the bedroom, all thoughts of our dinner forgotten.

Had it happened even earlier, while we'd been making love, my half-packed suitcase pushed off the bed and abandoned as he tumbled me back onto the mattress?

'We're going to miss our flight,' I told him as he unhooked my bra and lowered his head to my exposed breast.

'Do you want me to stop?' he asked, passion darkening the green in his eyes to a colour I'd never seen on any paint chart.

'God, no,' I murmured, my fingers already busy on the buckle of his jeans before rubbing my palm against the bulge that was straining against the denim.

I prayed it hadn't been when he'd been inside me, driving me over the edge as I gasped out his name. It would be all kinds of wrong if that had been the moment when his daughter had begun struggling to breathe.

It had been Rhys's idea for us to travel to Scotland three days before Jackson's wedding, which was being held in a genuine castle straight out of the pages of a fairy tale.

'If you can take time away from the agency, we could have a little mini break before the rest of the wedding party arrive,' he suggested.

Old me would have balked at just two days away from the office, let alone five. But she was a ghost who'd been properly exorcised. Learning that a business could still be a success if it didn't consume you 24-7 had been a revelation. Or that you didn't have to devote endless hours to social media to reach people, or that shutting the laptop and saying 'Enough' wasn't a bad thing . . . it was actually really healthy.

'I could do that,' I said, surprising me almost as much as him with my reply. 'Simon is scarily efficient and more than capable of holding the fort. I swear he's better than me at practically everything.'

Rhys had given me a long, slow smile, the crooked one that I really loved. 'Oh, I don't know about that. You have skills Simon could never match.'

I'd blushed then, like the lovestruck idiot I seemed to morph into whenever I was around him these days. I can remember smiling at his reflection in my bathroom mirror. He'd just emerged from the shower, but as he reached for a towel, it wasn't the droplets of water speckled across his chest that had snagged my attention.

'Your marks,' I said, turning towards him and studying his muscled torso. 'They're so faint I can hardly make them out anymore.'

A worried shadow had crossed his face. 'It's just the lighting in here. They're still there.'

I had run my finger over his body, starting at his shoulder and tracing the now indistinct markings all the way down to his heart, where I stopped.

'They're disappearing,' I said sadly.

'Not really,' Rhys said, but I think we'd both known he was lying.

We had seats booked on a late-evening flight to Scotland, and a cab arranged to take us to the airport. Despite getting deliciously sidetracked when a slow, lingering kiss had led to a bedroom detour, my case was finally packed and standing beside his at my front door when we headed to the kitchen.

The stir fry was sizzling happily in the wok, filling the room with spicy aromas that were already making my mouth water.

'It'll be all haggis and black pudding for the next five days,' I teased from my perch on a kitchen stool. He'd lifted me onto it, claiming he needed me on the opposite side of the room when hot food and sizzling oil was present.

'You're too much of a distraction when I'm cooking,' he said. 'I have a real problem keeping my hands off you.'

'Sounds like a good kind of problem to me.'

He laughed softly and shot me a look over his shoulder that stirred me up all over again. I smiled. Whatever the problem was, it appeared to be mutual.

He raised his glass of red wine to me, and I responded in kind with the can of cola I was sipping from. I wasn't always the best air traveller, and it had seemed safer not to have alcohol before flying.

'Just a minute more,' Rhys said, stirring the food and then frowning when his phone trilled from his back pocket.

He took one glance at his screen and that was all I needed to know the map of our evening was about to change. I just didn't realise how dramatically.

Rhys ran his finger across the screen and there was already a tight, concerned expression on his face. I stared at each individual feature, trying to ascertain the nature of the call. The one thing I didn't have to work out was who was calling. Annalise. It had to be. She was the only one capable of making him look the way he did right now. But seconds later, an expression I'd never seen before flashed across his face.

Rhys dropped the spatula as though his fingers had simply forgotten he'd been holding it and walked away from the stove. He was striding towards the hallway, igniting an immediate feeling of déjà vu, because this was exactly what he'd done on the day we'd met when he'd wanted privacy to take Tasha's call. But it wasn't his daughter on the end of the line tonight, it was her mother, and even though Rhys was walking away from me, I'd still been able to hear the distraught sobs coming from the phone pressed to his ear.

I immediately jumped off the stool and followed him. He was striding through my flat as though being pulled magnetically towards the front door. I tentatively touched his arm, but he just kept pacing, like a caged animal.

He was asking questions I recognised from the last time this had happened. But this time the panic on his face was dialling up and not down.

'Slow down, tell me exactly what happened.'

It seemed to take an eternity between gasping sobs before Annalise was coherent enough to relate even half the information he needed.

'Are you in the ambulance now? Where are they taking you?'

He looked around, searching for something to write on, and I was there with a notepad and pen that I'd already plucked up. It was a different hospital from the one he and I had been taken to.

'I don't know where that is, but I'll find it,' he said.

A piercing beeping filtered into the hall. I thought for a moment it was the ambulance siren, then I realised it was coming from the kitchen smoke detector. The room was filled with a haze from the stir fry we'd left abandoned on the hob. Even through the protection of an oven glove, the pan felt red hot. I threw it into the sink, drowning the burnt offerings in a gush of water from the tap.

By the time I'd smacked the smoke detector into silence and thrown open the windows to get rid of the smoke, Rhys had finished on the phone and was back in the kitchen, frantically looking around for the rest of his clothing – some of which I was still wearing. I tugged the t-shirt off and stooped to retrieve his hoodie, thrusting both into his hands.

'I have to go,' he said, looking dazed and distracted.

'Tasha?' I asked, wondering how it was possible for a single word to bear the weight of so much fear.

He nodded and I saw my terror was nothing compared to his.

'She's never had an attack this severe before,' he said, walking in jerky, staccato steps as he began looking for his missing shoes. I took over, finding one beneath my bed and the other behind his suitcase. I think he'd been seconds away from leaving the house barefoot.

'I have to get to the hospital,' he said, each word short and sharp, as though it had been severed from him.

'You do,' I agreed, tugging on leggings and a sweatshirt and ramming my feet into trainers.

He patted down his pockets and pulled out his car keys.

'What are you doing?'

He looked at me as though he genuinely believed I might be trying to stop him from leaving. That hurt.

'Driving to the hospital,' he said, his eyes already going to the door.

'Your car isn't here,' I reminded him gently. 'You left it at yours because it couldn't be parked on my road while we were away.'

Frustration flashed across his face, quickly followed by the solution he'd found.

'Can I take yours?'

'No. You're not driving in the state you're in, and besides you've had a couple of glasses of wine.'

I hated the desperation that was clearly consuming him. I took a deep steadying breath and reached for my own keys.

'I'll drive you there.'

Chapter Thirty-Nine

He ran so fast down my stairs I couldn't keep up with him. It wasn't that he was ignoring me, it was just the overwhelming need to be with his child. I understood that more than I thought I would. We jumped into the car like it was a getaway vehicle, and I rapidly keyed the hospital's name into Google Maps. As I drove, Rhys recounted everything Annalise had managed to convey between sobs.

'Tasha couldn't get any air. Annalise said her lips and finger-nails were turning blue.' He shook his head as though trying to dispel a mental image that I had a feeling was going to haunt him for a long time. 'That's never happened before. It's never been that bad and none of her medication was getting close to easing it. I think Annalise thought she was going to lose her before the ambulance got there.'

I'd already chewed my lower lip hard enough to make it bleed, but that last sentence chilled me to the bone.

'Did she say what triggered it?'

'I'm not sure. The weather has changed, and Tasha is always more prone to flare-ups when it's colder. And she's had a streaming cold this week.'

I felt as though my heart had literally come loose in my chest to plummet within my diaphragm. 'The cold she caught from me?' I asked, my voice small and riddled with guilt.

Something in my tone made him take his eyes from the road for the first time and look my way.

'She could have got it from anywhere: school, Brownies, or just in the air. It's that time of year.'

I shook my head while my right foot unconsciously pressed down a little harder on the accelerator. Whatever Rhys might say, it was impossible not to trace this back to me. Two weeks earlier, I'd been suffering from a lingering streaming cold when Rhys had swung by the agency with Tasha to drop off a client sketch.

His daughter had run across the room to throw her arms around my waist in greeting, something that still delighted me each time she did it. I'd been at the sneezy and coughing stage, still contagious, and even though I'd tried to distance myself, I clearly hadn't been successful.

'She caught it from me,' I repeated, dully. 'I'm the one who made her ill. This is my fault.'

'It's no one's fault,' Rhys said.

But it was.

We drove on in a silence that felt palpable. Every red light, every traffic queue, made his hands tighten into fists on his thighs. When the first hospital signpost appeared, he sat up straighter. We swung onto the hospital property exactly when Google Maps had said we would, but the journey felt like it had taken forever.

'Can you drop me at A and E?' he asked, already unbuckling his seat belt as though even the second it would take to do so once we'd stopped was time he couldn't afford to waste.

'Of course. I'll find the car park and be with you as soon as I can.'

He took his eyes from the approaching hospital entrance to look at me.

'You don't have to come in, Ellie.'

I couldn't tell from those seven words whether he meant I didn't have to, or he didn't want me to. I chose to believe the former.

'I do,' I said in a voice that made it clear this wasn't up for debate.

Rhys replied with a brief nod, and then his hand was on the handle and the passenger door was swinging open even before I came to a stop.

'I hope she's okay,' I called out, but he was already out of the car and running towards the person his world revolved around. My sigh sounded shaky as I pulled away from the kerb to look for the multi-storey.

I burst through the emergency room doors at a run, my eyes immediately going to the rows of chairs. Almost all of them were occupied, but not by the person I was looking for.

I was second in line at the desk, and the agitation of having to wait ramped up my anxiety even further.

'I'mlookingforNatashaDavies,' I said on a rush, forgetting to leave gaps between my words and rendering them almost indecipherable. Perhaps that happened a lot here, because the young man at reception appeared to have no trouble understanding me.

'Are you a relative?'

'Yes,' I lied, without even a twinge of guilt.

'She's still in triage. You'll find the rest of your family there with her.'

I followed his directions, rounded two corners, and then came to a stop so abrupt that the soles of my trainers probably left skid marks on the linoleum.

Standing outside a curtained cubicle were Rhys and Annalise. She was in his arms, sobbing against his shoulder. A wave of pure panic washed over me and for the worst five seconds of my life I thought we'd got there too late. Rhys's face was ashen, and when I looked closer, the arms he had locked around Annalise seemed to be the only thing keeping her upright.

He must have somehow sensed my presence, for he looked up and his eyes found mine. It was a moment I knew I would remember for the rest of my life. He read the worst fears written across my face and answered them with a small reassuring shake of his head. The relief was so great it rocked me on my feet.

I was still struggling to find my missing equilibrium when Annalise realised they were no longer alone in the corridor. She turned in Rhys's arms, and the look she gave me was so full of venom no antidote on the planet could have saved me.

'What's she doing here?'

'Ellie drove me to the hospital,' Rhys replied before I had a chance to defend my presence or apologise for it. I would probably have done both, but I never got the chance as the curtains of the cubicle were pulled aside and a medic in hospital scrubs addressed them.

'Okay, Mum and Dad, you can come back in now.'

Rhys shot a look my way which was too fleeting to interpret as the couple returned to their daughter's bedside.

Even from halfway down the corridor I could hear Annalise, her voice brittle with panic as she fired questions at the doctors. I strained to hear the answers, but they were speaking in low, measured tones, designed not to travel to the ears of outsiders.

And that was what I was here. I was under no illusions about that. This was a family drama, and the two lead roles had both been cast many years ago. I had no part to play. I turned to go, managed three steps, and then pivoted on my heel. I couldn't leave. Not yet. But I wasn't insensitive to what Annalise must be going through. She'd probably be surprised to hear it, but the last thing I wanted to do was make an awful situation even worse.

I found a vacant chair at the end of a row and claimed it. Minutes clicked past, turning into hours. I passed the time deconstructing the plans we'd made, cancelling cabs, flights, and then our hotel reservation. Even if this was another false alarm . . . please let that be what it is . . . there was no way Rhys would want to go away now. It had been the one non-negotiable I'd insisted upon from the very beginning of us: Tasha had to come first. Every single time.

I would have thought it impossible, given where I was and how uncomfortable the waiting room chairs were, but unbelievably, as the department emptied and grew quieter, I actually drifted off to sleep.

I woke with a start to the feel of a hand on my shoulder and jerked out of a dream, disorientated and confused until I looked up and found the one face that could always settle the worst of my panic.

'You're still here,' Rhys said, his voice a mixture of disbelief and gratitude.

It felt like someone had glued my tongue to the roof of my mouth while I slept.

'Of course I'm here,' I said thickly. 'I couldn't leave. How's Tasha?'

He looked bone-shatteringly weary but less distraught than before. I crossed my fingers surreptitiously and hoped it meant the news was good.

'They moved from oxygen therapy to giving her nebulised medication. Her last reading was ninety-six.' He was speaking a language I was unfamiliar with, but the relief in his eyes told me it was all positive news.

'That's good,' I said.

'They're keeping her in though. She'll be going up to PICU shortly so they can keep a close eye on her.' He read the confusion in my eyes. 'Paediatric Intensive Care Unit.'

I hoped I was awake enough not to let my concern show. If Tasha needed intensive care, she still wasn't out of the danger I was certain I'd put her in.

'But she's doing better? She's going to be alright?'

It was a total mix-up of roles. I should be the one reassuring him, not the other way around. But sick children were something I had zero experience of. I could scarcely cope with well ones. I was so out of my depth here, doggy-paddling like crazy and trying not to drown in unfamiliar waters.

'She will be, but I think we're going to need a more effective plan going forward.'

I nodded as though I understood what that would involve. But of course, I had no idea. Maybe that was just as well.

'Rhys?'

Our heads snapped around with perfect synchronicity. Annalise was standing at the entrance to the corridor. She was looking only at Rhys as though if she concentrated hard enough, she could simply pretend I wasn't there.

'They're taking her up now. Are you coming?'

His eyes went to mine.

'Go,' I urged.

Annalise coughed pointedly.

'Please go home, Ellie,' Rhys implored.

'I'm perfectly fine here,' I said, even though every vertebra in my spine was screaming out in protest.

'I don't want to worry about you too,' he said, quietly. 'And I will if you're down here for the rest of the night.'

Insisting on staying was selfish, I could see that. It was for me and not him.

'Okay,' I said, taking his hand and giving it a squeeze. 'I'll go. But keep in touch. You can phone me at any time. It doesn't matter how late it is. I won't be asleep.'

And I kept my word. I stayed awake, bolstered upright in my bed by a mountain of pillows and fuelled with strong black coffee until dawn painted the sky a lighter shade of grey. But Rhys never called.

Chapter Forty

'That has to be the fifth time you've checked your phone in the last hour,' Mel observed from the seat beside me. 'I've a horrible vision that right in the middle of the "I dos" and the "Does anyone here object" you're going to pull out your phone and start checking your WhatsApps.'

'I wouldn't do that,' I said.

She raised one of the eyebrows the make-up artist had just finished defining with a pencil. 'Only because our dresses don't have pockets.'

She made a good point, and I returned my phone to the dressing table to allow the hair stylist to continue trying to persuade my wedding curls to cooperate and fall where they were meant to.

It was hard being so far away from Rhys, so out of the loop, and he was understandably more concerned with helping Tasha and liaising with the doctors than updating me every five minutes. I just felt so helpless being half a country away from him and had to keep reminding myself that this was what he'd wanted me to do.

I hadn't seen him until mid-morning the day after Tasha's emergency hospital admission. He'd left her bedside briefly to go home for a shower and a change of clothes but had swung by my flat first.

He looked exhausted.

'Have you eaten anything? Can I make you some breakfast?'

'No thanks. I want to get back as soon as I can. But I'd love a coffee.'

He drank it scalding hot, as though even the minute or two it would take to cool was time better spent with Tasha.

'Have you spoken to her doctors yet?'

'We're meeting with them later this afternoon.'

He looked sad as he reached for my hand across the breakfast bar. 'I'm so sorry about messing up our plans.'

I silenced him with a finger pressed against his lips. 'Don't give it another thought. We've all the time in the world for mini breaks and holidays. Tasha is the most important thing right now.' A pang of regret crossed the features I'd grown to love. 'And Jackson will totally understand, I'm sure of it.' The pang rearranged itself into an expression of confusion.

'The wedding,' I explained. 'He'll understand why we can't come now. He'll be fine with it.'

'I can't go to the wedding—' Rhys began.

'I know that. Don't worry about it.'

Rhys shook his head. 'I can't go, but you still can. In fact, you have to.'

I stared at him for a long moment as arguments lined up in my head, jostling position to be the first voiced.

'You told me this wedding has been planned with almost military precision?'

'International coups have been organised with less fuss,' I said with a wry smile, thinking about the numerous late-night texts Jackson had sent over the last few weeks beginning with I've had another idea . . . or the laminated list of duties he'd handed to Mel and me. I'd surreptitiously swapped out many of the tasks, giving myself the most arduous ones. But if I wasn't there, Mel would attempt to take them all on herself, however pregnant she was. And I couldn't let her do that.

And what about Jackson? I'd vowed never to let him down again, and I was so close to doing so now it scared me. But leaving Rhys here when his daughter was still so ill felt like a betrayal.

His daughter. His responsibility. His life. And just in case you haven't noticed, he hasn't actually asked you to share any of those, has he? piped up Old Ellie from wherever it was I'd banished her.

I looked up at him with troubled eyes.

Ask me to stay. Ask me to stay and I'll find a way to make it work, I silently implored.

'You have to go,' Rhys reiterated instead.

I nodded sadly in agreement.

'I know you're right. And I do want to be there for Jackson and Mel.' I gave a sad sigh. 'But I also want to be close by in case you need . . .' I paused, not exactly sure what I was offering here.

'You,' said Rhys softly, slipping off the stool and pulling me into his arms. 'I'm always going to need you. But right now, Jackson and Mel need you more.'

'Are you sure?'

I could feel the warmth of his breath ruffling the strands of my hair as he spoke into them.

'I'm sure that I'm going to miss holding you in my arms for the next few days and falling asleep with your head on my chest. I'm sure I'm going to miss seeing how beautiful you look in your Groom's Woman dress and watching you get all sentimental when your best friend says his vows. But I'm also sure there'll be other weddings we'll go to together, perhaps ones that'll be even more special.'

My heart actually forgot to beat for a good ten seconds as one possible meaning behind those words filtered through. I drew back in his arms and saw something in his eyes that could have been a glimpse of a future I'd never dared to dream of.

'But for now the right place for me to be is here with Tasha and Annalise, and yours is in Scotland with Jackson and Mel.'

I'd only seen him once more before I'd left for the wedding. We'd squeezed in a quick meet-up halfway through the afternoon. Tasha had been in hospital for two days by then and was improving enough to start feeling bored.

'I've bought her some books and games,' I said, passing him a huge glossy carrier bag with a large furry cat sticking out the top. 'And something to cuddle,' I added.

'She'll love it,' Rhys said, his eyes warm as he took the bag from me.

'You don't have to say it's from me if that'll make things awkward with Annalise. You can say you bought it.'

'Absolutely not. Annalise is going to have to learn to get over that,' Rhys said firmly, which settled me more than he could ever have known. 'Besides, she's too busy being the most clued-up mother of an asthma patient in the universe to worry about anything else. I swear she must have read every paper in existence on the condition in the last two days.'

I laughed. 'I admire her for that. Tasha's a lucky girl to have parents who love her the way you both do.'

'I think that's possibly the nicest thing anyone has ever said to me,' Rhys said, his eyes molten emeralds. 'Thank you, Ellie.'

◆ ◆ ◆

'Breathe in,' I said, gently trying to persuade Mel's zip to fasten.

'I don't think baby bumps work like that,' Mel grumbled, hands on her hips to persuade the material to give her just another half an inch. Amazingly it took pity on her and I eased the dress closed with a soft purr of the zip.

'You'll probably have to cut me out of it later,' she said with a grin, stepping back to my side so that we could admire our reflections in the floor-length mirror.

'We don't look too shabby,' she said, smoothing down the fabric of the gorgeous silk dress with her hands. She turned ninety degrees and gave a small snort of laughter. 'Well, at least from the front.'

I put my arms around her and gave her as big a hug as my godchild would allow.

'You have never looked more beautiful,' I whispered.

'Well, that's gone and done it,' she said, stepping out of my hold and reaching for a tissue to dab at her now watering eyes. 'I told you not to be nice to me. Weddings always make me cry.'

I had a feeling they might do just that to me later.

I'd been feeling emotional ever since Jackson had pulled me aside the previous day to ask if I'd mind looking over the speech he was intending to give at the reception.

'You've always been good at that kind of thing, and I'd really appreciate your input on what I've written.'

'Can I edit out all the four-letter words?' I teased, secretly touched that I was the one he trusted enough to vet his speech.

'No, definitely not. They all have to stay,' he said with a wink, passing me his laptop.

I was teary-eyed before I was even halfway through. By the time I closed the document and passed the laptop back, I'd needed three tissues to mop up the mess he'd made of my mascara.

'That is absolutely perfect, Jackson. There isn't a single word I think you should change.'

The speech was an open love letter to his partner and a glimpse into my friend's heart. And he certainly hadn't pulled any punches.

'That bit about how you'd known the moment you first met Lars that he was the one you wanted to grow old with . . .' I said, my voice still wobbly with emotion. 'And how sometimes, when you least expect it, lightning strikes—'

'Ah, I thought you'd like that bit.'

I smiled. 'That's how you really feel, isn't it?' I don't know why there was a question mark on the end of that, because the speech made Jackson's feelings crystal clear. 'It really can be a love that will last, can't it? However fast you fall? That doesn't mean it's only infatuation or a fling?'

'Are you asking me, or telling me?' Jackson said, fixing me with a gaze that saw right through me.

'Telling you,' I said softly.

But this morning I'd woken up to a maelstrom of niggling worries. There'd been something distant in Rhys's messages the previous day. I'd spent the entire rehearsal dinner on edge trying to decipher what was bothering me. He was saying all the right things, but something was missing. Something was different and I couldn't put my finger on it.

'Perhaps he's worried about what will happen when Tasha is discharged,' Mel had suggested, which was certainly a possibility. The doctors had been hopeful that she could go home after one more night in hospital. 'It's bound to be tough for him not being with her, after spending so many days right beside her.'

'Perhaps he'll stay over at Annalise's place for the first night or two,' Steve had innocently suggested. He seemed oblivious to the death stare his wife shot him across the rehearsal dinner table.

'What? What did I say?'

'Too much,' muttered Mel.

'Nothing that wasn't already going through my head,' I assured him with a rueful expression.

Later, in the hotel bar when guests had begun peeling off to bed in preparation for the big day, Mel had swooped down to give me a kiss and caught sight of the internet page displayed on my phone screen.

She pulled the mobile from my hand in the way only a best friend has the nerve to do.

'Flights to London?' she said, rapidly scrolling down the page I'd been studying. 'You're going back down?' She turned to look over her shoulder and threw Steve a meaningful glare. 'This is your fault.'

'No, it isn't. I was just looking . . .'

'There's a flight in your basket.'

My cheeks heated up. 'I was just looking at the prices, that's all.'

'Prices for what?' Jackson asked, sauntering up with a swaying gait that suggested he'd enjoyed quite a few glasses of the excellent champagne that had been flowing.

'Ellie is worrying that something is wrong with Rhys and she's thinking of doing a runner from the wedding.'

'No, she's not,' I insisted, giving my friend a warning glare. The last thing Jackson needed to worry about was me going AWOL before all my duties had been carried out.

'Good,' declared Jackson, collapsing onto an elaborate brocade armchair beside me. 'Because it's the bride or the groom who's meant to be a runaway, not the Groom's Woman.'

'Not going anywhere,' I assured him, swiping the phone out of Mel's hand. I tapped the icon that emptied the basket and showed them both the screen. 'I promise I'm here for the wedding, and the post-wedding breakfast the next day. In fact, I might just be the very last guest to check out. How's that?'

Their laughter went a long way to assuage the guilt I felt about wanting to go home, but nothing was going to silence the niggling concern that something was wrong until I got to see Rhys again.

◆ ◆ ◆

It was a gorgeous wedding. Jackson and Lars looked equally handsome in their matching ivory suits. They exchanged their vows before a magnificent floor-to-ceiling stained-glass window, which threw jewelled fractals over them as they declared their love and promises to be there for each other for the rest of their days.

There were very few dry eyes in the house when the celebrant finally declared them husband and husband. Mine certainly weren't.

After being caught out in the bar the night before, I was determined to be the very best Groom's Woman imaginable. I circulated among the guests, introducing people to each other, ensured the catering staff were doing everything Jackson and Lars wanted, and that everything ran smoothly.

When they took to the floor for their perfectly rehearsed version of '(I've Had) The Time of My Life', thankfully minus the lift, I filmed the guests and their reactions, knowing the videographer would be able to splice it into his recording.

I did double duty on the dance floor, because by that point I knew Mel was just about done and had secretly kicked off her shoes. I did two rounds of the floor with both of Lars's uncles, neither of whom could speak a word of English, and then did even more with Jackson's slightly geeky nephew, who appeared to have taken quite a shine to me.

'Cutting in now, Neil, I'm afraid,' Jackson said, rescuing me from his nephew's slightly sweaty-handed grip.

He swirled me around three times, edging us closer and closer to the arched entrance to the room with each rotation.

'Thank you for taking Neil under your wing. He's at that awkward, gangly teenage phase.'

'He's very sweet. Reminds me of you in many ways,' I teased.

'The nerd gene runs deep in my family,' he said, shooting a huge beam at his new husband, who was deep in conversation with someone's grandmother. Lars grinned back and gave him a thumbs-up.

One more rotation and Jackson had swept me clean out of the room and into the medieval foyer of the castle. He released me from his arms, and I saw that Mel was already there, waiting.

In her hands was something that looked very much like my coat.

'Are you going somewhere?' I asked, confused.

She shook her head, the curls bouncing with the movement.

'No. You are.'

I looked from her to Jackson and there was an expression of shared mischief in their eyes.

'Your taxi is ticking over outside. I've put your suitcase in the back,' said Steve, striding up to join us and throwing his arm around his wife's shoulders.

'What's going on here? I don't understand.'

'You're leaving. You're booked on the ten-thirty flight home. It's going to be tight for time, so you'd better get a wiggle on,' said Jackson.

'But my things . . .' I began.

'All packed,' Mel said with a satisfied smirk.

'My hotel bill . . .'

'Settled,' Jackson said. He stepped closer and enveloped me in a hug. 'You're done, Harker. You're off the clock. Go fly back home to your man and set your mind at rest.'

I looked from one friend to the other, wondering how I got so lucky to deserve these people in my life.

'I can't believe you've done this for me.'

'I can't believe you're not in the taxi; the meter is running, you know,' joked Steve, earning himself an elbow jab in the ribs from his wife.

'I was such a bad friend to you both. I neglected you. I shut you out.'

'Oh, my God. Enough about that already,' Jackson declared dramatically. 'You were focused on your mum and making things right with her in the time you had left. We get it. A friend is someone you can ignore without them feeling ignored. That's right, Mel, isn't it?'

'Absolutely,' my friend said, throwing her arms around me in an enormous hug.

'Now get out of here before that extortionately priced airplane ticket goes to waste.'

Chapter Forty-One

Watery autumn sunlight filtered through the trees outside the kitchen window, making an abstract pattern of shadows dance across the breakfast bar. My eyes followed them, trying not to count the minutes it was taking Rhys to reply to my message. I was used to the immediacy of his response and the delay was making me nervous.

He might still be at the hospital, I reasoned, even though he'd sounded sure Tasha would be discharged the previous day. Maybe he's somewhere with no signal, or maybe his phone is dead, or he's lost it.

Pretty sure the only thing lost around here is your good sense, a snarky version of me interjected. I ignored her and spent the next fifteen minutes watching the hands of the clock move. When it gets to ten o'clock, I'll call him, I bargained with my conscience. Perhaps Rhys had been having the exact same conversation with his own, because before I had the chance to make the call, the phone rang in my hand, startling me enough to make me drop it onto the kitchen countertop.

I sounded every bit as anxious as I felt when I picked up the call. 'Hello, Ellie.'

His voice should have calmed me the way it always did, but today my nerves were strung taut, like tripwires.

'Hey, you,' I said.

'You came back early.'

There was definitely something weird in his voice.

'I did. How's Tasha? Is she home yet?'

'Yes, she is.' There was understandable relief in his reply. 'She's doing so much better.'

'That's wonderful,' I said. And it was. But I couldn't help thinking we were both standing beside an unexploded bomb.

'Is something else wrong, Rhys?'

Time seemed to stand still while I waited for him to answer with what I'd hoped would be an easy no. The birds outside my window ceased their chirping, the traffic stopped rumbling down the street, and my lungs forgot how to draw in my next breath.

Even though I'd been half expecting them, when they came, the words scythed me to the ground.

'I think we need to talk.'

In a moment of insanity, I considered hanging up on him, because if he couldn't say it, then none of this could be happening, none of this could be true.

'Okay,' I said, my voice decidedly shaky. 'What's on your mind?'

I heard his tortured sigh. 'Not on the phone. Can I see you?'

The coward in me wanted to tell him that I was busy all day, but we both knew that wasn't true. It was Sunday, the office was shut, and all my closest friends were still at the wedding that I now regretted having left.

'Shall we meet for coffee? Or brunch?' he suggested.

'I've already eaten,' I said, which was true. The fact that I now felt dangerously close to losing that particular meal was nothing I imagined he'd want to hear.

'I could come to yours, or you could come here?'

I considered both options, knowing neither location was right. There was really only one place where this conversation should be held.

'Why don't I meet you in the park?'

I heard him swallow and imagined him closing his eyes for a long moment before replying.

'Okay. Where do you want to meet?'

Did he really need to ask?

'By the tree.'

'Of course,' he said, already sounding more distant, like someone I used to know. 'See you there in an hour.'

My hands shook as I applied mascara and lip gloss in front of my bedroom mirror. Over my shoulder the empty room kept disappearing and a shimmering image of all the times Rhys and I had been together in this place glimmered in the glass. He was haunting me, and he hadn't even gone yet.

I chose my outfit with care, just in case this was going to be the last time I saw him. The thought caused a raw sob to escape. Old Ellie, the one Mum had shaped from the ashes of her own rejection, told me to get a grip. Ignoring her, I pulled his favourite top from my drawer. It was a shade of ice blue that complemented my colouring and went well with my jeans, the ones that hugged me everywhere they should. That was good, I thought, as I ran a comb through the wedding curls that still hadn't dropped out. I had a feeling I might need a hug before the day was over.

Sunday mornings in the park are always uplifting. It's impossible to escape the joyfulness, because it hits you from every angle: dogs leaping like acrobats for frisbees, parents playing ball with their children or pushing them to squeals of delight on the swings, breathless joggers gasping out 'good morning' as they pound past on the pathways. Even the herons living by the lake look happy.

I tried to draw in the atmosphere as though it was an antidote to the trepidation coursing through my veins, pushing the blood aside and making me cold in the unexpectedly warm October sunshine.

There was a feeling of serendipity in being here to learn what had been troubling Rhys for the last forty-eight hours. Time was spooling backwards; taking us back to where it had all begun.

Rhys was standing beneath the tree, facing away from me. My pace slowed, while my heart rate did the opposite. He was staring into the distance, following the flight of the lakeside's long-legged feathered residents as they settled in the trees.

I crossed the grass to reach him, my footsteps silent. Yet when I was still too far away for him to have heard my approach, Rhys suddenly stiffened and turned to face me.

The first thing I noticed was the two takeaway cups in his hands. One of them bore his name in scrawled black script. Something shifted inside me, as though a circle was closing.

The closer I got to his side, the more my heart felt like it was breaking, not because of what I feared was about to happen, but because here was the man I had come to love – even though I'd never once said those words to him – and he was hurting. Somehow that gave me the strength to summon up a smile from an almost empty barrel and paste it onto my face. This was horrible for him too. I could see that.

Very carefully Rhys set the cups down on the ground and stepped towards me, his arms open. My feet took over before my brain could override them. They ran to him. The hug lifted me from the grass, crushed my ribs, and made me wish that we could freeze this single moment and never let it go.

But he set me back down before gently lifting my chin until my face was tilted towards his. His lips were soft as they covered mine, but the kiss was bittersweet. It was over too soon, and I couldn't shake the feeling that the same was about to be true of us.

'You look tired,' I said, my gaze tracing new lines that I swear hadn't been there before. They ran like fantails from the edges of his eyes and drew a stack of horizons across his forehead.

'I feel exhausted,' he admitted. The smile I loved crept on to his lips. 'Turns out I don't sleep that well anymore when you're not beside me.'

'Ditto,' I said, noticing that the smile he was giving me hadn't reached his eyes, which were full of clouds darker than the stormy ones that had gathered on the day we'd met on this spot.

He bent to retrieve the coffees and passed me mine. I prised open the lid and saw a heart shape in the foam. It had broken down the middle, something I didn't imagine the barista had done. It felt like the entire universe was trying to prepare me for something I still didn't want to believe.

'Do you want to do the small-talk bit first?' he asked.

'No. All I want is to make sure this isn't a preamble to telling me something awful about Tasha.'

There was a look of quiet admiration in his eyes when I said that. 'You really are the best person I've ever met.'

I gave a rueful smile. 'Why do I get the feeling that isn't going to be enough?'

He winced then, as though I'd stabbed him.

'Let's walk,' he said, putting an arm around my shoulders and leading me away from the old, damaged oak.

I managed just five steps before I blurted out the horrible fear that I'd been trying my best to suppress.

'Are you going back to Annalise?'

His stride faltered, but he kept walking.

'No. Well, I don't know. Not really.'

'That's a piss-poor answer, Rhys. I'm going to need a better one than that.' I was trying to pry myself out of his hold, but his grip tightened and he wouldn't let me. That just wasn't fair; letting me go while still holding me close.

'You're right. But I need to preface what I'm about to say with something else.'

He stopped walking so abruptly the coffee in my cup sploshed over the rim in protest. He took it from me and once again set it onto the grass. His hands, now free, moved to my face, gently cradling it.

'I love you, Ellie. I know this isn't the right time or place to tell you that.'

'While you're breaking up with me? No, it definitely isn't.'

Old Ellie had leapt in with that whip-smart retort, but for once I didn't blame her or rein her in.

'I just needed you to hear it, to never wonder if I'd felt it. Because I have. I do. And I always will.'

'But you're going back to your ex?'

He looked away for a long moment, as though the words he needed to say were written on the horizon.

'Annalise is taking Tasha to Sydney.'

'For a holiday?' I asked, already knowing that couldn't be the cause of this angst.

'For good,' he said, tearing his eyes away from the park and returning them to me.

'But . . . but . . . why? This is Tasha's home. She's lived here all her life. She's got friends here, school, family.'

'We met with Tasha's doctors. I don't think I fully realised how touch and go it had been when they brought her in. They've put her on the highest dose of medication they can, but they warned us that children with asthma this severe, who've experienced an attack like Tasha's, are likely to do so again. It was devastating to hear, and our first question was what could be done to help prevent it. "Short of moving to a different climate, one with less pollution than here," the consultant told us, "the best advice I can give is to continue monitoring her closely."'

'Was he serious about the moving thing?'

Rhys's shrug looked hopeless. 'Annalise certainly took it as a plan of action. Perhaps because it confirmed everything she'd researched. "Would her asthma improve if she lived in Australia?" she asked him.'

I didn't need to be told his reply. The roots of it were buried in the conversation we were now having.

'But surely Annalise can't just run off to the other side of the world with your child. There must be laws, rules, or regulations that prevent that.'

'There are,' Rhys admitted, but the sadness in his voice told me I hadn't stumbled over a miraculous solution.

'Annalise is convinced the only way to keep Tasha healthy is for her to live in Australia and escape the cold British winters and pollution.'

'But this was only one doctor's opinion. Couldn't you see another specialist? Perhaps they'd have a different prognosis.'

'We saw a second one, the next day.' Rhys looked beaten, and that was a look I'd never seen on him before. 'She basically agreed that damp, cold weather is a real trigger for Tasha's type of asthma and that she'd most likely suffer less in a hot, dry climate.'

I swallowed hard, starting several opposing arguments in my head but never allowing them airtime. They all sounded selfish.

'Do you think they're right?'

With the kind of regret that rips hearts apart, he took my hands in his as he spoke.

'I don't know, Ellie, but I can't risk fighting her on this. Yes, there are laws that could force her to stay here. We share parental responsibility, so I could block the move by applying to the courts for a Prohibited Steps Order.'

I was nodding enthusiastically, holding out for a lifeline, only to see him reel it back in with a shake of his head. 'But what if I did, and Tasha had another attack here, one where the ambulance doesn't get to her in time?'

I was watching the systematic destruction of a life I hadn't even known I was trying to build, and there wasn't a single thing I could do to stop it, because Rhys was right. The risks to his child were too great. Tasha had to come first.

'Annalise has wanted to go back to Australia for a long time. Even before we broke up, she was talking about it. And now that her parents are moving back to Sydney, she thinks it's the right time to take Tasha to live near them.'

He must have read something in my eyes, something I would have been too ashamed to say.

'But her primary motivation is to keep Tasha safe. And I can't fight her on that. I just can't.'

He paused, and I braced myself, because I already knew what was coming next.

'She wants me to go with them.'

It was important that I said the right thing next. But the problem was, I had no idea what that might be.

I stumbled through my words like an actor who was on the wrong page of a script and had forgotten all their lines.

'But what do you want? What about your work? Your friends? Your life here? What about . . .' I bit off the rest of that question. I wouldn't go there. But Rhys did.

'What about you? What about us?' he said, so softly I almost lost his words on the warm breeze.

'I don't matter. I'm not a factor in this.'

'How can you say that? Of course you are.'

He sounded so emphatic that I should have felt comforted, but the break in his voice wouldn't allow me to count this as a victory.

'We're too new. We've only just begun. I shouldn't be a consideration here.'

'You will always be a consideration. Wherever in the world I live, my heart will always be wherever you are.'

'You have to go. You have to be wherever your daughter is. You and she have an incredible relationship, Rhys. Anyone can see that. Being separated would destroy both of you.'

'I know,' Rhys said, his voice hoarse. 'But so would losing you.'

There was a solution here and a question I knew he would have to ask, but I couldn't put him through the torture of wondering how to phrase it.

'I can't go with you, Rhys.' It was like an invisible bullet had just struck him. His face contorted in pain. 'I mean, maybe that's being presumptuous, because you haven't actually asked me to.'

He gave me the saddest smile in the entire world.

'I was going to, even though I already suspected you'd say no.'

My lip began to tremble, and I struggled to get it under control to reply, but it wouldn't let me. Rhys pulled me against his chest, my face finding the hollow of his shoulder, the place that felt more like home than anywhere I'd ever lived.

'I know you've only just found your father. He's the missing piece of your family and the only relative you have left. I could never ask nor expect you to walk away from him when you're only just getting to know each other.'

I buried my face in his shirt front, which I was horribly afraid was going to end up saturated with my tears.

'And then there's Mel. You're about to be godmother to her baby and she's going to want you to be here and be involved in her child's life as much as I know you want to be.

'And lastly, there's the business that you've worked so hard and for so long to make into a success. It's what your mum wanted you to achieve, and I know that getting where you are is tangled up in all she wanted for you. And that giving it up would be like severing your last connection with her.'

'How do you know me this well?' I asked hoarsely, lifting my teary face to his.

'It's easy. It's because I love you,' he replied simply.

More than anything, I wanted to say 'I love you too,' but what would that do, except make him feel even worse?

The seconds stretched on, taking me past the acceptable length of time to give him the response I knew he hoped to hear. Knowing I loved him back wasn't going to make any of this any easier. If anything, it would make it even harder for him to walk away. If I really loved this man, shouldn't I be doing everything in my power to lessen his pain, not add to it?

It was the hardest thing I'd ever done, but I dug deep and somehow managed to channel a strength I must have inherited from the woman who'd raised me. The woman who'd written the book on keeping your emotions tightly reined in.

'We had a good run, Rhys. But I think we both knew it was always going to end with something like this.'

'What?'

If I'd punched him in the stomach he couldn't have looked more winded. I had to focus on the tree behind us, because looking into his eyes would undo me.

'We helped each other get over something few people will ever understand or experience, and we had some pretty amazing times together. But let's not kid ourselves, your family was always going to come first. And that was just as important to me as it was to you.'

He was shaking his head slowly in denial, and I was so close to screaming, 'This is all rubbish. I don't mean a word of any of this' that the only way to prevent the words from escaping was to bite my lip hard enough to taste the metallic tang of blood on my tongue.

I was hurting him, but it was for his own good. I needed to help him walk away without looking back over his shoulder.

'I didn't want to be your everything, Rhys. Hell, I don't want to be anyone's everything. I don't want that responsibility. We said we'd give it the summer . . . and we did. Maybe we'd have lasted a little longer than this, but we always knew we had an end date.' I gave what I hoped was a resigned shrug. 'It just came a little sooner than either of us had expected. We should have known we were on borrowed time when your marks started to fade. The clock has been quietly ticking its way to the end of us for a while now. The best thing we can do is chalk this up to a lovely fling that ran its course.'

And just like that, I broke the heart of the only man I had ever loved.

Chapter Forty-Two

'You could have gone out there for a holiday. Just to see if you'd have liked it.'

My smile was sad as Mel continued to clutch at straws that I'd never allowed myself to hold on to.

'It's all sunshine and beaches and laid-back lifestyle. What's not to like?' I said, lifting the oversized coffee cup to my lips and sipping the contents slowly.

'Spiders,' Jackson declared with an exaggerated shudder. 'They'd be a major downside to living in Oz. And don't get me started on sharks. No, you're better off staying here.'

'Spiders don't worry me. I've stuck my head in too many dusty attics for them to be an issue.'

Jackson shook his head sadly. 'Then I'm all out of reasons why you're still here.' His arm came up around my shoulders and he pulled me in close. 'Except, of course, if you had decided to go, you'd have been a hell of a distance from Mel and me. And we wouldn't be able to descend on her and eat all her fancy biscuits whenever we wanted,' he added, swiping the last chocolate Hobnob from the plate and impressively managing to get the entire thing in his mouth.

‘Exactly,’ I said, trying to swallow the lump in my throat.

‘You’d better not be staying here because of us,’ Mel said, before taking a sip from the single cup of coffee she allowed herself each day, and sighing in bliss. ‘I mean it, Ells. Please tell me we’ve never been a deciding factor in any of this.’ She waggled her fingers between herself and Jackson. ‘Because I’ll disown you as my friend in a heartbeat if that’s why you’re not going with Rhys.’

Mel rested the cup on her impressive bump as though nature had handily given her a new and interesting lap tray. The liquid rippled in the cup as the baby moved, lightening the mood and making us all laugh. That was good, because over the last five weeks, since I’d left Rhys standing alone beneath the tree where we’d met, I was seriously beginning to think I’d forgotten how.

‘It’s not any one thing,’ I explained. ‘It’s too many things. It’s this little baby, it’s both of you, it’s Henry, it’s making my mum proud, and it’s the business.’

Jackson gave my hand the kind of squeeze that breaks fingers. ‘Glad to hear that one is finally at the bottom of the list, Harker. It’s about time.’

My smile was tinged with sadness. ‘I’m learning.’

‘Now!’ Mel cried suddenly, quickly passing Jackson her coffee and grabbing my hand and laying it flat against the tight-as-a-drum skin of her stomach.

Her eyes held mine with a look of dancing excitement. Unconsciously I held my breath as though trying not to spook the infant beneath my palm. Fifteen seconds later I was rewarded with a slight squirm and then a resounding tiny kick.

‘Oh my God. That’s incredible,’ I exclaimed, all at once – and totally unexpectedly – on the verge of tears. ‘How does that feel to you?’

‘Kind of wonderful.’

I thought I'd seen every expression on my old friend's face, but the one she was currently wearing was new to me. It was serene and suffused with joy. Just as surprising was a sudden longing that tugged at something deep inside me.

Mel had picked her moment well, catching me with my guard lowered. She covered the hand that was still resting on her belly with her own.

'I saw Rhys yesterday.'

'What? Where? How come?'

My head spun to Jackson, faster than a tango dancer. 'Did you know anything about this?'

He raised his hands in the universal gesture of surrender. 'Don't jump down my throat. This is breaking news to me.'

I turned my attention back to Mel, who was now looking far more Machiavelli than Madonna in my eyes.

'Did you arrange to see him?'

She shook her head. 'No. It was entirely accidental. He was coming out of the bank as I was going in. No one is conspiring behind your back, Ellie.'

I sat up slowly and tried to reclaim my hand, but Mel refused to give it up, threading her fingers through mine.

'He looked terrible.'

Despite the weeks I'd spent trying to exorcise him from my heart, he still haunted every chamber like a ghost. 'Do you mean sick? Is he ill?'

'If being heartbroken is a sickness, then I'd say he's got it every bit as badly as you,' she said, walking on ground that only a best friend would dare to tread upon. 'He looked kind of broken.'

I swallowed uncomfortably several times, not entirely confident I could use my voice without it cracking.

'Did he . . . ?' I stopped to clear my throat, which suddenly seemed to be full of gravel. 'Did he say anything about me?'

If Mel rolled her eyes any higher, they'd have disappeared clear into the back of her head. 'Of course he mentioned you.' She sighed like an exasperated teacher dealing with unruly children. 'He wanted to know if you were okay. That was the only thing he was concerned about.'

I didn't want to feel the all-consuming flash fire of love, but it was impossible to stop it.

Mel drew in a deep breath. 'He also told me that he's leaving in ten days.'

My stomach didn't really plummet within my diaphragm, logically I knew that couldn't happen. But it certainly felt as though it did.

'So soon?' Whose voice was that? Because it certainly didn't sound like mine.

Mel shrugged her shoulders. 'Apparently his ex and their daughter left several weeks ago.'

'Hmmm,' said Jackson, doing a very bad Hercule Poirot impersonation. 'That's interesting.'

'Not really,' I said, desperately trying to sound nonchalant and missing by a country mile.

Mel and Jackson exchanged a look that they didn't bother trying to hide. I saw it . . . just as they wanted me to.

Chapter Forty-Three

I didn't actually cross each passing day off the calendar. But that didn't mean I wasn't aware, down to the hour, how much longer Rhys and I would be in the same hemisphere.

'Please don't call me. Don't message me,' I'd implored him in the shadows of the oak tree. 'That would just be too hard. It's far easier if we make a clean break of it right now.'

The green light in his eyes had looked somehow dimmer. 'Nothing about any of this feels easy,' he'd said, shaking his head slowly.

'Please, Rhys. Just let me go.'

I could tell he hadn't understood my reasons. That made two of us, but I hadn't let my uncertainty show. And Rhys had done exactly what I'd asked of him. If he hadn't run into Mel, I wouldn't even know his departure was now just two days away.

I shivered, even though the heating in the office was set to a very comfortable twenty-three degrees. I was cold – I had been for weeks – but it was the kind of chill that came from deep within me, and no amount of radiators or extra layers could fix it.

'It'll be better when he's actually gone,' I murmured softly, but not quietly enough to have escaped Simon's attention.

He was sitting at the second desk I'd managed to squeeze into the office, looking far more productive than I'd managed to be all morning.

'Did you say something?'

I shook my head. I'd talked my reasons through with Mel and Jackson so many times that they'd finally stopped trying to persuade me to change my mind. I would get over Rhys in time, I kept telling myself, as though imprinting it in my head would make it true. I only had to get through another forty-eight hours, and then the healing could begin.

It was a plan that fell apart the moment the bell above the door rang and the man I was trying so hard to forget walked into my office. I gasped, losing any hope of trying to appear unaffected by his unexpected appearance.

'Rhys.' Just saying his name felt like a luxury that soon wouldn't be mine to claim.

'Ellie,' he said, his eyes devouring me with an intensity that made me feel naked.

The seconds stretched on, and I wanted to say, 'You shouldn't be here. We agreed not to do this to each other.' But I truly don't think I'd have been able to persuade my tongue to form those words. It felt wonderful and terrible seeing him again and I was hungry – no, starving – for just a glimpse of his face. Although what I saw didn't exactly comfort me. Mel had been right. If there was a contest for who had the most impressive dark circles beneath their eyes, it would probably be a draw.

A scrape of a chair made me tear my eyes from Rhys and I saw Simon getting to his feet.

'I think I'll pop out and get us some coffees,' he declared, blatantly ignoring the takeaway cups on each of our desks that were still hot enough to be giving off steam, and slipped out of the office. Maybe I smiled weakly in his direction, or maybe I just meant to. To be honest my eyes were having a hard time looking anywhere except at Rhys.

When we were eventually alone, I finally remembered how to make my vocal cords work.

'What are you doing here, Rhys?'

He shifted his weight from one foot to the other, looking uncertain. It was a look I'd never seen on him before, nor the broken one currently in his eyes. Guilt as powerful as a wrecking ball struck me. I had done this. I thought I was making it easier for him to leave, and look what I'd achieved. I didn't think it was possible to hate what I'd done any more than I already did, but it turns out there were sub-basements in hell that I hadn't even begun to explore.

'I know I promised not to bother you again.'

'Bother' hit me like a poison dart. Did he really think I'd wanted for a single minute to never see him again? I was trying to make things easier. But all at once I wondered if the price I was making us both pay was too steep.

'I won't take up too much of your time. I know you must be busy.'

Busy thinking about you. The words were right there, and for one dreadful moment I thought I'd actually said them out loud. But Rhys was still standing on the other side of my desk. He wasn't crushing me in his arms. His lips weren't frantically seeking mine. His tongue wasn't making mine wish it had never said all those awful lies.

'I can spare a couple of minutes,' I said, which sounded as prissy out loud as it had in my head.

He gave a ghost of a smile.

'I don't know if Mel mentioned that we'd run into each other recently?'

I nodded. I got the impression he was waiting for me to say something, but my lips felt as though they'd been superglued together. Beneath the desk my hands were tightly clasped, as though I couldn't trust them not to reach across the space between us and pull him to me.

'Then she probably told you I'm booked to leave in two days?'

'Yes, she said.'

I saw the shaft of pain that knowing his departure was imminent still hadn't prompted me to reach out to him. If he only knew how many times I'd summoned his number onto my phone screen and been on the verge of pressing the Call icon.

'There's something I wanted to give you before I left.' His lips twisted in something that was almost a smile. 'Kind of a farewell gift.'

I noticed for the first time there was a flat package tucked beneath his arm.

'What is it?' I asked, eyeing the package as suspiciously as though it was a bomb. I still hadn't freed my gripped hands to take it from him.

'It's just something of mine that I didn't want to pack into storage with the rest of my stuff. I thought you might like something to remember us by.'

As if there would be a single day for the rest of my life when I would ever forget him.

'That's very kind of you,' I said, reciting the words by rote, like a well-trained child at a party.

His eyes softened. Almost as though he knew that beneath the desk my nails were digging into my palms, leaving tiny half-moon wounds in the flesh.

Very gently he set the parcel down on my desk.

'Don't open it yet. Wait until I'm gone.'

Gone, as in out of my office – which looked like it was about to happen – or gone to the other side of the world, which was scarily imminent? Perhaps it didn't matter. Maybe it was best that he didn't witness my reaction to his gift.

'The rest of my things are in storage. I'll have them shipped out when I find somewhere to live.'

His words hung in the air between us. I knew what they meant, and I struggled not to let the reaction show in my eyes. He wasn't moving in with Annalise and Tasha.

'I'm going to look for a place where I can wake up and see the ocean.'

I tried hard not to let his words find a place in my heart, but they were already halfway there. Was he remembering how I'd once told him that one day I wanted to live beside the ocean? Or was I looking for hidden clues that simply didn't exist?

He took a step back from my desk and I felt it in my soul.

'I've already broken all the rules, so I don't have a problem in crossing one last line,' he said, his eyes travelling over my face as though memorising every line.

'I love you, Ellie. That's never going to change. I just wanted to tell you that one last time.'

Responding would have been impossible because my throat was too thick with tears. In any event he left me no time to even think about replying because with the words still echoing in my heart, he turned around and walked out.

I doubt Rhys was even halfway back to his car before I ripped the brown paper from the parcel he'd left me. From its familiar size and shape I was almost certain I knew what it was. It was the same as the many pen-and-ink drawings he'd done for my clients when properties were sold or rented out. Had Rhys done a drawing of my own home, I wondered as I freed the frame from beneath a second layer of tissue paper?

It felt like a very grown-up game of pass-the-parcel, one with hidden consequences. Perhaps that's why my hands were trembling when they finally revealed the drawing. It wasn't my house at all, but the image was as familiar to me as the place where I lived. Because I'd seen this piece of art many times before, only then it had been hanging on Rhys's wall.

I stared down in amazement at the detailed depiction of the oak tree where we'd both been struck by lightning. This was so much bigger and so much more important than a new piece of artwork. I knew how connected Rhys felt to this particular drawing, and it spoke volumes that he had given it to me.

Was that why my vision blurred and a single tear fell upon my desk, followed by another and then another. Or was the cause the small piece of card he'd taped to the edge of the frame. My fingers traced the bold strokes of his handwriting.

The start of us.

I carefully detached the card and lifted it to my lips as though it were his that I was kissing.

Simon would be back at any moment with the coffee neither of us needed, and because I didn't want him finding me sobbing over a drawing of a tree and asking questions I didn't feel up to answering, I went to rewrap the gift in the brown paper. That was when I noticed a second note tucked into the back of the frame. It was a single sheet of paper, carefully folded over and over until it was small enough to be slipped into the corner. I opened it carefully.

'Oh, Rhys,' I whispered as I looked at his second message. It gave the details of the flight to Sydney he was due to take in two days. Beneath the name of the airline, flight number, and departure time was another poignant sentence.

Please don't let this be the end of us.

I cradled the paper to my chest, close to my heart where all important decisions since the lightning were made. The only problem was I had no idea what to do.

Chapter Forty-Four

The canary-yellow building filled my entire windscreen. I peered at it through the rain, wishing I'd thought to bring an umbrella. I reached for the handle and opened the car door.

Keep moving. Keep busy.

It was a mantra I'd been reciting since about five a.m. when I'd finally abandoned all hope of sleep and climbed out from beneath the tangled duvet and twisted sheets.

I ran through the slanting rain towards the entrance of the storage unit which had just opened its doors. My plans for the day were already proving inadequate. How I'd ever thought that deep cleaning my flat would be sufficient to occupy my mind today, I'll never know.

As I stripped the sheets from my bed, I found myself wondering if Rhys was waking up for the last time in his empty flat.

As I polished furniture until every surface had a mirror-like glaze, was he looking around his denuded apartment now devoid of everything he owned.

I ran mindlessly through a puddle, not even noticing when the water splashed over the tops of my trainers as I headed for the building in front of me. Was this the same storage facility where his belongings were housed? Was I subconsciously trying to get close to the things he was leaving behind? Things like me? I shook my head. Rhys wasn't leaving me behind. I had chosen not to go with him.

Even if Rhys's possessions were here, he certainly wouldn't be. I consulted my watch. He'd be leaving for the airport soon. There was probably a taxi on its way to his flat right now. Would he pause before climbing into it and check the road one last time, hoping to see my car speeding towards his home? Or had he already given up on us and was thinking only about his new home, new life, new future? None of which would include me.

'Stop this,' I told myself angrily as I punched in the access code to the unit I'd come here to visit. I bent down and lifted the garage-style roll-up door. For a moment my senses were assailed by something powerful enough to steal my thoughts away from Rhys. The unit smelled like my mother's house. Months of imprisonment behind the bright yellow doors had done nothing to dispel the heartbreakingly familiar aroma. I breathed in deeply, hoping to absorb the old comfort of home.

I'd only been here once before, shortly after finding a folder tucked away at the back of my desk drawer. Within it had been sheaves of paperwork confirming I'd arranged for my mother's home to be packed up by removers and the contents put into storage. I'd obviously been preparing to sell it, and yet I'd never pulled the trigger; I'd never put it on the market. I had no memory of any of this. It was another of the permanently erased events that the lightning had claimed. They didn't bother me so much these days. I'd learnt to accept that some things might be forever lost.

Maybe I should try to get struck by lightning again, I thought as I flicked on the overhead fluorescent lights in the unit. Perhaps next time it could wipe my memory of Rhys, freeing me from the pain of loving, losing, and missing him.

'It could happen,' I told the multitude of storage boxes stacked before me. This morning's TV weather forecast had predicted thunderstorms later this afternoon. Not that I could imagine ever being brave enough to venture out when lightning was a possibility. I was still a long way from conquering that particular phobia.

The box I had come here to sort through wasn't hard to find. I'd seen it on my first visit but hadn't felt brave enough to rip it open. Photograph Albums was written on the label in a stranger's handwriting. My mother had never been much of a chronicler, so it had surprised me to find Box No. 34 – Photograph Albums listed on the remover's inventory after she died. I didn't know where she'd had them hidden, but I certainly hadn't seen them before.

Searching through the collection for the thing I'd promised Henry I would try to find seemed like a suitably diverting activity for a day when I'd have been worse than useless at work and poor company for anyone.

The brown tape made a satisfying cry of protest as I ripped it from the box. What lay beneath the lid was enough to steal my thoughts away from Rhys once again. I'd assumed there might be a couple of albums rattling around inside the box, but there had to be over thirty of them neatly stacked inside the container.

I dropped down to the floor, sitting cross-legged beside the box that my very unsentimental mother had kept hidden from me. The albums didn't appear to be in any particular order, so I reached blindly into the box and plucked out the first one my hand fell upon. Written on the inside cover was a year, penned in my mother's familiar script. Every album I pulled out was similarly labelled and beneath the pages of protective film were photographs that chronicled every important moment of my childhood. There were birthday parties where I saw myself morph from a toddler to a teenager. There were albums that covered a multitude of firsts: first steps, first day at nursery, then school, and finally university. Some of the prints I'd seen before; a few had made it into frames that had been dotted around the house, but the majority of the photographs had been kept here as an everlasting record by a woman who eschewed sentimentality as though it was a disease.

A gasp of realisation ran through me and ricocheted around the storage unit. These albums weren't for her. And they weren't for me either. They were for a person who'd been absent from my life, and who I'd only found after my mother was gone. They were for Henry. She'd collected every single moment he'd missed.

I'd come here today looking for photographs of her as a younger woman, because Henry had asked if there were any of her that he could have. But what I had discovered was far more revealing. Had she secretly hoped that he'd one day return and would want the missing jigsaw pieces of his daughter's life?

'Oh, Mum,' I said on a sigh to the empty room. 'Why did you never tell me?' But perhaps the even bigger question was: why did I find this hidden clue today, of all days?

That felt too important to ignore.

I got to my feet, wiping a film of dust from my palms before resealing the lid of the box to protect it from the rain. It was time to deliver these albums to the man who I had no doubt they'd been created for.

The rain was still falling hard as I drove to Henry's retirement home. Occasionally, when I stopped at a red light or a junction, my glance would go to the box on the passenger seat beside me. It was almost enough to distract me from continually checking the clock on the dashboard.

Rhys was probably halfway to the airport by now. He'd likely be chatting politely to the cab driver, because that was the kind of person he was: kind, thoughtful, and caring. What kind of idiot lets a man like that slip through their fingers? Me, apparently. I took another look at the box beside me. And also, my mother.

◆ ◆ ◆

'These are absolutely wonderful,' Henry exclaimed, pulling yet another album from the box. He'd already leafed through half a dozen volumes, his eyes growing a little mistier with each one. 'It'll take me weeks to look through them all properly,' he said, as though in apology.

'Take as long as you want. They're yours anyway. She left them for you – I'm sure of it.'

Henry looked truly wonderstruck by the find and it was nice to bring joy into his day when mine felt so full of sadness.

'This one looks a little more recent,' Henry said, pulling out a much slimmer album that had been slid upright at the back of the box. He opened it. I watched from across the width of his lounge as I sipped on the slightly too strong Earl Grey he liked to brew.

'Oh.' His smile was soft and full of an expression I couldn't quite identify. 'I think this particular one might be for you rather than me.'

He got to his feet and placed the leather-bound folio in my hands. I gave him a quizzical smile and opened the cover. Like all the other albums, this one had the year written on the inner sleeve. But unlike the others, it wasn't from far in the past. The date was just last year.

The first photograph was of Mum and me. I had no recollection of when or where it had been taken. But Mum must have been sick by then, for her head was covered in a silk headscarf, her treatment already underway. I tilted the photograph towards the window, trying to capture more light from the drizzly grey day. Henry switched on a table lamp and in the warm yellow glow I saw that behind us in the frame was a large ship.

I flipped through the pages, each one making my eyes grow wider and my mouth fall open in surprise. We were on a cruise. A cruise I had absolutely no recollection of taking. But the irrefutable evidence was right there in my hands. It had obviously been a mini voyage – I could see from our outfits we'd only been away for a few days. But we'd gone on a cruise together and had fulfilled one of her long-held dreams, even if I still couldn't remember a single moment of it.

Suddenly the travel pills in my bathroom cabinet, the cruise company emails in my inbox, and the curious three-day gap in last year's diary made sense.

'I can't remember this holiday,' I said, turning tear-filled eyes towards Henry, who was standing beside me, looking at the album.

His hand felt warm and comforting on my shoulder. 'Maybe now you'll be able to,' he said gently, 'now that the door has been opened. But even if you don't, these photographs tell you that the bridges between you and Bee had been repaired before she died.'

His age-spotted hand tapped one of the photographs in the album, one that I already knew was going to be my favourite. Mum and I were dressed up in evening finery, our arms around each other as we posed for what I imagined was an official ship's photographer. The portrait had captured us mid-laugh. I had no idea what had amused us, perhaps I never would, but the love that we felt for each other was there shining in both of our eyes like an eternal flame. Our relationship might not have been perfect – but whose is? We'd made peace with our differences and come together before it was too late to face a future filled with regrets.

It felt like an important message to learn today.

Perhaps Henry thought so too.

'Is it today that your young man leaves for Australia?'

I didn't bother correcting him that Rhys wasn't my young man anymore. He had been, but then I'd let him go.

I nodded.

‘I may be speaking out of turn here, Ellie, and please feel free to tell me to mind my own business.’

I looked up and gave him a gentle smile. ‘Can’t see me doing that somehow.’

Henry returned my smile, before his face sobered.

‘I know I have no right to be offering parental advice this late in the day. But I can see that whatever course you’ve decided upon, it isn’t one that’s making you happy.’

‘I’m fine,’ I said, so close to tears that there could be little doubt that I was lying.

‘Do you love this man, Ellie? Do you really and truly love him the way I did Bee and the way I believe she loved me?’

‘I do,’ I said, as though it was the vow I’d never get to utter before family and friends.

Henry took my hands in his. They looked so alike. And perhaps that wasn’t the only similarity in our lives.

‘Then don’t make the same mistakes I did, Ellie. Don’t tell yourself walking away from the person you’re meant to be with is ever the right decision.’ He lifted one hand and gently stroked my cheek. ‘Because there’s so much you risk losing by making the wrong choice.’

It was hard to speak past the lump in my throat.

‘But there are so many reasons to stay here—’

Henry shook his head, never allowing me to finish. ‘The people who care about you want only your happiness. Nothing else is important to us. We’ll find ways to be together as often as we can.’ He gave a gentle smile. ‘In fact, I’ve always wanted to see more of the world. And Australia seems like a very good place to start my travels.’

I gave a sound halfway between a laugh and a sob.

‘If Bee was here,’ he began, holding up a hand when it looked like I was going to interrupt him. ‘Not your Elizabeth, but my Bee,

I have no doubt what she'd tell you to do. She'd tell you – no, she'd insist – that you listen to your heart and take a chance on happiness.' His eyes went to the box of albums.

'I truly believe she somehow found a way to make sure you discovered this box today. She wanted you to know that beneath her tough exterior, some part of her always believed that one day I'd come back to her.' A single tear rolled down his cheek. 'And I did. I was just too late.'

'Oh, Dad.'

It was the first time I'd ever called him that, and the joy it brought to his eyes was something I would treasure forever.

Henry's hand covered mine warmly. 'I think today might be a very good time for you to be a little less like me, a little less like Elizabeth, and a whole lot more like Bee.'

Chapter Forty-Five

'Are you sure you won't wait until it eases off?' asked Henry, peering out beneath the covered porch of his building and shaking his head worriedly at the rain.

'I'll be fine,' I assured him, leaning in to give him a quick hug. That was a new development for us, and one I really liked. Was I ready to give it up so soon after finally finding it? 'I want to get home before the storm rolls in.'

Henry nodded, but the concern clouding his eyes mirrored the thunderheads gathering ominously overhead.

'And then what?'

It was an excellent question and one to which I had no answer.

'I don't know.' It was an odd response for a woman who'd always prided herself on knowing exactly which direction her life was heading. I felt weirdly untethered and couldn't decide if that was liberating or just plain terrifying. Perhaps both.

'Just trust yourself,' he said wisely. 'Whatever decision you make . . . it will be the right one.'

The roads had grown considerably more treacherous during my time at Henry's. I needed all my concentration just to keep the car travelling in a straight line as the tyres fought for purchase on the rain-slick tarmac and the wipers struggled to clear the windscreen. The twenty-minute drive took twice as long as it should, eating up precious minutes that I couldn't afford to squander.

I sprinted from the car to my front door fast enough to get a stitch that javelined into my side as I raced up the three flights of stairs to my flat.

I peeled off my wet clothes as I strode to the bedroom, trying hard not to let it remind me of all the times Rhys's clothes had lain scattered beside mine on a trail to my bed. Was this a snapshot image of my future? Was I destined to be forever haunted by memories of him and all the what-might-have-beens?

I pulled dry jeans and a jumper on but instead of sliding the dresser drawer to a close, I delved into the back, my fingers grappling until they found my passport. I slipped it into my pocket.

What on earth are you doing? I looked up at my reflection in the oak-framed mirror and came face to face with Old Ellie staring back at me as though I'd lost my mind.

Please tell me you aren't contemplating some crazy dash through the airport like in a sappy romcom.

I stared unblinking at my reflection.

For God's sake, at least phone him first and tell him you want to see him.

To be fair, it was sensible advice. But I didn't want to phone Rhys. That wasn't how this was meant to play out. I'd seen the movies; I'd read the books. I was supposed to run like a maniac through the terminal, leaping over luggage and security barriers, and rush straight into his arms. Calling him to say I was on my way was a last resort, just in case I couldn't get there before his plane took off. I had no chance of doing it if I drove, but there was a fast train that might just get me there in time.

It would have been easier if I had the faintest idea of what I would do when I saw him. The possibilities ranged from waving him farewell to asking if he still wanted me to go with him.

'Everything will fall into place when I see him.'

As plans went, it was flawed on too many levels to count, but it was the only one I had.

There was no time to pack a bag – and most likely no need for one anyway. But if I got to the airport before Rhys boarded his flight, if he forgave me for being too stupid to realise what I was about to lose, and if he wanted me to join him in his new life, then the day I'd been dreading for weeks might actually turn out to be the best of my life. But that was an awful lot of ifs.

Here's another if, said Old Ellie, who had sneakily been waiting for me in the bathroom cabinet mirror. If you are crazy enough to follow Rhys to Australia, what's going to happen to the business you've spent the last three years of your life building up?

'I don't have to decide that right now,' I said, opening the door and reaching for the packet of travel sickness pills on the top shelf.

I ran to the kitchen, pulled a rubbish bag from beneath the sink, and hurried to the fridge, quickly emptying it of all perishables. I got hijacked on my way to the bin by old me, who was hiding in the polished aluminium panel behind the hob.

Moving to the other side of the world isn't something to be taken lightly.

'I know that. But it was wrong to shut the idea down without considering all the options. He deserved that. We deserved that.'

I raced through the flat, pulling plugs from sockets and making sure the windows were locked. I was standing beside the lounge one, where rain was teeming down the pane, when a baritone rumble made me jump. As much as I wanted it to be the sound of a lorry trundling past, the road below was empty. The storm that wasn't meant to materialise for at least another hour was already here.

Fear made my hand tremble as I fumbled with the window key. I dropped it to the wooden floor when lightning speared across the sky.

No. Not now. Not yet.

I could see my reflection in the glass, not clearly, but sharp enough to read the terror upon it. If I was going to catch the train to the airport to intercept Rhys, I needed to leave now. Right now. But how could I when it meant venturing out into the very weather conditions that haunted all my nightmares?

It was a ten-minute walk to the station, down a tree-lined street. Doing that journey in a storm was foolhardy, especially if you knew – as I did – that sometimes lightning really can strike twice.

The lounge lamps flickered as thunder exploded above the rooftops. I raised my hand to the glass pane, and a trick of the light made it look as though there was another me outside the window, in the torrential rain, looking back in. Lightning illuminated her, and I saw there was a curious smile on her lips.

You can do this, Ellie. You're stronger than you know.

It wasn't OG Ellie staring back at me. Nor was it the new one I'd become in the months after getting struck by lightning. This was a different version. One who knew the importance of living and loving to the full. Who finally had her priorities sorted out. Who wasn't afraid to take a chance.

Without hesitation, I plucked up my coat and bag and ran out of the flat. I hurtled down the stairs, trusting fate wouldn't have brought me to this point only to have me end up in a crumpled heap in the hallway with a broken leg.

Yanking the front door open, I began to run. Freezing cold rain drenched me in an instant, but the fire burning inside me, the one no storm could quench, sped me across the puddle-strewn pavement so fast it felt like I was flying. Lightning lit the charcoal skies, momentarily dazzling me. I sprinted on, not allowing my eyes time to adjust. With my vision blurred by the torrential rain and the strobe imprint of the lightning, it took me several seconds to realise a shadowy shape was heading towards me at speed. The rain shimmered like a desert mirage as the figure swerved into the road to close the gap between us even faster. Puddles became waterfalls as pounding feet ploughed through them, following a pathway of petrol rainbows that turned the tarmac into something magical. I faltered for a second, unable to believe what I was seeing, and then I let the storm carry me forward as I ran faster than I've ever done before . . . straight into Rhys's arms.

We collided like magnets, his body crushing mine with an intensity that threatened to steal my breath away. 'Rhys. What are you doing here?'

I could feel him trembling against me, and although the rain was bitterly cold, I knew that wasn't the reason. I levered myself back to see his face. His hair was plastered to his head and there were raindrops clinging like diamond chips to his long black lashes while others coursed down his face in rivulets. His jeans and shirt were less than useless at protecting him from the elements, and shockingly he wore no coat, just the lightweight clothes he'd chosen to travel in.

'Your flight leaves in less than ninety minutes. Why aren't you at the airport?'

'I was. I was on my way to the gate when I realised I couldn't leave. I couldn't get on that plane and take myself away from you. It felt like I was leaving part of me behind.'

Above us lightning arced across the sky as though nature had launched a firework in celebration of this moment. And then a mouth I'd feared I would never kiss again claimed mine with a hunger and desperation that answered all my unspoken questions.

I was breathless when we broke apart.

'I was on my way to you. I had to speak to you before you got on the plane.'

A light that I'd been responsible for dimming slowly reignited in his eyes.

'Then there's still hope?'

'There was always hope,' I said softly, pressing a kiss on the lips I knew would be the last ones I would ever kiss. 'And love too.'

He pulled back, just a few inches so that my field of vision was filled with a pair of brilliant green eyes.

'I love you, Rhys. I have done for a very long time. I'm so sorry I never told you that before today.'

'You're telling me now, and that's all that matters.'

'In the pouring rain, in the middle of a thunderstorm,' I said on a sound halfway between a laugh and a sob.

'Where else could we possibly do this?' His arms tightened and he pulled me in closer, trying to shield me from the weather, from harm, from everything.

'Do you want to go inside?'

'In a moment,' he said, pressing me even tighter against his body. 'Right now, I don't want to move, because I really thought I'd never get to hold you like this again.'

Rain was steadily trickling down my neck, pooling in the small of my back, and yet all I could feel was a warm glow from his words.

'We've so much to work out. So much we need to decide upon. We—'

'Later,' he said, silencing my worries with another kiss.

I snuggled closer, my hands sliding from his neck down to his chest. As they did, my fingertips grazed something almost hidden beneath his shirt. I moved the fabric aside and saw the tape of a large wound dressing.

'You're hurt,' I cried, peering at the bandage that covered a large section of his upper chest, directly over his heart.

'Not exactly,' he said, taking the hand that was resting on the gauze and bringing it to his lips. 'It's a tattoo,' he said, sounding sheepish.

'A tattoo?' I returned my incredulous gaze to his chest. 'But you're terrified of needles.'

'I am. But this was something I had to do.'

Realisation dawned slowly in my eyes. 'The marks, the Lichtenberg figures. You've had them tattooed back on, haven't you?'

He nodded. 'We once said that you and I would last as long as they were there. I just took out some extra insurance.'

'You were always coming back to me, weren't you?'

He nodded again. 'And you were never going to let us go?'

I inclined my head in agreement. 'I'm never leaving you again or letting you walk away.'

I'd seen so many smiles on that handsome face, but this one was new to me. It was filled with tomorrows.

Then he bent his head and kissed me again, properly and thoroughly and yes, there was thunder and lightning exploding overhead, but all I saw were stars.

Epilogue

'Are you ready?'

'Just coming,' I called out, pausing for a moment to dab the tiny beads of perspiration from my upper lip. It was so hot. The heat didn't usually bother me, but today I was struggling.

I picked up the silver hoop earrings from the dressing table and slipped them on and stood back to survey my reflection. The blue sleeveless dress fell in soft filmy folds around my calves and went perfectly with my strappy sandals.

Rhys was waiting beside the floor-length picture window, silhouetted against the ocean. I didn't think either view was one I would ever tire of looking at.

'Sorry. Have I made us late?'

Rhys checked his watch. 'No. There's still plenty of time. It's not like they can start without me.'

I crossed the room to slide my arms around his waist.

'How are you feeling? Are you nervous?'

'Maybe a little.'

'Don't be. You've wanted this for so long and you've worked so hard for it. You deserve this. It's time everyone got to see just how incredibly talented you are.'

'You don't think you might be just a tad biased?'

I laughed. 'Trust me. It's going to be a fantastic night.'

Rhys lowered his head and pressed a kiss on my lips. 'I just hope you and I aren't the only ones who'll show up.'

I smiled into his shirt front. 'That's not going to happen. Louise told me they'd had more acceptances for your show than any other they've held this year.'

'Good to know, but as long as you and Tasha are there, that's all I care about.'

The small art gallery in a coastal town about a twenty-minute drive from our beachside home was owned by an elderly couple who were passionate about supporting local artists. Which, after living here for two years, Rhys was.

I was still a relative newbie to life down under. It had taken me almost six months to tie up the loose ends of my UK life and stitch the threads into a new tapestry. I had no Aussie twang, although I teased Rhys mercilessly at how easily he was picking one up. And Tasha sounded like she'd lived here her entire life. Seeing her sun-bronzed and healthy, playing soccer for the school's first eleven and joining the water polo team, felt like validation that we were all exactly where we were meant to be. And despite Mel's fears – which I'd secretly shared – Annalise had actually been far more amenable and reasonable since returning to her home country. Co-parenting always comes with glitches, but ours had all been minor, and the most important thing was that Tasha was happy and knew how much she was loved by all three of us.

'Your car or the ute?' asked Rhys, slowing his pace to mine as we descended the wooden steps that led from our deck to the parking area.

'Take the utility,' I said, my eyes twinkling, because I knew he'd tease me for refusing to shorten the word. Some of my mother's habits I'd carried with me to the other side of the world, and I rather liked that.

'Still so British.'

I gave a shrug. 'I think speaking to Jackson every other day has a lot to do with it. He wishes you luck for tonight, by the way.'

'That's nice of him,' Rhys said, manoeuvring the vehicle off the unmade road from our property and onto the highway. 'Are he and Lars still hoping to come out later this year?'

'They are,' I said with a smile. 'Although he said he'd have to clear it with his business partner.'

'I hear she's a real tyrant,' Rhys joked.

'Nah. Not anymore,' I said, turning my eyes to the passenger window to watch the sun slowly descend towards the horizon, painting the waves in molten gold hues.

Taking up Jackson's offer to become my business partner had been one of the easiest decisions I'd ever made. He'd taken over the day-to-day running of Ellie Harker Properties and loved dividing his time between my business and his own.

As much as I enjoyed my regular 'work' trips back to the UK, I think we all knew they were more to see the family and friends I'd left behind. It was six months since my last visit – the longest gap since I'd moved – and I was desperate to see everyone again.

In that uncanny way that always took me by surprise, Rhys had followed the direction of my thoughts. He reached across the centre console and took my hand. 'Did you speak to Mel today?'

I bit my lip, hiding a spasm of pain and not turning my face back from the window for a moment or two.

'We had a brief video chat earlier. Ava has grown so much since my last visit.'

'Babies do that,' Rhys said, and there was a look on his face that melted my heart.

'She'll be out here soon.'

I nodded happily. Mel, Steve and baby Ava – toddler Ava, I silently corrected – were coming out at the same time as Henry in about three months' time.

'I thought it might be best if I travel with them to give them a hand with the little one,' Henry had told me.

Whereas Mel's take had been'I think Henry should travel with us, so I can keep an eye on him.'

I loved how my UK 'family' all looked out for each other, even when they weren't actually related.

◆ ◆ ◆

The show was a resounding success. I was bursting with pride as I watched from the sidelines while Rhys spoke to customers, loving the enthusiasm that shone out as he discussed the pieces on display and loving even more the way his eyes kept coming back to me where I sat at a table near the counter.

I watched as sold stickers were pressed onto frames and gradually the crowds began to thin.

'Champagne?' asked one of the teenagers Louise had hired as a waitress for the evening.

I shook my head with a smile. 'Just a glass of water, if you have one.'

Despite the air con in the gallery, I was uncomfortably warm and the chair I was sitting on was clearly built for someone with an entirely different body shape than mine.

Finally, the gallery emptied of customers and Rhys strode across the room towards me, his eyes alight with excitement.

'It went well, didn't it?'

He nodded happily. 'So much better than I could have hoped for. What a night.'

'It's not over yet,' I said, as he pulled me out of the chair and into his arms.

'Is that a promise, Mrs Davies?' he whispered into my ear.

'It is,' I said, wondering if this was the moment.

But then Louise came over and I had to leave it a further ten minutes before letting Rhys in on the secret that I'd been quietly keeping to myself for the last twelve hours.

I waited until we were both in the car before turning towards him in the amber glow of a nearby streetlight.

'When we pull out of the car park, you'll need to turn left and not right.'

A puzzled frown creased his brow.

'Why's that?'

'Because that's where the birthing centre is.'

His eyes widened and then dropped down to my swollen belly. My hands went to my bump which felt drum-tight, uncomfortable, and totally wonderful. It was like touching a miracle and I couldn't resist the pull it had on me.

'Now? Tonight?'

I nodded with a serene smile that the next contraction tried to steal away.

'Why didn't you say anything? I thought we still had a couple of weeks to go. We should have postponed this evening.'

'Absolutely not. This was a big night for you . . . and now it's going to be an even bigger one.'

He leant across and kissed me tenderly.

'What were the chances of this happening tonight of all nights?'

'You know us . . . we like to beat the odds.'

'We do,' Rhys agreed, starting the car and giving me one last look filled with love. 'Now let's go and meet our daughter.'

THE END

If you loved The Wonder of You, read Dani's bestseller, Always You and Me.

Prologue

The bell announcing the end of visiting hours had long since been rung. I'd ignored it. I almost wished someone would come and challenge me about it, because I was spoiling for a fight. I was filled with red-hot rage, the kind that keeps threatening to erupt like lava from an unstable volcano.

'I hate you for this,' I told a God I didn't believe in, just in case – against all odds – he happened to be lurking on the other side of the water-marked mirror in the ladies' toilets.

He chose not to reply, and all I saw in the mirror was a woman who looked about a decade older than the thirty years on her birth certificate. I looked even worse than my passport photograph, which I'd always thought was physically impossible.

My eyes were no longer red-rimmed because there comes a point when you've cried yourself dry. All I could see in them was an aching sadness for something that hadn't even happened yet.

But it would tonight.

My hair was freshly washed, not because I cared how I looked, but because Adam had always liked to burrow his face in the long chestnut strands and inhale my apple-scented shampoo. We could at least still do that, although it had been weeks since he'd been able to pull me into his arms and kiss me until I was breathless, and even longer since he'd been able to lift me off my feet and carry me to our bedroom and lay me down on the cool crisp sheets and—

'Enough,' I told my reflection fiercely. 'Do not go there, Lily.'

The door behind me swung open and I immediately dropped my eyes when I recognised another regular visitor at the hospice. The woman was older than me, and we were on nodding terms in the lift or in the corridor, two refugees in a country we'd never wanted to visit. I didn't imagine I'd ever see her again after today.

I grabbed a handful of paper towels, in too much of a hurry to squander the twenty seconds or so the Dyson fan needed to dry my hands. As I slipped back into Adam's room my eyes automatically went to the clock on the wall. I'd been gone for six minutes. Six minutes I'd never be able to claw back.

Adam's eyes were closed, but they flickered open when he heard the scrape of my chair as I pulled it closer to the bed. He turned his head slowly towards me, as though the bones were fragile and the sinews rusty. When he winced, I felt the pain as though it was mine. 'Hey, beautiful,' he said in a voice that sounded about a hundred years old.

I smiled sadly. 'Only in your eyes.'

He swallowed uncomfortably and I was on my feet in an instant, reaching for the water glass and straw. I slipped my hand beneath his neck and lifted his head from the pillow because he no longer had the strength to do it himself. He'd carried an eight-foot Christmas tree up three flights of stairs to our flat just three months ago, and today something as simple as raising his head to sip from a damn plastic beaker was beyond him.

I turned to look out of the window for a moment, because I didn't want him to see the anger in my eyes. Adam was the best person I'd ever met – the best person anyone who knew him had ever met – and the fact that no one was going to get the chance to know just how totally incredible he was after today was nothing less than an outrage.

His eyes told me he'd drunk enough, and I lowered him back on the pillows.

'Are you in pain? Shall I get someone?' My hand was already hovering by the Call button.

He shook his head. The drugs made him drowsy, and over the last few days, since we were told that the sand in the hourglass was finally running out, he'd refused to take them at all.

'I'm not wasting a single second being spaced out. If this is all the time we have—' I'd sobbed then, I couldn't help it, and he'd taken hold of my hand before continuing. 'If this is it, then I want to be here in the moment with you, right up until I draw my very last breath.'

'You're going to be with me for longer than that. We said forever, remember? We wrote it into our vows. You don't get to wriggle out of it now, buster.'

'I'm not sure dying is wriggling out of it,' he'd said gently. 'But I am reneging on our deal. And I'm so, so sorry to do that to you, Lily. I think perhaps you should sue.'

That was Adam, determined to make me smile even when my heart was literally being torn in two.

'Is Fletcher still here?' he asked unexpectedly.

I swallowed uncomfortably before answering. Adam's short-term memory had begun to waver, like a radio signal that kept slipping off station into a different frequency.

'No, hon. Raegan took him back to her place a few hours ago. Remember?'

I watched as the man I loved, with a Mensa-level IQ, tried to gather up the fragments of his fractured memory and piece it back together.

Fletcher was Adam's dog. He'd been in Adam's life even longer than I had, and I really didn't know what I would have done if the hospice had denied my request to bring him in for a final visit. The nurse I'd asked had drawn in her breath before replying, and I was ready to launch in with every persuasive argument I'd spent most of the previous night compiling.

'Yes, of course you can,' she'd said. 'I think maybe you should bring him in tomorrow.' And instead of thanking her for her kindness I'd immediately burst into tears, because I knew what the concession meant. The clock ticking away the time we had left suddenly got a little louder.

Fletcher was not a particularly intelligent border collie, with a tendency to eat slippers, incoming mail, and even the occasional sock. I'd had no idea how he'd react in an alien environment with so many unfamiliar sounds and smells.

He'd sat beside me on the passenger seat today as I drove to the hospice, for once not fidgeting, pawing at the window, or trying to climb on to my lap. As we pulled into the car park, he sat up higher in his seat and looked directly at the low red-brick building that had been home to his owner for the last four weeks.

He gave a single soulful whine.

'Can you sense him, Fletch? Can you tell that he's in there?'

Fletcher looked at me with eyes that suddenly seemed knowing.

'You have to be good today,' I told him as I clipped the lead to his collar. 'You mustn't upset anyone.'

Adam's dog looked at the tears coursing down my cheeks, as if to say that ship might already have sailed.

'You're here to say goodbye to him, boy,' I whispered brokenly.

Fletcher watched me with an almost human expression of empathy.

'But I think you know that, don't you?'

For two hours Adam's dog sat beside the bed, within easy reach of the hand that fondled his silky ears the way it had done a thousand times before. And would never do again. As much as it broke my heart, I think having his old friend there helped heal something in Adam's.

Towards the end of the visit, I lifted the dog on to the bed.

There were intravenous drips and wires everywhere, but Fletcher, who was possibly the clumsiest hound in the world, didn't disturb a single one. He simply lay down on the mattress and stared up at his owner with a devotion that matched mine. We both loved this man with all our heart. And tonight we were both going to lose him. The hospice staff were invisible angels, slipping unobtrusively in and out of Adam's room throughout the night, checking him, checking me, tweaking machinery, and then silently disappearing back into the shadows. Someone had turned off the harsh overhead lamp, leaving the room bathed in the subdued glow of the panel light behind the bed. It was still bright enough to see every detail of the face I'd planned on waking up beside for the next sixty years or so. The thought caught me unawares, and whatever I had been saying was lost in a broken sob.

'Oh, babe,' Adam said, managing to lift his arm off the mattress with a strength I thought he'd already lost. 'Come here.'

I went to him, negotiating my way through the tangle of wires and tubes to lay my head on his chest. It was my favourite place to sleep, with the reassuring steady thud of his heart beating beneath my ear. Tonight its rhythm was off, like a song being played at the wrong tempo. It came fast in a flurry of beats, and then slow with excruciatingly long gaps before the next reassuring thump.

'Adam will slow down,' they had told me. 'He'll become drowsy and may sleep for long periods of time. He won't want to eat or drink. Gradually his body will begin to shut down.'

'Will it . . . will it hurt?' I'd asked, my face awash with tears that I hadn't bothered trying to wipe away.

'We won't let it,' the doctor had told me gently. 'We'll give him whatever he needs.'

Later I would replay those words over and over again. Because what my husband needed was the one thing that no one could give him: a miracle. A cure for the disease that was stealing him away from us.

'Climb under the covers,' Adam said now, his voice low.

'I'm pretty sure that's not allowed,' I whispered, already kicking off my shoes and glancing worriedly towards the door as they hit the floor with a noisy clatter.

'I don't think they'll throw me out for misbehaviour.'

'Are we going to be misbehaving?' I asked, trying to make him smile. Adam had the best smile of anyone I'd ever met.

'I wish,' he said with regret, his eyes looking deep into mine.

It seemed beyond wrong that even after all these years I could still remember the first time we'd made love and yet I couldn't recall the last time.

All I knew was that it had fallen somewhere between growing vaguely concerned about Adam's niggling symptoms, and the day we'd sat, white-faced and terrified, in an oncologist's office.

'Can you please just give it to me straight?' Adam had asked him. 'I don't want some dressed-up version of the truth. Just how bad is it?'

The doctor had paused for a long moment. He hadn't needed to look down at the test results or refer to the X-rays fanned out on the desk before him. He'd locked eyes with Adam.

'Bad,' he'd said quietly. 'It's bad.'

The minutes slid silently into hours. Staff changed shifts and the corridor outside Adam's room grew quieter.

'Talk to me,' Adam said, as I lay pretzelled against him.

'What about?'

He gave a ghost of a smile. 'Anything. I just want to hear your voice. Tell me what you thought of me the first time we met.'

'That's easy. I thought you were a bit of a knob. Far too overconfident.'

He gave a low chuckle, which turned into a worrying coughing fit. His lungs were compromised now. His breathing was no longer silent. There was a rasp to it that I knew wasn't going to go away. I did as he asked, telling stories that all began with the words 'Remember when . . .' They made us smile, they made us cry – but that was okay too, because we were doing it together. And 'together' was a luxury we wouldn't have for much longer.

Almost as if he sensed the dark avenue my thoughts had turned down, Adam's arms tightened around me. It was after midnight and the hospice was silent except for the occasional quietly trodden footsteps travelling the corridor.

'Lily, I have something I need to ask you. Something I want you to promise.'

'More promises?' I said, trying to keep my voice light, but there was something about his tone that made the hair stand up on my arms. There had been a whole collection of things he had wanted me to promise over the last days and weeks. Most of them were pretty doable.

'Promise me you'll remember to get the car serviced regularly.'

'You're worried about the car?' I'd asked incredulously.

'I'm worried about you. I don't want my time in the afterlife ruined by stressing about you driving around with dodgy brakes.'

Behind the humour in his eyes, I had seen the genuine concern.

'Okay, babe. I promise I'll visit the garage regularly.'

But not every promise was so easy to make.

'Promise me you'll still take that trip to Australia next year like we planned.'

I'd shaken my head sadly at that one. 'I don't want to do that without you. That was our dream.'

Adam had taken my hand between his and squeezed it gently.

'It's still our dream. And when you stand on the top of the Sydney Harbour Bridge, I'm going to be right there beside you. That's my promise.'

I kind of liked that, so I'd said yes to that one too.

'Go on then,' I said to him now in the quiet of his hospice room.

'This one is really a two-part promise, but it's the most important one that I've asked of you.'

He looked so serious as he stared down at me. It was almost as though he already knew how I'd react.

'Okay. Whatever it is, I promise I'll do it,' I said, gently running my fingers over his furrowed brow.

'Good,' Adam said with a slow nod. 'Because I want you to find Josh and fix things with him.'

'No.' The word shot out of me before I had a chance to censor it. 'Absolutely not,' I added for extra emphasis. I struggled in his arms but his hold on me was surprisingly strong, in every sense of the word.

'I need to know you'll be alright when I'm gone, Lily. You need to go to him.'

'No, I don't,' I said, gentler this time but just as firm. 'I will be alright, sweetheart. I've told you that. I will be sad, and my heart will be broken for a very long time, maybe forever, but I do not need to go and find the man whose last words to me were that he never wanted to see me again.'

'That was my fault,' Adam said, his voice cracking.

'I chose you, not Josh,' I reminded him, pressing a kiss on his lips, which felt as dry as sandpaper. 'I will always choose you. In this life and the next.'

Adam shook his head and one of the machines he was attached to started to beep alarmingly. He was getting agitated, and that was the last thing I wanted.

'Please, Lily. For me. Go and see him. Listen to what he has to say. And then, when you've heard it . . . forgive him. And then forgive me.'

'You're not making any sense,' I said, my voice wobbling. Was this the beginning of the end? They'd warned me that Adam might become confused, or even delusional, and instructing me to go to the man who I'd turned down to be with him was about as deluded as it got.

'You don't have to understand now why I'm asking you to do this, but you do have to promise me you'll go.'

My sigh was long and heartfelt. 'Alright. If it means this much to you, I'll do it.'

'And don't wait too long. Go to him soon. Promise me.'

'I promise.'

There is probably a special place in hell for people who lie to someone who's dying, and I was already halfway there.

It happened in the dark, middle-of-the-night hours, when so many warriors finally lose their fight. I knew it was getting closer by the worried expression in the eyes of the nurses as they came in to check on him.

I struggled to slip out of the bed but a senior nurse, one I'd never really warmed to, stopped me from getting up by placing a firm hand on my shoulder.

'You're fine just where you are,' she said quietly.

The lump in my throat was almost impossible to swallow past.

'Would you like someone to stay in the room with you?' She turned her head and nodded to a shadowy corner. 'We could sit quietly over there.'

I shook my head. 'I think I'd like it to be just the two of us.'

Her hand was back on my shoulder, gently squeezing it.

'That's okay. I understand. You can buzz if you change your mind.'

Adam fought to keep his eyes open for as long as he could; fought to stay with me for every single second we had left. But his body was struggling, and I was hurting him by wanting him to hold on a little bit longer, just for me.

'Close your eyes, sweetheart.'

'I don't want to. I want to see you.'

I leant up and gently kissed him again. 'I'm there behind your eyes, whether they're open or closed.'

'You are and always will be the love of my life, Lily.'

'And you are mine.'

His eyes closed briefly. 'Please remember what I asked tonight.'

'I remember. I remember everything,' I said. That much at least was no lie. There were some things that would stay with me for all time.

'I am going to close my eyes now,' he said, his voice so weak I could hardly hear it.

'Good idea.'

'I'll see you soon, Lily.'

'You sure will.'

But that was the second lie I told him that night.

Fifteen minutes later, the gap between his breaths grew longer and longer, and then quietly, with that was uniquely his, Adam Tennant – my husband, my best friend, and the love of my life – simply stopped being.

I stared down at his face which, for the first time in months, looked free from pain. From the corner of his eye a single tear had escaped and sat on his cheekbone like a dropped diamond. I bent down and gently kissed it away.

ABOUT THE AUTHOR

Photo © Hannah Cousens

Dani Atkins is an award-winning novelist. Her 2013 debut *Fractured* has been translated into over twenty-three languages and has sold more than half a million copies.

Dani was born and has lived in various parts of Hertfordshire all her life. Before the arrival of her two children, she worked for many years as a secretary/PA in London in a range of diverse organisations, including the BBC, a car dealership, and an international engineering corporation. Books were her constant companions on the daily commute, and she never let go of her secret dream that one day she too might become an author.

A long and happy marriage, two children who have now grown up and left home, and a great many much-loved pets later, Dani still has to pinch herself to realise that she is now, quite literally, living the dream.

Follow the Author on Amazon

If you enjoyed this book, follow Dani Atkins on Amazon to be notified when the author releases a new book!
To do this, please follow these instructions:

Desktop:

1) Search for the author's name on Amazon or in the Amazon App.
2) Click on the author's name to arrive on their Amazon page.
3) Click the 'Follow' button.

Mobile and Tablet:

1) Search for the author's name on Amazon or in the Amazon App.
2) Click on one of the author's books.
3) Click on the author's name to arrive on their Amazon page.
4) Click the "Follow" button.

Kindle eReader and Kindle App:

If you enjoyed this book on a Kindle eReader or in the Kindle App, you will find the author 'Follow' button after the last page.

Follow the Author on Amazon

If you enjoyed this book, follow Dani Atkins on Amazon to be notified when the author releases a new book!
To do this, please follow these instructions:

Desktop:

1) Search for the author's name on Amazon or in the Amazon App.
2) Click on the author's name to arrive on their Amazon page.
3) Click the 'Follow' button.

Mobile and Tablet:

1) Search for the author's name on Amazon or in the Amazon App.
2) Click on one of the author's books.
3) Click on the author's name to arrive on their Amazon page.
4) Click the "Follow" button.

Kindle eReader and Kindle App:

If you enjoyed this book on a Kindle eReader or in the Kindle App, you will find the author 'Follow' button after the last page.